A PIRATE'S WIFE FOR ME
The Governess Brides

By
Christina Dodd

A PIRATE'S WIFE FOR ME

Createspace Edition
Copyright 2015 by Christina Dodd
ISBN 13: 978-0-9960859-2-2

A Pirate's Wife for Me is a work of fiction. All characters and events portrayed herein are fictitious and are not based on any real persons living or dead.

CHAPTER ONE

Poole, Dorset, England, 1843

In all his degenerate life, he had seen only one woman who walked like that — like a great cat, pacing along, stretching out her legs in a slow, pantherish stride that made a man turn and look, and wonder with fascination how it would be to part those legs and ride.

Would she scratch? Or would she purr?

Like all the other sailors in the pub, he turned to watch her stroll past, a flowered carpetbag clasped in her narrow fingers. He saw the auburn hair, tucked tightly into a chignon, the tall, lithe figure with its tiny waist and high breasts, and the green, lucid eyes which wavered neither right nor left, but gazed directly at Cleary, the pub owner.

And he knew she would scratch. And purr.

What in the hell was Miss Caitlin MacLean doing at night in the roughest dive on the Poole docks?

Silence assaulted Cate as she made her way across the uneven wooden floor. She ignored the aggressive masculine stares. She was used to attention. One didn't get to be twenty-five, six feet tall, and blessed with red hair without knowing that when one stepped into a room of strangers, a hush would fall, followed by a flurry of whispers.

She never took notice. Nor did she now.

She kept her gaze fixed on the large, battered, middle-aged man behind the bar. He stood polishing a glass with a grimy towel, staring at her with his mouth hanging open. The stench of body odor, ale and cigars assailed her. Cheap candles smoked in their sconces set on ash-darkened walls. Placing her hands on the battered plank that was the bar, she leaned forward, and in a low tone, asked, "Are you Mr. Cleary?"

His piggy eyes narrowed. He examined her from top to toe. "Aye, that I am." He bent toward her until his bulbous, red-veined nose almost met hers. "Who the hell are ye?"

She'd found him. She adjusted the heavy traveling bag in her grip. "I am Miss Cate MacLean, and I am to rent a room for the night."

He rocked back on his heels. "No."

Startled, she blinked at him. "No?"

"Get out of here. I don't keep doxies in me pub."

She couldn't help it. She laughed. "Don't be ridiculous, my good man. I am most certainly not a doxy! Unless doxies have taken to dressing in black bombazine." Black bombazine that buttoned all the way up to her throat, she might add. "You're expecting me. I'm – " She glanced around. Every eye was fixed on her. In a voice pitched to reach Mr. Cleary's ears alone, she said, "Mr. Throckmorton sent me."

He froze. He darted a glance over her shoulder. As if receiving a command, he nodded. She wanted to look behind, to see who directed him, but he returned his attention to her. "Up the stairs, last chamber on yer left. Lock the door, don't open until the Cap'n comes up."

"The cabriolet driver needs help getting my trunk down and into the pub. Please send a man out to assist him."

"A trunk?" If possible, Mr. Cleary looked even more stunned than when she identified her sponsor. "Ye brought a trunk?"

"Yes, and it's heavy."

"A *trunk?*"

"Yes! And I'd appreciate your assistance in taking it to my chamber." What kind of man questioned a lady about her luggage? She looked Mr. Cleary over, seeing the round belly beneath the stained apron, the broad, stumpy arms, the gray stubbled chin. The man was a town-dwelling provincial with no manners and less class. She always found this sort interesting, usually possessed of a variety of knowledge, and at any other time, she would have insisted on a chat. As it was now, she had more important beasts to smoke out.

Turning, she sought the man who had commanded Mr. Cleary. The man who would command her. She looked through the pall of smoke at the gauntlet of sailors and drunkards, thieves and fools, seeing each one, but allowing her gaze to linger on none. In the eight years since she'd lost her reputation, she'd perfected the trick. Only the most degenerate of men could imagine that cold, impersonal appraisal indicated interest. Unfortunately, as she'd discovered, a great many degenerate men inhabited the world.

Even now, in her peripheral vision, she could see about six of them grinning at her. Perhaps a dozen tried to hide their fangs and claws by bowing in her direction.

A thin-faced, hook-nosed fellow with a Scottish accent called out, "If ye need a man for any reason, lass, me name's Maccus."

All the men, the flirts and the stallions, snapped their fingers and made clicking noises with their tongue as if she were a bird to be coaxed into the net. She could have sworn they believed a woman found such insolence seductive.

Only one, a broad-shouldered creature with black hair to his shoulders, stood with his back to her, talking in a low tone to a shorter fellow. Was he the man she'd been sent to seek?

Perhaps. Perhaps not. In this underworld of criminals and spies, she dared not make assumptions.

Mr. Cleary thrust a lit candle and a large, iron key at her. "Take this and go upstairs right quick, Miss. Ye'll cause a fight if ye don't."

She clasped the iron ring and strode across the taproom to the stairwell.

The cacophony of laughter and drunken revelry rose in a wave and carried her up the stairs to the second floor; she squirmed at the words she chose not to acknowledge and the speculation she couldn't avoid.

The corridor was silent and dark, with four doors on either side. She heard no sound from any of the rooms, but light shone around the casement on the first door.

Don't call unnecessary attention to yourself, Mr. Throckmorton had instructed, *yet always maintain an imposing demeanor.* His gaze had flicked over her. *But you already know that.*

She did know it. She had learned much in the long, lonely years while all her playmates met and married. A single woman could go all the places that a married woman went, but she had to move with confidence, as if she owned the very earth.

Going to the last door on the left, she opened it cautiously. Surprisingly, it smelled of nothing more virulent than lavender and wood smoke. Her raised candle illuminated a small, well-maintained bedchamber with a fireplace, a narrow bed, a straight-backed wooden chair and a bed table with basin and pitcher. Shutting the door behind her, she fit the key in the lock, and turned it. She made her way to the bed and pressed hard on the thin mattress. The ropes squeaked, but the thick blankets would protect against the chill off the ocean, and when she peeked at the sheets, they looked relatively clean and vermin-free.

She deposited her traveling bag and her candle on the table and removed her black leather gloves. Walking to the window, she looked out over a bleak alley at the back of the tavern. Here and there, light spilled from the windows of other taverns, and every place rocked with the laughter and shouts of sailors. Across the way, the back door opened and a pail of slops were flung into the mud.

She tried to open the casement. Damp made it swell and stick, and she first pushed with her hands, then put her shoulder into it. It wouldn't budge. Finally she backed up and took a run at it. The window gave all at once, and she barely caught herself before she toppled out into the alley. Going to her bag, she removed the rope ladder and placed it beside the open window.

There. She dusted her fingers. So far everything about her assignment had gone flawlessly. Of course, that included nothing more than traveling from London to Poole on the train, finding the tavern, and getting a room, but each success built her confidence. She could do this. She had to do this. She owed it to her brother. To Kiernan.

The docks of Poole were rough and lawless, and Mr. Throckmorton had impressed upon her the perils of her mission. He'd given her instruction before she rode the train up from London, but the most important directive, he'd insisted, was that she should always have an escape route planned.

A knock sounded on the door. She jumped.

The Cap'n. Or perhaps … someone less benevolent.

Going to her bag, she pulled out her derringer – loaded, for she hadn't dared to come to the docks unprotected – and slid it under the pillow. Accessible, but not obvious.

Gliding to the door, she leaned against it and asked, "Who is it?"

A deep voice answered. "The Cap'n."

She turned the key, opened the door, and stepped back. In the darkness of the corridor, she could see nothing but a tall, broad outline of a man in a collarless white shirt and black, form-fitting trousers. He was taller than she was – a rarity. His shoulders spanned almost the entire doorway.

Then he strode into the room, and the pale light of the candle illuminated his countenance. Gray eyes, chilly as sea fog. Black hair, straight, grown too long, and tied at the back of his neck. Features sculpted by noble heredity and harsh experience. A trimmed black beard. Wide, plush lips that looked as if they knew how to kiss a woman to ecstasy ... as she knew very well they did.

She had hoped never to see his face again.

Taran. Taran Tamson. Her friend. Her enemy.

Her first and only lover.

And the man who had broken her heart.

CHAPTER TWO

Cate didn't think. Her fist shot out toward his stomach.

Taran tightened his muscles and took the strike, and if he felt pain, he didn't show it. Then, as she used the flat of her palm to try and break that aristocratic blade of a nose, he caught her wrist and coiled her toward him. She landed, her back to his chest, with a thump that knocked the breath out of her. With her free hand, she reached up to grab his hair. He caught that wrist, too, and pulled it around her. Now he held her against him, trapped with her arms wrapped around her waist.

Leaning down to nuzzle her ear, he crooned, "Ah, darlin', I'm the one who taught you those moves."

She struggled. "Swine."

"That wasn't what you called me the last time I held you."

She hated him so much. The hatred twisted in her gut, depriving her of everything but pure, unreasoning instinct. She slammed her booted foot down on his instep.

He grunted in pain. "Damn it!"

Releasing one arm, he twirled her like a dancer into her bedchamber, and followed behind. Without taking his eyes off of her, he slammed the door with his boot.

She was strong, with long fingers and wide palms, and shoulders that looked broad and smooth on those rare occasions when she wore an off-the-shoulder ball gown.

He was stronger, with callused hands and shoulders that strained at the seams of his plain white shirt.

She was independent, used to defending herself if she had to, and she frequently had to.

He ... she didn't know what he was.

He stood with his fist on his hip. "Do you like what you see?"

He wore black trousers that molded to his narrow hips and muscled thighs, and scarred black boots that looked as if they'd seen adventure aplenty. "No."

"That's too bad, because I like what I see very much." His gaze slid up over her like a warm, soft caress. "You've changed, darlin', and all for the better."

She calmed herself and weighed her odds. He was inside the room with her and obviously bent on mischief. She needed a cool head and a sensible strategy to come out of this unscathed. She could do that. These last years had been spent teaching herself how to think before she spoke, how to look before she leapt. "You have no idea how happy it makes me that you, of all men, so choose to honor me." Deliberately, she took a stance to challenge his. "Or maybe you do. What brings you here?"

"I brought your trunk up." He gestured toward the door at his back. "You attacked me and I was forced to abandon it."

"I meant here, in Poole."

He smiled, if that slight upturn of the lips could be called a smile. "I told you. I'm the Cap'n."

The Cap'n. The man whom Mr. Throckmorton said she should serve? No. Oh, no. "I don't believe you. Why would you be the man I should … I should … ?"

Now he smiled for real, his teeth sharp and white. "Obey?"

Without expression, she retorted, "Report to."

"Because I'm the leader of this mission. Because I know how to prepare. I know how to fight." He strolled to the center of the chamber. "I'm the captain of a ship."

"I suppose, knowing your character and proclivity for wickedness, that your ship would be a pirate ship?"

"Of course. Fight and steal. It's what I've learned to do well."

"My brother was the most honorable of men. He educated you. Trained you. Then you betrayed him with me, and betrayed him yet again by becoming a common thief." She paced her words judiciously, wanting to impress on him her meaning — and her resolution. "If fighting and stealing is all you do well, you're a disgrace to Kiernan's name."

"Ah, but I do one other thing well." Taran smiled again, this time a smile that sent a warm warning. "You can attest to that, can't you?"

His cavalier reminder of a time long past, made her want to attack again.

But no. She would not give him the further satisfaction of knowing how easily he could still stir her to passion, even if that passion was purely rage. As warm as his smile was, hers was chilly.

"A gentleman would not remind me. But I forget. You are not a gentleman."

"If you think a gentleman wouldn't remember that day, and that night, you are still a little innocent. I remember every moment." His every word mocked, yet he managed to sound sincere. "Your untutored eagerness. Your tongue in my mouth. Your naked body, twining around mine."

She wanted to cover her ears, to block the madness he evoked, but that wouldn't block the memories.

The firelight flickered on the walls of the small hut. Taran lifted her above him, placed her on his hips, and in a guttural voice commanded, "Take me."

Eagerly, she obeyed, caressing his sculpted chest with her fingers, smoothing his abdominal muscles with her flattened palm ... wrapping his penis in her hands and stroking it while the man below her strained and cursed. Rising over him, she slowly, gently, placed him at the entrance of her body and sank down ...

Crisply, she said, "You are an ass."

"You told me you loved me. You begged me to teach you everything I knew about the love between a man and a woman."

"You knew nothing about love and everything about treachery."

In the voice which, like fine wine, had grown richer and deeper with age, he said, "I've continued to learn ... about love. Let me redeem my reputation."

"No. I thank you." She took a breath. The room was stifling, small and cramped with Taran taking up the space. She had come here wrapped in her hard-won confidence. He sought to strip it from her. He would not succeed. "A pirate can't be working for the British Home Office."

He circled the room, looking at the bed, fiddling with the catch on her carpetbag ... not knowing a pistol resided beneath her pillow. "The English will use a thief for their own purposes."

So Throckmorton had said. "But surely the Home Office desires to utilize Englishmen."

"The Brits only care that I'm useful." He moved again, this time toward her. "You're not English, either, my sweet."

She slid away. Some might call it retreat. She called it good sense. "No, Scottish born and bred, but you're not even that."

"What am I, then?"

She didn't answer. She couldn't. His faint burr was imperceptible to the ear ... unless you were Scottish. And she *was* Scottish, born on the isle of Mull into the Clan MacLean and raised as the treasured sister of the respected clan chieftain. Men and women from all over Scotland came to visit Castle MacLean, and none of them sounded like Taran. He spoke English, Spanish, and French like a native, yet buried deep in his voice was the faintest wisp of an accent she could not place.

Strolling toward the window, he looked out, and she had the impression he saw much more down there in the muck and the dark than she did. "Three years I lived in your household," he said, "and you never asked me where I was born."

"You wouldn't tell me." In truth, she hadn't cared about his nationality. Her only care had been his fine young body. "So where *are* you from?"

"Cenorina."

She stared at him. Cenorina. An archipelago of islands east of England and south of the Channel Islands. An independent principality ruled by the same family for four hundred years. The place where she must go to complete her mission.

She actually felt the blood drain from her face. Her lips moved. "Cenorina." But she made no sound. Her lungs weren't working. She couldn't get air.

He observed every fluctuation of color and every change in respiration.

She hated that. She wanted him to know nothing about her. Nothing.

His eyes were as cool and gray as the winter sea. "Perhaps you ought to sit down."

"No." Sit, recline, relax in any way in his presence? *No.*

"Aye, I'm from Cenorina." He seemed proud of his heritage, and bitter, too. "That puts a different complexion on it, doesn't it, my lamb?"

The air came rushing back into her lungs. "If you had a lamb, you would roast it and serve it in a stew."

"You judge me harshly."

"I judge you fairly." She judged him as he deserved to be judged.

"I know every inch of Cenorina terrain. It is a place of mountains and hot springs, of wild shorelines and herds of deer. I know the palaces and the villages. I'm Throckmorton's main contact for this mission." He pulled the window shut and loosely latched it. "So it would be best if you went back to London and told Throckmorton to send me the proper staff."

How dare Taran presume to know what she was capable of? "I am the only one who can complete this task. I have entry into the governor of Cenorina's household. Sir Maddox Davies sent to the Distinguished Academy of Governesses for ... staff."

"Sir Maddox Davies, the governor of Cenorina, who has no wife or children, sent for a governess?" Taran voice rose incredulously.

"For a housekeeper. The academy provides all kinds of services, and has a reputation for providing excellent domestics. I am the new housekeeper."

"You?" He burst into low, scornful laughter. "A housekeeper? You don't know the first thing about --"

Two long steps brought her to stand in front of him. Poking her finger into his shirtfront, she said, "Yes ... I ... do. When my mother remarried, the burden of caring for Castle MacLean fell on me. Just because you weren't there to witness it, Taran, doesn't mean I didn't succeed."

He stopped laughing, but he surveyed her with an intimate smile that sent shivers down her spine. "That's my Caitlin. You always recover quickly."

"Cate."

"What?"

"I am Cate now. Not Caitlin. Not the little fool you knew before. I am Cate."

"Cate," he repeated. "I like that. It fits you. And ... Kiernan would kill me if I allowed you to go on this mad adventure."

All unknowing, Taran had jabbed at a tender spot. Abruptly, her fingers shook, and she tucked them behind her back. "Kiernan spent years wanting to kill you. Why should anything be different now?"

"Why, indeed?" Taran caught her shoulders in his grasp. He gazed into her eyes as if he would hold her through the power of his words. "Nine years. Nine years is a long time. I thought I'd forgotten you, Cate. when I saw you walk across the tavern tonight, I knew I was only fooling myself. I could never forget you."

CHAPTER THREE

Cate stood unbending, holding every muscle rigid. "Am I supposed to be impressed that you remember me at last?"

"You were always one who valued action above all." Taran lowered his lips toward hers. "Darlin', remember this?"

She slammed her forehead toward his mouth.

He jerked his head back barely in time. "A tussle, lass? Is that what you like now?"

"I don't like anything now." With a swift upward swing of her fists, she broke his grip on her arms and strode across the bedchamber. "Since you left me tied to that bed, I've spent half of my time evading jackasses like you who think I need a man. I don't need any man. Certainly not one who abandoned me, never to return."

"Yet you still want me."

"I would have to be a mooncalf to still want you." …Yet she did. And she hated him for it.

Her heart raced as he stalked her across the room. Her body remembered what it was to be his, and that body, too long without the touch of a man, hummed with excitement. She had thought she was long past the time when everything in her responded to a man. She had thought loneliness, humiliation and defiance had replaced every sweet, womanly need. But her heart pounded, the fine hairs all over her body rose, and a fine sheen of perspiration covered her skin. Her agitation was all Taran's fault. No other man had ever made her want with all the fierce desire in her nature.

But these years of independence had taught her to think on her feet. Briefly, she considered the rope ladder. No. The window stuck. So she moved toward the bed. Toward the pistol.

"I was kidnapped." He watched her with anticipation gleaming in his gray eyes.

"Kidnapped? You mean someone wanted you dead beside Kiernan and me?" she jeered.

"Yeah. It was my —" He took a dive at her, caught her around the waist, tumbled her on the bed.

She landed face down, head toward the foot of the bed —

not what she'd planned – kicking and screaming like some helpless maiden in a morality play.

He landed on top of her, his front to her back, spoon-fashion. Using his whole weight, he subdued her until her struggles had stopped and she could only yell.

"Do you think that shrieking will bring someone running?" He laughed. "Listen to the men. My men."

The music from below got louder, and from the stamping and cheering, she guessed they were dancing.

"The taproom is lively now, and likely to get livelier. The doxies have arrived, those sailors know the danger of this mission, and they're determined to wring every drop of enjoyment out of each remaining moment."

She was a sensible woman. She stopped screaming, and concentrated on her options. She had only one: the pistol, which remained far away, at the head of the bed.

His hand skated between her neck and the mattress. His fingers caressed the vein that pulsed in her throat. He slid his fingers into her hair, held her so that one side of her face was turned to his, and kissed her forehead, her eyelid, her cheek, her jaw.

The faded, striped coverlet stretched endlessly away from her. Far beyond the reach of her fingers, she could see the pillow. She wanted so badly to be there, to hold the smooth cold metal in her fingers and with it force him to leave.

His warm breath slithered across her skin, and the scent of peaches and brandy formed an intoxicating mix. He glided close to her lips, but she bared her teeth and with a chuckle, he moved on. He kissed her neck: the sensitive place behind her ear, the pale, soft skin that showed above her collar. His tongue, that wicked tongue that had taught her so much about pleasure, slid along her earlobe, and he drew it into his mouth and lightly scraped it with his teeth.

Damn him. He remembered all the tender places. The places that made her want to turn into his arms and welcome him between her legs.

"Stop that!" She knew it was useless, but she tried to climb out from under him. The sheets and blankets slipped free from the mattress, sliding toward her. Wisps of her hair came loose from her chignon and fell around her face.

He picked up one and slid it between his fingers. "You cut

your hair." He had the nerve to sound hurt, as if she'd done it to spite him. "How could you cut your hair?"

"With scissors." Her breath rasped in her lungs. "I will never, ever open my door to you again," she said. "Never. I swear it."

"Your door." He chuckled and pressed his knee between hers. "I promise, you will open your door to me." His voice grew husky. "Caitlin. Dear God, Caitlin, how I've missed you."

He'd lost that undercurrent of amusement which so annoyed her, and he sounded … intense. Appealing. So much like the lad who she'd loved that, for one moment, she was swept back to the days when every breath she took, she took for him.

No. She would not fall into that trap again.

"Don't," he said. "Don't think of the old days. Think of *now.*"

Now, when she hadn't experienced the weight of a strong, healthy man atop her for nine long years. When the way he held here recalled the dreams that had haunted her and given her the only pleasure she ever dared take. His thigh pressed against her bottom. He thrust against her as if trying to ease the eagerness of his erection, and deep inside, desire spread its undeniable dampness.

"Think of you and me." His lips moved against her cheek. "You and me, alone with nothing more important than to live for this moment."

"Don't!" Her voice grew from a whisper. "I'm not one of your men. This mission is going to succeed, and I'm going to go on to another mission, another success."

He stopped kissing her. He laid his head next to hers, so close his breath touched her lips. "Tell me, darlin'." His cheek stroked hers. "What does Kiernan think about you working for Throckmorton … as a spy?"

He sounded calm, but her heartbeat picked up. Amazing how he could make her feel uneasy. "Kiernan knows what my life has been since my disgrace. He knows how I've searched for a way to give my life meaning." She stared straight ahead, ignoring the man above her. "Now I've found it."

Taran wouldn't allow her to distance herself from him. Of course not. He flipped her over to face him, imprisoned her hands, sprawled atop her again. "You must be jesting. You're a gently bred female, the daughter of a Scottish laird. You can't really be a spy for the English."

If she hadn't been in such an untenable position … if he hadn't been imprisoning her hands … if his scent didn't fill her nostrils … she would have rejoiced to see him so incredulous. "Do you think Mr. Throckmorton would send me as a jest? I am a spy."

"This is an aberration. A lark!" He stared down at her, his gray eyes hypnotic with conviction. "You can't possibly plan to make a career of this."

She stared back at him, strengthened by her own fervor. "Just like you, Taran Tamson."

"Like me? You've got it wrong."

"Then tell me how it is." She smiled, mocking him with her refinement. "Enlighten me, oh most mercenary of pirates."

"I'm not going to be a spy forever. I'm going to—" He shook his head, as if he couldn't believe their dispute. Yet he had to know she was serious. He did know she was serious, for he muttered, "Reason never worked with you."

And he kissed her. Kissed her with all the passion and warmth of summers long gone. On his lips, she tasted the sweetness of cherries, the freshness of the wind, the joy of first love. Her eyes filled with tears at the delight of having a male body – his male body – atop of hers once more.

Was she so susceptible to his touch, his concern, the history they shared? Apparently so, for her body warmed and softened. Desire arrived, fresh as the spring grass where they'd lain to consummate their union. All those old feelings of sensual pleasure and anxious longing flooded back, and with them the physical symptoms. Her fingers wanted nothing so much as to seek the hard planes of his chest and find the long-forgotten nipples that lay hidden in the rough curls of hair. Her breasts grew swollen and tender, and she moved beneath him, trying to ease the ache.

Yet no matter how much he coaxed, she wouldn't allow his tongue in her mouth. She'd learned hard lessons, and she wouldn't be used again. Now she lived for herself and her family, and her family … for her brother.

Oh, Kiernan.

Pain swept her. She whimpered.

"What?" Taran whispered against her lips. "Tell me what's wrong."

She would not. Years ago, he'd lost the right to comfort her. But she did want surcease from anguish. "You owe me," she muttered.

"Aye, but what's wrong?"

She pressed her mouth to his. She kissed him, slipping her tongue between his lips. Questions forgotten, he opened for her. That was how it should be. He had no right to question her about her pain, her joy, her sorrow. She explored the sweet cavern of his mouth, and his tongue twined around hers, a sweet struggle for supremacy.

Neither won.

Both won.

She struggled against his grip, but only because she wanted to run her fingers through the feather-soft length of his hair.

His beard softly rubbed against her chin, a new sensation both irritating and thrilling. He was a new man, harder, stronger, more dangerous, yet at the same time she recognized his body, his scent … his being. He gave to her with a passion that filled the empty hollows of her soul.

How could she have forgotten? They were lovers, bodies singing in tune: pleasure and pain, joy and sorrow.

His hands slid up her arms to her body, smoothing the black bombazine and delighting the flesh beneath it. Free to touch him at last, she caressed his cheek with the backs of her knuckles, and allowed him to press kisses on her palms. The caress of his lips, the brief, erotic touch of his tongue, made her gasp and sigh with enchantment.

His eyes flashed, alight with eager passion. Impatience pulled at the hollows of his cheeks and lit his tanned skin with a faint glow. That face, the one she had loved so long ago, had matured to a masculine beauty that made her throat grow tight.

She moved restlessly beneath his weight, wanting more, always more. A familiar longing, yet made different with the passage of time. Lifting himself, he looked into her face, then down at her breasts straining against the black fabric that covered them. "You are so beautiful." He brushed his palms against her nipples.

She hadn't been touched like this so long. She was starved for pleasure.

He fed her with his eagerness and his skill. He opened the

top button of her bodice and petted the hollow of her throat. "Like the finest silk from China," he muttered hoarsely. He opened another button, and another, revealing her chest, the beginning of her chemise, her corset ...

No warning bells rang in her mind. Her flesh was starved for him, and she fed on his touch without thought. Experience assured her he would bring her pleasure, and she sought pleasure ruthlessly. She clutched his shoulders, taking joy in the width of them, the heavy muscles that layered his arms and weighed her down. He kissed her flesh with slow, languorous strokes, tasting her skin at each stop, moving ever closer to her breasts. Her nipples beaded with anticipation; soon, so soon, he would suckle with all the purpose of a man bent on gratification. His ... and hers.

He drew back the light cotton of her chemise. He gazed on her with all the power of a conqueror. He reached with his fingers, circled her nipple, touched the tip lightly with his callused thumb.

Pleasure struck like lightning. She arched up, flung her hands out...

She touched the hard metal of cold reality.

The pistol. When she tore at the sheets in her futile effort to get away, she had pulled the pillow toward her, and beneath it rested her salvation. *Her pistol.* A chill worked its way up her spine. She shuddered as odious deliberation worked its way through the haze of sensation.

She'd put that pistol there to defend herself. Defend herself from men like Taran.

What was she doing? Yes, if she made love with him, she would feel better ... while it was happening.

Afterward ... oh, heavens, afterward! How could she have forgotten? Afterward, he would laugh and be off, once again leaving her in the wreck of her dreams.

No. Never again. Before she could entertain second thoughts, she smacked his temple with her elbow.

With a roar, he clutched his head.

Shoving him off her, she rolled to her feet and out of his reach. She ran backward toward the window. She raised the pistol. It shook in her hand, but she pointed the barrel at his chest and in a level voice, said, "Get out of my room."

He bounded up, still holding his throbbing temple. "What

the hell did you do that for?" Seeing the gun, he stopped, swaying. "Where did you get that?"

"From under the pillow." She supported her firing hand with the other. "I want you out of my room."

"Are you joking? A minute ago you wanted me. In fact" – his gaze sharpened as he looked at her bosom, displayed like a shopkeeper's goods – "in fact you still want me."

All the wispy remnants of pleasure dispersed under his scrutiny and his sarcasm. "You know I know how to use this. Get out of my room and don't ever come back."

"You don't mean that." He started walking toward her slowly, speaking in the soft tones of a wild animal trapper. "You love me. You've always loved me."

The room wasn't big enough for the two of them. The world wasn't big enough for the two of them. She steadied the gun, aimed it. "Don't make me do this."

"Caitlin, darlin' …" He moved closer. His eyes gleamed.

She knew that expression. He wasn't going to stop.

So she pulled the trigger.

CHAPTER FOUR

The blast spun Taran around. The bullet ripped through his right upper arm, barely missing the bone. Blood blossomed. He yelled as he hit the floor, tumbled sideways, and held the wound as if he suffered in agony.

As Cate supposed he was. "I did not enjoy that, but I hope this taught you a lesson on the futility of wagering with me while I hold a firearm."

He writhed on the floor.

Damn him. Why had he forced her to take such drastic action? If he'd endangered the mission, she would personally tear him limb from limb. Or at least complain severely to the Home Office. With deadly calm she walked to the door and opened it. "I want you out of here. Now."

Taran stared out the door. The flush drained from his face, leaving it the color of parchment. His lips moved, although Cate didn't know what he said.

She didn't care. She wanted him to leave her alone to face the ugly truth … that she still wanted this smug, lying, despicable pirate who had loved and abandoned her. Gesturing toward the corridor, she said, "Out."

She watched as he lurched to his feet. Saw that he wasn't watching her, but stared outside the door. Turned to look…

A woman of perhaps fifty years stood beside Cate's trunk. She was short and plump, with a round face lined by harsh experience, and a head of snowy white hair crowned with a dowager's lace cap. The style of her plain black clothing echoed Cate's, but while Cate's was a hardy bombazine traveling outfit, this lady's dress was a finer, newer mixture of worsted and silk called barathea. She wore a double strand of pearls in an old-fashioned twist, and the clasp of silver and tiny diamonds sat at the side of her sagging throat. She carried in her slight form a dignity and authority that made Cate gulp and Taran … goodness, Taran was blushing.

Cate fumbled to cover herself.

The lady stared at Taran, her mouth a grim line. With a distinguished French accent and in a tone of ominous fury, she snapped, "I heard the gunshot and rushed down in fear and trembling ... and what a sight meets my eyes! You are here, in a young lady's bedchamber, and by the manner in which she is clothed or unclothed and clutching that pistol, and you are clutching your shoulder, I would have to say you are unwelcome." Her gaze flicked to the rumpled bed. "Taran, what have you done?"

"Made a tactical error," he admitted.

"Such a mistake could get you killed." Sweeping in, she walked to where he stood, swaying. "You're not badly injured," she stated in a manner so decided Cate thought his bleeding would cease.

"No, ma'am. Caitlin is a crack shot." His lips were white. He held his arm, and blood seeped through his fingers. "She chose not to hurt me badly."

Eyes narrowed, the lady looked Cate over, and such was the strength of her pale blue gaze that Cate found herself making an explanation. "I shot him in his right shoulder because he's left-handed. I didn't want to incapacitate him."

"Why not, young lady?"

"Because he's —" She looked to Taran for guidance.

"Because I'm the Cap'n," Taran said. "She *knows*. Caitlin is the picklock we've been waiting for."

"They sent us a *girl?*" The lady didn't even try to restrain her incredulity.

Cate stiffened. She didn't care how imperious the lady was. She didn't care that the circumstances couldn't have looked worse. She was tired of having her abilities questioned. "I'm the best."

"We'll see." The lady pointed toward Taran, then toward the door. "Now get out and don't come back until you can behave with more propriety."

"Yes, ma'am." He bobbled his head. "As you say, ma'am."

Cate watched the little scene, her hand at her throat. Who was this woman who so intimidated Taran? And why was Taran abandoning her to the lady's stern care?

He stopped in the doorway. "Trust her as you trust me."

In a low tone, Cate said, "That is not a reassurance."

She could see by the lines that creased his forehead that he was in pain. But he laughed. "Then trust her more than you trust me." He left without looking back.

Cate released the breath she'd been holding. Placing the pistol on the table, she buttoned her bodice all the way up to her throat. Then she dove toward her trunk, grasped the handle, and dragged it inside. The weight made her gasp for breath; she saw no reason to go on an adventure without the proper clothing.

With restrained violence, the lady shut the door behind Cate, then sent a hard look toward her. "You're observant, to so quickly see that Taran is left-handed."

Cate didn't see any reason to lie. "We knew each other ... before."

"Did you? Where?"

"In Scotland. Years ago."

"I thought I detected a Scottish accent. Your name is ...?"

"Miss Cate MacLean."

The lady, who had been demanding and overbearing in a way sure to get up Cate's nose, lost color. Her mouth grew pinched and the wrinkles at her brow bit deep into the pale skin. "MacLean?"

The lady's fifty years had not been easy ones, Cate realized. She looked as if she might faint. Cate placed a chair behind the lady. "MacLean."

The lady sank down and fanned her cheeks with her hands.

Cate flipped open the latches of her trunk and found her array of fans, packed firmly below the curve of the lid. Opening one, an ivory fan carved with gold curlicues, she set to work cooling the lady.

The lady said, "The MacLeans have been hereditary allies in the struggle to keep Cenorina independent."

"I don't know about that, ma'am, but I suppose you're right." Of course, she had to be right. But in those years, Cate had been young and almost as arrogant as this lady. She hadn't asked why Taran had been educated and trained with such care. This evening had made her think that her lack of curiosity had been an ill-fated oversight.

"There's a connection between you and the Cap'n." The lady stared down at the floor and shook her head. "And I didn't think the situation could get worse."

Cate bristled.

But the lady at once realized how that must sound, for she

looked up and caught Cate's hand. "Not that there's anything amiss with you. It's Taran with whom I'm displeased."

Cate didn't quite believe her, but this lady obviously played an important role in this mission. Since Cate thought it bad form to shoot their leader *and* alienate another member of the mission on her first night, she accepted the conciliation. "I'm sorry, but I don't know who you are."

"Of course you don't, dear. That dreadful lad didn't introduce us. You may call me … let's see –" the lady pressed her finger to her lips in thought – "you may call me Sibeol."

Only Sibeol? Not Her Holiness Sibeol? But the lady seemed to think she had granted Cate quite an honor, so Cate responded accordingly. "Thank you … Sibeol. But I was also wondering what you do."

"Do?"

"As in … for this mission, I'm the lockpick. What do *you* do?"

"Oh. Dooo." Sibeol laughed merrily. "I serve as the voice of good sense. You might say … I'm the matriarch of this expedition."

Cate had met her share of domineering women – her mother was one – but she couldn't continue to interrogate Sibeol. For all her small stature, Sibeol dominated the room. She acted as if she had rights granted by God Himself. Cate would have given much to know if that attitude could be acquired, if one had to be born with it, or if it could be purchased.

As Sibeol looked Cate over, her severity eased. "I spent my youth envying tall, willowy women, but I'm too old to want to be anything but what I am. So I can look on you and think how lucky you are."

Cate fumbled for words as she had fumbled with her buttons. "Some people would tell you I'm too tall."

"They are jealous."

Without fondness, Cate remembered the girls who had taunted her when she was twelve and towered over the lads. "They are fools."

"You're quite comely." It was clear Sibeol considered hers the deciding opinion. "You could use some polish, but I'm sure that will come with time."

"I don't know why you believe me to be unpolished."

"You shot the Cap'n."

"That was not an ill-mannered action, but one of necessity, and I warned him clearly enough to desist before I put the bullet in him."

"Those are good manners, indeed."

Sibeol could be as sarcastic as she liked. Cate didn't care, as long she understood the circumstances and Cate's quite practical defense.

"When I was young, I had hair as beautiful as yours. My husband used to brush it before we went to bed." Sibeol stared at Cate, but Cate would have sworn she didn't see her. "More than ten years he's been gone, and I still miss the old devil." Sighing, she brought her attention back to Cate. "Why don't I brush your hair?"

Discerned, Cate touched her chignon and the wisps of hair hanging around her face. "I … thank you. That would be lovely."

"Get your brush."

Cate did as she was told. Despite Sibeol's attempt to set her at ease, she couldn't have felt more awkward.

Sibeol indicated Cate should sit on the chair. "Did Taran … harm you?"

Cate had traveled to London by herself. She had found her way into The Distinguished Academy of Governesses, and convinced Adorna, Lady Bucknell, to take her in and then to recommend her to the Home Office. She had endured an interview with powerful men, and convinced them she should be chosen for this task. She had traveled to Poole. She had, at night, entered a pub filled with men. She had shot her former lover. But never had she been as intimidated as she was now. " I didn't let him."

"So you shot him *first*. Good for you." Sibeol's thin, grim mouth lifted in a smile. "But if you will allow me to pretend I am your mother, I would remind you that a young lady doesn't allow a man into her bedchamber. It's not proper, and it leads to this kind of unseemly behavior."

With unnecessary force, Cate sat on the straight-backed chair. "I did not *let* him in. He *came* in."

Sibeol gently pulled the pins from Cate's mussed hair, and placed them in a tidy pile on the nightstand. Holding Cate's shoulder-length hair in her hands, she said, "Lovely. Like liquid copper trouble." Sibeol smoothed the brush through the tangles. "I can't help but wonder about your presence here. What is a MacLean doing working for the English? I would have never thought a MacLean would so lower himself – or in your case, herself."

"Sometimes it is necessary to join with one's enemies for a common cause."

"That I understand. But surely your mother isn't happy about your role here."

In the understatement of her lifetime, Cate said, "My mother breaks every mold." Cate's mother smoked cigars, wore fashions that were thirty years out of date ... and disdained undergarments. Lady Bess would never venture to advise Cate on her choice of occupation.

"What about your brother? Kiernan, I believe his name is."

Cate pressed her hand over her heart. "Kiernan could never say no to me."

From the taproom below, they heard a crash loud enough to make them jump, and boisterous laughter. In her most acerbic tone, Cate said, "I knew all the lads in the MacLean clan, and from what I've observed, when men gather in a group, they become collectively stupid."

Sibeol laughed, and as if the sound of her own merriment startled her, she laughed again. "I've had a husband, and I've got a son, and I must agree with you."

For the first time since Taran had left, Cate relaxed. Funny, but even after she shot him, she had feared he couldn't be stopped. The boy she had known had grown into a man steeled in ruthlessness, and the danger of the mission paled in contrast with the danger he exuded.

Sibeol brushed some more. "How old were you when Taran seduced you?"

Cate refused to lie, or hide her face in shame. Lifting her chin, she said, "He didn't seduce me. I took advantage of his unhappiness and seduced him."

Sibeol caught a tangle in the brush, apologized, then asked, "Why was he unhappy?"

"I don't know." But his unhappiness had made Cate's heart ache, and she had thought she could cure him. "We shared a tutor and we raced to see who could learn more quickly. We were always neck-and-neck. My brother praised him as a great warrior, and the other lads admired him. But I think he missed his home."

"So you seduced him." Sibeol brushed some more. "He didn't have to take advantage of your offer."

Cate held her head carefully erect, letting Sibeol do her job. "As afterwards, my brother pointed out to me repeatedly."

"Hm. Aye. So Taran left, and you paid the price."

"Left, with promises to return. He never did." Even now, the knowledge that he had willfully lied made Cate want to find him ... and shoot him again. Lower, and toward the middle of his body. "I learned a lot from Taran."

"Nine years ago?"

Swinging around, Cate snatched the brush out of Sibeol's hand. "Are you pretending ignorance, then? Do you already know the whole, sordid story?"

"No. I only know Taran's story." Sibeol's voice was tender and sad. "You see, I'm his mother."

CHAPTER FIVE

"His ... mother?" Cate searched Sibeol's face, searching frantically for a resemblance. "You don't look… I mean, he doesn't look…"

"Taran looks like my father, except for his square jaw. That he got from my husband, his father. Except — his father was never shot by a woman." Sibeol put her wrinkled hand to her cheek. "Although I *am* a very good shot, and there *were* times Tonio certainly deserved it."

"Men," Cate said.

"Precisely."

Cate felt funny about meeting Taran's mother. Well, of course she did. She'd talked with Sibeol about the fact she and Taran had … had …

Cate made it a policy not to blush. Pink cheeks clashed with her red hair. But she blushed now, cleared her throat, and deftly avoided the one subject guaranteed to make her blush yet more. "If you are his mother, then you can tell me who he is, and why you sent him to Scotland to be fostered, and how he came to be a pirate."

Sibeol cocked her head and studied Cate as carefully as Cate had studied her. "Actually, I can't. The information is his alone to disclose, and he has good reasons to conceal his past. But I can tell you this, my dear. No matter what passed between you in the past, no matter what happens in the future … he can never be yours."

"I don't want him."

Cate's assurance did not deter Sibeol. "He is betrothed to another."

Cate groped for her throat. *Betrayed. Again.* She had known Taran was a lying swine, but this … this fresh evidence choked her.

Then the choking sensation became a laugh, short and sharp and loud. "Betrothed? That's rich!"

"I know he broke your heart and took your virtue —"

"You know *nothing.*" Cate rose and paced away to the window. She pretended to stare out into the dark.

Sibeol picked her words carefully. "His betrothed is a

woman of good character."

Cate swung to face Sibeol. "And a virgin?"

Now Sibeol looked concerned, as if she feared Cate would faint or shout or … behave in an unseemly manner. "She is well-guarded."

"How … glorious … for her." Cate laughed again, more quietly, and to herself, she said, "What a relief this is for me. Yes. A relief."

"I'm glad that you are taking this so well." Sibeol didn't seem convinced Cate was taking it well at all.

"Yes. I am. Taran's fiancée is what I should remember as we go forward with this mission. Isn't she?" Cate didn't wait for an answer. "Remembering her place in his life will strengthen me and keep me from having to put another bullet into your son."

"That would be pleasant." Obviously, Sibeol had stayed behind to give Cate that piece of information. Now that she had done so, she rose and moved toward the door. Opening it, she turned, steely-eyed, to deliver another message. "The mission is all important. Our personal feelings and desires are nothing compared to taking Cenorina back from Maddox Davies, and returning it to the caring arms of its rulers. Let us all remember that, and proceed with that goal in mind." Sweeping from the room, she shut the door behind her.

Cate rushed to turn the key in the lock. "Yes. Let us all remember that." She tried to concentrate on that. But her heart ached too much for such wisdom. Leaning her hot cheek against the rough wood, she said, "I only wish I could forget why Taran once meant so much to me."

The Isle of Mull, Scotland, 1831

Clutching her best glass marble, thirteen-year-old Caitlin knelt on the hard-packed dirt and lowered her cheek until it rested on the ground. She sighted along a straight line, right at Graeme MacQuarrie's blue-swirled marble, and with an expert flick of her fingers sent his spinning out of the circle. The lads gathered around gave a groan. Graeme fell backward, clutching his head in pitiful despair. Sitting up, Caitlin flung out her arms, and gave a shout. "Ha! I told you I would beat you, Graeme. I told you. Now give me that marble!"

Her brother's warm, laughing voice intruded on the moment. "Such overweening conceit isn't pretty in a girl."

She twisted around to see Kiernan, standing by the edge of the stable, with a slight youth slouching beside him, eyes on the ground, lips sulky. "The lads would behave the same toward me."

"So they would." Kiernan moved forward, the youth straggling after him. "The more fools, they." He nodded at the boys, then with his hand on the strange youth's shoulder, he said, "I'd like you all to welcome Taran Tamson to Castle MacLean. He's come here to complete his education and learn how to be a warrior. Taran, this is our neighbor, Graeme MacQuarrie, his cousin, Will, our own cousin, Jimmy MacGillivray, the Buchanan twins, Morgan and Gunn, and Douglas Ross, another lad like yourself I'm pleased to foster." The boys stood up as he introduced them, nodded their heads, and scrutinized the young man.

Taran stared back, examining them with a cool interest that seemed at odds with his shoddy demeanor. He was shorter than her, and so thin his chest was almost concave. His shirtsleeves were too short for his arms and his ankles shone beneath the hems of his trousers. Kiernan always said the way to judge how a lad would grow was to measure the size of his hands. Well, Kiernan topped six-foot-two, and Taran's hands were as huge and raw-boned as Kiernan's own.

Kiernan smiled down at her. "And, Taran, this unpleasantly victorious girl with the dirt on her cheek is my sister, Caitlin."

Taran scarcely flicked her a glance. "I'm pleased to meet all of you, and I look forward to furthering our acquaintance."

Caitlin tilted her head and studied him. He spoke with a slight accent, one that wasn't quite Scottish and certainly not English. "You sound funny," she said.

For the first time, he looked down at her.

She almost fell backward from the shock. His broad, bony face was austere, unsmiling. His nose was thin and too long. His black hair was shorn, and his ears stuck out. But his bleak gray eyes were rimmed with the most beautiful fringe of black lashes, and the rage there burned red and hot and passionate.

A kindred spirit. She recognized him.

But he didn't seem to recognize her. Without interest, he

replied, "I'm from south of here."

Rising to her feet, she scrubbed at the dirt on her cheek. She had already gained her full height, and her figure had a way of making men stare.

Taran looked without interest at the dust on her skirt, then turned to Kiernan. "I thought you said your sister was thirteen."

"She is."

"She's horribly tall for thirteen."

Caitlin wanted to wilt into the ground.

But Kiernan wrapped his arm around her shoulders and clucked her under the chin. "Aye, she's a long-legged beauty with a mind that will outwit you if you don't study hard, Taran Tamson. Best take the warning and make the best of yourself."

"I will." Taran spoke the words like a vow. "I'm here to learn to fight."

Kiernan's face grew grave. "Not merely to fight. To speak Latin, French and Italian, to study mathematics, history, music and dance. I have a grave responsibility toward you, Taran. And you, too, Douglas."

Douglas nodded, but Taran said fervently, "I'll learn everything you can teach me, sir."

"Good." Kiernan leaned down to Caitlin and whispered, "You, minx, you are to treat Taran as your own brother. He's far from home, his father very recently passed on, and he misses his home and the rest of his family."

Then Taran and Kiernan walked on, and the lads followed as if mesmerized by the new boy.

Caitlin stood rooted in place. Always before, male attention had annoyed her. She preferred to run, to shout, to fight like a man. Nothing, she declared could make her simper around with a parasol and flutter her eyelashes at the stupid lads when she'd as soon trounce them in a horserace.

Now, in an instant, everything had changed. She wanted Taran to see her, to notice the way her breasts filled out her bodice and her waist curved in. She wanted to sit at his feet and stare into his smoky gray eyes surrounded by such lovely, long, dark eyelashes.

She put her hand over her fluttering heart.

She wanted him to take her in his arms and declare his

undying devotion. She didn't know why or how, but there could be no doubt.

She was in love with Taran Tamson.

CHAPTER SIX

Clutching his gory, shattered arm, Taran staggered down the corridor toward the stairway. Below him, in the taproom, the revelry continued unabated. The merriment and the music, the laughing shrieks from visiting ladies of the night.

Blood slid down to his elbow and onto the floor, but the bullet had gone right through the muscle. If a man had to be shot, this was the wound he wanted.

Taran had been shot before in battle, and suffered while a clumsy quack surgeon had dug the bullet out. Unfortunately, familiarity did not make the experience any easier to bear.

Damn it. *Damn it.* He had to jettison Cate. Since seeing her in the taproom, getting rid of her had been his only desire.

Well, not his *only* desire. But the other wasn't a desire, really. More of an instinct, a sense, a need …

He started to descend the stairway, then paused to lean against the railing and breathe … deeply. His head was swimming…

In 1831, King Edward Antonio Dashiell Kane of Cenorina died, his mother was struggling to maintain control of the country, and on her insistence, fourteen-year-old crown prince Antonio Raul Edward Kane was given an alias, smuggled out of the warm, sunny islands and sent into bleak and lonely exile in Scotland.

Taran Tamson was that alias. Taran was that crown prince.

At the time Taran left Cenorina he was still a scrawny youth who, except for the characteristic Kane family jaw, looked like no one else in the Kane family. His mother claimed he looked like her father, but the comte of Gramont had been dead for thirty years, and no one else remembered him.

During his first year in Scotland, Taran's voice deepened, he shot up seven inches in five months, and his feet grew so quickly the boot-maker was tearing his hair.

Now, twelve years later, Taran disguised his jaw with a short black beard. He had continued to mature until he stood six foot four in his stocking feet and outstripped everyone in his family — except for, perhaps, the comte of Gramont — in height and breadth.

Women in ports as far away as Istanbul and Bombay had avowed they would never forget his pale gray eyes, but he'd seduced not a single lady since returning to England. No one recognized him here. He took care to keep it that way.

Now Cate MacLean had arrived, and like a cat in the chicken house, she'd set loose chaos.

What kind of man was he? He had a mission. For years, he had dreamed of, imagined, sought to right the wrong done to him, his family and to Cenorina. Now, at last, he had his chance ... and he had allowed himself to be distracted by a female.

The trouble was, Cate was no mere female. When he had lived on the Isle of Mull, she was the woman who had haunted his dreams. Then, for the first five years on the pirate ship, he'd scarcely thought of her and never dreamed of her. Hell, he never got enough sleep to dream at all. There'd been no women; in the hierarchy of the ship, he was on the bottom rung with no power to claim a captive for his own nor even any money to buy a dockside whore.

When he'd become captain ... how well he remembered the girl his crew had brought him. Blowfish and the others had chipped in to get him the fanciest piece of English ass in Singapore. A thank you, they said, for ridding them of the blackguard who had commanded them for so long. Taran had gazed on the girl's lush curves, golden hair and pale skin, and for one moment he'd been transported back to Scotland and to Cate's arms.

He didn't know why. That female bore not even the slightest resemblance to Cate. But he'd seen what he wanted to see and he'd found a passing pleasure in her arms.

After that, he had picked his own fancy pieces, and they'd always looked like Cate. Every woman he had kissed had Cate's delicately-boned face. Every body he caressed was tall and sleek. He could not claim the real Cate, not while keeping faith with the mission to recover Cenorina, and the world had been bleak and colorless.

Tonight, it was as if a rainbow had exploded in his mind.

He looked down at his arm.

But no. A rainbow had exploded in his flesh. Red for the blood, blue and yellow for the bruising. Blowfish would have to care for him now. He only hoped he didn't make the mistake of falling down the stairs in a faint. His men would never let him live it down.

Leaning his weight against the railing, he descended into the taproom.

His men were drunk, every man Jack of them.

Quicksilver held a doxy on his lap.

Dead Bob was leading a lady of the evening toward the kitchen.

Lilbit was intent on proving to a whore his nickname involved his age and not his physique.

But Blowfish ... where was Blowfish?

Taran spotted a fully dressed female who appeared to be in the throes of ecstasy. Moving closer, he observed the soles of a pair of shoes sticking out from under her lumpy skirt. A man's pair of shoes, wiggling enthusiastically.

He'd found Blowfish. He aimed a kick at the largest lump. When he connected, he heard a yelp from beneath her skirts.

Blowfish emerged, fists up, eyes belligerent, until he saw Taran. "Cap'n?" His gaze fell on the burned and bloodstained shirt, and Taran saw sobriety strike him.

For that reason, Blowfish was his first mate. This man, sun-spotted, middle-aged and reaching no taller than Taran's chest, could be depended upon in a crisis.

"What happened, Cap'n?" Blowfish demanded with a great measure of hostility.

"I faced off with the wrong enemy." Taran indicated the back room. "Fix me up?"

Blowfish got to his feet.

The prostitute gave a shriek of dismay.

Taran asked, "Did you let her down, man?"

Blowfish snorted. "She's got nothing to complain about."

They entered the room they'd turned into the men's barracks, and Blowfish pulled his medicine bag out from under his bunk. "Ye might want to lie down," Blowfish suggested. "Ye're looking peaked."

Torn between tumbling onto the mattress and the pain that doing so would cause, Taran lowered himself inch by laborious inch. The gunshot wound burned like fire, each movement jolted his entire body, and when he finally reclined full length on the mattress, he closed his eyes and fought to control his churning stomach.

Blowfish leaned over him. With his knife, he cut away Taran's shirt, baring the wound. In a low, intense voice, he said, "Tell me who did this, Cap'n, and I'll kill the bastard."

Reluctantly, Taran looked up at his first mate. The temptation to lie was strong, but the truth would out and the razzing would never cease. "Remember that woman who came into the taproom?"

"The tall one with the shock of angry red hair? That lass?" Blowfish cackled. "That *girl?*"

The ridicule had started already. "I didn't think she'd really shoot me."

"How did she surprise a man such as yerself — an important man, a Cap'n — with a gun?"

Taran didn't know if the pain was worse from his shoulder or from his humiliation. "She didn't surprise me exactly."

Like a whale blowing at the surface, Blowfish breathed loudly through his nose. "What, exactly, did she do?"

"When last I saw her, nine years ago, she was wild, but sweet. Now she's a termagant."

"Ye knew her before tonight?" While Taran winced, Blowfish cleaned the entry wound and pressed a clean pad over it. "Why didn't ye say something in the taproom?"

"It's not that simple, Blowfish." Tonight when he'd first seen Cate, he had planned to go to her. Introduce himself. See if the mere sight of him would discourage her from pursuing this madness.

It hadn't. She'd been highly perturbed, as she had the right to be, but she hadn't seemed unduly discouraged.

Then he'd planned to invoke the use of good sense, logic, and family loyalty to convince Cate to leave. He thought he'd done a reputable job of that.

But he had known she wouldn't listen. Stubborn as sin, was his Caitlin, and he'd doubted the passage of time could change that. He'd been right, of course. Cate had gotten a mulish expression on her face, an expression with which he was too familiar, and she had declared she would stay.

"Let me get this straight. Ye saw she had a gun. She pointed it at ye and threatened to shoot ye. But ye didn't believe she'd go through with it?"

"It sounds stupid when you say it that way."

"Say it so it doesn't sound stupid," Blowfish challenged.

The door opened. Taran twisted his head to see who it was — and realized that tonight was most definitely not his night.

Sibeol came in and shut the door behind her.

Blowfish bowed deeply, his awe of the queen not lessened by knowing her son.

Always gracious, she said, "Mr. Blowfish, it is a pleasure to see you." Then, without waiting for a greeting, she asked, "Taran? She says she's a MacLean. You seduced a MacLean and promised to come back for her?"

"Ye seduced her?" Blowfish asked in amazement.

"Years ago," Taran said.

Sibeol tapped her foot. "And afterward disappeared without a trace."

"I thought I would keep that promise." Taran didn't know why he bothered to defend himself. He couldn't win this argument. "You know why I didn't return."

"Did you truly intend to?"

"Aye, I intended to."

"For what purpose?" Queen Sibeol demanded. "To have her as your mistress? You know who you are. You understand your duties. That girl is noble, but you can't marry her!"

Taran would accomplish nothing by alienating his mother now, yet he had to speak. "I know you have chosen a royal maiden for me, Mother, but the young woman must be released from any agreement you have made. Whoever she is, I cannot wed her!"

"Wait a minute." Blowfish lifted his hand away from his task. "That woman up there, the woman who shot you — she's a MacLean?" His voice rose. "That is Caitlin MacLean?"

Taran started to answer.

Blowfish didn't wait. "Of course she is. I shoulda recognized her. She has the look of all those wenches you —"

Taran glared at him.

Blowfish swallowed his words.

It would not do to speak of Taran's dockside loves in front of his mother.

"She looks like the type of lady you favor," Blowfish said sedately. Then, as if he were puzzled, which he certainly was not, he scratched at the gray stubble on his chin. "So ye're telling me that years ago, ye seduced the young miss upstairs and left 'er alone to deal with the consequences."

In profound irritation, Taran snapped, "I was kidnapped and sent off to be murdered!"

His mother gave him no reprieve. "This is no excuse! You should never have taken her in the first place. As for the present state of affairs — her bed was rumpled. Tonight you tried to seduce her … *again.*"

And he got caught by his *mother*. Taran had lived through every man's worst nightmare — *his mother* had caught him bedding a woman. No, worse — trying to bed a woman and failing.

"I want Cate to go away, and I thought the best way to frighten her was to … to …" To threaten her … with himself. Taran had thought if he took her in his arms, held her struggling body against his, and forced his kisses on her, she would recall the disgrace their liaison had brought her, and run away.

Instead, he was the one who had remembered. Remembered her silky skin against his, the scent of her hair, the passion and the fire of her body.

Blowfish helped Taran to roll over and started on the exit wound.

In a voice that was worse than severe – in a voice that was saddened – his dear, darling mother who had undergone so much, said, "I am disappointed in you."

"Ma'am, truly, no more disappointed than I am in myself. The first time, I was …" He turned his head to the wall. "I was angry at myself for being such a coward, for not returning to Cenorina and doing my duty."

"And ye were seventeen," Blowfish said. "The selfsame definition of stupid."

"Yes, thank you, Blowfish," Taran said in profound irritation. "We have established that I was and am stupid!"

Blowfish applied such pressure to the wound Taran's eyes rolled back in his head. "Ye *are* stupid to give grief to the man cleaning this pitiful little hole in yer arm."

When Taran had ceased writhing, Sibeol asked, "Your father and I tried to impress on you your noble obligations."

"You did," Taran admitted. "I knew right from wrong. I have

no excuse except ... that last year in Cenorina, Father was sick and you were busy with him, and Mr. Davies was my tutor. He ... he encouraged me in every foolish endeavor, in every dissipation and careless emotion."

Sibeol took a wavering breath.

Cautiously Taran reached out to her to touch her hand. "But between the pain at losing my father and knowing you were imprisoned, and the MacLeans and their good teaching, I swear to you I thought I could make things right with Cate ... somehow. And Cate ... she was sixteen and so beautiful, and she loved me. Truly loved me for myself. She saw no blemish, no corruption, no *stupidity*. She soothed me, pleased me, gave me happiness where all was a desert..."

CHAPTER SEVEN
The Isle of Mull, Scotland, 1834

Sweat dripped off of Taran's forehead as he slashed with the claymore, using the heavy steel blade with the skill Kiernan had taught him and an aggression all his own. He drove Graeme MacQuarrie back toward the fence, and it took Kiernan's shout before he would back away.

Kiernan removed the handle from Taran's sweaty fingers. "Damn, lad, you've got no enemies here. If you've got a fire in the gut, save it for true battle."

Taran nodded, his chest heaving. But he didn't really listen. It had been three years since his father, the king, had died. Three years since his mother, the queen, had sent him away from Cenorina, and since then he'd heard not one word about his kingdom, not one word of his mother. His heart ached to see her, to hold her in his arms and comfort her in her grief and loneliness. But he didn't even know if she was alive; he only knew that she wouldn't leave the country she had adopted with her marriage. When she saw him onto the ship, she had sworn to stay and lead the fighting, and to bring him back as soon as she could.

But he had heard no word. So probably ... probably ...they held her in prison.

Or... or she was dead. He never dared think much about it, but at night he dreamed, and his dreams were horrible. He wanted to cry. But men never cried.

Caitlin's strong voice shouted, "'Twas a good battle, lads! I could watch you both all day."

Unhurriedly, Taran turned his head.

Caitlin was sitting on the fence, her skirt tucked around her, grinning at him like a brownie bent on mischief.

As she was. Kiernan's gangly, graceless sister had grown into an exquisite young woman of sixteen, and she knew it. Knew it, and used every one of her feminine wiles to trap him.

He couldn't allow himself to be trapped. He was a man who had no future, because he was a man too cowardly to do what should be done – to return to Cenorina and face the villain who had stolen his home and sent him into exile. Aye, he should go to Cenorina, march up to Maddox Davies, and demand the return of his kingdom. Although Davies claimed to have noble English blood, he was nothing but a common tutor, and a coward. Davies would not dare harm Taran ... his student. Although Taran half-hoped he would try, for then Taran would fight him as he had found Graeme, and no one would stop him when he delivered the final blow.

Kiernan was talking to Graeme, demonstrating how to parry those slashing blows.

Caitlin jumped off the fence and sauntered toward Taran. Her long, auburn hair was tied back in a bow, and the wind ruffled the wisps that came loose around her face. Her complexion glowed with a touch of the sun, and her rosy lips smiled at him as if he were the only man on earth.

She had a way of making him feel like that.

Gripping his shoulder with her gloved hand, she whispered, "Take me to Granny Aileen's hut in the mountains across the water. We could meet there and you could teach me everything about making love." Her green eyes glowed with excitement, and she caressed his flesh with a subtle touch.

Instantaneously, his cock stood up and crowed.

How could she do this to him, every time, everywhere, no matter who was watching?

To hide his condition, he turned his back on Kiernan.

Aye, Caitlin was the most beautiful thing he'd ever seen, and he wanted her more than any other woman in the world. But he knew in his mind she was the one willing woman in Scotland he couldn't carelessly bed.

If only he could convince his body!

Caitlin didn't seem to notice. She stared at his face in adoration.

And he loved it. He had become addicted to her saucy wit, her husky voice, her swaying hips and glorious, long body. But he couldn't allow that to continue. He had duties to fulfill ... someday. Surely someday he would have duties once more.

When he danced with Caitlin at parties, or conversed with her after horse races, or played cards with her on long winter evenings, he forgot his guilt, his rage, his frustration, and for one moment in time was no more than a young man fascinated by a stunning young woman. If things were different, he would wed her. He would make her his princess, and she would charm everyone on the four islands. But that wasn't possible. He couldn't wed her. The future king had a duty to advance his country's wealth and position, and he could not do that by marrying a Scottish laird's sister, regardless of how attractive she was.

But did it matter, when he didn't even have the stomach to demand the return of his kingdom?

Other lasses came to him, offering themselves, exclaiming over his brooding gray eyes and his braw body. He took them. He learned what they had to teach him. He was seventeen. Ruefully he admitted his weakness. He could turn down no offer.

Except Caitlin's. She wanted him, and tormented him until he couldn't sleep at night, until the other women lost their savor and he pretended it was Caitlin's thighs he caressed, Caitlin's lips he kissed, Caitlin's who he rode.

Now he was a victim of his own disgraceful fantasies. Stripping off his leather gloves, he wiped his forehead on his sleeve.

Then, at last, she removed her hand from his shoulder.

Taran said, "Kiernan MacLean has provided me with shelter, food, clothing. He's taught me and protected me. If I seduced his sister, I would be the worst kind of man ..." If he brought disgrace upon Caitlin, Kiernan would flay him and chase him away like a mangy dog, and then ... then Taran would be forced to return to Cenorina and act as a crown prince should, with bravery and daring.

He stared straight ahead.

He couldn't lie to himself. Dishonoring his benefactor's sister to force himself into action would be the worst kind of cowardice.

She tugged at Taran's arm until he looked back at her. "Taran, you mustn't vex yourself." She gnawed on her lower lip as if she were shy.

He knew very well she was not. But he watched, fascinated beyond wisdom.

If only there was a way to have what he wanted and what Caitlin wanted, too.

In a soft voice, she said, "When we came together, it would not be a seduction. You see, Taran ... I love you."

CHAPTER EIGHT

Cate hesitated in the doorway of the taproom.

Gray sunlight, softened by the liberal application of fog, seeped through the windows. The two dozen men who had been so boisterous the night before sat eating in morose silence about a long plank table. The odor of kippers and bacon mingled with the stale scent of last night's ale.

The pirates were an unkempt bunch. Grimy scarves kept their lanky hair out of their eyes. One man wore an eye patch. One man had a hook where his arm should be. She recognized Maccus, the tow-headed Scot who last night had offered his services. For the first time in her life, she saw a man whose complexion was sooty black. He must be from Africa — a Negro. She wanted to stare, but these men — they were rough. They belched and scratched body parts she preferred not to notice. They spoke in growls and ate with their fingers except when they wanted to fillet a fish, then eight-inch long knives flashed out of their belt to be used with a skill that brought her heart to her throat.

These were Taran's men. He'd lived and fought and robbed with these fellows, and as she gazed at them, she could see into his past. If she used the proper approach, if she asked the right man, she might discover information necessary to handle Taran in the days ahead. The more she thought about the events of last night — and as the hours had ticked away and sleep remained elusive, she had thought long and hard — the more she became convinced Taran had deliberately planned each move on her.

If, at the first sight of him, she had turned tail and run, he wouldn't have given chase. He would have considered her flight a job well done.

He had already caused her one sleepless night. That would not do. She was a sensible woman on a mission. She needed her slumber.

So she stepped into the taproom, armed with questions.

At once the squint-eyed sailor spotted her. In an accent that sounded as if it had come straight from the back streets of London, he announced, "'Tis the lass what shot our cap'n."

In unison the benches scraped back and every man stood.

Placing her fist on her waist, she looked them over. It would not do for them to think they intimidated her. "Why, gentlemen. Your manners are impeccable. Methinks pirates have been maligned … and I would have thought you'd take it ill that I'd shot your beloved captain."

"It's not like ye killed 'im or anything." The squint-eyed fellow lithely leaped over his bench and came to her side. "Or like ye used a real gun. Hell, that li'l popgun ye used couldn't take down a turtle. But the point is, ye made 'im bleed and if you'd had recourse to a real gun, you'd have hobbled him considerable." Taking her hand, he pressed his lips to her knuckles, and looked up at her with twinkling brown eyes. "'Course, then we'da had to kill ye."

She removed her hand with alacrity. "You could have tried."

The men oohed and cackled.

The top of Squint-Eye's head was shiny and bald, which she noted readily for he reached no higher than her chin, but his bushy eyebrows rose long and high on his face. Blotches on his cheeks and ears marred his tanned skin, he was missing a top front tooth, and she would be hard pressed to guess his age. Forty, perhaps. Or fifty?

Did pirates live so long?

He scratched his stomach and grinned. "Aye, ye're a sharp un. No wonder ye put a bullet in the cap'n. I'm Blowfish. Blowfish Burnham, at yer service."

"Don't ask him how he earned the name of Blowfish," the sailor with the eye patch advised in an upper class British accent. "Or he'll tell you."

She glanced around, not understanding, and that was a cause for more laughter.

"Now hush up, men," Blowfish said. "She's a lady. Any damned fool can see that, and ye're all damned fools." To her, he said, "I'm the first mate of the Scottish Witch, the sweetest sailing ship ever to cruise the seas."

"The Scottish Witch is Captain Taran's ship?" As if Cate had to ask. Of course it was Taran's ship, and obviously, he had named it after her.

The louse.

"Aye, and she's as lithe and lovely as ye are." Blowfish put his hands to his cheeks and sighed as if overwhelmed by her beauty.

Which he might well be. She knew she looked her best in her stylish pelisse-robe of a striped taffeta in alternating shades of dark green. Her small squared collar was neat, and the trim of black velvet allowed her to wear mourning without actually advertising her grief. She worse a reticule belted at her side, one large enough to carry the essentials to grooming in such a rough environment — and, when necessary, her lockpick tools. Right now, she considered it necessary, and the tools rested snugly inside. On Mr. Throckmorton's advice she'd sewn a pocket in each of her skirts. But she would keep that a secret. She knew of no reason why Blowfish should know she kept a thin, sharp knife with her at all times.

Going to the head of the table, Blowfish clapped his hand on the one-eyed sailor's shoulder. "This smart-mouthed young feller is Quicksilver. A lady, disappointed in love, named him."

Quicksilver grimaced. "Pay no attention to Blowfish, ma'am. He imagines himself a wit, but he's only half that."

Blowfish rolled his eyes. "Very amusing, my good man." He was trying to do an imitation of Quicksilver, but he couldn't wrap his tongue around the noble syllables. "This is Dead Bob. He was named fer his sparkling personality."

Dead Bob nodded at her, his unlined, handsome face deadpan.

"We've got a reward fer the first person who can make him laugh," Quicksilver said.

"This is Mucus," Blowfish introduced a remarkably clean-nosed sailor.

"Maccus," the sailor muttered.

"Mucus," Blowfish insisted.

Color rose in the sailor's thin cheeks, and he looked up at her. "Beg pardon about last night."

The man obviously needed help. She was willing to provide it. "I would hope so. You'll never get a girl by offering yourself to her in a pub. If you'd like advice on courting, I'd be happy to assist you."

Dead Bob gave a crack of laughter.

Silence fell on the table. Everyone stared from her to Dead Bob and back again. Then, reluctantly, they dug out pound notes and gold coins and, as if she were a vendor, they tossed them at her.

"Everyone." Blowfish added his grimy bill to the growing pile. "You, too, Lilbit."

Lilbit was the cabin boy: youngest, blondest, and quite the tallest of the sailors. He hung his head and tossed in his coin.

Delighted, Cate considered the pile of money. "Is this truly mine?"

The men nodded glumly.

"Well! Thank you." Her first earnings! She gathered up the coins and bills and poked them in her reticule. "Although I still don't understand what you find so amusing in my offer to assist Maccus. It was sincerely made."

Dead Bob's expression was once again deadpan. "That's why it's funny."

When she had filled her pockets, Blowfish began introductions again. "This is Plum, this is Italy, this is Dove ..."

Dove was the black man. He spoke in a soft, oddly accented voice, his fingers fluttering as he spoke.

And so it went, down the line until she'd been introduced to every one of the sailors. At the top of the table, she looked them over again. "Don't any of you use your real names?"

Shoulders shrugged up and down like a wave.

"A bad notion when ye're a pirate," Blowfish explained. "Me mum would be mortified."

"Your mum," Cate said faintly. He was worried about his mother's opinion. As foul pirates went, these lads were failures.

Blowfish shoved Italy off his stool, then with a bow indicated Cate should seat herself there. "Lilbit, grab the lady a plate an' some rations from Mr. Cleary in the kitchen. Shooting the Cap'n is hard work."

The men cackled again, and Cate realized that with a single gunshot, she'd won their hearts. She thanked Lilbit for the plank of food, most of which appeared edible, and dug her fork out of her reticule.

"Oo, she's prepared," Blowfish marveled.

She said, "I like my dinnerware clean."

"Here in Cleary's Pub, 'tis spittin' clean." Blowfish spit on the floor in lieu of demonstration, placed his foot on the edge of her stool and leaned his arm on his thigh. "We've told ye our names."

He grinned as if he knew a huge joke. "So, li'l lady, introduce yourself to the men."

"I'm not little." With her elbow, she knocked his leg off the stool.

The pirates roared with laughter.

She waited until the commotion had died down and Blowfish had stopped faking distress. "I'm Cate MacLean."

All merriment stopped. All heads turned. All eyes stared — at Cate.

"What?" she asked.

"Cate? Caitlin?" Maccus spoke at last. *"Ye're* Caitlin MacLean?"

CHAPTER NINE

Blowfish cackled. "Thought that would knock ye men back onto yer conch shells!"

Some of the younger men looked confused.

But the others, the ones who looked as if they'd been around the globe a few times, exchanged glances and nudges.

Blowfish waved a hand up and down beside her as if selling her on the auction block. "Tall. Bit on the bony side. Red hair. Fair skin. Aye, she's Caitlin MacLean, all right."

"My God," Maccus said.

So they'd heard of her. She would love to know what Taran had told them, but in the end, what mattered was how she performed her post. "Thank you for assuring me of my identity."

Blowfish didn't notice her irritation. Or he didn't care. "The Cap'n runs to type, he does. Appreciates ladies of yer general stature and, shall we say, curvature."

"Does he keep them or does he sell them?" she snapped.

Blowfish exchanged a glance with Quicksilver. Quicksilver shook his head, and Blowfish said, "The Cap'n's all fer trading goods. He don't keep anything if he can help it."

"Then he hasn't changed a bit." She vigorously polished her fork on her handkerchief. "A good reason to shoot him. I'm surprised to hear I'm the first woman to do so."

"Not the first to try, but definitely the first to succeed," Quicksilver assured her.

She tasted the egg. Surprisingly, it was good. She took a bite of golden-brown biscuit. The crust was flaky, and from the inside steam roiled up like froth from a crashing wave. The bacon was crisp, not burned, and the potato patties contained a hint of parsley. She looked up, amazement plain on her face, and the men burst into laughter.

"Why do ye think we stay here when we're in port?" Blowfish asked. "Cleary cooks like a dream, and after a long sea voyage, all we asks of life is a pat of butter an' a frothy pint of ale."

Cate considered them skeptically. "Is that *all* you ask?"

"That's all we can tell *you*, ma'am." Lilbit spoke with an odd accent. "The Cap'n says we're not supposed to talk about whores in mixed company."

Dead Bob smacked Lilbit on the back of the head.

Blowfish sighed. "Ye'll have to excuse the lad. He's as strong as a winch, but his mechanism is wound a little loose."

"It's all right," she said to Lilbit. "After a long sea voyage, I'd worry if you weren't interested in women."

"See?" Lilbit smacked Dead Bob right back.

Cate smiled at him. She wanted information about Taran and she thought Lilbit was the man to provide it. She told herself it was good to know your enemy, especially when you were to work closely with him. She told herself that knowledge was power. Most of all, she told herself that after her ordeals, she had a right to her curiosity. "You're so young. This must have been your first sea voyage."

Lilbit straightened his shoulders. "No, ma'am. I first put to sea outta Boston Harbor when I was nine."

"An American! That explains so much." She scrutinized him. Strong, virile, with blond hair that flopped in his bright blue eyes and the kind of wide open smile that made a woman want to hug him. "You must be … eighteen or nineteen now."

"Nineteen, Miss, that I am." Then he had been aboard when Taran had arrived.

"Did you first ship out with the Cap'n?" she asked.

"This Cap'n? No, we had a different cap'n then. This Cap'n was a fellow we were supposed to dump as soon as –" Nobody hit Lilbit on the back of the head this time, no one made a motion or said a word, but he stopped. He glanced around at the censuring faces, and the whites of his eyes showed. Ducking his head, he mumbled, "I forgot."

The silence that fell was ponderous, embarrassed, and filled with sidelong glances and disconcerted nudges.

Oh, no. Lilbit couldn't fall silent now. Not when she was on the verge of discovering how Taran had come to be the captain of a pirate ship. "So the Cap'n came on board as a sailor, too?"

"No." Lilbit jumped as if he'd been kicked. "Dunno."

Cate pressed the matter. "Is he related to one of you?"

Blowfish snorted. "Not 'ardly."

"How long ago did he come on board?" Cate insisted.

Quicksilver looked at Cate from the corners of his eyes. "Years ago."

Men were louts. They banded together to keep her in the dark about a matter that was surely of no consequence to any of them – and was a matter of much curiosity to her.

Then Blowfish roared, "Look lively, Cap'n's on board!"

As they had done when she walked in, the men rose in unison, but this time their respect was real and reverential. The Cap'n was their leader; they honored him as such.

From the stairwell, Taran said, "Be seated."

With a clatter of boots and a scraping of benches, they obeyed.

He bowed to Cate, a great, sardonic obeisance. "If you want to know how I came to my present position, Miss MacLean, ask me."

Actually, she wanted to ask him how, with a mother like his, he had come to be such a cheating betrayer of women and all-round snake in the grass. But last night she had resolved she would do her job with dignity and honor, and that meant she could not fight with the big liar, at least not in front of his men. "Certainly, Cap'n, I'm glad to ask you," she said. "Would you like to have this conversation now or in private?"

Blowfish chuckled, then sobered and cleared his throat. With his gaze on Taran, he pulled the single thin wisp of hair that hung over his forehead. "Sorry, Cap'n. Not funny at all."

Taran wore the somber black jacket and trousers of an English businessman, and the dark material contrasted with his pallid complexion. His white shirt was crisply pressed. His arm was in a sling. His boots were polished to a shine.

When she scrutinized him, she clearly saw the differences nine years had wrought.

His body had been honed to hard muscle held in coiled power. His cold gaze and stern lips were those of the Cap'n, leader of a pirate ship and of a mission that could end in death for all of them. His youth had been burned away in some great, harsh crucible of command, leaving only a hard man untouched by compassion or generosity.

And she knew if she was not fit to do her part, he would eliminate her. In fact, he intended to eliminate her.

It was up to her to convince him otherwise. She had no doubt she would do so, for Kiernan's sake.

And for her own.

CHAPTER TEN

Taran marveled at the scene in the taproom. At the long table his men, scourge of the Seven Seas, lolled about, staring at Cate as if they hadn't seen a woman for years — and after last night, he knew they'd all seen at least one each, both inside and out.

At the head of the table sat Cate, her plate pushed away, her elbow resting on the table, her chin perched on her fist. She looked at ease … until she gazed at Taran. Then her spine straightened, her shoulders squared, and her gaze cooled.

There! That was the woman who, the night before, had calmly shot him. His arm ached like hell this morning, but as Blowfish had pointed out, he would probably escape without an infection, and that was more than he deserved for being devilishly reckless. Although Blowfish had used a different adjective…

Taran would have told any man the same thing. He knew well enough that folly always extracted its price, and he wondered — what madness had caused his carelessness last night? He was a man in control of his emotions.

No. More than that. Those whirlwinds of fear and joy, happiness and grief did not influence his clear thinking. He determined a goal, he weighed the results of achieving that goal, and he either proceeded, or not. When unexpected trouble arose, he made logical, lightning-quick decisions, and they were always the right ones. He did not so lose himself in a woman's arms that he forgot good sense and forced her to shoot him. Moreover, he didn't lie to himself. If Cate hadn't shot him, he *would* have lost himself in her arms.

He could not afford such mistakes.

She must be replaced at once.

"Miss MacLean, come with me." He turned and mounted the stairs.

She followed him, the tap of her boots loud on the steps.

Behind them, in the taproom, a buzz of speculation rose.

He entered his bedchamber, the second largest in the inn. He walked to the table, cluttered with sea charts and roughly sketched maps of Cenorina, and turned to face her.

She did not enter. She was wary of entering any confined space with him, especially one with a bed.

So. She had learned her lesson, too.

She stood framed in the doorway, pulled a handkerchief out of her sleeve, and while she maintained eye contact, she meticulously wiped off her fork.

If he was reading her correctly, she was warning him she had a weapon. Not so great a weapon as her pistol, although perhaps she had that secreted on her body, too. But in skilled hands, a fork could cause considerable damage. A smile twitched his lips. Cate had always known how to wield a fork, especially when challenged by a roasted spring lamb.

She stuck the utensil in her reticule, and in a level voice that scorned him and his amusement, she said, "Tell me all, Cap'n. How did you come to your present situation?"

"Stupidity and luck, Miss MacLean. Stupidity and luck ... and some planning."

"That's not an answer," she said precisely. "I want an *answer*. Last night you said you were kidnapped. By whom?"

She wanted to know what had happened to him nine years ago when he left her. He couldn't tell her all of it, of course. He didn't talk about the first five years — not to anyone. But he could give her the bones of his story. Perhaps he owed her that. "I returned to Cenorina, to my home, but someone was not pleased to see me once more."

"Sir Maddox Davies?"

"When I knew him, he was plain Mr. Maddox Davies. But I failed to realize that during my exile in Scotland, he had taken all power into his hands." What a young fool Taran had been. He had actually gone to his former tutor and ordered Davies to leave Cenorina. It ever crossed his mind his tutor could use his sword so skillfully, nor that he would dare harm someone so noble as Crown Prince Taran of Cenorina. "He had me permanently removed from the islands ... by pirates."

"Those gentlemen downstairs?" Cate was making fun of him. She'd met Blowfish and Lilbit and Dove, and she'd seen only the surface. She didn't know the dangers they'd faced, the scars they carried, and how very dangerous they could be.

Right now, it suited Taran not to tell her. "Aye. Some of

those men were on board."

"Why does Sir Davies hate you so much?" Doubt weighted her voice.

He smiled gently, thinking of his ex-tutor and how very much damage Davies had wrought. "I don't know that he hates me. Perhaps he does. But looking back, I would say he is an opportunist, driven by greed. My family was wealthy and influential. I stood in his way."

"But he *must* hate you! To give you to the pirates … not all boys who go to sea even on the ships of Her Majesty's Navy are treated well, and some die! Did he not know that?"

"Indeed he did. Unfortunately for Davies, I have a strong survival instinct, something that I intend to explain to him myself at some time in the not-too-far-distant future." He seated himself at the low table. "Now. We have more important matters to discuss than my past."

She clearly debated whether to ask more questions. Then she nodded.

"Now please, Miss MacLean, enter and be seated." Odd to sound refined when for years he left the trappings of civilization so far behind.

She looked him over, her green eyes cataloguing him, taking into account his resolve. Her gaze went to the bed and lingered there. "The only thing we have in common is a desire to see this mission completed successfully."

Clearly she chose her words with the intention to aggravate. Or maybe it was a natural talent. "You make me want to shut your mouth with kisses," he said.

He gave her credit. She barely flinched, then entered in that long, stalking, cat-like walk. "So I'll leave the door open, then, shall I?"

"Of course." Sibeol bustled in, holding her bag of knitting and smiling graciously. "We established that it's improper for a young lady to be behind closed doors with a young man, especially in a bedchamber."

Ah, yes. In the nick of time. His mother.

He stood.

Sibeol had been resting in her room until he'd gone to get Cate. She must have heard their voices and decided to provide him with a chaperone, when a chaperone was the last thing he wanted.

Because unfortunately, he still wanted Cate. On the Isle of Mull, she had spent three years teasing him, and he had desired her with every fiber of his flesh, every drop of his blood, every thought, every breath. Craving Cate had become a habit.

A sensible man can break a habit.

Apparently, he wasn't as sensible as he had hoped.

Last night he had demonstrated that his wit and sense was not proof against Cate's siren call. He'd also proved that she still wanted him. That was a dangerous piece of knowledge.

Sibeol seated herself in the rocking chair by the window. "We can't afford to have you shoot Taran again, Miss MacLean."

"Especially since, this time, I'd aim more toward the center of his chest," Cate answered.

"This time," he said gently, "you wouldn't have time to reach for your pistol." Indeed, if not for Queen Sibeol and her relentless demands that he comport himself as the crown prince of Cenorina, he would leap at Cate, subdue her, place his mouth on the soft skin of her throat to mark her as his, and teach her to love him once more.

Apparently Cate found comfort in the click of Sibeol's knitting needles and the creak of the rocking chair, for she readily sat in the only remaining empty chair, facing the two of them, the light from the window shining on her face.

The years had left their mark on her features. She had a scar on the left side of her forehead. The plump cheeks of youth had slimmed to a starker beauty. Most of all, her eyes no longer watched him with adoration. Quite the opposite, it would seem, and if he were a good man he'd be glad she was so suspicious.

Instead, he found that insulting directness to be a challenge.

Yes, she was attractive. Too tall for a lesser man to handle, and her direct gaze discomfited lesser men, too, but he liked a woman who wasn't afraid to meet his eye. Her hair made him want to play in its fire. Her breasts, her hips ... Why did his body remember her? Why did he lust after her while his mind rejected any current entanglement?

"What is it you wished to talk about, Cap'n?" She was calm, polite, distant.

Even the way she said *Cap'n*, as if she didn't know his

Christian name – even that posed a challenge. He began to roll up the charts before him. "The time has come to talk seriously about the mission."

"Very good," Cate said. "That *is* why I came."

"I appreciate that." He looked down at the letter he had received this morning by courier. "Throckmorton briefed you on at least part of your responsibilities."

She recited, "I am to report to the Cap'n, which I've done. Then I'm to go to Cenorina by public transportation – there is a ferry that leaves three days hence, I believe – then to the Davies's Giraud estate as the housekeeper."

"Ah. Giraud." Taran's hands were steady as he placed the charts into his captain's case behind him … Giraud. He knew it well. In that great house, he had been born, had rocked in his cradle, had as a lad run free, learned to ride his first pony, studied the duties of royalty with his father and his mother … and had been led into the first steps of dissipation by his tutor, Maddox Davies.

Of course, Davies would choose Giraud as his main residence. Every evening, he must sit at the long, polished dinner table, preside over his guests, and gloat over his successful coup.

Hate clawed at Taran. But he would not allow hate to control him, any more than he allowed fear or love or joy to have power over him.

His mother said, "Miss MacLean, you'll be pleased to know that although the royal family made Giraud their home, it is really more of a manor house than a palace. The setting is exquisite, and when you're not busy with your duties, I do hope you have the chance to explore the estate."

Cate's gaze flicked from Sibeol to Taran. "I would like that, but I expect this masquerade to take all my attention, and when I am done, I will go on to another task."

Like hell you will. But Taran wisely kept that thought to himself. "Cate, do you understand why England is interested in Cenorina?"

"Yes. It's located south of England, and I believe the English are concerned that as governor, Sir Davies's loyalties to Britain are not as stellar as one might have hoped. No one quite seems to know exactly what he intends, and previous attempts at intercepting his correspondence have been unsuccessful. I'm to see if I can find written evidence of his plans ... whatever they are." Her brow knit. "I do remember from my studies that Cenorina is a principality, and although Mr. Throckmorton didn't say so, I surmise the English want the queen removed."

"Why?" Sibeol asked sharply.

Cate said, "For cooperating with Sir Davies, and possibly for directing him."

"That is not true! The queen would never stoop to voluntarily deal with one such as *Sir Maddox Davies.*" Sibeol spoke his name like a mockery and a curse.

"I'm sorry." Cate looked discomforted and apologetic. "You're obviously loyal to the queen."

"I know the queen!" Sibeol jammed her knitting needles into the ball of yarn. "She is a person of moral, upright character, and her relationship to Davies is —"

Taran placed a warning hand on her shoulder.

Sibeol swallowed her words, and said softly, "The relationship is difficult at best."

"Of course. I'm sorry. I was told ... but that doesn't matter." Cate shook her head.

Taran could only imagine what she'd been told. "The royal family has been a pawn in this game" — how it galled him to admit that! — "and they are of no concern to you. My intention is to restore them to power. For you, it is Davies who must be misled and defeated. Did Throckmorton explain how Davies came to his attention in the first place?"

Cate shook her head.

"I didn't think so." Taran paced back to the table. "In this case, Throckmorton is not pleased with his own gullibility. You probably know that Throckmorton commands a large and varied network responsible for the nation's safety through the use of ... shall we say ... diplomacy?"

"Espionage," Cate said.

"Well put. After the deaths of the king and crown prince of Cenorina, Davies stepped into the role of governor. No one knew that what he'd done was a coup, and of course, although England was initially interested in the shift in power, once they realized Davies was an Englishman who gave a good accounting of himself, he was forgotten." Taran grew ever more grim. "Until he brought himself to Throckmorton's attention by asking for help ridding the islands of pirates who he said were using isolated harbors for rest and recreation, and as a jumping off place to raid English coastal towns. Because there had been raids, the English sent in militia, two ships were sunk, and Davies was in Throckmorton's good graces."

"I'm confused." Although Cate did not look so much confused as accusatory. "You said Sir Davies sold you to the pirates. If that is true, why would he report them to the English and ask for help in eliminating them?"

"So that when they returned," he said, "the English would sink them, they would die in battle, and no one alive would remember what happened to *me.*"

"That's diabolical." Cate stood quietly, her brow knit. Then, *"Who* did you say you are?"

"He's my son, the son of a very wealthy, influential family," Sibeol said.

"I know that. My brother took in noble young men to train, and from the way the other boys followed Taran, I knew he was used to leading." Cate examined him as if seeing him once more for the first time. "But for Sir Davies to be so afraid of his influence that he would use him so vilely!"

"Sir Davies *is* vile." Sibeol's eyes grew flinty. "He is an assassin of lives and reputations. He has destroyed my family, my country, all that I love. Should you go on this mission, I would ask you to be very careful of him."

Impressed by Sibeol's vehemence, Cate nodded.

As Taran expected, she believed Sibeol to be incapable of deceit. Sibeol had that effect on people. And, of course, Sibeol wasn't lying. She simply wasn't telling the whole truth.

Taran said, "The English are, in their own charming way, naïve in many ways. For years, I've been watching Davies from a distance. He has been wandering into England, buying his way into rich and noble homes with his money and his phony title, and gathering any information that will weaken the British cause abroad. He sells that information. He is responsible for numerous English and Scottish deaths in both battle and in espionage."

Cate's eyes developed the glaze of tears. "I know. Believe me, I know."

Apparently she had the good sense to be frightened — how

else to explain her quivering lips? — so Taran bent his most serious gaze upon her. "Now he moves in different circles. He travels abroad for reasons unknown."

"What is your speculation?" Cate asked.

He waved away her query. "Speculation is useless. We need facts, and that is what we seek in Cenorina. Yet if Davies or his mercenaries discover you are a spy — if they have the slightest misgiving about your performance — they will torture you until you blurt out every bit of this plan, and when you are of no further use to them, they'll kill you."

Cate said, "I would think they have trouble keeping help."

How odd and almost funny she was, as if the existence of such evil was nothing new to her. But she was a sheltered young woman — or she had been.

"Your family will never know what happened to you," Taran said.

"Then like Caesar's wife," Cate said, "I must be above suspicion."

Why had he imagined he could terrify Cate? Long before he appeared in her life, she'd earned the reputation of a girl who would take any challenge. After he arrived in Scotland, she had learned the gentle art of flirting for the sole purpose of seducing him. Now, nine years later, she was a spy. She would always go after her objective, and if she didn't succeed, if everything didn't turn out as she planned, she would make another plan. She was fearless and far too forthright to play the game with the guile that it called for.

"Tell me one thing," Cate said, "when Davies took power, was all law abandoned?"

"He brought in foreign mercenaries to control the population. For the most part, the aristocrats fled. Many of the villages disappeared altogether. At this moment, Davies is making a tour of the Mediterranean countries, using his position to gain entry into the homes of wealthy aristocrats, generals and *nouveau riche*. We don't want him in Cenorina when we're searching for proof of his wrongdoing, but we want him trapped when the time comes to arrest him."

Cate tapped her fingers on the arm of the chair. "I don't completely understand. Does Sir Maddox Davies have any inkling the English are on to him?"

"No," Taran said.

"But if he believes the English have discovered he's a spy and a traitor, isn't it more likely he'll escape to France, or Italy, or Russia? Somewhere where England has no influence, nor are they likely to have?" She watched Taran intently.

"During his sojourn as governor, Davies has been mining Cenorina for every bit of wealth. He is a very greedy, very expensive person." Davies's greed had gutted Taran's nation. For that reason alone, he would destroy his former tutor. "Cenorina has been Davies's sanctuary – and the greatest part of his money and the belongings he has acquired remain on Cenorina."

Cate chuckled. "How delightful. He must return to collect his wealth. So in my capacity as housekeeper, I'm to look over every bit of his home and discover where he hides his secret documents."

"And his wealth," Taran said. "For the royal family to regain their influence, they must be able to restore Cenorina to prosperity. What better way to do that than to use the fortune Davies stole from the Cenorinian people?"

Taran could see Cate's mind working. "The timing seems delicate."

"Yes." *Yes.* Taran had waited years for this moment. He had plotted every possibility. And one of the possibilities that existed was the chance that the housekeeper would be trapped if Davies arrived too soon. He'd been sanguine about the possibility before. After all, the housekeeper knew the risks she took.

But he hadn't known the housekeeper would be Cate.

"What means will Throckmorton use to send Sir Davies scuttling back to Cenorina?" she asked.

"I do not know," Taran said. "I can only hope it is painful."

CHAPTER ELEVEN

Sir Maddox Davies woke to a blast of Italian sunshine as the maid drew back the curtains and in execrable English, said, "Rise, you scum of an Englishman! The count has ordered his coach will take you to your next place of staying."

Maddox rose onto his elbow, protecting his eyes with his hand, and squinted at the maid.

She wasn't the pretty little thing who had sneaked in every day for the last week to offer him tea, assemble his clothing, and ride him for the price of one gold coin.

This was a coarse, earthy woman with big hands and broad shoulders. He had no desire to be ridden by her. He sank back onto the bed. "It's early. Shut the curtains."

"No." She cracked her knuckles. "The count says *now.*"

Hm. Last night, Maddox may have indulged in too much of the fine Tuscan red wine and been a tad too friendly with the countess. But how was he supposed to know what was too friendly? The woman had been flirting with him from behind her fan. But perhaps wrestling with her in the corner had been against some rule of Italian culture. Foreigners were free with their escapades. He never could tell what was going to set them off...

"Now!" The maid advanced on the bed and stripped off the blankets. "Now!"

In horror, he tried to cover his morning erection with his hands.

She snorted derisively and made a gesture that gave him to understand she considered him a lesser man. "Skinny," she muttered. "Freak. Upstart." With too much vigor, she started throwing his belongings into his trunk.

He didn't chide her. The woman looked rough, like she could knock him out the window onto the piazza below and dust her fingers after a job well done.

Upstart. Parvenu. Vulgarian.

Bastard. That was what his noble grandfather had always called him.

In deference to the spinning room, Maddox rose slowly,

groped his way to the cupboard, got out his clothes and went into the dressing room. A man of his stature should have a valet. But a man involved with his kind of commerce trusted no servant. When he appeared, properly attired, the ugly maid said, "You! Leave!"

He followed her through the empty, echoing rooms and out into that damned bright Italian sunlight. His trunk was attached to the coach. A footman held the door.

Maddox climbed the steps. When he was balanced with one leg inside, the maid put a hand in his back and pushed. When he fell forward, she shut the door. The driver whipped up the horses. Maddox crawled onto the seat and braced himself as the coach careened around the corners, taking him away from the villa and toward the seacoast.

Sometimes his departures were precipitous. But no matter how disgruntled the Tuscan count might be, he would not actually harm him, for Maddox held something the count wanted very badly, and that … was Cenorina.

Maddox coolly smiled and relaxed into the luxury of the velvet seat.

He was selling Cenorina. Selling it as a base to spy on and attack England, to interrupt established trading routes, to establish a petty régime where any man could be king. Or woman, if she had the money and the ambition. Every despot in Europe vied for the chance to own his own country. The wealthy and the discontented fought for the chance even to bid.

Maddox flexed his hands. And he held them all by the balls.

Genius. He was a genius.

The count's coach stopped at the inn where, three days hence, Maddox would meet with Mrs. Abigail Cabera. The footmen tossed him and his bags on the doorstep, and the coach left before he had even dusted himself off. He obtained the finest chamber in the inn, then concentrated on enjoying the warm afternoons and cool evenings in the tiny town overlooking the sea. He ate well-prepared foods and drank good wines, and was pleasantly surprised when Mrs. Cabera appeared a day early, dressed in an attractive gown and twirling a parasol.

When she spotted him seated at a table in front of the tiny local *ristorante*, she startled him by smiling. Hurrying over, she offered her hand. "What a delightful surprise!" she said. "I didn't yet expect you."

He stood and bowed over her glove. "My mission is completed, and I grow bored with Tuscany," he said. "Please. Take a seat."

Mrs. Cabera lowered her voice. "My mission is completed, also."

"So you have something for me in your bag?"

"I do indeed." She smiled again, and slid her hand along her neckline.

He blinked. Mrs. Cabera was Spanish, the well-to-do widow of a Cenorina tradesman. When the aristocrats had fled and businesses failed, she had been left destitute. Two years ago, when he had conceived his plan to sell Cenorina and realized he needed an employee to visit potential buyers on the continent, he had approached her to work for him, for like him she spoke Italian, French and English, and she could also make herself understood in German. In addition, she understood bookkeeping and would never allow herself to be cheated by a crafty or bullying patrician.

A ruthlessly practical woman, she had accepted his offer, and because she was a mature and handsome woman, he assumed he would also have bed privileges. She informed him she would do whatever he required of her in the way of underhanded dealing, spying, and passing information, and never betray him. But she would as soon sleep with a poxed pig.

He had tested her allegiance, and as long as he paid her without quibble, she was completely loyal ... and absolutely uninterested in him as a man.

Now she smiled, her rich red lips curving upward, her dark lashes fluttering. "I don't know what I'm going to do. The inn is full. It has no rooms."

"That is miserable luck," he said. "Perhaps one of the farmhouses will rent out a room."

She put her hand over his. "I was hoping to share."

"With who?"

"With you."

He prided himself on being a gambler, a man with a cool brain and the ability to weigh the odds. If he had a weakness, it was his ready response to the female form. But Mrs. Cabera's curious behavior put him on his guard. "Share? What is your intention?"

She wet her lips with a slow, sensuous slide of her tongue. "That we ... *share.*"

He could think of only one reason why, after so long, she would be making up to him. "Did you lose the money?"

She drew back, affronted. "Lose the money? Sir! I have not! It is in the purse attached to my waist beneath my skirt. I will retrieve it for you. Right now, if you wish." She rose.

Now he put his hand over hers. "You have never wanted to share a room with me before."

She waved a hand at the view. "Never before have I been inspired by such magnificence. The sunshine. The food. The wine. And you are looking ... very healthy. Very strong. It is all ... warming."

Despite his suspicions, his cock stirred.

She said, "And in Italy, you are different. Less careworn from your duties as governor."

Now his vanity stirred, as well. "The populace does not appreciate it, but I do work hard to rule Cenorina."

She veiled her eyes. "Here, in these balmy lands, I can almost see the burdens lifting from your broad shoulders."

"Yes." He gestured widely. "I think when this is over, I shall buy a villa somewhere close."

"The air would do you good." She looked up again, her eyes dewy with adoration. "But if you have changed your mind about your desire for me, we will conclude our business as usual and I will proceed to the next mission."

"No. I ... I am interested." Very interested, although after she made him wait for so long, he would not admit that.

"Then let us drink and eat, and you can tell me about yourself. Afterward, we will adjourn to our room, and there pleasure each other."

By God, when she yielded, she yielded generously.

She inquired about his past, asked why he seemed intent on selling Cenorina to foreigners who wanted to use the islands for a base to raid England, and generally create chaos in the richest country in the world.

He said he was not interested in those things, only that the richest bidder would win. Then, after she plied him with wine and fed him truffles from her own fingers, he admitted he had no loyalty to dear old Britannia. His mother had yielded her all to the romantic dancing instructor, and found herself abandoned and with child. She died in the birthing of Maddox, and of shame, so his grandfather told him. Abandoned to indifferent nannies, Maddox stubbornly survived, so for his fifth birthday his grandfather sent him away to a Norfolk boarding school. Maddox fought his way through years of short rations, freezing cold, and a brutal headmaster with a stout cane and a strong arm until, at the age of seventeen, he graduated with the credentials to be a tutor for young men.

Maddox finished that part of his tale, and Mrs. Cabera begged for more. How had he moved from such lowly beginnings to his present position of power and wealth?

Maddox admitted he had an eye for advancement. His first position was not gained by his teaching credentials. No, at last his mother was of use to him; she conferred upon him a whiff of the upper class. Mr. Carter, a wealthy Liverpool merchant who held high social aspirations, imagined that Maddox Davies, bastard grandson of an English lord, could polish his image. Mrs. Carter was not so naïve, but she was willing to put Davies in the position to teach her sons ... and in the position to visit her bed.

When Mr. Carter discovered the affair, Maddox Davies found himself abruptly on the street corner without baggage or wages. Yet ever resourceful, he sneaked back into the house to enjoy one last romp with Mrs. Carter, and to get a farewell gift of coin, jewels, and his baggage. Then he sent Mr. Carter a message demanding a letter of recommendation, or Davies would inform the scandal sheets of his liaison with Mrs. Carter, making Mr. Carter a laughingstock among his colleagues.

Not surprisingly, Mr. Carter complied. The letter arrived with a one-way ticket to the continent.

Mrs. Cabera seemed awed by Maddox's cleverness.

A doubt niggled at him; why was she willing to cast aside her steadfast aversion to him now? Why now was she so interested?

The answer was almost too easy.

Money. Mrs. Cabera was an excessively practical and intelligent woman, and she now realized his wealth would be without measure, and that he would want a mistress. He leaned back in his chair and in the light of the sunset, he looked her over. Yes. The two of them were alike. They would manage well together.

He suggested they go up to the room now.

She ran her hand down his thigh, fetched him a glass of port and asked how he had found his way to Cenorina.

She made talking about himself a pleasure, and he sipped his port and became even more expansive.

Maddox had taken all his ill-gotten gains and left for Spain where, within a year, he was not only broke again, but he had another angry husband after him — and this was no civilized Englishman. This husband was out for blood, so Maddox left on the first ship out of Cadiz, landed in the rough English harbor town of Poole, and at once looked for a position. When the cuckolded Spanish husband arrived with murder in his eyes, it was immediately clear to Maddox that he longed for the solitude of the island kingdom of Cenorina, where he would apply for a position teaching a young man languages, mathematics and social skills. Maddox slipped away under cover of night, arrived in Cenorina, and made a splendid impression by arriving in person to apply for the position. Mr. Carter's glowing letter of recommendation and Maddox's newly-acquired polish and fluency in languages stood him in good stead. Of course, he was delighted when he realized the family was the *royal* family.

In young Prince Taran, Maddox saw the potential for advancement. The lad was spoiled, proud, chomping at the bit for experience with wine, women and song, and Maddox knew those subjects all too well. He tread cautiously at first, testing the waters to see if anyone would notice he taught debauchery to the young prince.

But Queen Sibeol was oblivious to anything but her husband's failing health, and within a few months Davies had expanded the young prince's education to include dissipations that made the lad despised throughout the land. With the king's death, Maddox moved quickly and quietly, securing his position and imposing his rule. By the time Queen Sibeol realized what he had done, she was completely in his power.

Yet somehow she managed to send Prince Taran away. That knowledge had been a thorn in Maddox's side … until the lad came back. Disposing of the arrogant little ass had not only cleared the way for Maddox to rule without fear, but had also given Maddox a great deal of personal satisfaction.

Mrs. Cabera leaned forward and placed her breasts against his arm. "Learning more about you has been a delight."

Yes. She would be a very good mistress, indeed.

He let her lead him up the stairs to his room. He watched as she lit every candle so the chamber blazed with flickering golden light. Then she drew him toward the window, seated herself on the sill, and as he did her, she screamed in lusty appreciation. It was fast. It was wild. It was good.

And when he was done, she pushed him away.

He staggered back, surprised to discover he was unsteady. "Why so abrupt, my love?"

"Get on the bed." She stood in the window, slowly drawing the curtains. "A quick snooze will revive you for another round."

He extended his arm. "Join me."

She began extinguishing the candles. "Of course. Let me prepare."

But when he awoke it was morning, and she stood beside the bed. When she saw he was awake, she placed the bag of coins beside him.

At once he realized he had been double-crossed. But how? If she was leaving him the money... "What are you doing?"

In her usual contemptuous tone, she said, "Here's the payment for the last bid I will take for you."

He grabbed her wrist. "What do you mean, the last? We have four more bidders to visit."

She yanked herself free. "I quit."

He cut a significant glance toward the window, the seat of their mutual pleasure. "Surely you cannot claim you were dissatisfied last night."

"I did what I set out to do, and that is convince Mr. Throckmorton that our alliance is nothing but lust and loins."

"Throckmorton." Maddox's breath caught. He knew that name. He had once tricked Throckmorton, used him to eliminate a problem. Had the man discovered the truth? Did he harbor a grudge? "Why do you imagine Throckmorton is interested in ... us?"

"Someone was watching me. Following me. I couldn't shake her."

"*A woman?*" Maddox wanted to laugh. "You thought *a*

woman was following you?"

"I do not *think*. I *know*. When I managed to turn the tables and follow her, she was having an assignation with a man. I eavesdropped, and heard her give a report of my every movement." Her voice trembled. "Then ... I heard your name. Apparently, your actions, and thus mine, have caught Throckmorton's interest. I, for one, do not care to spend the rest of my life looking over my shoulder waiting for the stiletto to slide into my back."

"You're imagining things." Mrs. Cabera was hysterical.

"Believe what you like. Lucrative as it has been, our association is over. Farewell, Sir Maddox Davies. I hope to never see you again." She caught up her cape, donned it. "You may keep the salary you owe me." She slammed the door after herself.

That was what convinced him. Unless she was running scared, Mrs. Cabera would never, never have walked away from her salary.

Rising, he prepared to escape, to run back to the arms of his one true love — the fortune stashed at Cenorina.

CHAPTER TWELVE

"I know the palace." Sibeol dropped her knitting into her lap. "Before you go, I'll draw you a map. I'll let you know where the most likely hiding places will be."

Cate considered Sibeol, looked down as if thinking, then glanced at Taran.

What conclusions did she draw? Did she realize she faced the queen and the crown prince of the principality of Cenorina? Or did she believe Sibeol was a Cenorinian aristocrat and he a nobleman's son?

He couldn't tell.

The young Caitlin would have blurted out those questions. This Cate kept her own council. "I thank you, Sibeol," she said. "I appreciate any direction you might give."

Sibeol said, "Remember, when you meet Sir Maddox Davies, he will be charming and apparently witless."

"It's a front?" Cate asked.

"Because Davies seemed so dimwitted, the young crown prince ignored signs of imminent trouble," Taran told her. "Don't be fooled. Davies is sly and cruel."

"What is his weakness?" Cate looked to Sibeol as if she would know.

Sibeol answered as if she did. "He thinks he is more intelligent, more cunning, more exciting than any other man on the planet."

Cate smiled. "Then should he arrive before I expect him, all I have to do is convince him I believe it, too."

Taran began, "I don't want you—"

Sibeol interrupted, "That is correct."

Damned annoying females. "Miss MacLean, how do you expect to convince Davies you think he is so…?"

Cate lowered her head. She tilted it. She looked up at him through her lashes and smiled, quirking her full lips a little. At him. As if she liked him, admired him, worshipped him.

For a moment, Taran forgot what he'd asked, why he'd asked, and that his mother was in the room. He was in thrall.

Then Sibeol chuckled.

Cate straightened, got serious, and snapped, "Like that."

He shut his mouth and pretended as if he was unaffected. "Of course. That should work. Now — you must gather the evidence Throckmorton wants. How?"

Cate examined her fingertips, one by one, then rubbed them with her thumb.

Her every movement, her impenetrable confidence fascinated him — and he didn't have time for fascination now.

"Throckmorton told me to collect documents which Davies guarded. If those documents are under lock and key, I'm to open those locks. After perhaps a week, the Cap'n will arrive. I'm to lead him to the documents, wait while he translates them, and if they're the right documents, my part of the mission is finished." Cate's chin stuck out as it did when she got stubborn, and she burst out, "Why do I even need you, Taran Tamson? Why can't I translate the documents? I learned from the same tutor you did. I can read Latin and Greek, French and Italian, and speak English and Gaelic. Tell me one language you speak that I can't!"

He experienced a great, dark satisfaction when he answered, "The language we speak on Cenorina."

"It can't be that different from … all my other languages!"

He wanted to smile at the flash of the old Cate. He missed that Cate, for the more he saw of her, the more he realized she had changed in ways he couldn't yet define. He sensed depths of emotion, sparks of fury, an abundance of confidence, and beneath it all a well of sorrow. He didn't know what caused that sorrow, but he would find out. He would discover everything about her – no matter how many times she shot him for trying.

Leaning back in his chair, he rubbed the twinges in his arm. "On Cenorina, we lived in virtual isolation for a thousand years. You will be able to hold a conversation — our people are seafarers and speak English, Spanish, French with varying forms of ease — but the native language is difficult, and the written language hasn't changed since the monks developed it in the tenth century. It's perfect for use as code. When one of Throckmorton's men got a glimpse at one of the documents, he had no idea what he was looking at."

"I could do it," she insisted.

"You could?" Reaching behind him, he plucked one of the ancient texts from his bookshelf and handed it to her – upside down.

With a sneer at his impudence, she turned it the right direction and randomly opened to a page. She studied the letters. "I can read this!" She mouthed the words, then frowned. "But it doesn't quite make sense. I can't ... what ..."

Before he could smile his *I-told-you-so smile*, his mother explained, "Cenorina's original language might have been equal parts Portuguese and Spanish. Then in the tenth century, the Norsemen rampaged all the way up and down the French and English coasts, into the Mediterranean, and even as far as Cenorina. Before they departed in the eleventh century, they had left their shipbuilding skills, parts of their language and, it is rumored, more than a little drop of Viking blood in the Cenorina royal family."

"They rampaged through Scotland, too, but they did something very odd to your language." Cate blinked as if the letters weren't in focus.

"Exactly!" Taran removed the book from her hands before she deciphered enough to declare herself skilled. "So I will be the one going to Cenorina to read the documents. You, however, are not a good candidate to find them. You're a gently bred young lady, not a picklock."

"All the more reason I should be sent. I am not a suspicious character." Cate smiled, a lopsided, provocative smile. "Mr. Throckmorton examined my picklock credentials thoroughly."

"Perhaps you could demonstrate for us." Sibeol pointed to the door. "Could you open that?"

Without even glancing at the lock, Cate said, "Yes."

Taran wanted her to fail. "Open it in less than a minute."

She reached into the black velvet reticule that hung around her waist, and pulled out a battered brown leather workman's kit tied in a ribbon. She placed it on the table and opened it to reveal narrow, sharp and shiny implements.

He wanted her to fail very badly. "Let's say that your tools are out of reach, and you have to work without them." He pulled out his pocket watch and glanced at the face. "Starting now."

Cate's air of assurance didn't dim. Her gaze swept the room. "Very well." Leaning across the desk, she took his perfectly sharpened pen and, from the nightstand, his best scissors, the ones he used to trim his beard.

He winced. That her machinations would ruin his pen was without question. That the edge on the scissors would be sacrificed, he didn't doubt. Cate would make him pay for his doubt, and she would enjoy every moment.

Sibeol took the large key off the corner of Taran's desk. "I'll turn the lock from the outside, and wait for you to open it." On the way out the door, Sibeol patted her on the arm. "I have every confidence in you, dear."

Taran shot his mother a glance of moody reproval.

With a smug smile, she sailed out the door.

"Thank you, ma'am." Cate waited with her implements while Sibeol left and the sound of the tumblers fell into place.

Cate pointed to the lock, and in an instructional tone, said, "From the shape of the key and sound of the lock, I can say this is a ward lock. The oldest ones were easy to pick, and you'd be surprised at the number of old ones still in use. The newer ones – this is one – have double tumblers. They're a little more difficult." She knelt before the lock.

Taran strolled over and knelt at her side. Her feminine scent rose in waves from her body. Orange soap and sandalwood perfume, and underlying them was the warm, spicy aroma of Cate. Those scents carried with them a memory that even now brought him to eager readiness. Cate's power over him had not diminished with the years. If anything, it had increased, and he … well, he was grateful his mother had removed herself from the room and was not here to examine the fit of his trousers.

Leaning close, he spoke so that his breath brushed Cate's ear. "Tell me, how did you learn such a skill?"

She shot him a scornful glance. She realized his ploy.

She would try to break the lock.

He would distract her.

She didn't waste time slapping him. She inserted first the pen, then the scissors, in the keyhole. In short bursts of speech, she said, "When I was eighteen, I caught a fellow burglarizing our house in Edinburgh."

Taran touched the short wisps of hair that had fallen from her chignon with the palm of his hand. Then he fingered the silky locks. He'd forgotten how very much he loved to play with her hair, to see the contrast between each strand — some almost blonde, some vibrant red, some richly auburn. Together they made up the glorious color of autumn leaves, and when he closed his eyes, he could still see the waist-length strands spread across a white pillowcase.

But what had happened to make her cut it? "This burglar awakened your curiosity, but nevertheless you turned this thief over to the authorities." He tugged at her hair until she had to turn her head and look at him. "Tell me that is what you did."

Those green eyes weighed and dismissed him. "Over to the authorities? Not at all. I made a pact with him."

She chilled Taran's blood. "You haven't changed. You're still the same daredevil Cate."

She turned back to her work, but her tones were crisp and forthright. "It was stupid. I admit it."

She admitted it, did she? "Thieves have no honor."

Even more crisply, she said, "As much honor as some pirates I can mention."

He wouldn't win that argument. "Was he old?"

"Who? Billy?" With a reminiscent smile, she glanced at Taran, all the while fiddling with the internal lock mechanism. "Only five years older. Charming. Handsome. He'd been caught before, but by ladies, and always he'd talked his way out."

This woman tripped along the high wire as if her future wasn't ticking off in seconds on his watch. "A seducer?"

"Billy?" She laughed, wealth of affection in her tone. "No, not my Billy."

Taran didn't believe her.

"But I demanded he teach me his skills, or he would be in such a deep prison he'd never dig his way out." Her cool tone told Taran how ruthless she had been.

"Did Kiernan know about this?"

"I did not wish to worry my brother any further. He was the laird. He had duties, and the fulfillment of those duties kept him working more nights than I care to recall."

"Did you ever tell him?" Taran heard a clinking in the lock.

"Later." She sounded grim.

Taran hoped that meant Kiernan had taught her a lesson she wouldn't soon forget. "This picklock taught you his vile skills while in your home."

"Not at all." She twisted her instruments. "I went with him on his jobs. I picked locks on some of the best homes in Edinburgh. The secrets I could tell! Did you know the mayor spends all his money on show, and none on his family's comforts. It's shoddy upstairs, and cold. He skimps on the fires."

"I don't care about the bloody damned mayor!" In his imagination, Taran could see her as she had been then. Twenty years old, bold as bedamned, going to hell in her own way with no one to stop her. She made him break out into a sweat. "You're lucky you weren't killed."

She gave an elegant shrug. "I was shot at a few times."

He wanted to shake her. And hug her. And lay her naked on a bed and affirm life with her in the most primitive method possible. All that stopped him was the memory of the wild lass she had been – and the pain from the gunshot wound she'd inflicted the night before. "What were you thinking?"

She spoke rapidly. "I was thinking my life wasn't worth living because my lover had taken my virtue and my love and left me with nothing but a scarred reputation and a broken heart. My friends dropped me for fear they'd be tainted with my character. I was not invited to parties or for visits. I was lonely. And I was furious." She handed him his pen with its nib destroyed and his scissors with the point bent.

"But to try and get yourself killed –"

"I wasn't trying to get myself killed. I was proving to the world I was as bad as they supposed." Her nostrils widened as if she smelled something nasty. "It took one close call before I realized that, as long as I'm busy, I could live very happily as a spinster; indeed, much more happily than most of my married friends. As I'm sure you realize, that's one of the reasons why I've come here to work." She looked him over as if *he* were the source of the rot. "It's only bad luck that I have to work with *you.*"

He fingered the instruments. "Are you giving up?" He glanced at his forgotten watch. A minute and five seconds. "No matter. Time's up."

Agreeably, she reached up and turned the handle.

Sibeol walked in. "The door is unlocked."

CHAPTER THIRTEEN

For a brief, a very brief, moment, Cate relished Taran's astonishment.

Then she stood and shook out her skirts. She gathered her lockpick kit and placed it in her reticule. She curtsied to Sibeol, nodded to Taran, and started out the door.

"Wait a minute, Miss MacLean!" He caught her arm, and his tone raised goosebumps. "What do you mean, one extremely close call?"

Cate bit her lip. As soon as she had said that, she knew she should have kept her mouth shut. Impetuosity had brought her years of loneliness and heartache; now she tried always to guard her tongue. But sometimes, she spoke without thought, especially when she was angry — and she was always angry around Taran. "I should go."

"You should tell me what you meant by *one extremely close call.*"

She would tell him nothing more. Folding her hands at her waist, she said, "By word and deed, I have proved myself capable, and I will no longer answer your questions."

He dared to point his finger at her. "You will do as I tell you, and I say —"

"Taran!" Sibeol interrupted. "Stop badgering Cate. She can do the job." Going to her rocking chair, she picked up her knitting, seated herself, and set to work.

He straightened. He paced away again, then back to Cate, and he loomed once more. "How many other missions have you worked?"

"How many?" She almost told him the truth, if only for the fun of goading Taran into another frenzy of anxiety. But she wouldn't be left behind in this pub while Taran went off to do her job, so she looked him in the eyes and lied. "This is my third mission."

Swinging toward Sibeol, he offered his hands outspread. "Mother!"

"It's too bad she's so inexperienced," Sibeol said. "But she's still the only picklock we have."

"I can solve that." He fixed Cate with a stern gaze. "I want you to teach me how to pick a lock."

In her slowest, most sarcastic drawl, she said, "Yes, and I want to learn to be a pirate captain. Can you teach me everything I need to know before I leave for Cenorina?"

"If I knew how to open locks, you wouldn't have to go to Cenorina."

"If I knew how to be a pirate captain, England wouldn't need *you.*"

He towered over her again, doing his hawk imitation, and glared down his beak of a nose.

Unfortunately for him, she had no fear of hunting birds; she'd trained her own. "I would expect a more reasoned response from a man who carries the responsibilities you do, even if those responsibilities are outside the bounds of morality." She caught herself before she went too far, said too much. "After all, if picking locks were that easy, anyone could do it, and then what good would a lock be?"

"You learned."

God's teeth, he was insulting. "So it must be simple?"

"I did not say that. I merely meant that, as you've pointed out, I am a pirate and a thief." He smiled, all self-deprecation and charisma. "I can surely acquire the knowledge of picking a lock."

It was almost a decade too late for him to charm her. "Learning took me two years. I have a touch for it." Again, she rubbed her fingers together. "And an ear, Billy said, that listens to what the lock tells me."

"Dear, she's right." Sibeol knitted and rocked, the squeaking of the floorboards an accompaniment to their conversation. "You know she is. We'll have to think of a way to keep her extra safe."

Stubbornly, Taran said, "I still want to try."

"All right." Cate dragged the words out. "I'll show you, if you'll show me more ways to defend myself."

He lifted his eyebrows. "Do you feel the need to defend yourself?"

"I'm a woman going into a dangerous situation. I can depend on the element of surprise only once. After that, I have to somehow win my way free – and last night you proved to me I don't know enough."

He nodded slowly, and the way he watched her made her want to squirm. "Yes, I'll teach you."

Cate hoped she hadn't made a mistake. She'd lost the fight last night for more reasons that simple ineptitude. When he'd put his arms around her and he wrapped her in his dark spell, she had lost her formidable good sense and became, again, that girl who lived and breathed for the touch of one Taran Tamson. She shouldn't test her will power again, but what was her choice?

Sibeol came to her rescue. "Better yet, Taran, have Blowfish teach her. He's small, he's fast, and he's tricky — and you are busy with the plans for Cenorina."

"Hm." Taran stroked his beard, then strolled back behind his desk. "A good thought. Yes, Blowfish it shall be."

Cate kept her backbone straight. It wouldn't do to show her relief. "I'll go then." She stepped toward the door.

He stopped her. "Before you leave, Cate, I would very much like to impress on you the peril we'll face on this mission." When she would have spoken, he held up his hand. "Please. Let me finish. We have lived in the same household. Together we have a history that includes your whole family, and we have a history between the two of us."

She hated the blush that lit her cheeks. The prudent responses she had so painfully taught herself disappeared when he spoke, for she lived in fear he would reveal all of the truths between them. And one of those truths loomed like a monolith, always there, always waiting to fall, to crush her.

Of all the men in the world, why did this man have to be directing her first mission? Was it fate mocking her, or God reminding her of her duties and her sins?

No. She would not believe that. She would not fear her past. She had learned never to look back, always to look forward. One day soon, she would be done with this, done with Taran, and she would go on to her second mission, and her third, and maybe after a dozen missions, she would feel she had her revenge.

In the meantime, she needed to view Taran, with his false concern and his studied trepidation, as a test, one would she would pass.

In a voice warm with concern, he said, "I wouldn't be a man

if I didn't worry about your safety."

Ah. A new tack to dissuade her. "How did you show your concern these last nine years?" Finger against her cheek, she pretended to think. "Oh. By being invisible."

Sibeol watched them, her serious gaze so different from her son's. Yet they shared an intense bond, one of goals and intent, and in that they were obviously mother and son.

Leaning forward, he pressed his palms flat on the desk. "All right. I can't convince you of my apprehension, but what about your mother, Lady Bess? What of your brother, Kiernan? You know they would be terrified if they knew what you were doing. Abandon this mission and leave it to us."

But at Kiernan's name, Cate's fingers had clenched so tightly they tingled from lack of blood. "It's for Kiernan that I do this."

Taran pushed a careless hand through his hair. "What do you mean?"

With an intensity borne of grief, Cate told him, "Kiernan was murdered in the Crimea. Killed by a bomb, in a trap set by English traitors. I will hunt them down. I will not be satisfied until they are all dead ... or I am."

CHAPTER FOURTEEN

Taran reached for Cate.

Cate held out a hand to ward him off. "No. It is far too late for any comfort you might offer me."

Cate curtsied to Sibeol, walked to the door, and closed it behind her.

Sibeol stared at her son, heart aching. Cate had lost a beloved brother, but Taran, too, must feel the loss of a friend, his mentor, the man who had taken him in when the world turned against him. She wanted to go to her boy, put her arms around him and tell him it was all right to cry.

But she already knew he would stare at her as if she spoke a garbled tongue.

Taran didn't cry. As far as she could tell, Taran didn't *feel*.

Taran lowered his arms, his face blank. He gave nothing away: not what he was thinking, not his lusts, his fears, his affections.

All the time of her imprisonment, Sibeol had prayed every night that her handsome, impetuous son had survived against all odds. She'd been afraid to pray for more; she had believed that life itself was the great gift.

Now that he was back, she realized she should have asked for more.

When he returned from his sojourn with the pirates, he had embraced her. He let her hold him. But she hadn't really touched him. She didn't dare think of the trials he'd been through to transform him from her impetuous, confident crown prince into this monolith of strength and cool deliberation.

His comrades, the pirates, treated her with the greatest of respect, but they were rough in manner and common in speech. And they held Taran in awe. Not because he was a prince, but because he had fought at their sides, led them through storms, found them prizes in ways she didn't want to contemplate. But no matter what he had done in the past, he *was* the crown prince of Cenorina. He had duties to fulfill. For those, he needed compassion. He needed statesmanship.

He needed a wife who would bring diplomatic ties and honor to the kingdom. He *knew* that.

Oh, *why* were men so difficult? She wanted a wife for Taran who would restore his soul and teach him to love again. At the same time, the one woman who showed promise was not royal, nor was she chaste and sheltered.

Picking up her yarn, Queen Sibeol automatically set to work, so used to knitting during the long years of imprisonment that she no longer had to think to make a sweater or turn a sock. "What are you going to do about Miss MacLean?" She meant, *Are you going to treat her with honor, then let her go?*

Naturally, he heard — or pretended to hear — only the words, and not the intent. "I have no choice. I will send her to Cenorina. If what she said is true, if Kiernan is dead" — Taran's voice was steady and without a wisp of grief — "I could no more stop Cate from going than I could halt the tides."

But Sibeol would not allow him to prevaricate. "That's not what I meant. I wasn't in prison so long I don't recognize a young man stricken with desire."

Shuffling the stacks of papers that awaited his attention, he said, "You were held for more than nine years. That's a very long time. Perhaps you don't remember."

"I most certainly do. Your father used to look at me that way." She still missed her old prince. Their marriage had been arranged by their families, but their affection for each other had been the cause of gossip in the court. Whipping out her handkerchief, she dabbed at her eyes. "When we fought—"

"It was the clash of titans."

"If he hadn't died when he did —"

"But he did, and so this crisis is ours to solve." Just as Taran had always done when he was troubled, he pushed his hair off his forehead, but he didn't use his old impetuous gesture. This indicated thoughtfulness and a disconcerting deliberation. "If everything is going as planned, if Throckmorton managed to successfully send Davies scurrying back to Cenorina, he will be back there within the fortnight. He will be proud of his plan to hold you hostage as a way to ensure his escape. If he finds it's not you in that prison —"

Sibeol crumpled the handkerchief in her palm. She had viewed the spite that rotted in Sir Maddox Davies. He hated her. He hated Taran. And why? For no better reason than their noble birth. He imprisoned her in the fortress overlooking the sea in a damp cell, with mercenary jailors to watch her every move. He sent her son away to die.

No one could ever comprehend her own pain and guilt, for it was she who had chosen Maddox Davies as the most respectful, considerate, and intelligent of the recommended candidates. All her life, she had been vigilant about those she allowed close to her and her family. Then, because Davies was charming, and she hadn't taken enough care to look beneath the surface, she had plunged her kingdom into despair.

The argument might be made that her husband had grown ill not long before Davies's arrival, and that had occupied and distracted her. But she was the queen. She did not accept excuses for her own negligence, nor could she abandon her responsibilities now. "Davies will kill the young lady who took my place," Sibeol said.

"Miss Bennett knew the risks when she volunteered for duty."

"That doesn't absolve me of responsibility. Miss Jeannette Bennett is the daughter of one of my loyal ladies who was forced to flee Cenorina to the safety of England. The child would not be there if I hadn't ignored the oncoming danger."

Taran did Sibeol the honor of neither arguing nor agreeing. He understood the consequences of neglecting duty, of not preparing oneself for every eventuality. "I'll make sure Miss Bennett is rescued."

Queen Sibeol had despaired under the restrictions of her arrest. Decrees were made in her name. She left the fortress only when Davies wanted her to be seen. Then he placed her in an open carriage and drove her around the countryside to assure the people of Cenorina she still lived and was in charge. An elaborate charade, one that ground her pride into the dust, and always she feared she would be smothered in her sleep and buried without rites or justice or any mark that she had ever passed this way.

She'd seen her son, the crown prince, one time. Nine years ago, in his youthful bravado Taran had returned and been captured. Davies had allowed one brief reunion marked by happiness and marred by hopelessness, before he had sent Taran away to be murdered.

Three years ago she'd received word through the network of spies still loyal to the royal family. Taran was alive. He was the captain of a ship. And he was working on a plan to free her and take Cenorina back, to restore the family and his country's prosperity. She was to be patient. So when, a fortnight ago, a woman of about Sibeol's height had been smuggled in to replace her, Sibeol had escaped without a protest. But the memory of that girl's face intruded on her sleep. One did not live as princess of a principality for thirty years without developing a sense of obligation. It was her sense of obligation that made her speak to Taran when she would rather have not.

"I like Miss MacLean. She's brave. She's intelligent. Her family is good, not noble, but good, and one of our ancient allies." Sibeol recognized the mask Taran wore. It was the same one his father had always donned when he planned to ignore good sense and do what he pleased. Yet she had to speak. "If you are to maintain your grip on the throne, you need a female of impeccable virtue. Miss MacLean's virtue is lost, and everyone knows it."

"That's my fault."

Her exasperation broke through. "Yes, of course it's your fault! I'm not excusing your behavior which was ungrateful and abused every law of hospitality and if your father were here he would take you by the ears and shake you until your teeth rattled!"

Taran considered his mother as if uncertain how to take her outburst. "I am sorry to have caused you distress."

"But you're not sorry you did it." Before he could speak, Sibeol made a gesture to cut him off. "But what can be forgiven in a man and a prince cannot be forgiven in a woman and a princess. In addition, she *steals*."

"I believe you should say — she has stolen. She no longer steals."

"We don't know that. She might take what we seek and hold it for ransom."

He folded his hands on the desk before him and considered her steadily. "Mother, I'm a pirate. I also have stolen."

She dismissed that. "That's different. It was not a lark. You had to steal to survive." But she was uneasily aware that Taran and Miss MacLean had more in common than a shared background.

They both had been thieves, and that Taran had stooped to such a foul crime and even now expressed no remorse — his only explanation had been, *Mother, we weren't stealing from the poor* — showed her how truly Taran had changed.

She hurried into speech. "We have already discussed that you need a bride with ties to the powers of France or Spain or Portugal, countries who desire to thwart Britain in any plans she has to occupy Cenorina."

"Mother, I respect you and your opinion completely, but my wife will want me to fight for my kingdom."

"Yes." Sibeol nibbled on her lip. "But you heard Miss MacLean. She believes the English plan is to depose the royal family."

"That was speculation on Cate's part."

"That is what I fear."

Taran folded his hands. "Prince Albert seems a level-headed chap. He's not interested in invading and keeping Cenorina as an English province."

"Queen Victoria is his wife. She is ambitious, and England is always greedy."

"Always greedy for the great, rich lands like India. Cenorina is prosperous, but not wealthy, and has proved time and time again that a nation of small, mountainous islands is difficult to conquer. We have to trust that once England has what they want – the knowledge the islands will not be used as a base to attack Britain – they'll once again ignore us as if we don't exist."

"But the risk!"

"Mother, I had no choice." He was patient, and calm — and emotionless. He had weighed the risks and he gambled without the doubts that plagued her. "I couldn't get my country back with a single ship under my command. I had to ally myself with Britain."

She took a breath. "I know. But I remember all the times they've tried to conquer us, and we're inviting them in to help in the final fight!"

"They can't win against us. We know the terrain, we're defending our homes, and we don't fight by the rules."

He meant *he* didn't fight by the rules. That worried her, too. That streak of ruthlessness which ran through him like a vein of hard, solid gold. "You're right. I know you are, I just … I don't sleep well, and I worry."

"There's no use worrying, Mother. The plan has been set in motion. We'll succeed. One way or the other, we'll succeed."

"And Miss MacLean?" Sibeol held her breath.

He considered Sibeol for a long time.

She could almost see him weighing options and discarding them. She said, "You don't mean to take the daughter of our old ally as your mistress!"

Without changing expression or raising his voice, he laid his claim. "Cate will be mine until the day I die."

CHAPTER FIFTEEN

Here in the common room in a corner tucked away from his men, Taran stood and concentrated as Cate untied the ribbon that held the battered brown leather workman's kit together and unrolled it on the table. Tucked in the pockets, two dozen metal instruments gleamed in the candlelight. Today she had sent Blowfish out, and he had returned with exactly what she asked: two locks set in wood as they would be in a door, and one that was stark and bare.

She pointed to several straight tools with slightly curved tops. "These are feeler picks." She showed him four simple wrenches. "These are tension wrenches. An accomplished lockpick can open most ward locks with two of these tools."

"Then what are the rest of them for?"

"Different sized locks. Different kinds of locks." She looked up at him through her eyelashes. "Showing off."

He noted a small, jealous twinge somewhere in the region of his heart. "Is that how your friend Billy captured your attention? By showing off?"

"He captured my attention by being wicked and being there." She sounded cross and looked cross, not surprising after the day she'd had.

Taran had done as his mother suggested, and turned Cate over to Blowfish for lessons in self-defense. After a tough morning in the pub spent learning to escape an assailant's hold, how to make weapons where there were none, and how to hide weapons so they would be available, Blowfish had taken her out into the streets of Poole. He had been relentless, taking her to the meanest streets, lecturing her on how to avoid attack, then jumping her when she least expected it. It wasn't kind of him, but Taran wanted to chuckle. Cate had always hated to be bested; she really hated to be bested by a man half a foot shorter. But she'd learned. She would learn more tomorrow. As he would learn tonight.

Cate pointed at a variety of keys. "Picking locks is difficult and unpredictable, so first we try every key in our stockpile. Even if they're not right, sometimes with a little jiggling we can get them to work." Nimbly, she took apart the stripped lock and pointed out the parts.

Wisps of hair fell out of her chignon, and she tucked them back with a gesture of annoyance.

He would pay a hundred guineas to discover why it had been cut — or why she had cut it. Young ladies did not do such a thing, and Cate had been proud of her hair, loosening it for him in a ritual that bound him as firmly as any vow. Now he wanted to hold the ends in his hands, marvel at the color, breathe in her scent.

"Are you paying attention?" Cate's voice was sharp. "Because I'm tired, I don't want to do this, and if you don't stop staring at my neck, I'm going to show you a trick I learned from Billy that you don't know, that Kiernan didn't know, and that made Blowfish wince when I told him about it. I call it the nutcracker."

The girl she had been was flirtatious, open and enticing. This woman with her narrowed eyes and her flared nostrils was intimidating … he wanted to know when that had happened. "Please." He gestured to the lock. "Proceed."

She scowled as she put it back together, bolted it, and showed him how she held the pick and tension wrench.

Under her control, the lock sprang open so quickly he couldn't follow the steps. He picked up the candle and held it so it shone on her fingers. "Do it again."

She did. "You feel for the pressure here, and shove here …"

She showed him as slowly as possible.

"I understand. This doesn't look difficult." She'd been lying when she said it was.

She handed him the tools. "You try it."

His fingers seemed as big and clumsy as sausages, and when he stuck the tools in the small lock hole he couldn't tell what they were touching. He concentrated, remembering what the lock looked like, and thought he had it.

He didn't.

He tried again, and again.

He stopped, puffing with frustration, and stared across at his men. Thank God, they weren't paying attention to him. They were sitting in the far corner, discussing the fine details of the plans he'd worked out, and he wished he was there with them.

"It takes a while to get the hang of it," Cate said encouragingly. "Here, look at it from the side. Then you can see what you're doing."

He did as she suggested.

It didn't help.

He could steer a ship laden with goods through the trickiest channel, climb the highest mast and mend a sail, and sleep through a hurricane on a hammock — but he couldn't get the feel for this delicate work?

He could not believe it.

Increasingly annoyed, he watched the wrench and pick slide across the wards, and suspected Cate of laughing at him.

A glance up proved him wrong. She looked as discouraged as he felt. "Billy said ..."

"What did Billy say?" he snapped.

"It doesn't matter." She touched the wrench and guided it to the tumbler. "Put a firm, twisting pressure here."

He did. At least he tried.

With a cry, Cate jerked her finger back, looked at it, and stuck it in her mouth.

He dropped the tools and took her hand. "I'm sorry. Let me see."

"It's nothing. Just a scratch. Try again."

It wasn't just a scratch; he'd slipped the point beneath her fingernail. Blood oozed dully from her cuticle, and crimson traced a path beneath her nail. He slid the bench under her and pushed her down on it. "To torture prisoners, they used to shove slivers under the fingernail."

Her complexion was pasty. "I'll confess to anything right now."

"Really? Such an opportunity." He put a firm pressure on her nail and held it between his fingers. "What did Billy say?"

"He said you were a jackass."

"Nay, he didn't."

"Aye, he did. He said the man who'd sent me on such a streak of wildness ... was a jackass. That was you." She smiled at Taran, but pain made her lips narrow and bloodless. "Don't worry, I didn't let him blame you. I told him I'd gone bad on my own. You were no longer the impetus."

"Faint praise. I thank you." He glanced at her nail. The bleeding had slowed, but her fingers still trembled. "I'm surprised, though. I thought you blamed me for every misstep along your way."

"Not in my saner moments. I brought disaster on myself. I know it."

"Then what were you thinking? You were raised with good values."

"So were you, but you cheated at cards."

He remembered at once the game she spoke about. "I did not. I corrected a mistake."

"You had discarded and you no longer touched the card. You had no right to seize it back."

How they'd fought about that card! He'd known even then that she loved him, but she didn't back down to please his ego. A girl like that could drive a man mad. "My mother worries that, since you once stole for pleasure, you might steal from us."

Her round-eyed dismay was almost comical, and all too real. "Have you noticed how much your mother is like mine?"

Startled, he mentally compared the flamboyant Lady Bess to his own dignified Queen Sibeol. "How?"

"They don't look alike. But they have the same strength of character. They'll do what's right no matter what the cost to them or anyone else. I tell you the truth, Taran. It was one thing to tell Kiernan what I had been doing during my months with Billy. It was another to tell my mother."

When he had seized that card from Cate, Lady Bess had touched one finger on his sleeve. In her husky, smoker's voice, she had said, "God hates a cheater." Taran didn't know if God hated one, but he knew Lady Bess did, and he'd given up the card without another word. "Aye, I see your point."

Cate stared at their joined hands. Her finger still throbbed, Taran still pressed on it, and she wished she could remove herself from the area — and temptation — but she had an explanation to make. "Tell your mother I didn't keep the things I ... acquired. I gave them to Billy, who sold them. He was a kind thief. He had friends he helped support, and ..."

Head tilted, lips twisted, Taran watched her. "Are you trying to say you were supporting Billy as you would a charity?"

She inclined her head graciously. "An excellent way of putting it. I will never steal from you or anyone. When I was with

Billy, I was ... confused."

"What lifted your confusion?"

Cate didn't want to tell Taran this tale; not because she'd been reckless, but because she'd been foolish, and her foolishness had resulted in tragedy. More than that, she didn't want to remember. But she'd learned that sometimes a mistake could bring one eternal remorse. Because sometimes that same mistake could cost a life. With her hand at her throat, she said, "I ... Billy and I broke into a lovely home, for a lark, really. I saw a scarf worn by one of the women who'd scorned me – who'd been happy to cut me, because I –" She hesitated.

"Who was it?" Taran asked.

"Sarah Barry."

"She always envied you."

"Yes." Sarah had not been as pretty or as popular as Cate. She'd been spitefully rapturous by Cate's downfall. But her perfect little life had been ruined by the events of that evening, too, and Cate couldn't bring herself to exult. "I wanted her scarf. I thought it would be funny if she lost something she treasured." Cate rubbed her hand over her lips. She could remember that scarf even now. The rest of the events were fuzzy, but she could remember that scarf. Every swirl of green and purple, every ripple ... every puncture of the knife.

"So you were going to keep that scarf for yourself," Taran observed. "It wasn't going to the charity of Billy."

"I've always thought of that. I've wondered if I was pulled back from the brink of iniquity by some Celestial hand." Sweat broke out on Cate's brow, and she tugged at her collar. "But someone had to pay."

"You?"

"Not me. Unless I paid the coin in guilt." She took deep breaths, trying to calm her queasiness. "Billy and I waited until the house was asleep. We picked the lock at the window. Billy said we should always plan an escape route. We did, out through the servants' quarters. But we didn't think we'd need it. The job was easy. She'd left the scarf on the banister. We were giggling. We didn't know her husband was sneaking in to catch her with her lover. Instead, he saw Billy, assumed the worst, stabbed him –" The scarf. The colors. The knife wounds.

In a quiet voice, Taran asked, "Did they catch you?"

"Billy died almost at once." Writhing in pain and agony. No goodbyes. No chance to apologize, to grovel, to beg him not to leave her. Only blood everywhere, and a furious nobleman shouting that he'd teach Billy to sleep with his wife. And on the landing above, Sarah Barry, accompanied by her real lover, screaming that single, long, high-pitched shriek. "It was almost completely dark. Only a couple of candles lit. I was dressed like a serving maid. I slipped away." She hadn't wanted to. She'd wanted to stay there and cradle her friend.

But Billy had trained her well, and she heard his voice in her head.

"Get oot. No matter what happens, get oot. Ye don't do yer friends any good by going to the gallows with them." Leaning down, he caught her chin. *"And ye – fer sure, don't let a flatfoot catch ye. They'll find out who ye are. They'll make an example of ye and ye'll do the hangman's dance for sure."*

In her fury and her anguish at losing Taran, she had done a great many wrongs. She had lashed out at her family. She drank too much, laughed too loudly, had been too wild. She had stolen. She was responsible for the death of a dear man, her friend … everybody's friend.

Two days after the inglorious robbery, she'd sneaked away to attend Billy's rag-tag memorial service. His comrades had pelted her with garbage.

She'd gone home to the Isle of Mull and closed herself in her chamber. She had mourned. She had wept. She had done penance. Finally, her mother came to her and demanded, not an explanation, but labor. Cate threw herself into the task of creating a pauper's garden in the rocky soil of the island, and while she did it, she thought, very hard, about her life. She needed a vocation.

With this mission, she had found one.

Taran didn't understand. He could not dissuade her. Events – fate – had pushed her toward this moment, this obligation, and she would complete her task.

Kneeling in front of her, Taran asked harshly, "Was he your lover?"

She blinked at him. "Who? Billy?" She laughed too long and too hard.

The pirates in the corner stopped murmuring among themselves and stared.

Her nausea retreated. "Billy was the handsomest man I ever met. Charming, sweet, brave, savvy, street-smart -- the kind of man every woman dreams of meeting. Yes, of course he was my lover."

Taran stared into her face, examining each emotion with the care of a surgeon. "You're lying."

She was. Of course. But that he dared ask, after all he'd done, make her so mad she wanted to spit. "Shall I interrogate you about *your* lovers?"

"You can if you want. I don't remember any of their names." He gave an elegant shrug, so smooth, relaxed and indifferent Cate pitied the women who had loved him. *"Why* wasn't Billy your lover? Obviously he adored you."

"He loved women … but he loved men more. I was never in danger of seduction by Billy." *And he died because of me.* But she didn't say that, because she'd given up on melodrama.

Apparently Taran had not. He stood, loomed over her like a great dark hawk. paced away from her, and paced back. "You've lost your nerve," he stated.

"You weren't listening. This is not the truth. It's what you hope. And hopes are fragile things, unlikely to be fulfilled." How dare he behave as if he could read her heart and her soul? "I have not lost my nerve. I have lost … hope."

Leaning over her, Taran took her arm. "Think of what it will be like to again face a situation where you might be killed. You'd panic again."

He made her want to slap him. "I didn't panic," she said tartly. "I did as Billy had instructed me. And while I am as afraid of death as the next *man*," – she taunted him with the word – "it was the loss of Billy that I mourned. I assure you, I have waited for this assignment. It proves that my time with Billy happened for a purpose, and that purpose was to teach me to pick a lock, rescue a nation — and avenge my brother. Tragedy has made me strong."

His expression and his stance didn't change, but Cate would have sworn he made a decision.

"My mother is waiting upstairs to show you the layout of the palace." He gestured toward the table. "Gather up your tools, Cate. I concede defeat."

She wanted to crow, and indeed, she couldn't restrain a single, large smile. Taking his hand, she shook it heartily. "You won't be sorry. I promise you that."

When she tried to withdraw her fingers, he clasped them a little closer, engulfing her in the warmth of his grip. "Yes, you are the company picklock."

"I'll do my job."

"Aye, I know." He released her at last, and in a voice that sounded quite different from his usual tone, he added, "May God have mercy on both of us, my dear. Fate has caught up with us at last." He walked away.

She watched him, and whispered, "No. It doesn't have to be so. If only you would agree to forget..."

CHAPTER SIXTEEN

On the third evening of her training, Cate watched as, like a
bantam rooster, Blowfish strutted across the candle-lit taproom.
"Every time ye walk into a room" — he swung on her and pointed
his finger in her face — "any room, ye look fer the weapons. Ye
look fer the possible villains."

"I know."

"Oh, ye know, do ye?" He cracked his knuckles.

In the daylight, he dragged Cate up and down city streets
while lecturing on likely escape routes and hiding places.

She was not a woman who took kindly to being lectured, nor
was she a woman who enjoyed having her ignorance pointed out to
her, especially when she prided herself on having had experience
with the seamier side of life. But she listened intently, because she
knew every time Blowfish taught her something new, she had a
better chance of completing her mission alive and going on to
another. She would not fail Kiernan ... or herself.

In the evenings, Blowfish grudgingly allowed her to spend
time with Sibeol, learning the layout of the palace.

Taran had remained conspicuously absent from all lessons.
Men arrived, went up to his bedchamber, and held low-voiced
consultations with him. Sometimes he summoned Blowfish or
Quicksilver. But he didn't speak to Cate. He scarcely glanced at her.

Yet ... he stalked her.

Not physically. Not at all. Still, he was aware of her in a way
that made her skin prickle and her heart race. She dreamed of him at
night, and looked for him by day.

They shared a secret she dared not allow him to reveal.

Knowing he was in her vicinity disturbed her in ways she
refused to examine. On her treks through the city, she had found
herself catching glimpses of Taran – but it was never Taran. It was
some stranger with the same build, or the same hair color, who
never even glanced at her. Her own irrational behavior worried her;
why should she see Taran everywhere when in real life she prayed
never to see him again?

When she went to bed at night, before she took the

precaution of placing the rope ladder by the window, she locked the door and shoved a chair beneath the handle.

"What do ye do if someone grabs ye like" – Blowfish snatched her arm and wrenched it around to her back – "this?"

Giving a cry, she struggled against his hold. "Ouch! That hurts. Ouch, ouch, let go!"

The pirates gathered around the perimeter to enjoy the spectacle. Quicksilver leaned against the wall, an elegant figure in a pirate's rough clothing. Dead Bob sat at a small round table, drinking an ale, his mouth a straight line. Maccus and Italy desultorily tossed the dice, while Lilbit rocked from toe to heel in a constant motion. Even Mr. Cleary stopped to watch.

So she resolved to provide them with a spectacle.

"What have I taught ye to do now?" Blowfish demanded. "Think, woman! Use the weapons available to ye. What should ye do?"

She sniffled. "I don't know what to do. I'm just a girl."

Blowfish sighed mightily. "'Ere in Mr. Cleary's fine establishment, what could ye use fer a weapon?"

Cate sniffled again. "The fireplace poker, a burning brand … my arm hurts, Blowfish, please won't you let me go? The bottles behind the bar." She'd learned so much. Today the ship that ferried goods and people back and forth to Cenorina had docked. Tomorrow she would be on it, and soon, so soon, Kiernan would be avenged.

She squirmed in Blowfish's hold. A lock of her hair shook loose from its chignon. She shook it, for she knew the strand would catch the firelight, and shine, and distract them. "Ow, ow, it really hurts –"

Blowfish let her go. Leaning his hand on the table, he said, "Blast, woman, ye've got to stop whining, else no one will take ye seriously."

She pounced on the silverware, snatched up a fork, and stabbed it right between his spread fingers.

He yelped and leaped away.

Coolly she looked into his eyes. "A woman's weak tears make a man underestimate her, and a fork makes a fine weapon."

The silence in the taproom was awesome.

Then the pirates fell on each other with laughter.

For one moment, she observed a flash of hardnosed rage in Blowfish's features.

And it was gone.

He chuckled. "All right," he said. "I deserved that."

She looked at him more carefully. He seemed the genial sailor he'd always been with her, but that expression ... was that the pirate who had survived so many years at sea?

"Ye're a crafty lass, and ye'll do fine in a fight, except fer one thing."

She glanced around at the men she thought of as her friends. Beneath their welcoming exteriors, did they all hide a pitiless streak that made them pirates feared throughout the world?

He snapped his fingers under her nose. "Pay attention!"

She blinked at him. "What?"

"Ye'll never really 'arm a soul."

She could scarcely sputter from indignation. *"What?"*

"Have ye ever, in yer whole life, ever really 'armed anything? Shot a deer? Skinned a bunny?"

How had he guessed? She hated hunting, and on butchering day, she worked hard in the garden, and plugged her ears when the pig   squealed.

"Caught a fish?" Blowfish asked hopefully.

The men quieted as they listened to the argument.

She folded her arms and lifted her chin. "I shot your Cap'n!"

"She did that," Quicksilver defended her.

Blowfish cast him a scornful glance and retorted, "With clear intent to do no harm."

Lilbit chewed his lower lip. "In the mission, she's not supposed to have to hurt anybody, is she?"

Dead Bob clouted Lilbit to the side of the head.

"Wha ... at?" Lilbit sputtered.

Dead Bob nodded at Mr. Cleary, who watched them wide-eyed and fascinated.

"Oh." Lilbit rubbed his ear. "I forgot."

"He's going to forget us into a trap," Blowfish muttered to Cate.

"Me?" Mr. Cleary pointed to his barrel chest. "I don't tell anyone anything!"

Quicksilver rose, his gentlemanly upbringing evident in the

way he moved and in every word he spoke. "Mr. Cleary, let me assist you with clearing the boards. Lilbit, Mucus, give us a hand."

Within minutes, the pirates had hustled Mr. Cleary and his crockery out of the taproom and into the kitchen.

Troubled, Cate asked, "Isn't he trustworthy?"

"He is. He can be trusted to accept any bribe." Blowfish tossed his arm over Cate's shoulder. "A man who always behaves the same way, even a bad way, is trustworthy in his way. Right?"

"I suppose." She'd never thought of it that way.

"Lass, do ye know there's evil in the world?"

"Yes." She'd seen evil in the slums of Edinburgh. The killers, the whores, the pimps. But she'd seen evil among Edinburgh's finest society, too. The women who ignored their children. The men who beat their wives. The people who murdered and betrayed their country for a sack of gold. "I recognize evil when I see it."

"If ye knew ye would save a 'undred lives by ending one, would ye do it?"

She struggled with the answer. "Nay. For what if I judged badly, and that person was the one who could save a hundred lives?"

"Soft," Blowfish scoffed.

In the dark of the night after she'd heard the news about Kiernan, she had sworn this vow that whoever had caused his death would pay. "I will do everything possible to incarcerate the villain."

"Incarcerate? That's a mighty fancy word fer *no.*"

"It's not *no,* it's … well, it is *no.* But I'll still be a good spy." She hated to disappoint Blowfish. "I'm sorry."

Blowfish gave her a squeeze before he let her go. "Don't be sorry, lass! Most people would as soon whack ye as look at ye. But ye – ye're a good woman, so ye've got to be extra prepared. When ye meet with the evil ones, cry and pretend to be weak, if that'll disarm 'em. Then kick 'em in the nuts. Lock 'em in a closet. Gag 'em. Knock 'em out. Most times, the important thing is timing, and if ye ruin their timing, they'll get what's coming to 'em somehow. Now" – he grinned wickedly, showing his missing tooth – "we got the final test before ye go off to do yer dooty fer God and country."

She didn't like the way the men gathered around her in a circle. Quicksilver, Maccus and Lilbit had returned. Everyone was *leering.*

"What?" she asked.

"Ah, she sounds suspicious, don't she, me hearties?" Blowfish walked around her, looking her over. "D'ye think she'll struggle? Shall we tie 'er arms to 'er side?"

"It's all right, Miss MacLean. I survived with scarcely a scratch." Lilbit towered over the others, and he looked as if he wanted to laugh.

Surely that was a good thing. Surely torture wouldn't make Lilbit merry.

But they *were* pirates.

"I'm sorry, Miss MacLean." Quicksilver's melodious tones rang heavy with regret. "I tried to talk them out of it, but it's a pirate custom that can't be ignored."

Was she supposed to fight them? *All?*

She assumed a battle-ready position. Balanced on the balls of her feet. Hands relaxed and free of any encumbrance.

They'd cleared the table. The bottles, good for smashing and slashing, were at the bar. She had her knife in her pocket, but that would help her for about one second.

Expressionless, Dead Bob stood, his arms crossed over his chest. "If grown men can survive this, Miss MacLean, you can, too."

Her heart beat in her throat. Were they going to brand her? Beat her?

Blowfish backed toward the bar. "If ye're going to be one of us, ye'll have to do this."

"Cap'n said we could do it," Maccus said. "An' a fellow Scot like yerself'll have no trooble showing them yer mettle."

"The Cap'n knows about this?" Cate would make sure the Cap'n paid for not warning her.

"Only lost one sailor in all the days we've been doing this rit-oo-al," Blowfish reassured her. "He couldn't ... dance."

"What?"

Blowfish pulled a squeezebox out from under the bar, and it gave a squall. "What do ye say to a party?"

CHAPTER SEVENTEEN

Cate stared at the accordion, at Blowfish, at the grinning circle of pirates. Lilbit shoved his dice in his pocket and danced a jig. Quicksilver bowed as elegantly as any gentleman in a ball. Dead Bob folded his arms over his chest and without a twitch of a smile gave the impression of happiness. Maccus joined Blowfish at the bar and brought forth a violin.

"A party?" Cate's smile quivered. "Really?"

"We couldn't allow our best girl to go beard the lion in his den without a proper send-off," Blowfish said.

"You are a dear, dear man, my favorite pirate ever." Overwhelmed by a wave of affection, Cate kissed his whiskered cheek.

Blowfish's dark cheeks turned darker. Putting his hands on her shoulders, he put her away. "Enough of that. We've got some dancing to do."

Blowfish and Maccus tuned up while the men formed two rows facing each other. Quicksilver bowed, took her hand, and led her to the top of a line. In an undertone, he said, "The dance isn't difficult. In fact, it's not even arranged. Do your best country dance with the occasional spin and everyone'll be pleased."

The music started, a jig with a lively rhythm, and Cate observed as the first two pirates pranced along. One of them lifted his legs high, skipping like a schoolboy. The other kept the rhythm with a combination of taps with his heels and toes. Everyone clapped in time to the music, so Cate clapped too, and laughed to see the fearsome pirates frolicking like children. Two by two they danced past her, each of the men she'd come to know this past week.

Finally it was her turn. She curtsied to Quicksilver, placed her hands on her hips, and capered with him down the aisle formed by the clapping pirates.

White and dark, tall and short, young and old, these men were her friends. She knew what it meant to them, to give up women on one of their precious nights in port to celebrate with her before she left.

Once, they liked her because she'd had the audacity to shoot their Cap'n.

Now, they liked her for herself.

The lines broke up as restraint broke down. The squeezebox squawked and the violin moaned, and each man danced his own dance, occasionally hooking arms and swinging each other around so aggressively the dances became wrestling contests.

Cate didn't care. She spun alone, her hands over her head, more and more of her hair falling around her shoulders.

The pirates whistled as they watched, singing vulgar songs she didn't want to know the words to.

Mr. Cleary returned from the kitchen and assumed his place behind the bar.

When she finally stopped and held the stitch in her side, laughing, the pirates passed her a mug of ale and she swallowed it down. Then she twirled back onto the dance floor – and came face to face with Taran.

Taran, tall, dark and bearded, his arm freed from its sling. He extended that hand to her. "May I have the pleasure of this dance?"

The noise around them faded. Conversations died as the men watched Cate watching Taran.

She considered him and his invitation.

In these days of preparation and waiting, she had studied her mission. The layout of the palace. What to look for. How to fight if necessary. But she was a creature of emotions as well as of thought, and always beneath the concentration was an awareness of Taran. He was here. He was alive.

She wanted him.

Funny, the way a woman's heart worked. There was no sense to it, no logic, but her body operated on a primal level. He had abandoned her all those years ago. Yet still she longed for him. He was her mate, the man who should father her children, sleep beside her every night, fight with her and feed her and care for her.

Moreover, she didn't doubt that he also wanted her. He wanted her the way most men wanted a woman. Lewdly, without affection or care. With Taran there would be no children, no sleeping, no fighting or feeding or caring. He'd proved he could walk away from her and never come back. Moreover, he was dangerous, a man without emotions, a man who would do his duty even if it meant sacrificing his most beloved possession — for he did not love.

No one had to tell her. She already knew. He had never loved her, but now the years of separation and experience rose between them like icy mountains, and she would freeze to death if she tried to cross them.

Moreover, he would let her freeze.

Yes, he wanted her. Every day he watched her, his dark eyes hungry. The tension wound around them, strangling them with need. Now he wanted to touch her hand, to lead her in a freewheeling dance guaranteed to free their inhibitions and leave them … breathless.

So be it. She had things to show him. Things like control, defiance, and the intelligence that kept her from stepping in the same trap twice.

He might entice, but she would not respond.

With a superior smile, she curtsied and put her hand in his.

He led her into the intricate steps of the Highland Fling.

Of course. She'd taught him the steps, and he wanted her to recall what they had in common. He wanted to share the movement, the joy, the pleasure of a dance shared.

And they *were* good together. The men stopped to watch them, clapping in time to the music as they bowed and stepped high, gamboling around each other like lambs in the spring.

A competition developed.

The accordion and the violin kept playing faster and faster, following each other through frantic rhythm.

Cate and Taran danced faster and faster, their eyes flashing, their feet leaping, and all the while watching each other in challenge. Finally, just when she thought she would gasp her last, Taran wrapped his arms around her waist and swung her around and around until she ached with dizziness and laughter.

He swung her up against the wall and leaned her there.

The music stopped.

The men cheered enthusiastically.

She saw two dozen smiles flash beneath two dozen scraggly beards. Then they turned back toward the bar, leaving their Cap'n and Cate in relative quiet.

When she had caught her breath, she said, "They're good men."

He leaned against the wall beside her, a smile as sharp as a razor playing on his lips. "The best. They're putting their lives on the line for this job. If it succeeds, if Davies is caught and we rescue Cenorina, they'll get a pardon from England and all their crimes against the crown will be forgiven."

"Is that why they're doing it?"

"No. It's an adventure. They love adventure. And they're doing it for me." Turning his head suddenly, he caught her watching him. "Bless them. I needed them, and to a man they said *aye.*" He used charm like a knife and authority like a bludgeon.

She had forgotten how the movement of his lips fascinated her, how every time he spoke she dreamed he put those lips to her skin and caressed her with them. Mayhap part of his danger rested in, not his coldness, but the heat he could generate. He used touch and memory like flint and steel, igniting a spark, one that burned her with desire, but could never give off warmth.

"We'll be done, one way or the other, by Michaelmas."

In four weeks or less, they'd have found the evidence which would convict Sir Maddox Davies — or they would have failed and possibly died.

Her smile didn't falter.

Bless the pirates, indeed, for showing her a good time before she faced the deadly business ahead. "Aren't you going to try and convince me not to go to Cenorina?"

"No. You were right. I can't learn to pick a lock in less than a week —"

She could be gracious. "It would be a rare man who could learn how to pick a lock in such limited time, much less a leader with so much to do with the planning that will ensure the success of this mission."

He waited until she finished before he added, "— any more than you can learn to kill a man."

She stiffened. "Blowfish told you?"

"I remember you and your aversion to killing." He touched her cheek.

She jerked her head away.

His hand dropped to his side. "You used to turn green when

Kiernan and I brought in a dressed deer."

"Years and events might have changed my predilections."

"Nay. Thank God." His gray eyes watched her from beneath lids made heavy with dark lashes. "There are still a few things I can depend on."

Some subjects she would be smart to let drop, and this was one of them. "Good. I'm glad you've decided to be reasonable about my part in this mission. I'm capable and I'm intelligent, and I'll find those letters." She smiled with determined amiability.

His mouth, so plush, so made for passion, did not smile. "I'm going with you."

CHAPTER EIGHTEEN

She straightened away from the wall. "What do you mean, you're going with me?" Her voice rose.

The conversations at the bar faltered.

She used her firmest tone. "You most certainly are not. As you yourself pointed out to me, until the plan comes to fruition, you are needed here."

The pirate captain, the ruthless gentleman, was much in evidence with his quiet tone and his uncompromising gaze. "If you're going, I'm going."

"How? As my half-witted brother?"

"Not as your *brother.*"

The way he said that … the way his stare swept her …

She froze. He didn't mean … it had been three days, and he hadn't … but, oh Lord, she'd been afraid of this every moment of every day. Her blood cooled to shards of ice, and she pointed her finger at him. "You had better not be thinking what I think you're thinking."

He caught her finger. He shaped her hand into a fist, then clasped it in both his hands. "As your husband."

"No." She had sworn she would never let him into her bedchamber again. If she let him do this, he would have succeeded by stealth — by making her bedchamber his. "No!"

"I am not leaving you alone, not even for a moment."

"No." She tried to yank herself free of his grip.

He held her easily, dragged her toward him.

She resisted every step. Her husband! He would tell everyone he was her husband! The scent of his body brought forth memories she wanted buried, and his heat warmed her when she would remain cold. She pressed her free hand against his chest to hold him off, and desperation made her thoughts leap to a logical argument. "What explanation would I have for dragging my husband along to my position as housekeeper? There was no mention of a husband. A housekeeper doesn't suddenly acquire a husband."

Throughout her speech, he shook his head implacably.

She cast about in her mind. "Your presence will endanger the mission. Davies will be suspicious."

"He will not recognize me."

"Why not?"

"I have my ways." His assurance was absolute.

The men surreptitiously watched them fight.

She glared at them until Blowfish picked up his accordion again. "Let's dance some more, lads!" he shouted.

Maccus picked up his violin. The men gave a cheer, and the dancing started once more. This time, they carried their mugs and slopped ale onto the floor. They'd drunk enough that they sang louder and sounded more like the braying of donkeys, but her affection was unchanged — for them.

For Taran, she felt only a burning in the gut. In a low, disgusted tone, she said, "You're from Cenorina, you said. Won't you be recognized?"

"I have taken that into account."

"No." She stomped her foot in frustration, then groaned at her own impetuosity.

He brought it out in her. Taran Tamson, with his perilous gaze and his absolute pronouncements, carried her to the edge of passion. This would never do, but — it felt good, this once, to let go, especially when she knew she was right. She stomped her foot again. "No, no, no! What right have you to jeopardize the mission because you believe me to be an incompetent? I'm not."

"You're not. I agree. But you're going with me as your husband, or not at all."

"But —"

"With me as your husband, or not at all," he repeated, and she thought he would repeat it over and over until she heard it in her sleep.

She tugged at her hand again, and this time he let her go. She made the pronouncement. "I am not sleeping with you."

"Do you think I still want you?"

"You do."

"You can tell by your feminine intuition."

"I can tell because your trousers fit too tightly. And you are conceited. You think, because I adored you before, that I can be made to adore you once more. It won't happen." She was so angry, she shook from head to toe. "I won't be used again."

"Maybe not. Maybe I can't make you adore me again, maybe I can't make you love me again —"

Oh, why did he have to use the word *love?*

"But you're right about one thing." He leaned his arm against wall by her head. His lips barely moved as he spoke, but his eyes gleamed with a blatant assurance. "I want you in my bed all the time. I'm not going to force you. I don't have to. Our flesh almost sizzles when we stand close, and one night soon you'll come to me and offer yourself."

"Nay." *Nay.* She wanted to cover her ears. He was saying exactly what she feared.

"Every moment, every day, every time we see each other, the craving grows. You won't be able to resist for much longer. I'm going to have you again, Cate. You're going to give yourself to me as freely and as generously as you did at the hut in the Scottish mountains."

"I'm … not!" He wasn't doing anything. Just standing, leaning close, looking down at her, but her breasts grew heavy and the lace of her chemise seemed tight and scratchy.

He moved closer, crowding her with his scent, his strength, his heat. "Think of it, Cate, you and I sweaty and passionate, our naked bodies moving together in a dance without music."

She lifted her fist, ready to punch him in the shoulder.

He blocked her blow, grabbed her hand, and leaned close enough to speak right in her ear. "We'll spend days in bed, nights in bed."

"I don't need you." She sagged against the wall.

…She wanted to kiss him right now.

His breath caressed her neck and his lips moved across her skin as he spoke. "I'll worship your body and you'll worship mine. I'll taste you and you'll taste me." He caught her other hand and kissed the back of her fingers. "And it's right and proper, is it not? For in truth, darlin', I remember the day. I remember the hour."

She struggled to remove her hands from his. "Don't say it!"

He was relentless. "Whether you like it or not, on a bright morning in Oban, we stood in that tiny church and said our vows before that old, old clergyman."

"Don't remember!"

"Don't remember?" He was incredulous. "I can't forget. My darling wife, in the eyes of man, and law, and in the eyes of God, we *are* married."

CHAPTER NINETEEN

This was what Cate had dreaded since the moment she had seen Taran. This nugget of truth, hidden from the world, known only to the two of them. She stopped struggling and stared urgently into his gaze. "No one need ever know."

"We know." His voice curled around her mind like sweet, thick applewood smoke, confusing her, making her tremble. "That minister knows."

"He's dead." God forgive her, she'd been glad to hear that that sweet, fragile old man had gone to his reward, for she had wanted no one to know the depths to which her idiocy had descended. "I lived in fear he would realize who I was, but if he did, he never told anyone, and now he's dead."

"*God* knows."

She took hard, desperate breaths, trying to bring in enough air to banish this faintness that threatened to bring her to her knees. "Then it's between you and me and God. I don't want the world to know. I can't believe you do, either."

"How desperate are you to keep it a secret?" Taran murmured. "What will you pay to make sure I tell no one?"

Her voice rose. "I'm not fornicating with you!"

A few of the men looked around, grinning.

He didn't smile as he shushed her. "Fornicate with me? As a bribe to keep me quiet? Certainly not. You'll fornicate with me because you want to. I meant — will you take me along as your husband because you're told to, or will you take me along as your husband because I am?"

She had no choice. She knew it. He knew it. But she would bargain anyway. "So if I take you as my husband, when this mission has been completed, do you promise to let me go my own way without interference from you?"

Throwing back his head, he laughed long and hard. "A woman without a husband is like —"

"— A bird without a corset."

He cocked his head, a faint smile still caressing his lips. "That doesn't make sense."

"Isn't … that … the truth." She didn't need a man. She'd proved it time and time again. Now she had to prove it to Taran, that ultimate arrogant male beast.

"You'll take me with you to Cenorina, because it's the best chance the mission has of succeeding."

"You'll disappear from my life when Davies had been captured?"

He stroked one side of her jaw with the backs of his fingers. "I suspect I can safely promise that."

She considered him suspiciously. Was that good enough?

Probably not.

Would she get more from him?

Definitely not.

But why did he look like that? As if he'd been presented a choice between a cup of poison and a rusty blade? "I want more. I want your vow that you'll disappear from my life forever. I want never to see a man who resembles you. I want never to hear a voice that reminds me of yours. I want to know —"

Sliding his arms around her waist, he swung her body up to meet his. "You never did know when to shut up."

He leaned her back and kissed her with all the finesse of a pirate intent on victory, with his tongue and, when she wouldn't cooperate, with the gentle scrape of his teeth against her lower lip.

The taste of him. The scent. The warmth. The texture of his lips, the nubby surface of his shirt beneath her fingertips, the press of his chest against hers.

All around them, the party continued, but they were instantly, totally involved in each other. She wanted him, now, on the bench, on the floor, in her bedchamber …

Dimly, in the recesses of her brain, she heard the slam of a door.

The roar of a gunshot sliced across the squall of the accordion, through the singing and the thumps of men's boots.

Chips of wood and plaster fell like hail.

Silence descended.

Taran lifted his head and stared down at Cate, and for a moment he looked as dazed and overwhelmed as she felt.

Reality returned in a rush.

She gasped and shoved him away.

He smashed her against the wall and swung to face the room. She could see nothing of the tavern but Taran's back. But she did hear the scrape of knives being drawn. The click as pistols left their holsters.

A harsh male voice shouted, "I 'eard there were terrible pirates in Cleary's pub, but I see only cockless cowards too afraid to dance with wenches."

Cate strained to peek around Taran's shoulder.

As a group, his men stepped forward and in front of her.

Only Taran hung back to thrust a pistol into her hand. In a low voice, he commanded, "Get to your room as fast as you can." Then he shoved his way through his men until he reached the front.

In a voice as loud and rough as his unknown assailant, he roared, "Gerry Williams. You worthless arse-sucker! I should have known you were in town. I smelled the stench of rotting fish."

Cate sidled over to the stairwell. Sliding inside, into the dim interior, she stood on the lowest step and looked over the top of the men.

An enormous, bald, bug-eyed pirate stood just inside the taproom. His hands were the size of serving platters. His still-smoking pistol was twice as long as Taran's. His clothes were every color of the rainbow, but smudged and torn, and blood smeared his face. His teeth were black, his scowl dreadful to behold, and in his ears he wore delicate gold earrings. Incongruous, but all the more frightening because of that.

Surrounding him stood two dozen of the dirtiest, meanest-looking sailors she'd ever seen. They, too, looked as if they'd fought other battles this night. One man's eye was swollen shut, another had a cut across his cheek. Knives hung in a shining array across their chests, except the ones they clutched in their hands.

"Your ship is called the Floating Twigger." Taran's voice dropped to a sympathetic croon which he somehow managed to project through the pub. "But tell the truth. You haven't had a stand out of old Horny since dirt was young."

"Oh ... yeah?" The pirate fixed his bulging gaze on Taran, and if looks could have killed, Taran would have exploded into bloody fragments.

Taran swaggered toward Gerry Williams. "You've got no money in your purse, no ink in your pot, your sails are limp and your mast is broken. You couldn't board a ship, must less occupy a woman. That's why you came looking for a fight, you –"

With a roar, Gerry threw himself at Taran.

Taran's crew flung themselves at Gerry's crew.

They clashed amid shrieks of rage with knives and punishing blows.

Cate lifted the pistol, prepared to defend her men, but she couldn't see Taran, couldn't tell one pirate from another. The noise was deafening as they overturned tables, threw chairs, broke glasses.

Mr. Cleary came rushing in from the kitchen, waving a towel, and went down under the mass of humanity like a sand flea beneath an ocean wave.

Every other moment, Cate saw one or the other of her pirates, swinging his fists with a madness that looked like pleasure. *Was* pleasure. Her mouth puckered. Yes, she'd grown up with enough boys to recognize when they were having a good time. They punched each other's brains out with glorious good will. She craned her neck, trying to get a glimpse of Taran.

The crowd parted.

Taran fought Gerry Williams like a man baiting a bear. Gerry outweighed him by four stone, and one good blow would have finished the fight. Instead, Taran danced in and out, slapping him, tweaking his nose, and occasionally giving him a good clobber on the ear. Gerry shouted and fought, punching at him, but never landing a straight hit. One blow, even half-struck, from that beefy fist would have knocked Taran into next week. Gerry never had a chance to land that blow.

At the same time, both men observed the brawls going on around them, for occasionally they would step into another fight and knock the stuffing out of someone else.

It was, Cate decided, like the dance, only without rhythm or beauty.

Taran was good. He was accurate. He was savage. He fought as he made love, with precision and grace. He made every movement count, and Cate's mouth dried as she stared. Every time she met him, she recalled how good it had been between them, and once again she wanted him. Every time, the desire increased, smoldering like a spark ignited by bellows. If she didn't stay away from him, she would willingly step into the fire and be incinerated by the passion between them.

Taran's fist met Gerry Williams's face, knocking him flat onto his back. He slid along the floor, right into the shadowy stairwell. Head back, face bloody, he looked upside-down at her. Smiling his black-toothed grin, he roared, "Hey, little lady, come out and play!"

She lifted the pistol, cocked it, and pointed the barrel right between his eyes. Some hint of her cool intention must have percolated through to his pirate's drunken brain, for his eyes widened, he got to his feet, and he flung himself back out into the fight.

She heard him shouting unintelligibly. "Female! Damned red-haired female! Almost blew me head off!"

Taran skittered into the stairwell. "Blast! Cate, can't you ever follow directions?"

She glared at him. Blood oozed from his swollen lip. He had the beginnings of a black eye and he sucked on his bleeding knuckles.

It wasn't fair, knowing what she rejected, seeing how he moved … knowing he was right, that the two of them together made a team that would avenge her brother's death and bring the traitors to justice.

So he would go to Cenorina as her husband. She would do her job. And if he tried to take advantage of their proximity, she would utilize the knowledge Blowfish had taught her. She couldn't kill Taran. Oh, no. But she could knacker him and throw his acorns to the pigs. She nodded. "Yes, I will."

"Get upstairs!" he shouted, and jumped back into the fray.

Carefully, she eased the flintlock back into place, pocketed Taran's pistol, and on wobbly knees went upstairs to bed — alone.

No matter how he kissed her, no matter how incredible the heat between them, that was the way it was going to stay.

Nine years ago, he might have wed her before bedding and abandoning her. But she'd changed in nine years. Now she was determined to preserve her sanity and her virtue. He would never again share her bed.

CHAPTER TWENTY

Nine years ago...

Nine years ago, when Cate and Taran left the isle of Mull for their lovers' rendezvous, Cate had wanted to scamper away from Castle MacLean.

Taran insisted they stroll as if they were going for a walk. Taran carried a leather bag with him.

Cate wondered what wonderful gifts he had obtained for her.

He allowed her to hire the fisherman to take them to the mainland. He had arranged for a frail old minister in a village outside of Oban to wed them, and that moment, as they stood in his parlor while he blessed them, had been the happiest of her life. She would never forget the way the daisies trembled in her arms or the single, passionate kiss of claiming Taran pressed on her lips.

Then he insisted they separate and make their way to their rendezvous separately.

She was glad to do anything he asked. Their flight had all the earmarkings of an escape. She thrilled at their great adventure, for she knew, without a doubt, how it would end. With happily ever after.

Now Cate chuckled bitterly. Down in the taproom, the fight roared on. Without taking off her clothes — one never knew if the idiots downstairs would set the place on fire — she reclined on her bed and covered her eyes with her arm.

Nine years ago.

Nine years ago, she had been so incredibly, mightily naïve, that even now it hurt to remember. She tried never to recall those moments, but now ... between Taran declaring himself and the flutterings of her own foolish heart, she forced herself to remember all the passion, all the recklessness ... all the pain.

Years of pain. Years of loneliness.

Nine years ago ...

Granny Aileen had died, leaving a well-tended valley hidden in the folds of the mountains. Kiernan stocked it with firewood and dried food in tins, intending it as a refuge for travelers. Birds nested in the orchard, and deer brought their young to feast on the new young buds. Few human travelers followed the path here, but when they did they were rewarded with a sense of security, of eternity captured in one protected corner of the earth.

As Cate slid down the steep path, she smelled spring green grass and heard the tinkling of the tiny spring into the sand-lined pool. The gentle sunshine caressed her face, and for the first time since her father had died, she was totally, completely happy. She loved Taran with all the passion of her young heart, and now she had him for her own, forever and ever.

She knew he didn't love her. But he wanted her. Once their bodies had joined, his heart would change. Instead of that look that so often of late had flattened the color of his gray eyes to muddy despair, he would gaze at her as she gazed at him — with adoration. He'd smile ... more than once a month. With her love, she would cure all his unhappiness, and he'd stay on Mull with her forever. She knew it. She did.

When he arrived, he would take her in his arms. They would undress and press themselves together ... she shivered and fingered the buttons on her blue-flowered muslin frock. Whatever pain her virgin body might experience would be worth it, to be with him.

Opening the door to the hut, she raced to open the shutters. Sunshine streamed in, lighting the single room. In Granny Aileen's time, the place had been spotless. Now dust covered the tiny table, the benches, the bed covers.

This called for action — and action would cure Cate's attack of silly nerves. She discarded her bonnet and with the supplies she found in the tiny cupboard, she dusted, she swept, she shook out the blankets. She went down to the spring and filled the pitcher with water. She plucked daisies out of the overgrown garden and arranged them in Granny's tin cup, and put them on the table. Then she stood back and admired her handiwork ... and allowed herself a moment of worry.

Where was Taran? The marriage had been hasty, almost dreamlike, and nothing like she'd ever imagined for herself.

Had he changed his mind?

She placed her hand on her chest and took a breath. If he had, he would be the fool, for what she had to give him would be the greatest gift of his life. She nodded her head decidedly.

Of course, her mother declared men were fools.

Opening her bag, Cate brought out her change of clothes, shook them out and hung them on the nails pounded into the wall.

She brought out the food: a loaf of bread, yellow cheese, last years' dried apples, oat scones baked this morning and two bottles of stout red wine. A thought struck her, and she hurried out to the tiny orchard. The cherries were red and luscious, hanging from the towering tree in bunches. She plucked them into a basket, and somehow, every other one found its way to her mouth.

When Taran drawled, "Charming," she swung around in surprise.

He stood, framed by tall granite boulders on either side of him and the mountain looming behind him. He wore a sturdy, dark traveling suit, his newest boots and a broad-brimmed hat that hid his features in shadow. He'd grown since he first came to Mull; his shoulders had broadened and he'd shot up so quickly Lady Bess had jokingly complained he split his shoe leather on a regular basis. But he still had the same black hair and gray eyes with which Cate had fallen in love. His full lips still settled in that adorable pout, and when he moved, she watched him and sighed with what Kiernan called "silly lass longing."

But Cate was no silly lass. She knew what she liked, and she liked Taran. His every movement pleasured the eye. Grace tempered his strength, and the coil and uncoil of his muscles as he exercised, or fought, or simply walked, made her think of a wild stallion. She tried always to walk behind him so she could watch his bum; of course, all the other girls did the same. But none of the other girls had Taran with them now. He was hers. Her husband.

"You're here!" She laughed from the pure joy of seeing him and, dropping the basket, she ran to him and jumped into his arms. He was the only man tall enough and strong enough to catch her and not stagger backward. She loved that, and loved the way his arms wrapped around her and hugged her to him as he swung in a broad circle.

Now everything would be all right.

She kissed him, mashing her mouth on his, and he kissed her back with a lad's enthusiasm for his own dear lass. Then he put her down, and he looked as happy as she'd imagined. "You taste of cherries." Wiping his finger at the corner of her mouth, he showed her the stain.

She grinned up at him. "Do you want some?"

They collected cherries, eating as many as they put in the basket. They had spitting contests, seeing who could get the cherry pit over the top of the largest boulder. When she succeeded, he declared her the best spitter the isle of Mull had ever produced and gave her a kiss in reward.

That kiss ... he held her head in both his hands and tilted it just so. Their lips met at the perfect angle, without a single nose bump. He caressed her mouth with his, brushing it, until her eyes closed, her breath came faster, and she wanted more. But still he held her back, forcing her to withhold her eagerness, seemingly happy to explore the lightest touch. Her puppy-like eagerness faded as she relaxed, content to follow his lead, to concentrate on the dark thrill that shivered along her nerves as he kissed her, lips closed. Only their mouths touched; his hands held her head, but he kept their bodies separate. She hadn't known so many experiences could occur from the touch of lip to lip, nor had she realized that, after an acquaintance with that simple pleasure, that she would want more.

To hold him in place, she grasped his wrists in hers. Thick wrists, with muscles built up from swinging the claymore, from riding, from lifting a heavy pistol time and again, aiming it at a target, and shooting until he hit dead center.

But he kissed her more and more lightly, then eased away. He touched her mouth with one finger, and as he gazed at her, his chest rose and fell as if he'd been running. He sounded slightly out of breath when he said, "In Oban, I bought a roast chicken, and I've smelled it all the way up here. Shall we eat?"

"That sounds wonderful." She wasn't at all disappointed to have him draw back. Everything sounded wonderful today. Taking his hand, she led him along the path. "Did you go to the hut already?"

"I went looking for you. I thought you'd changed your mind."

Stopping, she faced him. "I could never change my mind about you."

"Back on Mull, you claimed you loved me." He watched her tautly.

"I do." She said it as fervently as she had said their wedding vows.

"Forever?"

"Until the day I die."

He nodded as if satisfied. "No matter what I do?"

She grinned and walked backward. "No matter how much you tease me, or nag me, or fight with me. I'll always love you."

"Even if I ..." He hesitated as if searching for the right phrase.

"What?" She hopped along, trying to watch him and behind her at the same time.

"Even if I tickle you?"

That hadn't been what he was going to say. She was sure of it.

But he started toward her, fingers outstretched.

She shrieked, turned and ran for the hut.

He caught her, of course. She let him. She struggled, but not too hard, as he ran his fingers over her ribs, and she didn't struggle at all when his knuckles brushed against her nipples.

Taran and Cate stopped laughing. They stared at each other, and Cate thought she could fall into his gray eyes. They were deep, intense, yet at the same time, like fog, impossible to see through. His soul was well hidden from her.

Breaking away, she said in an unsteady voice, "You wanted to eat."

"Aye. I want to eat." His soft, guttural voice made her think he meant something else entirely.

But they went into the hut and gathered the scones, the wine, and the chicken. The rich odor of rosemary and garlic rose from the brown-paper wrapped fowl, and her stomach growled.

That embarrassed her, too. What if she broke wind?

This love-making business was more fraught with difficulties than she realized.

Back out into the afternoon sunshine, they spread a blanket on the grass under the giant fir. The spicy scent of crushed needles rose as they seated themselves, one on each side of the blanket.

The silence turned awkward, and she couldn't think of any clever way to break it. So she said, "It smells fabulously good."

"A feast fit for a king." His voice held utter satisfaction, and she looked up to see him staring at her.

He looked almost dangerous, like a starving brigand presented with a meal — and she was the main course.

She blushed. Silly, really. She'd lived with him for three years now, longed for this moment absolutely forever, but now that the time was upon her, she suffered tiny, quibbling fear, a mere virginal bit of silliness. A fear of the unknown.

Not a warning from her conscience. Not good sense rather than emotion. She was a wild lass. Everyone said so. So she had proved all the nasty gossips right, and eloped. When the truth came out, she would be the envy of every female in Scotland.

He interrupted her reverie. "Can I take off my boots? They're new and they rub on my heels."

He sounded so prosaic, so normal, that she laughed. "You'll do anything to try and avoid serving. Very well, but you'll have to clean up."

Grasping his boot, he struggled to pull it free. "I promise."

She snorted. All the men said things like that to get their way. They never actually did a bit of cleaning, although they were perfectly capable.

The fat from the roasted chicken had soaked through the paper, so she peeled it free and placed it on one of Granny's tin plates in the middle of the blanket. She laid out the scones. She filled one bowl with cherries and one with last fall's walnuts in the shell, and laughed when at once Taran cracked a nut with his boot heel. He cracked one for her, too, and fed it to her. The touch of his fingers on her lips gave her a thrill she didn't expect. There seemed something symbolic about the act. He acted as if he was doing more than simply feeding her, as if he had taken responsibility for her well-being, her hunger, her thirst, her body and her mind.

Did she want that?

Yes. Of course. As long as it was Taran.

But ... but she had fought all her life to be independent.

She tried to put her thoughts together.

Would Taran demand so much of her? Did he want to possess her completely?

More important, did she want to give herself completely?

Of course she did. She was Cate MacLean. For her, it was all or nothing.

His thumb sketched her lower lip.

And she forgot her qualms.

CHAPTER TWENTY-ONE

Instinct brought Cate's tongue curling out to brush the callused whorls of Taran's fingers.

He sucked in his breath. His gray eyes glowed almost blue, as if coals burned within. Hastily, he drew his hand back and stared at his fingers as if they were scorched, then looked at her, and she could have sworn they communicated without words. He would provide for her. He would feed her, clothe her, make her his mate.

Her chest rose and fell, and life pulsed through her veins.

They drew apart.

They looked down at the food.

And as if such transcendent moments were commonplace, they filled their plates and ate while chatting about their friends, the upcoming Johnsmas bonfire, and whether Lady Bess would ever wear clothing which didn't embarrass her daughter to death.

Taran said no.

Cate was inclined to agree. Cate was convinced her mother lived to embarrass her.

All the while she cast him tiny, amazed glances. All her dreams fulfilled.

The chicken was tough and juicy, and he finished it off, ate three scones, cleaned up the cherries and cracked more of the walnuts and put them on her plate. Then he actually did as he said he would. He cleaned up.

She helped him balance the plates on the way to the hut, and as he wrapped the food, she looked at the meager remnants of the feast. "What will we eat tomorrow?"

With gravelly finality, he said, "Darlin', we'll be lucky if we have a tomorrow."

"Yes, we will." She flung her arms around his waist. "We're young. We're married. We'll have a thousand tomorrows. A million!"

He stared down at her, his eyes in shadow. Finally he said, "Go on back out to the blanket. When I come out, we'll talk about tonight, instead."

She glanced at the bed with its wooden frame and its straw mattress. Tonight. He meant they would make love tonight.

She caught her breath on an unconscious sigh of relief.

Taking her hand, he kissed the back, and all the warmth of his mouth flooded her with happiness. That, and the fact he was putting the food away.

With a skip, she hurried back outside, shook the crumbs off the blanket, and spread it out once more. Seating herself in the middle, she wondered how best to entice Taran. She pinched her cheeks to make them pink. She unbuttoned the two top buttons on her bodice. No, she would unbutton three. She slipped off her boots and neatly placed them off the edge of the blanket, then pulled off her hose and stuffed them into the boots. In a rush of wickedness, she pulled the pins from her hair, let it drape over her shoulders, and tossed her locks until they looked artfully tousled.

At last she was ready, or as ready as she could be, so she looked around at the valley, slung like a hammock between mighty granite mountains. The wind sang softly through the narrow crevasses in the rocks, and over her head, the pines creaked. Flopping onto her back, she stared at the hypnotically swaying branches. The clear, blue sky was garnished with the occasional clouds floating past to build white pillow castles in the air. In the stillness, nature's splendor sang to her soul, and the peace — and the wine — tamed her restless spirit.

A prickle of warning ran up her spine. Turning her head, she caught Taran watching her. His dark eyes gazed on her as if she were the most glorious female on earth, and her instincts stirred as she stretched, spreading her hair across the blanket, giving him a sultry smile.

He didn't smile back. His head lowered, his nostrils flared. He looked furious, or ... not furious, but pained. As if it hurt him to look at her here.

"You don't even understand a smidgeon of the power you hold," he said, and his guttural voice puzzled her.

Her smile faltered. "What do you mean?"

He shook his head. "I shan't tell you. I have to save myself somehow."

She still didn't understand, but she so seldom understood men and their vague pronouncements.

Coming to her side, he dropped to his knees. He picked up one of the locks of her hair and rubbed it between his fingers. "You have the most beautiful hair I've ever seen. You must never cut it."

"Some people disdain red hair as immoral." She let her eyes twinkle up at him. "But I know my hair gets a man's attention."

"That it does. Too many men's attention."

"Better yet, all kinds of stories circulate about a woman with red hair — that she's tempestuous, spirited and given to wicked thoughts." Cate grinned at him "You lads can think what you wish, but I'm no more tempestuous than the next girl."

"And I think" — he leaned down and kissed her lightly — "that you don't know yourself at all."

She circled his neck with her arms.

Stretching out beside her, he gazed into her face. "You're a peculiar girl. You say whatever you think."

"Only to you! You understand me."

"No. I don't."

"What don't you understand?"

"You say you love me, but I don't know why."

"All the lasses love you. Don't they?" She felt her smile dip and quiver. "Kiernan says you've bedded half the maids."

"I pride myself I've given them the best thirty seconds of their lives."

She didn't really understand, but she laughed because she thought he wanted her to.

"But they don't love me," he said. "They say they like my accent. They say I'm big and strong and handsome."

She touched her fingertips to his lips. "You are."

He kissed them. "You always loved me, even when I was skinny and scared and mean. I don't understand why."

"Because you're like me. You want adventure. You want to be strong and brave." She plucked at the buttons on his shirt. She couldn't look at him. Not when every word she spoke was torn from that secret, earnest corner of her soul. "You're more than merely an orphan fostered by the MacLean clan. You can do great things, and you will. I know I can do great things, too, and I'll do them at your side." She peeked up at him.

He stared at her, his mouth slightly open. "By the saints, Caitlin MacLean, you're a marvel."

She could see maturity in the shading of his black beard on his chin, the bushy line of his eyebrows, and his shoulders, which were broad enough to block out the sky. Yet remnants of boyhood clung in the smooth, unmarked skin and in the way he stared at her, as if she were someone unique and wonderful.

Sliding his arm under her head, he kissed her. Not a kiss like the one in the orchard, but a real kiss this time like the ones the other girls — the ones who had lived in Edinburgh and thought themselves so chic — talked about. He opened her lips with his. He sought her tongue. It felt odd, this melding of their tastes, but after a moment of indecision she decided she liked it. Shutting her eyes, she let him feast on her. Dimly, she could still hear the wind in the branches and the singing of the lark. Her arms encircled his neck, his torso pressed against hers, and she liked that, too.

Lifting his head, he flicked his finger at her open buttons. "Did you think to seduce me?"

"Yes." She grinned saucily. "Is it working?"

"Everything you do is a seduction." He smiled. A slow stretch of the lips, all temptation and promise. "Do you remember on Midsummer's Eve when the clans went out to the hills to light the fires, and you fell asleep on that rock?"

"Yes." She had the feeling she wasn't going to like this.

"I found you. You were sleeping so hard you were drooling —"

"Taran!" Humiliated, she tried to shove him away.

He wouldn't let her. "Still I wanted you. I want you when you're yelling at Graeme for not letting you play cricket. I want you when you've been carrying wood for Cook and you have smudges all over your face and wood chips in your hair. I want you when you're returning from a crofter's cottage, alight with the miracle of helping deliver a wee babe. You're tall and you're beautiful and you're kind. I want to absorb you into my soul."

CHAPTER TWENTY-TWO

Taran's intensity frightened Cate. She tried to turn her head away, but he kissed her cheek and the corner of her mouth, and she found herself turning her face to his like a daisy toward the sun. This kiss was deeper, warmer than any other that had gone before, and she experienced the beginning of a sea change. Like the tide, she moved inevitably and intuitively, concentrating completely on the sensations that welled in her heart and in her body. Taran unbuttoned her bodice past her waist, and she didn't really even notice until he spread it and her chemise apart. Then she gasped, and looked at herself, at her pale breasts exposed to the sunshine.

She blushed again, such a foolish reaction, but the way he stared at her!

"Taran?" Her voice wobbled. "What are you ... what are you thinking?"

He didn't answer. He lightly touched the tips of her nipples with his fingertips. Color burned hot in his brown cheeks, and his chest rose and fell in hard jerks, as if the effort of breathing required attention, and he had no attention to give. All his concentration was on her.

A combination of embarrassment and agitation made her push his hands away.

Instead, he caught her and pressed her fingers to her breasts. "Show me what you like," he whispered. "At night, when you're alone in your bed and want pleasure, what do you do?"

She was afraid she would succumb under a fit of mortification. "Taran! I don't —"

He smiled at her. "Don't you?"

"I can't show you ..."

But he began to move her fingers for her. He pressed her breast, then lifted her fingers to circle her nipple. "Like that? Do you do that when you think of me?"

"Y...yes. And ... this." Closing her eyes, she wet one finger in her mouth and touched herself.

He caught his breath harshly, then his mouth closed on her other breast.

Her eyes sprang open. She was horrified and ... dear God, that felt like heaven. The suction, the dampness, the warmth ... he suckled ruthlessly, caressing every nerve. His tongue revolved around her nipple, and dimly she heard herself gasping. It wasn't horror anymore. No, it was sweetness and heat, deep inside. Her legs moved restlessly as between them, she grew moist.

Then she was horrified and embarrassed again, and she pressed her knees together to stop the flow. But as long as he kissed her there ... his hand plucked at her other nipple. That doubled the sensations flooding her. And when she pressed her knees together hard, she wanted ... her back arched, offering herself to him.

Above her, the branches waved, green needles and brown bark against a blue-and-white sky.

On the blanket, she writhed beneath his touch, and he ... he pressed himself against her, moving his hips strongly against her side. He groaned deeply. "Caitlin. I want to be ... I want to love you." He tugged at her skirt, lifting it.

Now? Did he mean ... now? With her skirt around her waist and his trousers around his knees?

Cool air washed across her bare legs.

Shoving him away, she sat up. "No!"

Shock blanked his face. He looked as if she had slapped him, but she didn't have time to kiss his brow and soothe his feelings. Instead, she tore at the petticoat ties at her waist. Kneeling, she pulled her arms out of her gown. Stumbling to her feet, she dropped the gown, the petticoats to the ground.

A different kind of shock held him now, and he watched her as he would a pagan fertility goddess.

Clad in only her pantalettes and her chemise, she spread her arms wide and stared upward, asking for a benediction. She found it in the sunshine on her skin, the breeze in the trees, the blue sky that stretched to infinity.

Then she shimmied out of her chemise, dropped her pantalettes, and stepped out of them.

She wore nothing. In this beautiful day, in the sunshine and the breeze, she was as God had made her.

She looked down at Taran, still a little fearful, but proud of her body and determined to fling herself into their joy.

"I've never seen anything as lovely in my life as you are

right now." He spaced each word as if he had to think before articulating the syllables. His hand slowly reached for her inner thigh. He laid his palm against the skin, then slid it in a spiral up to her hip and around her waist. He cupped her buttocks at the bottom where they met her legs, and he squeezed gently, rhythmically.

She felt it between her legs. The tugging of the skin, the wonder of his intimate touch ... she was aware of heaviness in her loins, and once again she was damp and aching.

His finger slipped between her legs.

She stiffened her knees, closed her eyes, and braced herself.

He barely touched her. Only the ends of her hair, little touches that transmuted themselves into great thrills of pleasure.

How could he do so little and she feel so much?

By the time his thumb glided along her folds and opened her to his touch, her knees were ready to collapse. But with his other hand he held her steady, and began a slow, soft exploration of such sensuality she found herself sliding her hands into her own hair and holding her head. For balance, perhaps. Or sanity.

He caressed all around the important parts — the nub she touched when she thought of him, and the entrance to her body. His fingers would get close, and she would tense with anticipation. Then they'd glide away, and she wanted to scream at him for being so ignorant. Didn't he know ...? Should she tell him ...?

But she couldn't. She couldn't tell him ...

She couldn't bear it any longer. "Please, Taran."

"What?" He kissed her hip. "Tell me what you want."

"Please.   Touch   me."

"I am." The hand on her hips, that one held her steady, rubbed her in a circle.

"Not there. Not there."

"Where?"

Exasperated and desperate, she pressed her hand over the top of his, over her clitoris. "There!"

"Ohh." His voice was deep and almost amused. "There."

He was teasing her. The bastard was teasing her. She would have aimed a roundhouse at the side of his head ... but suddenly, he got it right. He found her nub and stroked it.

She whimpered and tried to stifle it with her fist. Inside her, pressure grew for what reason she did not know. She only knew her hips rippled in some primitive dance that she somehow recognized.

Then he found her. The center of her. The dampness. The tightness. The almost-pain of desperate arousal.

He entered her with his finger. She didn't notice the intrusion, or the oddness of having an alien being — a man — touch her there. She only cared that he eased that ache that made her shiver in the bright sunshine. His finger went deep, then out, then deep.

Her knees gave out.

He caught her on the way down, stretched her out on the blanket. He tore at his clothes, but she no longer cared whether he took the time to undress. She wanted him now, there, between her legs.

She lifted one knee.

He paused in the act of pulling off his shirt. He stared, and cursed. The shirt went flying.

She rolled one hip off the ground, the movement like a voluptuous ocean swell along her body.

He dropped his trousers and underwear.

In the dappled sunlight, he was beautiful, an unknown landscape of relentless splendor. Muscles knotted his shoulders and changed into smooth cords along his arms and chest. Dark hair covered his brown skin, lightly along his powerful arms and legs, then gathering in the middle of his breastbone and growing in a column down to his groin. From that thatch of hair thrust his manhood, hooded, rosy at the top, blue-veined ... and large. Larger than she'd expected.

Too large?

But she had no time for second thoughts. He was there, his knees between hers. A weight on her body, warm and musky, a dangerous male atop her.

Scent. Strength. Passion. She was drowning in her senses. The rough blanket scratched her bare back. The crushed grass barely cushioned her.

He braced himself on one elbow. He fumbled below with the opposite hand, his knuckles brushing at her until she thought she would go mad.

She combed his hair with her fingers, leaned up and kissed his face, doing anything she could imagine to entice him.

He found her. She felt the pressure, the sense that the final assault had begun. Her eyes slid shut as she concentrated on controlling her intuitive withdrawal. She would not draw back now. Skimming her hands down his body, she grasped his hips and urged him steadily closer.

"Caitlin?" He tilted her chin up. "Look at me."

Reluctantly, she opened her eyes.

His silky hair hung around his face. His eyes smoldered, holding her with their ardor. She could see it. He wanted to hurry, like a bull in rut. Instead he whispered, "Watch me. Let me watch you."

He advanced inside her. Vaguely she was aware of burning, of pain, of the shattering of her maidenhead. But more than that, she acknowledged their joining. He laid claim to her body. She did the same with him. She shifted her hips, brought her legs up to hold him, saw the change in his features as he recognized her entreaty.

Take me. As I take you.

At last he was seated in her. She had accepted him, all of him.

His chest heaved as he watched her face, waiting for ... she didn't know what he was waiting for.

He smoothed the hair back from her forehead, kissed her brow, her cheeks, lingered on her lips. "Caitlin ..."

Only her name, but it was enough.

The movement started. Slowly at first, a slight withdrawal, then a firm forward pressure. That forward pressure ... at the return of satisfaction, her eyelids drooped again. "That feels ... good." Her voice was slurred, as if she'd been drinking strong spirits, and that startled her.

"How about this?" He pulled out farther, then came back in an even more leisurely manner, drawing out the anticipation until she panted from eagerness.

Then that pressure again. Her hips rose of their own volition, pushing against him, seeking gratification for the whole of her body. The hair on his chest rasped against her breasts. Heat from inside scorched her skin. She wanted ... she wanted.

He set a rhythm, deliberate and steady. She held his shoulders, traced the length of his spine. Her fingers skidded along on a fine sheen of perspiration, and he trembled with the difficulty of holding himself back. He wanted so much more, he wanted it quickly, and she loved him all the more for his care of her newly-created womanhood. She wished she could watch him, see his enjoyment, tell him how much this meant to her, but one by one, the needs of her body conquered her ability to speak, to see, even to move with volition.

It was the length of him inside her and the motion of his hips that commanded her. Her breath came in moans that gradually grew in volume and intensity. She clutched at his arms. She braced her feet on the ground. Deep within her, desire coiled and heated, generating more moisture, making her urge him on.

The pace increased in purposeful measures. He hunched over her, intent on her, only her. He drove forward, lingered for a moment deep within her, then drew out. In and out, over and over — and finally, finally lightning struck. She convulsed, helpless, insensate, desperate and pleasured. She clawed at his back, thrust herself upward, clutched him tightly between her thighs. The spasms swept her again and again. She quivered, suspended for one long moment in an agony of pleasure.

And he lost control at last. He plunged into her, lost to anything but his own satisfaction.

She allowed him gladly. She wrapped him in her embrace, reveled in the failure of his restraint. He gritted his teeth, the muscles in his neck strained, he groaned.

His enthusiasm took her to another climax, longer than the first one, more restrained, searing in its sweetness.

They finished together. Sank down onto the blanket. Clung together as their breaths slowed. Sank into sleep and woke to the onset of evening, a fire in the hut, and more love-making. More ...

CHAPTER TWENTY-THREE

In the wee hours of the morning, Taran put down his pen, rose from his desk and stretched, and groaned as every bruised and battered muscle in his body protested.

He was too old to fight like a maniac, with no thought of tomorrow or anything beyond the pleasure of letting loose that primitive fury which raged in his soul. The younger men were faster. They took the punches better.

He grinned.

But older warriors like Gerry Williams — and Taran — were well-versed in the tricks that had eventually given them the upper hand.

As Gerry, that whey-cocked old salt, had finally shouted, "Old age and treachery always wins out over youth and enthusiasm."

Of course, then Lilbit had hit Gerry and knocked him out, but the fight had been fun while it lasted.

Taran went to the window and looked out. Morning was two hours away, but no sign of the sun pierced Poole's stinking black fog, formed half of cloud and half of coal smoke. He hated this city; longed for the fresh air of Cenorina.

Tomorrow, after so many years, he would be there, standing on the shore, looking up at the mountains, smelling the freshness of home. He closed his eyes against the great wave of longing that struck him and tried to suck him under.

When he opened them, he gingerly touched his throbbing, swollen lip and the cut on his chin. He couldn't imagine what Cate would say when she saw him in the morning. Something scathing, he was sure.

Speaking of Cate … returning to his desk, he picked up the sheet of paper, pursued what he had written, and nodded. He folded it, set his seal on the seam, took it to his mother's bedchamber and slipped it under the door. In the missive, he confessed the truth about his marriage to Cate. He was very glad he would not be here when she received it.

Then he took to his bed for a few hours of much needed rest.

The sky was gray, winds puffed at the small ship's sails, and Cate clutched the rail and fidgeted as she watched two sailors stagger up the gangplank under the weight of her trunk. The trunk was the last of the freight; no other passengers traveled to Cenorina or on to the other ports of call. With any luck at all, Taran would miss this sailing and she would be free to go to Cenorina and do her job without interference. She didn't need him tagging along in some ridiculous costume. She didn't want him watching over her, threatening to seduce her with every touch, every glance of his dark gaze. She didn't deserve that kind of distraction when she was desperate to prove herself brave, strong and intelligent enough to warrant another assignment in the netherworld of spying.

She watched a poor, haggard blind man make his way along the dock. He had obviously once been tall, with broad shoulders and a handsome face. Now he wore a bandage over his eyes to protect them from the light, and his face was bruised and cut. He shuffled along, his left arm in a sling that covered him from fingertips to elbow, a cane hooked on his elbow, leaning heavily on the arm of his shorter companion. Both men wore clean clothing of middle class styling, and short, gentleman-like haircuts. The blind man wore brown wool trousers, a brown coat and had a knit shawl of brown and maroon stripes laid across his slumped shoulders. Still he shivered as if chilled by the fresh wind off the Atlantic.

Cate wrapped her own green wool greatcoat tighter about her. It wasn't stylish, but when a woman lived on the coast of Scotland, she sometimes had to eschew fashion for warmth. At least, Cate did. She expected the day's journey south on the open ocean to be chilly, and beneath the greatcoat she wore her black traveling gown, her corset, her warmest chemise, and underwear made of the warmest, thickest cotton. She nodded firmly. Let Taran try anything while she wore all that!

Below her, the blind man and his shorter companion were deep in conversation, the companion nodding in vigorous agreement.

Then he glanced up at the ship, and Cate gasped.

It was Blowfish. He touched the brim of his hat in greeting, then indicated she should come to the top of the gangplank.

Her gaze flew to his cohort. It couldn't be…

It was.

Taran. He'd cut his hair.

An inappropriate dismay filled her. He'd cut his beautiful hair, black and straight, shining like a beacon, beckoning her to touch. She should be glad he had cut it and removed temptation, but she wished she could run her fingers through the strands one more time for the pure tactile joy of it. Now it was gone, sacrificed for the mission, and she doubted he would ever grow it again. Shoulder-length hair was barbaric, the mark of a medieval warrior or a pirate captain, not of a civilized man.

Taran. Civilized. What a joke.

He'd dressed like a wounded soldier. He even carried a short sword in a leather scabbard hanging from his belt. So many men had gone to war. Many of them had been hurt, had scars, were blinded. In his costume, he wouldn't warrant a second glance. More than that, the indignity of his wounds made people reluctant to look closely at him.

He'd said he had a masquerade; she hadn't imagined it would be so effective that she wouldn't recognize him.

Without enthusiasm, she moved into place and watched as Blowfish led Taran toward her. Taran's blindfold covered his eyes completely. He couldn't see where he was going. At the top, Blowfish directed his feet, then placed Taran's hand on her arm. "There ye are, Madam, 'e's 'ere safe and sound and ready to sail."

"Oh." Cate's voice dripped sarcasm. "Thank you."

"Darlin', I'm ready to go anywhere you take me." Taran ran his hand up her arm.

She swatted him away, then glanced up to see one of the ship's sailors glare at her, scandalized. "This will never do," she said.

"It will do very well." Taran took her arm again.

She asked, "Don't you think it's dangerous having Blowfish bring you down here? Doesn't everyone know him?"

Taran laughed. "Contrary to what you might believe, my love, pirates and sailors mix as little as possible. The pirates are afraid of being recognized. The sailors don't want to be conscripted – or tempted by sin."

Because no one she knew was as tempting as Taran Tamson.

In a lower tone, he said, "Blowfish, you've got your

instructions."

Blowfish recited, "Sail in a week. Wait offshore fer the beacon. If in four weeks no beacon is lit, well then, you're taking the long dirt nap —"

The long dirt nap? What did Blowfish mean?

"— and we are to come in and rescue the Caitlin and take out Sir Wicked Britches." Blowfish nodded in satisfaction.

The two men were discussing Taran's death. "No one is going to die," she pronounced.

"Dying's never *in* the plan, young mistress. At least, not for us." Blowfish seemed unduly cheerful. "But it's a hazard of the job, ye know, and we plan fer all eventualities."

"Death is unacceptable," she told them.

"Ye just remember all them fightin' skills I taught ye, and ye'll do fine," Blowfish said.

He was trying to comfort her, as if she faced death, too. She was merely the thief. Taran was her escort. "Neither one of us is going to die. Of that I am determined."

"Aye, ye're a grand woman," Blowfish said to her. To Taran, he said, "I do now understand yer nine-year Cately obsession, Cap'n."

Taran wore a ghost of a smile. "Blowfish, I always knew you to be a man of intelligence." He sobered. "Now — you know what to do if, while I'm gone, trouble starts?"

"That I do, sir." Blowfish's sharp eyes got sharper and bluer. "But I hope ye're wrong, sir."

"As do I."

Blowfish tipped his hat. "Farewell, Madam. *Bon voyage.* Best of luck."

She watched him make his way down the gangplank. "What was that all about?"

"Instructions."

"What trouble are you expecting?"

"Have you heard the expression, *When the cat's away, the mouse will play?* I'm the cat." He certainly smiled with a cat's complacency. "Blowfish is my first mate. He is a good sailor, an excellent pirate, but he's past his prime and some might think to take advantage of that, and of my absence."

She thought of his crew, of the men she had met, and how

much she liked them all. "You suspect someone of mutiny."

"Aye."

"Who would do such a thing?"

Taran shrugged. "No point in speaking evil of a man based on a mere suspicion."

"'Scuse me, Madam." Two of the sailors waited to carry another trunk onto the ship.

She turned away, dragging Taran after her.

At once, he tripped on a coil of rope.

Appalled, one of the sailors gasped and frowned mightily.

"For heaven's sake!" As she helped Taran recover, she tried to look suitably contrite. In an undertone, she asked, "How much can you see out of that thing?"

"Nothing at all." He adjusted the kerchief over his eyes.

"If you could, you wouldn't tell me. You're enjoying this far too much."

"What man wouldn't?" He pecked at her in the general direction of her forehead.

She wanted to slap him down, but a quick look around proved that the sailors watched them and whispered, and from their glares she could imagine very well what they whispered about.

This isn't how she'd planned it. If she did have to sail with Taran, she had intended to keep a good distance from him at all times. She wouldn't touch him. She would speak to him no more than necessary to ensure the success of their mission.

But the swine had thwarted her. With this disguise, he would always be close to her, holding her arm, pretending affection, filling her nostrils with the scent of clean male and passionate memories.

Too many memories, too recently evoked. Recalling that brief time of their loving had been a mistake. She should have left those memories sealed in her brain forever. She *would* forget … if she could…

"Weigh anchor!" the captain called.

The sailors pulled the gangplank back. The anchor chain rattled.

Taran pressed himself against her side, leaned down as if kissing her cheek. He bumped into her bonnet.

Triumphantly, she adjusted it. "It appears you'll have to behave yourself."

"I wouldn't know how." His heat warmed her unwilling body as he drew close again, this time with more care, and murmured in her ear, "Didn't Blowfish tell you? I'm good with disguises. It's one of my many … talents."

Something about the way Taran spoke made her draw back suspiciously. "Do you disguise yourself frequently?"

He followed her movement, but slowly, clumsily. "It's easy to discover a ship's cargo if I don't ask as the Cap'n — most sailors are reluctant to disclose information, especially to a pirate."

"I can understand that." She walked toward the forward railing, the deck swaying beneath her feet.

Taran trailed behind her, hanging on her arm, his cane bumping on his shin, his sword's scabbard striking his thigh.

She thought he appeared to be a one-man percussion band, with too many instruments and not enough talent. Without a doubt, that was the real disguise, for she knew if needed he could use both the sword and the cane as weapons.

He said, "When I'm in camouflage, I discover gossip about who ships out with who, where the ships are bound, whether they contain any secret treasures or extra passengers. Useful in this business of spying."

"You find out whose ship you want to attack?"

"Exactly. Most of all, I've found disguise a useful tool to discover whether my crew will be able to perform their duties as I require."

Memories of the past few days paraded across her mind. A tall, dark man on a Poole street corner. A staggering, drunken sailor at a pub. A withered old man eating soup at an outdoor table. All of them with beards. Black beards, gray beards … "You've been watching me!"

"My love, keep your voice down. The sailors will hear." Amusement vibrated in his voice.

She grasped the railing hard and in a furious whisper, she said, "As Blowfish dragged me through the streets, I kept thinking I saw you, then thinking I made a mistake, but I didn't, did I? You *were* watching me."

"I wanted to find out how your lessons were progressing. I couldn't ask Blowfish; he likes you. I knew he would cover for you if your performance was abysmal. So I tagged along a few times."

He frowned. "Although I'm disappointed that you identified me. What was it? My walk? My height?"

"Your *stench*." Folding her arms over her chest, she tried to catch a calm breath. If she didn't, she would box Taran's ears, and she could only imagine how that would scandalize the sailors who worked aloft.

Waves slapped at the ship as it rose and fell with the freedom from its anchor. The breeze picked up as they nosed their way through the harbor toward its mouth.

At the inn, Queen Sibeol finished dressing and prepared to go out and bid her son farewell and Godspeed, to gaze on him and know... know it might be the last time she saw him alive...

She wiped the blur of tears from her eyes. She was the queen. She would not cry. Not now. Not when at last her son had returned, determined to win at all costs.

As the queen, she approved. As his mother ... she feared, and prayed, and —

What was that by the door?

A paper, folded carefully, sealed in red wax, and had been slipped into her room while she slept.

Foreboding embraced her as she walked across the floor and picked up the letter. She broke the seal and read the lines:

Dear Mother and Majestic Queen Sibeol of Cenorina, Before I sail, knowing the peril I face, I must tell you a secret of most importance and request your understanding, your Christian kindness and royal forbearance for both me and Cate, my bride of nine years...

The paper fluttered from Sibeol's nerveless fingers. She stood immobile, shocked to her core. Snatching up her shawl, she opened the door, ran into the corridor and down the stairs.

As a man, Taran's pirates looked up, and stood up.

"Is he gone?" she asked. "Are they gone?"

The somber-faced one, the one they called Dead Bob, said, "Yes, ma'am. Gone this hour."

"Will the ship have sailed?" she demanded.

With the unerring instincts for the tides that all good sailors possessed, he said, "Another few minutes."

"Take me to the docks. I must ... I must tell him..." What

could she tell him? The damage was done, the marriage performed and consummated years ago. What could she do? Nothing. So before the young couple sailed into danger, she needed to offer reconciliation and her blessing. "Take me to the ship!"

"As you wish, ma'am." Dead Bob offered his arm.

Maccus called a cab.

The pirates went out on the street to block Sibeol from the common run of rough, rude pedestrians.

Mr. Cleary stood behind the bar, wiping the scarred wood, and when he believed he was alone in the taproom, he put down his rag. He moved quietly for a big man, up the stairs and to the threshold of Taran's door. He tried the handle, and when he couldn't open it, he pulled out his keys and fitted one into the lock. An ugly expression crossed his face when he realized Taran had thwarted him; the lock had been changed.

But in the open door of Sibeol's room, opportunity beckoned. He walked in and stepped on the discarded letter. The crinkle of paper made him look down. Leaning down, he examined the seal and the handwriting, then as he read, he frowned and moved his lips. As the information percolated through to his brain, a smile blossomed and grew — until a cudgel smacked the back of his skull and sent him sprawling to the floor, unconscious.

The lone pirate leaned over and plucked the paper from Mr. Cleary's lax fingers. He read the letter. Read it again. Laughed softly, let the letter drift to the floor once more, and nudged Mr. Cleary with his toe. "Sorry, old man, but *I'm* going to use this, not you." Going to the window, he opened it. Grabbing Mr. Cleary under the armpits, he dragged the unconscious man over and with a grunt, hefted him up onto the sill. While Mr. Cleary hung there by his belly, arms dangling outside, legs dragging the floor inside, the pirated pulled his dagger from his belt, leaned out, and cut Mr. Cleary's throat. He cleaned his blade on Mr. Cleary's shirt, then shoved him out face-first into the deserted alley.

Still smiling, the pirate left Sibeol's bedroom.

CHAPTER TWENTY-FOUR

When Cate once more had her temper under control, she looked at Taran, the low, conniving dungworm who played the part of her long-suffering husband so well. "How dare you spy on me?"

He shed amusement as he would a cloak, and she caught a glimpse of the duty-driven Cap'n. "Make no mistake," he said. "This is my operation, and if you had proved unable to learn what Blowfish had to teach you, I would have found *someone* to replace you. Too much is at stake. We will not fail."

His low-voiced intensity silenced her complaints. She had family honor and a desperate need for retaliation against her brother's killers. Taran had ... "What is it to you besides a pardon from the British government? What *do* you have at stake?"

"Cenorina is my home. I left when I was fourteen years old, and I've missed it — its mountains, its forests, its stubborn, stiff-necked, proud people — every day since I've been gone. I want to go home, and when I vanquish Sir Maddox Davies" — the name was a sneer on Taran's lips — "I will go home. I'll live there for the rest of my days and I'll never again take for granted my freedoms or my duties."

As they cleared the harbor, the sails unfurled with a crack as loud as a gunshot. The wind, laden with the tang of salt and sea, filled them, and the ship lifted like a bird about to fly. Taran groped for the railing, found it, and turned his face into the wind as if trying to catch the scent of Cenorina.

Home. He wanted to go home.

While she ... she never wanted to go home.

Oh, she was homesick for her mother, a forthright woman of uncommon good sense, and she was still welcome at her family home on Mull. But when she visited neighbors or went to a party, she could be sure the whispers would start. Some intoxicated jackass would call her a whore, and someone in the Clan MacLean would be forced to jump to her defense — and none believed she deserved such a defense. Except for Kiernan, of course. He had forgiven and forgotten her trespasses.

She sighed.

How she missed him.

How she mourned him.

"Are there seats?" Taran asked.

She glanced about. Here and there, a plain wooden pew was screwed to the deck facing outward. "A few."

He gestured in toward the center of the ship. "Shall we sit?"

She wished she could tell him to go away, but he had outflanked her so magnificently with his helpless disguise, she almost wanted to laugh. She *would* have laughed, except she seemed to have lost her sense of humor — and like everything else, that was his fault. She led him to the forward bench, the one protected from the worst of the chill wind. He fumbled for the back of the pew, and with a hiss of disgust she helped him lower himself onto the seat.

He caught her hand before she could move away. "Sit with me."

"I don't want to."

Like a supplicant, he kissed the back of her fingers, looked up with apparent wistfulness in the direction of her face, and in a tone of quiet command, said, "Sit down or I'll make you sit down."

She knew how it looked to the sailors — the callous wife disdaining her blind and crippled husband. She knew, too, that for all Taran's placid tone, he meant what he said. To lose a wrestling match with a blind man who had his arm in a sling would be humiliating and demeaning. Taking a frustrated breath, she demanded, "Why do you insist when I so blatantly don't want to be with you?"

"You haven't told me what happened to Kiernan." He sounded implacable.

Her knees weakened, and she sank down beside Taran. "No. I don't like to talk about it."

"Because you don't want me to see you cry, I ken."

If he only knew!

"But I can't see you, so tell me."

Sorrow gathered thick in her chest. "Why should you care?"

"He was my friend."

She snorted. "Some friend you were."

Taran wrapped his arm around her stiff shoulders. "Tell me."

She shrugged, trying to dislodge him.

He slid closer and held her tighter.

He had isolated her on a ship with no one around them except for sailors. She had nowhere to go even if she managed to get away from him.

After all, what difference did it make? Kiernan was well and truly dead, and it wasn't as if she would break down in front of Taran. She hadn't cried for her loss even yet. The Clan MacLean had held a memorial service, and while all about her women had sobbed, Cate had stood dry eyed, staring at the flowers that surrounded her brother's portrait, and wanted nothing so much as revenge. The women had whispered that she was unnatural, and maybe she was. She only knew hatred burned in her, and the tears would not come.

So she yielded, and told Taran, "Our cousin Stephen managed to disappear at last."

Taran knew Stephen, knew well that her cousin was a wastrel and a coward. "Stephen's gone? That's no surprise. Unless he had changed, he was always off on some exploit or another."

"This time he sent no word, not even to beg his mother for money."

"A bad sign." Taran's hand moved up and down her arm, rubbing warmth into her flesh.

She ignored his unwelcome comfort. "Indeed. At last Aunt Catriona begged Kiernan to go and seek her worthless son. Kiernan agreed, and went off to England. We got a letter from Kiernan in Suffolk, telling us Stephen had gone abroad and Kiernan was going after him. Then — nothing." Cate could scarcely breath at the memory. Kiernan had been so alive, so vital, the man against whom she measured all other men. "Nothing for months. At first we thought ... *he's abroad, he's busy.* Next we said — *perhaps there's been a storm, some interference with the post. It happens.*"

"Frequently," Taran assured her.

"We worried, Mama and I. We worried and worried ... then we got word from a Mr. Throckmorton. Kiernan had traced Stephen to the Crimea, a bit of a strip of land in the Black Sea. He'd gone after him. There was an explosion. A bomb. Set by the wretched Russians to kill the spy who lied to them and lied to us. To kill Stephen. But Stephen survived." Her voice grew thick with rage. "Stephen, as useless a bit of flesh as ever walked this earth, is alive and at this moment is being nursed to health in Suffolk, while my brother rots in a grave far away from the land he loved so much... We didn't even get his body to bury." She shook with rancor.

With a soft murmur, Taran slid his arm out of the sling and gathered her close. "Poor lass." He rubbed his hands over her back. "My poor, poor lass."

"So now you know the tale." Taut and unbending, she sat there, waiting for him to release her so she could leap up and stride away. If she could do something — move, walk, work, anything — the hurt would lessen and she would be relieved.

Or so she always thought. Always, she was disappointed. Running away didn't help with this. Nothing seemed to help, but she always had to try.

Taran didn't understand. He held her as if waiting for her to melt into a sobbing puddle. He untied her bonnet and dropped it on the deck. He pulled her into the heat of his body, rubbed his cheek against her head, and in a gruff voice, murmured, "I can scarcely believe it. Kiernan. I looked up to him. I wanted to be him. He was strong and true, a master of his fate, yet he understood kindness."

"It was his kindness that killed him."

He shook her gently. "Never believe that. It was the bomb that killed him. He once told me that kindness was the requirement of every man for his fellows, especially for those who were smaller and weaker."

Kiernan had told her that, too. He had taken his duties as older brother seriously. After Taran left, after her reputation was in tatters and she'd fought her way through rebellion and into depression, he'd come to her and told her the only way to be happy was to make someone else happy.

These last few years, she'd tried. She'd succeeded, too, with her family, with the crofters, with the servants. She'd resigned herself to a small life lived in a small way.

She didn't know how to do that anymore. She only knew how to hate. She couldn't even grieve, but being in Taran's embrace brought up emotions she hadn't experienced in ... well ... years.

The first night in Poole Taran had swept her into his arms and seared her with the fires of passion, and reluctantly, so reluctantly, she had burned with him. Last night he'd held her, danced with her, and for the first time since Kiernan's death, she had laughed, freely and without guilt.

Now, today … well, today was different. Today she felt … she moved restively within his grasp, wanting to escape.

Taran wrapped her closer. "Recounting the tale of his life will make his spirit live."

She didn't want to struggle. Didn't want to make more of this emotion than it was worth. But she knew now she had been stupid. Last night, she had deliberately recalled their past; that day and night at Granny Aileen's hut when Taran's every touch had brought her ecstasy.

Oh, yes, that had definitely been a mistake, because now it felt right to have him console her. The young fool she had been believed she could bind him with her body and keep him by her side for all their lives, and right now that body which she believed she had schooled to stern chastity … her own body seemed convinced she'd succeeded. As she listened to his voice, smelled his scent, gathered his warmth, her body softened. Her head drooped onto his shoulder. Tears burned her eyes.

"No." Before, she would have given anything for the solace of tears. But she didn't want to cry now. Not here, in Taran's embrace.

More important, she didn't want to feel anything in his arms. It wasn't so much she didn't want him to see her weakness. She didn't want to have weakness. Not when weakness meant she had responded to *him*.

He rocked her back and forth, murmuring soft, indistinct words of reassurance. "When I was living with you, I used to think Kiernan was stiff-necked and far too honorable, but after I left Mull, whenever I didn't know what to do, I would ask myself what Kiernan would do."

"Become a pirate?" she mocked, but the pressure of tears behind her eyes grew. Her heart beat heavily in her chest, and she tried to breathe evenly, sucking salty air into her laboring lungs.

"Aye. When I took over the pirate ship, I was doing as Kiernan advised. Survive, he said. Survive at all costs." Taran's fingers stroked the side of her face. "Then do what is right. What we're doing today is a tribute to Kiernan."

Her breath scalded her lungs. She didn't want this.

"He wasn't that much older than I am, only six years, but he was years ahead of me in wisdom. Do you remember what he said to us when first we met? That we should be as brother and sister?" Taran laughed softly. "If he had only known, he would have struck me down at that moment."

The tears branded her skin. She pressed her cheeks against Taran's shawl, trying to blot her face before he realized how she had crumpled in the onslaught of grief.

He knew. Of course, he knew. He pressed a handkerchief into her fingers. "One of my greatest regrets was losing Kiernan's friendship, but I never could regret the pleasure I found in your arms."

My God. Her brother was dead, and the only person who understood her grief was her most dire enemy. Cate wept into the handkerchief, each tear an agony that offered no relief. No matter how much she cried, Kiernan was still dead, his life wasted in the service of his family. The anguish grew so strong, she coughed and wretched, and the only thing that kept her from collapse was Taran's strong arms swaddling her in the only comfort to be had on this earth.

He didn't try to stop her crying, but gradually she ceased. Her eyes drooped. And right before she dropped off to sleep, she told him, "Kiernan forgave you. He even missed you." On a sigh, she added, "But I never did."

CHAPTER TWENTY-FIVE

For nine years, Taran had been consumed by one goal. Going home.

Now he *was* going home. Home to deceit, war and possible death. He'd taken all that into account. He'd been willing to fight, to die, even to sell his soul and lose whatever lousy crumb of honor he had left. Anything to return the Kane family to the throne. And it wouldn't be so difficult, really. The years he had spent at sea had gradually stripped him of all … oh, what had he heard his mother say? That he'd been stripped of his humanity.

She might be right, for even her condemnation had failed to move him to anger or to tears.

What was wrong with that, really? To suffer no fear, to be immune to affection, to make logical decisions unmarred by messy emotions. He'd lived with the highs and lows of love and terror, and he remembered well the absurdity of his decisions, the mistakes he'd made.

During his first weeks with the pirates, he had been wretched with homesickness. Consumed with fear. Constantly on guard. He'd been desperate with hunger and damp all the time. His face sunburned so badly his skin peeled off, then peeled off again. His fingers blistered from working with the ropes. He tasted brine every time he opened his mouth. When the sun rose in the morning, he wanted nothing so much as to still be alive when it set.

After four years, he'd woke up one morning from a doze high in the rigging and realized — he didn't feel anything anymore. His body had adjusted to hardship. He didn't miss his family. He didn't care if he lived or died. The heights of emotion were freezing cold and lonely, and while up there he lost his youth. He lost his ideals. He knew one thing and one thing only — he was the crown prince of Cenorina, and to right the great wrong he had done, he would sacrifice himself for his people.

Emotions. Years ago, that great emotion, lust, had led him to take advantage of Cate when he knew he would not stay. Then another emotion, pride, had sent him back to Cenorina to save his country from tyranny. Instead, Maddox Davies had showed him what an arrogant young fool he was, and sent him off on a voyage to hard-won maturity.

Now, many years had gone by and Cenorina had been gutted and left bleeding.

Today, the ship sped through the waves, a voyage that would take no more than a day and yet would transport them into a different place, a different world. Taran cradled the sleeping Cate, protecting her against the wind and the sea spray, and wondered savagely how one little woman could destroy so many plans. He had fancied himself protected against emotions by a sheath of steel indifference. Now he saw that sheath was no more than a knitted blanket, unraveling in uneven holes and leaving him open to the cold.

Why? What was it about this woman that clung to his mind through fire and water, days and years?

The kerchief completely covered his eyes. He couldn't see her, and he had to trust in her guidance.

But he could rest his cheek on the top of her head, and inhale the scent of her hair. She smelled of orange and sandalwood, and mixed with the perfume was the faint, elusive odor of Cate.

She burrowed deeper into his chest; thumped her cheek against his muscles as if trying to soften her pillow.

He wanted to laugh, and that was curious, too. For the second time in two days, to laugh out loud in pure amusement — it had been years!

Before Cate arrived, he had given himself no better than a fifty percent chance of surviving the takeover of Cenorina. He planned to be on the front lines, rallying his people to the cause of freedom. Now he had his duty to his people, *and* his duty to Kiernan, and that duty was to keep Cate safe. She would not die in Taran's fight.

He ran his hand down her spine and cupped her buttocks. Beneath the coat, the gown, the corset and the corset cover and the chemise and all those other preposterous items of clothing women used to disguise their flesh — was Cate. Her long, strong limbs, her breasts, the nipples tinged a dusky rose, her narrow waist and that grand flare of her hips. It was all there, he knew it, and he wanted to remove her garments, lie down with her, taste every bit of her silken skin, caress every inch of her glorious limbs, wrap himself in the warmth of her body and let the world fall away. Left alone with her, he would win her back. It would be a battle. It would take time. But before it was over, he would once again find pleasure with her such as the world had never known.

Of course, he would give pleasure with the same munificence.

He wondered if she realized how thoroughly she'd betrayed herself. She had informed him, and shown him, too, that she had grown to be a woman of sense, not given to flights of great emotion. Yet every time he'd taken her in his arms, she had demonstrated to him the passion and the fire of the younger Cate. Yes, she might wish to be the prosaic female who had learned her lesson in a hard school, but when he scratched the surface, he found the same girl he'd fallen in love with all those years ago.

He unbuttoned the middle buttons of her coat and slipped his hand inside. She was warm. So warm. He pressed his fingers up her ribcage and that damnable restraining corset to her breast. She filled his hand to overflowing, a flawless size and shape, and when he slid his thumb over her nipple, it tightened to a bead that would fit perfectly into his mouth. She moaned, a sweet, half-sigh of a moan, and she rolled her cheek on his shoulder.

He let his head fall back on the bench. He was so hard he could stand on a board, tie a sail to his mast, and cruise to Cenorina by himself.

He shouldn't renew their liaison. Yes, they were married, but no honorable man would act in such a disgraceful manner. But he'd lost his honor the first time he'd taken her to bed. Now, he had her in his arms again and, because of her, the flame of his desire to live flared high. He wanted to explore these emotions, to feel the pain, the joy, the pleasure — one last time.

He'd made his vows. He had reparations to make. Probably he would die. But by God he would taste life first, and he would take the memory of Cate with him.

With difficulty, he withdrew his hand from her coat and slid it up to her neck. There he stroked the soft skin at her nape, and tilted her chin up. She frowned and wrinkled her nose in her sleep, and he brushed her mouth with his. Her frown smoothed; she took a long, deep breath. He ran his tongue along the seam of her lips, and when she parted them, he kissed her as he had wanted to. He went deep, tasting her, loving her with his tongue, giving himself over to the complete enjoyment of this preliminary claiming.

For many years, sex had been an agreeable exercise, a slow, gratifying thrill, a piece of action greatly enjoyed and quickly forgotten.

Kissing Cate was a courtship, a reacquaintance with passion, love-making in its purest form. The sweet liquid of her mouth joined with his to form a promise, jointly given. Her tongue rose to meet his; he touched it, caressed it with his own.

She shivered.

He felt her breath catch as she came awake, felt the jolt that struck her body as she realized that he held her in his embrace. She tried to pull away; he kept his hand on her neck and shushed her, his lips still against her lips. "It's just a kiss. We're married." He might have got away with that assurance if he had left it at that, but he had to add, "You liked it."

Her fist came up and struck him on his gunshot shoulder.

"Blast it!" He let her go and grabbed his wound, doubled over with pain. "Why did you do that?"

She launched herself to her feet. "Why did *you* kiss *me?* You took advantage of me. Took *advantage* of me."

She hadn't done permanent damage to his arm. "I'm probably going to bleed to death on this ship before we dock."

"You're a lecherous, two-timing louse!" Either she didn't believe him — smart girl — or she didn't care if he bled to death.

"You're cold-hearted," he observed. Crossing his legs, he leaned back against the seat in a commendable imitation of relaxation. "I can't take advantage of you while you're awake. You won't let me." Obviously, his admirable logic meant nothing to her, for she sputtered like a tea kettle coming to full boil. He only wished he could see her — to fend off further blows, of course.

"You, sir, are a despicable cad with no morals or manners!"

"You were better with an insult when you were sixteen, my Cate."

Dropping into the accent of the Edinburgh tenements, she said, "Black-'earted bastard wi' a dung worm where yer John Willie should be." Whirling away, she stomped off leaving Taran sitting with his mouth hanging open.

Obviously, just because the lass didn't commonly use

vulgarity didn't mean she didn't know it.

With so little time left, he was a fool to so anger his wife. Taran laughed at himself. Before it was over, he would anger her even more. And pleasure her, and teach her, and learn from her.

Taran heard the squeak of boards as someone — someone big, with a limp — approached. He tensed. Without his vision, he was impaired, and some sailors, even on the most honest of ferries, could be dangerous.

CHAPTER TWENTY-SIX

"Bit of a handful, is your wife." The voice was deep, resonant, with the slightest inflection.

Like his, Taran realized. This man came from Cenorina.

"That she is. She'll settle soon enough." He extended his hand. "I'm Taran Tamson."

It was taken in a firm grasp and shaken. "Captain John Dunbar, formerly of the Royal Navy."

Taran rose to his feet. "You retired to command this vessel?"

"Retire?" Captain Dunbar snorted. "I guess you can say I retired. You can't see, but I suffered a skirmish off of Morocco. Didn't amount to anything, but I got lead in my leg and there's no way to remove it, so I was mustered out. Fifteen years ago, that was."

Shocked, Taran realized he knew this man. He hadn't known his name; the conceited, egotistical youth he had been didn't care about a mere captain. But fifteen years ago, Captain Dunbar had had brown, straight hair, firm blue eyes and the tanned skin of a career sailor. And a limp.

"Damn pirates," the captain said.

The captain didn't seem to know Taran. Of course, Taran had been seventeen when he made the crossing to Cenorina that last time, but what a test for his disguise!

"I'd kill every one of them pirates with my bare hands if I could. Sent me from a great ship to this little dingy with a single shot."

Taran nodded with appropriate empathy.

The captain took Taran's hand, placed it on his arm, and led him toward the port side of the ship. "Was it pirates who caused your problems?"

The wind blew at Taran's back. His hair, suddenly so short, whipped at the edges of his face. "Never grappled with the lowly scum, myself. I got sent home from India blind and enfeebled because some rajah got it into his head he could defeat the whole British army."

"Idiot."

Cautiously, Taran placed the blame, hoping for information without betraying himself. "'Twas the Russians' fault." They reached the railing. Taran grasped it and used it for balance. "They told him we were weak, gave him ammunition, and then left him to it."

"Russians." Captain Dunbar spit without deep and throaty vigor. "Bastards have spoiled this route with their comings and their goings. Them, and the Spanish, the French, the Portuguese. Every week, I used to ferry wealthy Cenorinians to Ireland or England or anywhere else I put in. They went to visit relatives, or shop, or whatever rich people do to entertain themselves. Now not a one of them has a ha'pence to rub together — but Sir Maddox Davies still goes to England. He still visits."

"What's that got to do with the Russians, the Spanish, the French and the Portuguese?" Taran asked.

He heard the hiss of a match and caught a whiff of pipe tobacco. "I shouldn't say anything. It's my job if I do."

"I'm going there to live, man. I'm blind already, dependent on that lass for my sight and my living. You can't send me in not knowing what the damned foreigners have to do with Cenorina." When Captain Dunbar still hesitated, Taran added the clincher. "Not if there's danger. I've got to care for the wife."

"Ach. Very well, then, but you didn't hear it from me, and I don't know a half of it, I'm sure. Foreigners come in to the harbor in their own ships, little, swift sloops that whip in for a few hours. When they're there, I have to hold out on the ocean. I'm not allowed into harbor. Those foreigners come after Davies visits England, and I suspect he goes over and spies a bit, then comes back and sells the secrets. Why else would they bother to come and go so quick?"

Taran couldn't believe it. The best men of Throckmorton's English spies had not been able to grasp the idea of such a bold plan, and this backwater captain had watched and learned. "Have you told the authorities?" Taran asked.

"What authorities? The idiots in Poole? I'm nothing but an old sailor in charge of ferrying goods back and forth until my eyes roll back in my head from the boredom." Captain Dunbar's scorn oozed from his tone. "What do I know?"

Taran was taut with tension. "Are you saying you told people in England, and they didn't listen?"

"Told the head of the harbor and the captain of the local militia. Laughed in my face, they did." Captain Dunbar spat loudly.

When Taran told Throckmorton about this miscarriage of justice, Throckmorton's wrath would be strong and terrible. "You should have insisted on talking to their superiors."

"I'm married. I've got three daughters yet unwed and a son to put through school. I can't risk this job for a hunch."

"Nay, I can see that." Unfortunately Taran could. The man was caught between drowning and the sharks. "You really think Davies is selling English military secrets?"

"I don't know. I only know Cenorina is changed. No one goes in and out without permission, and I'm not allowed to set foot outside of the harbor area. Sir Davies seems like a gentleman of sorts, but there's something havey-cavey about him, make no mistake about that."

"Thank you for warning me."

Captain Dunbar's voice turned away from Taran. "Your missus is coming around the stern. Are you newlyweds, then?"

"No, but we weren't married long when I shipped out, and I think she had greater hopes than to be married to a blind, half-crippled man."

"Will you take some advice from an old salt?" Taran smelled strong puffs of smoke. "Take your belt to her now. She'll shape up, and you'll both be better for it later."

"I just got back from India. Tonight'll be our first night alone together. She'll be fine in the morning."

"Ah. Aye. A woman alone in bed is prey to all kinds of foolish fancies. She needs a man to keep her occupied." Captain Dunbar nudged Taran. "You look like the type to keep her busy half the night." He cackled.

Taran grinned modestly.

Captain Dunbar raised his voice. "Here's your missus, back from her refreshing stroll."

Cate came to Taran's side and placed her hand on his arm. "Thank you, Captain, for entertaining Taran while I walked off my sickness."

"A bit of the *mal de mer*, was it? I'm glad you're better now." Captain Dunbar nudged Taran again. "In an hour, we'll be docking in Cenorina. Must go take care of duty. Happy hunting, Mr.

MacLean."

The captain's limping shuffle had not yet died away before Cate demanded, "What were you two smirking about?"

"He was giving me marital advice."

"Is there any man in the world who isn't a fool?"

Taran decided to treat that as a rhetorical question. "He suggested beating you."

"That would not be a good idea."

"No." He clasped his hands and leaned on the rail. To his surprise, he found he was enjoying himself. "I know more enjoyable ways of subduing you."

"If you don't stop making such intimations, I'll become discomfited and unable to complete my mission."

"You mean you wouldn't be able to pick a lock?"

"Exactly."

"My dear, I saw you work, remember? You were unshakable, and you proved without a doubt you could open any lock in the dark, in a storm, during a ball, on your head, even if we were … well, no, not then, but at any other time."

He heard her take a long, exasperated breath. "I'm going for another walk."

He caught her by the arm. "You heard the captain. Stay. I haven't seen my home in nine years, and I'm blindfolded. I want you to be my eyes."

She didn't refuse.

He had known she wouldn't refuse him. She might think she hated him, but she wanted him, too. He could almost feel the tug of the chain that bound them as she pulled back from her own desires.

"What am I looking for?"

"Islands. First they'll look like a drop of green mist on the edge of the world. As we approach, they'll take shape, growing tall into the air, and the green will separate into trees and you'll see the white spray of the waves on mossy rocks …" He was either a fool or a poet, and he no longer knew the difference. He only knew he so desperately wanted to see his home he made music with his words, and opened himself up to her laughter.

But she didn't laugh. She said only, "I can see three islands."

He grasped the rail tightly. "There are four. The other, Luxúria, is over the horizon, small, warm, rugged, beautiful. Like all my islands."

"The ship is flying across the water, but I still can't see it. The others are coming closer, getting larger."

"Rugosa Antigua is the farthest, not large, and the holiest spot on Cenorina, with a monastery that's falling down and a few monks still living there, scraping out a living. The royal family is buried on the island, and you can almost smell the sanctity there among the ruins." When, with God's help, he'd won back the kingdom, he would make a pilgrimage and say his thanks. Or, if he didn't live, he would be buried beside his ancestors.

"It sounds … beautiful."

"It's lonely." He'd grown used to loneliness, even in a crowd, and for years the idea of Rugosa Antigua had tempted him with its isolation.

Now Cate stood beside him, dragging him back to life.

"The island to the left is small and far off, a sandy brown at the waterline with patches of green as the island climbs."

A picture built in his mind. "That's Namoradeira."

"We're closing on the one directly ahead. I can see a fishing village. There are nets drying on the fences and the cottages are thatched. It looks … poor."

He didn't move, but he was angry. Poor. How could it be poor, when the sea swarmed with fish and tall mountain walls protected the interior valleys from poor weather so that crops grew there in abundance? "The island is Saint-Simone."

"But now we're headed straight back out to sea."

"The pilot is following the channel to the capital. The capital city of Arianna sits in a cup, embraced on all sides by gentle mountain slopes. Overlooking the harbor on one side is the old royal castle, a battered wreck abandoned for two centuries. On the other side, guarding the harbor, sits a fortress bristling with stone battlements and a tall watchtower." He didn't need his vision to know where they were. Cate — and his heart — told him.

Perhaps Cate and his heart were one and the same.

"Arianna has long been a jewel in the royal crown, known for its fine homes and quiet culture. You'll see. It is a beautiful place." He wanted her to see his home, to take it to her heart. "We'll make the turn soon."

"We're slowing. You're right!" With more than a trace of

suspicion in her voice, she asked, "Are you sure you can't see through that blindfold?"

"I'll not tempt fate until I have to." For all his dislike of being so hobbled, he knew his own weakness. If he had left the slightest gap so he could see, he would look, and by his actions everyone would know the truth. "No, I can't see."

"This island is like the hump of a great, long, green dolphin slipping through the mist. It appears whenever the fog parts, then slides back. It's tall — so much taller than the isle of Mull. The beaches are rocky, when I see one, but mostly I see cliffs that stagger down to the ocean. And there's a thin silver waterfall. Oh, there's another one! And another one! The island is so beautiful."

"Can you see Arianna now?"

A hesitation.

"Cate? Can you?"

"Yes. The city is not quite so splendid as you described."

He caught a whiff of something foul. Rotting garbage and sewage left in the streets. "Is it as bad as it smells?"

"Aye. It is a wasteland, a once grand place now gone to the pigs."

CHAPTER TWENTY-SEVEN

No one was there to meet them.

Cate and Taran stood on the dock, her trunk and his bag beside them. The sailors trudged back and forth from the ship to the large storehouse.

Cate wondered what she had got herself into. The town had looked bad from a distance, but this was more than poverty. This was hopelessness, abandonment, despair. The fishermen's' homes clustered around the harbor. As the streets wandered up the hills, the houses became larger, wealthier, and everywhere she could see signs of a former prosperity. Now doors hung crooked on hinges, the thatch roofs had holes and refuse littered the streets. The homes above looked abandoned, with shuttered windows and peeling paint.

Taran's mouth was one thin, angry line. "Is it as bad as it smells?"

"Aye." No one was in sight. She supposed that was as it should be, with the men out fishing and the women inside working, but … "Where are the children?"

Taran held his head at an angle as if listening. "I don't know."

That was the problem, really. She could hear the lapping of the waves on the round, gray rocks, the calling of the seabirds, the faint whistling of the wind through the rocks. But no children ran and played. No older sister stood with a baby on her hip. No young lad carried a bucket of water for his mother. The place was deserted.

The captain stepped up beside them. Hands on hips, he looked around. "Frightening, isn't it?"

"Where is everybody?" Taran asked.

"Hiding in their huts. Gone, if they could afford it. Dead, if they're lucky."

"I understand why they'd leave. I understand they would die. But why are they hiding?"

"They never know who'll come in with us. Sir Maddox Davies keeps mercenaries up there" — Captain Dunbar gestured — "in the old fortress."

The gray stone fortress was more stern than Taran had

described. It frowned down on the town, a medieval declaration of hostility to the pirates and conquerors who would seek to acquire the Cenorinian islands. Cate could see battlements, and cannons pointed out to sea, and two men looking down on the ship, the sailors, and them.

"Are the mercenaries a problem to the townspeople?" Taran asked.

"Only if they want something the townspeople have. And the women make it their business to never walk alone," Captain Dunbar answered. Then, "Hey!" He raised his voice in a shout and hurried toward two of the sailors. "Be careful with that rug or Sir Davies will slice out my liver!"

"Sir Davies is in for a big surprise," Taran muttered.

A ragged woman peeked out the door of the public house and, seeing them alone, trudged toward them. "We have a visitor," Cate told Taran.

"What does she look like?"

Taran had come from here. He probably knew this woman. Hopefully she would not recognize him.

"I would guess our visitor is my age, but she's ..." The gown had gone beyond dirty to grimy, and the hem reached the woman's knees. She wore rags around her ankles as if to disguise her immodesty, but her feet were bare. She had that shamed look about her, as if one day in the past she had worn clean clothes and leather shoes. "She's tired," Cate said softly.

The woman curtsied. "Are you going to Giraud?" Her gaze flicked toward their faces, then back to her feet. "Because I'm supposed to take a guest there." Her English was accented, but Cate perfectly comprehended her.

"Thank you. We'd appreciate that. I'm Miss —"

"Mrs." Taran interrupted, then groped for Cate's hand and squeezed it warningly. "Mrs. Tamson. I'm Mr. Tamson. Mrs. Tamson is the new housekeeper at Giraud."

It wasn't, Cate realized, that the woman didn't want to look at both of them. Taran intimidated her. She repeatedly peeked at him, then glanced away, as if the sight of his scarred and blinded face both fascinated and frightened her. "I'm Zelle. But I don't know ... there was no mention of a husband with the housekeeper."

"He just returned from war," Cate said.

Zelle glanced at him uncomfortably. "I'm not supposed to take without permission."

Taran pitched his voice to a comforting timber. "We'll speak to Sir Davies. I'm sure he'll allow a poor, blind soldier wounded in the battlefield for England to help around his palace."

"Ye don't know him," Zelle muttered, then shrugged. "I'll get the cart."

When she left, Taran turned to Cate and in a low voice, warned, "You must remember to call yourself 'Mrs.' It won't do to betray yourself with such a simple mistake."

"I didn't forget. Claiming I was your wife stuck in my throat."

He squeezed her hand again. "Shrew." But for now he seemed unconcerned.

"Do you know her?" Cate asked.

"Zelle? Aye, and she knows me well. Did she act as if she recognized me?"

"She could scarcely look at you."

He smiled, that coldly sardonic smile. "A good disguise, then."

His cynicism sent an uncomfortable prickle up her spine, a sense that he read other people better without his sight than she did with hers.

"There's the cart," she told him. "The sailors are pulling it out of the warehouse, and Zelle is leading the horse. Obviously both belong to Sir Davies. The cart is a handsome, open, two-wheeled vehicle, and the horse is a gelding, strong and tall. Zelle must regularly exercise him, for he's steady as she harnesses him to the cart. They're riding to the dock. Two of the sailors strapped my trunk up on the back and flung your bag atop. All right, Taran, here we go."

When Zelle pulled up, Cate assisted Taran up the step and into the narrow cart, then seated him facing the front while she took the backward facing seat. In a normal situation, the female always rode facing forward, but there was nothing normal about her situation. She had to indulge a perfectly healthy man because everyone thought him an injured, blinded veteran of Queen Victoria's wars. The deceit made her want to slap him; she could imagine what the sailors would say about her then.

They waved as they drove off, Cate smiling with as much gracious courtesy as she could muster. On the road through the town, no one stirred in the huts or loitered in the shade; the air of desolation was so marked Cate wanted to take Zelle by the shoulders and explain how to fix matters ... Surely there was a way to fix matters.

But Cate wouldn't be here to help. She would be off on to another adventure, and Cenorina would have to recover on its own.

The road climbed past a large church, a cathedral, where boards cover the windows and the doors. They passed closed store fronts, then more and more wealthy homes, then turned into the pristine forest. The trees enfolded them in their branches, rich with blue-green needles. The road twisted, allowing Cate glimpses of the bright blue sea sparkling through the pines on one side, of streams sliding down the mountainside on the other. The cart rattled through the streams, the wheels flinging up water in a slow splashing.

Taran tapped Cate's knee and indicated Zelle's hunched back.

Cate turned to face front. "Zelle, do you make this drive often?"

"Often enough." The woman spoke with forbidding reticence.

But Cate would not be forbidden. In a firm tone, she asked, "How many servants will I command?"

"You've got sixty-two maids, footmen and kitchen folk, the crazy old butler — he drinks, ma'am, but there's no harm in him — and Signor Marino, the cook."

"Sixty-two!" Good heavens, Cate had known this would be a large responsibility, but she'd thought to discharge her duties efficiently and spend her time in searching for the book.

"Used to be twice that in the days when His Majesty was alive." Zelle said nothing for so long, Cate took a breath to ask another question. Then Zelle said, "No one wants to work at Giraud anymore. Got to, of course, there's no other way to feed the mouths at home. You'll be sorry there's not more servants, ma'am."

The scent of loam and road dust mixed with the spicy scent of pine, and Cate caught sight of a red deer, staring at them from a brushy bower. Forgetting that Taran couldn't see, she exclaimed, "Oh, look!" and pointed.

"What is it?" Taran asked.

"A doe, with its beautiful brown eyes big and fascinated by us."

"Zelle, do the villagers hunt the deer in time of need?" Taran asked.

Zelle swung her head back and forth in denial. "The deer are fer the noble folk. We're not to touch them. 'Tis *Her Majesty's* pronouncement."

"So you have a queen?" Cate asked.

"Aye, ma'am. We see her occasionally, riding by in her grand carriage, bedecked in jewels and waving at us. She's not like the king. When he was alive, he pretended to care, but not now, not about us common folk."

Taran's fingers crushed Cate's. "Why do you think that?"

With a wealth of bitterness, Zelle said, "She's not starving, that's fer sure."

"Where does she live?" Taran asked.

"In the old fortress, at the top of the tower where she can see the destruction she has wrought and gloat."

"In the fortress?" That Cate did not understand. "Captain Dunbar said the mercenaries live in the fortress."

"She has to have someone close to protect her. Her ... and her friend, Sir Maddox Davies." Zelle's resentment was almost a living thing. "They work hand in glove to tax us to death."

"Is there no one who can help?" Cate asked.

"Only a few of the old aristocracy are left. They hide in their valleys, conceal their wealth, keep their firearms close. If a Cenorinian is lucky enough to be one of their servants, they are fed and cared for." Zelle laughed without amusement. "Then there is the prince. Some say he's is dead, taken by the pirates. Most say he's alive somewhere, rich, fat and happy. He cares nothing for us."

A wicked suspicion coiled like a bit of dark smoke through Cate's mind. Sibeol had been so regal... "What is her majesty's name?"

"Queen Rayne Chantal. She's French." Zelle made her loathing clear.

Still Cate wasn't satisfied. "Her Majesty is here? On this island?"

"Aye, ma'am."

"Now?"

"Aye, ma'am. I saw her yesterday with me own eyes, her head wrapped in a rich silk scarf, riding out in her fancy carriage."

Suspicion was vanquished, and Cate grinned at the silliness of her thought. Yes, Sibeol was imperious, but at the same time she had brushed Cate's hair and counseled her on the proper etiquette when dealing with a former lover. No princess would be so common.

And no husband of Cate's could ever be a prince.

She eyed Taran coldly.

Certainly not this one.

CHAPTER TWENTY-EIGHT

Taran seemed unaware of her thoughts, intent on discovering all he could from Zelle. "My wife was told Sir Davies is away from home."

"Aye, on one of his … missions, he calls 'em, and he'll return all smiling and happy, with coins jingling in his pocket that we'll never see." Zelle shifted, a sudden restive movement. "Ignore me. And don't stick your nose in where it don't belong. You'll get it cut off."

Cate chuckled. "Not literally, I don't suppose." An uncomfortable silence followed, and she realized — that was exactly what Zelle meant.

"What happened to the last housekeeper?" Taran asked.

"Gone." Like Zelle's burst of eloquence.

"Did you drive her back to the ship to leave?" he insisted.

Zelle shook her head. "Stupid woman. Liked to snoop. Liked to gossip. Don't gossip, Mrs. Tamson. Not healthy."

Cate turned to Taran and squeezed his knee.

Did Zelle mean the housekeeper had been murdered?

He picked up her hand and entwined their fingers.

"I'm very discreet," Cate assured Zelle. "Is there a constable who could investigate her disappearance?"

"A week ago, a woman's body washed up on the far side of the island. Bones broken. Fell off the cliffs onto the rocks. Couldn't tell 'twas her fer sure." Zelle's voice was flat and cold. "But who else could it be?"

Cate was sickened. The woman had been murdered. What a place Cate had come to. How desperately they needed her!

"Where is our bedchamber?" Taran asked. "Is it surrounded by other servants?"

Cate looked at him in astonishment. What an odd question.

"Signor Marino has his quarters by the kitchen, and he keeps his sous-chefs and scullery maids close. He fears nothing, and protects his staff. Harkness the butler sleeps where he falls. But the maids come back to the village at night, and the lads who are footmen, too, if they can get away."

All the way to the village? Cate looked back down the steep, twisting road. "They leave? They walk? Why?"

"The men who visit Sir Davies bring their filthy foreign liquor and get stinking drunk. They fight with wicked long knives and rape the lasses." For the first time, Zelle half turned to them. "'Tis a good thing you have your husband, ma'am, fer you're too pretty fer your own good."

"That she is, but I'll protect her," Taran agreed.

"You be careful, too, sir." The road climbed, the horse labored, and Zelle slapped his back with the reins. "They'd not hesitate to destroy a man who cannot see."

"Thank you for warning me. I will be careful and stay out of their way," he said. "Are there visitors there now?'

"Nay, not a one."

"Then why don't the maids stay at night?" Cate asked.

Zelle coughed as if the dust got in her lungs. "The lasses like to come home."

They broke over the ridge, turned a corner — and looked out over the most beautiful sight Cate had ever seen. "Halt!" she called.

The cart lurched to a stop.

Zelle gestured with her big, rough hand. "There she is."

"Cate, describe it." Taran's voice sounded gravelly, and he had an expression on his face … as if he could see through the blindfold. He'd been here before, Cate knew that he had. Right now, here in the middle of the road, she wanted to question about his family, his father, who they had been, why Taran had come to stay with the MacLeans. There was a mystery about Taran, one she'd allowed her resentment to dismiss as unimportant.

Still she didn't dare to ask, for if she did, if she discovered he truly loved his family and suffered from their loss, she would began to feel empathy for him once more. Ah, dangers lie in that direction.

Cate said, "Below us stretches a valley, long and narrow, sliced by a giant's knife between two sets of high mountains. There at the top of one I see flecks of snow still nestled in the shade, so it is very tall indeed."

"That is Trueno Ridge," Zelle told her. "In times past, when danger threatened, beacons covered the island, ready to be lit as a signal in case of danger. Now no one bothers to keep those beacons ready, for the danger is *on* the island."

"What danger?" Cate asked.

"Sir Davies's mercenaries. Sir Davies himself." Zelle spit on the road.

"What if pirates attack?" Taran asked.

"Chances are, we'd welcome them," Zelle said. "They couldn't be worse, could they?"

"No. No, they couldn't." Taran leaned close to Cate, and with a voice pitched to reach only her, he asked, "Can you see the peak that rises, like a narrow spear thrusting up from the valley floor?"

"Yes." It stood apart from the mountains, with a stairway that spiraled around, climbing ever upward.

"That is Giraud's beacon, lit to summon help from the Arianna harbor town, from the other aristocrats ... and from the sea." He ended on a significant note.

Cate realized — he would light the beacon to call in his pirates. She nodded her understanding.

Zelle was leaning back, her head turned. *"What* did you say, sir?" She must have caught a wisp of Taran's comment.

"Since I cannot see, I wanted to know more about the rest of the land here." He elbowed Cate.

Cate hurried into speech. "Forest climbs the hills and settles in dips on the valley floor, but most of the level land is given to gardens and fields, except where there's the most beautiful — oh, Taran, I wish you could see it — a beautiful, still, glacial green lake with the mountains reflected so clearly I can't tell where water leaves off and the earth begins."

A hungry pleasure, akin to love, seized his features. "Yes."

"The lake nestles right up against the mountains, with waterfalls plunging directly into it, and on the other side is the house. A palace." Her throat hurt from the splendor of it, and she wondered how to find the words to describe the scene below. "The house is ... perfect. Whoever designed it wanted it to be a part of the landscape, a miracle of unerring magnificence. The walls are pale rose stone, rising four stories, decorated with white stone above the window and around the roof. The main part of the house is square with the lake, and a narrow lawn separates the palace from the water. The north and south wing are each set at an angle to follow the shoreline, and there are so many windows that look out at the vista! Every room must be a pleasure."

"Think of all that glass to keep clean," he reminded her.

Silly ass. "There's a broad veranda set with tables and chairs so one can sit there and look at the mountains and the lake and simply think …" Her voice faltered. She wasn't here to stay, to sit and think. She was here to get those letters and get out.

For no reason, Taran asked a stupid question. "Zelle, is the house haunted?"

Zelle shuddered. "Nay! Nay, sir, why would you think such a thing?"

"Because the maids would rather walk two hours home than stay the night."

Cate should always remember how perceptive he was.

Zelle was silent so long, Cate tore her gaze away from the view and gazed at the woman's profile.

Reins clasped loosely in her hands, she sat looking down at the palace, her tanned face work worn and pensive. "'Tis not haunted. Just empty, so empty. One of the maids is a fey girl, and she says the house is grieving. Told her 'twas impossible, but she says at night you can almost hear the house sigh." She slapped the reins on the horse's back and the cart jolted on. "Silly lass. Houses don't feel."

CHAPTER TWENTY-NINE

The gravel crunched beneath the wheels. They descended the mountain and entered the valley, and beneath the bandage, Taran could see the flashes of light and dark as they passed in and out of the shadows of the trees. The ocean breeze didn't reach over the hill; here it was warm and still, and the scent of ripening apples scented the air.

"The drive is beautiful with great oaks on either side," Cate told him. "I can see glimpses of the house, growing ever bigger as we approach. Hang on, there's a rut."

Taran clung to the seat as the cart dropped, then labored back out. In his time, the road had been a smooth sweep for the carriages to travel. He shouldn't be returning like this. Like a stranger to his own home.

He tasted the bitterness of knowing that before him stood Giraud, his family's favorite residence — and he couldn't see it. He remembered swimming in the ice-cold lake while his parents watched from the veranda. He remembered walking the rail, how irked his mother had been when he fell into the shrubbery and broke his arm, how his father had laughed and said, *Boys will be boys.*

"We're about to clear the trees," Cate told him. "I'll get my first good look at the house."

The setting sun shone full on his face.

Cate fell silent.

"Well?"

"The house is ..." Cate hesitated.

He still held Cate's hand, their fingers entwined, and he gained strength from that small touch. "Tell me."

"It is sad. I can see the signs of former splendor, but now it's ill-kempt, like a strong beautiful woman neglected in her old age, and always more time is passing." She shook her hand free. "Here we are."

The cart jolted to a halt.

The springs jiggled as Zelle descended. "I'll rouse someone."

Rouse someone? How could they drive up to a former palace populated by over sixty servants and have no one come out to greet them?

Cate opened the door of the cart and descended also, when if all had been right and proper, she would have sat and waited for him to pick her up out of the cart and carry her across the threshold. He had brought his bride home. More than he thought possible, he regretted the loss of that opportunity.

Groping, he found the opening and slid out, onto the step, then to the ground.

Above him, he heard Zelle's footsteps ascend the stairs, then her fist rapped on the door.

Cate was suspiciously silent, and he wanted to tear the bandage off his eyes and see for himself the damage Davies had wrought.

Instead, he ran his hand up her arm and onto her face.

At his touch on her bare skin, she jerked away.

"Talk to me," he said. "Tell me what you see."

In a tone as prosaic as only Cate could be, she said, "I was wishing for a bucket of soap and a broom to clean the grime and moss off the stone façade. The window sills need paint."

He took a step in the direction — he thought — of the stairs. Something crunched beneath his boot.

She caught his arm. "Be careful. One of the flagstone steps has broken off."

"So the place needs repair."

"Yes." Her voice was aimed right at him, so he knew she was looking at him. "I wonder why you care so much."

Ah. It had finally occurred to her to probe beneath the surface of his role here. Better that she didn't know who he was — or rather, who he had been. For Cate, ignorance provided protection; the simpler their charade, the easier their roles were to play.

But more than that, most women would be pleased to discover they were married to a prince.

He had no such illusions about Cate. She would be livid, and he both dreaded and relished the thought of telling her. For if he came through this ordeal alive, then ... then his whole life would unexpectedly be laid out before him, and he would have decisions to make. Decisions about his family. Decisions about his marriage. Decisions that would involve Cate — and probably a lot of yelling.

"Cenorina is my home, and I would rather die here than live anywhere else."

"You're not going to *die* here. We're going to successfully do our job."

He rather liked the fact that she briskly chided him for his grimness. "I would have thought you'd want me laid out in a coffin."

"I don't have time to organize a funeral."

"I'm touched."

"Besides, I don't wish you dead. I simply don't want to be married to you."

"Give me an hour, and I can change your mind."

"An hour? You flatter yourself." Her hand tightened on his arm. "A drape twitched in the window. The door is opening. A gentleman in a black and white costume has come forth. He staggers … whoops!"

Taran heard a thump and a clatter.

"He must be the butler." Cate sounded amused and dismayed. "Come, Taran, let's go and greet him."

In excessively loud and ponderous tones, the butler demanded, "Who are you?"

Cate led Taran to the stairway and placed his hand on the rail. She kept pace with him as they slowly climbed up the steps. "I'm Mrs. Tamson, the new housekeeper. And you are …?"

"I'm Harkness, the butler." He staggered sideways one step, then righted himself. "Where did you come from? Who sent you?"

"I'm from England. Sir Davies sent me."

"Ohh. Sir Davies." Harkness slurred his words.

She realized he was not only drunk, he was completely incompetent. "Zelle, would you have someone bring in our bags?"

Zelle nodded, and stomped in through the open door.

"The housekeeper, heh? I'll have to let you in, although it's none too healthy a climate for housekeepers here." Harkness transferred his gaze to Taran, stumbled, leaned against the wall. "Who's that?"

"That's Mr. Tamson, my husband."

Harkness squinted at Taran.

They reached the porch and she led Taran forward.

"What happened to him?" Harkness asked.

Cate waited for Taran to answer, but he stubbornly remained silent. Glancing at him, she saw that his chin almost rested on his chest. "He was in Her Majesty's army and injured in India."

"Why's he wearing the bandage over his eyes?"

Cate began to lose patience with both the inebriated Harkness and her mute husband. "He's blind. He also lost the use of his arm, and he is horribly scarred. All over. One big solid mass of ugly, oozing scabs..."

Taran tightened his grip on her arm.

She smiled. Annoying him was such a pleasure.

As they were about to enter the house, Harkness asked again, "Who sent you?"

Cate whirled on him. "Sir Maddox Davies."

"Oh." Harkness gripped the door casement. Glancing fearfully behind him, he asked, "Is he here?"

"No." Cate led Taran inside.

Harkness thought long and hard, as if he had to process the information and decide what he should do next. "May I take your outer garments?"

"Yes," she said crisply. As she removed her bonnet, gloves and coat, she glanced about the palace.

The house smelled musty and unaired. The huge foyer rose two stories above the black and white marble floor. Far above them, the domed ceiling was painted a pale blue and trimmed in gold and decorated with clouds. Rooms opened off the foyer and off the galleries above. The sun poured light through the windows and made Cate blink as it struck the etched-gold porcelain vases, gold-trimmed furniture and gold knick-knacks. Tapestries, plaques, and gold-framed portraits littered the walls in such profusion, she could not focus on one to the exclusion of another. As housekeeper for this huge manor, Cate had her work cut out for her.

Beside her, Taran struggled to discard his shawl and coat, managing to snarl himself up in the material. With a tsk, she untangled him and handed his garments to Harkness.

Giraud was quiet; far too quiet for a house of this size. Footmen should stand at the doorways. Serving girls should be dusting. The cook should be yelling. The gardeners should be knocking on the door with bouquets of flowers. And guests ... there should be guests, laughing, gossiping, bustling upstairs to change clothes and outdoors to ride. She could tell that once it had been that way. Now Cate could hear only the echoes of life.

Zelle was wrong.

The house truly was grieving.

CHAPTER THIRTY

Cate saw heads popping out of the many doorways; her staff had found her.

"Sit here," she told Taran, and helped him into a chair.

He sat, shoulders slumped, knees and ankles together, one hand in his lap, the other in the sling. He looked cowed, as if she regularly beat him. If only he realized how tempted she was…

She swept to the middle of the foyer and clapped her hands. "Come out, please! I wish to meet you all."

It took a moment, but sheepish servants filed into the foyer and lined up in order of rank.

Zelle joined the line at the very end.

Cate doubted Zelle was truly so humble; for all her grime and poverty, intelligence lit her eyes and the other servants treated her with wary respect.

The cook was Signor Marino, a massive Italian of impressive dignity. His staff seemed less cowed than the others; Cate thought she would get along with him.

Harkness did not put in an appearance; Cate heard the occasional snore issuing from the library. She hoped her bonnet had not become his pillow.

Cate did her duty, greeting each one of the servants, learning their names, then giving a lively speech designed to put them at ease and inspire them to work at her bidding. Judging from their shifting gazes and nervous shuffling, she had not succeeded.

She indicated Taran, and told them, "This is Mr. Tamson. He'll be spending most of his time in our bedchamber as he heals from the wounds he garnered fighting in Her Majesty's army."

"Her Majesty?" Gracia, a petite chambermaid of perhaps sixteen years, scratched her head. "Has Her Majesty started a war to save us at last?"

"Not *our* majesty, stupid." The lad next to her, obviously her brother, Gillies, pulled at her brown hair. "Mrs. Tamson is talking about Queen Victoria of England. She's a real queen. She takes care of her subjects."

"I'm sure better times are coming for Cenorina," Cate said

crisply. The Cenorinian queen had obviously alienated her subjects and Cate thought it would be difficult for the royal family to regain its position. But that part of the mission would occur after Cate's departure. For now, she would concentrate on locating those papers. "It's late and we've journeyed far. I would like to see the housekeeper's bedchamber."

Gracia stumbled forward, propelled, Cate was sure, by her brother's hand. A fierce blush rose in her brown-freckled cheeks, as she curtsied. "Please, ma'am, allow me."

"Thank you, Gracia." Cate pointed to Gillies. "You may bring up my trunk and Mr. Tamson's bag." That would teach him to torment his sister.

Gracia's wide smile offered thanks. Like all the servants, she was dressed in proper, humble, black garb. But also like all the servants, her clothing was old and worn, her white apron permanently stained at the knees.

As she approached, Taran stood, and knocked the chair sideways with a teeth-jarring rattle.

Gracia seemed unfazed. She stopped beside him and touched his shoulder. "If you'll follow me, sir, we'll get you to your chamber and you can rest."

Taran hung his head and muttered thanks, then placed his hand on Gracia's arm and allowed her to lead him up the stairs.

Cate climbed after them, watching him and marveling that the arrogant, conceited Cap'n could, through his own acting, become the object of a young girl's compassion.

Below them, the servants dispersed, and the murmuring rose upward toward the gallery. They were anxious, Cate knew, to see if she would bring stability or more confusion to their already misaligned world. She would not, but if she succeeded in her mission, stability would eventually follow.

As they walked along the gallery, Gracia spoke to Taran. "The housekeeper's chamber is on the fourth floor where the maids' rooms are. Quiet up there it is these days since we've all started going home fer the evenings, so you'll have peace in which to recover."

"I'll like that," Taran said. "Since I was wounded, I don't like to leave my room."

"Ah, you wait and see. As soon as those bruises go down

and you're feeling more like yerself, you'll want to sit on the veranda and soak in the sunshine. Me grandda was blind, and that was what he liked to do."

Taran turned toward Gracia with an expression of horror.

Cate smothered a laugh.

At the ripe old age of twenty-six, Taran had been compared to a grandfather.

They arrived at the back of the gallery, and started up the flight of stairs toward the third floor. Two walls enclosed the broad steps, carpet ran up the middle of the risers, and high-set windows let in the sunlight. "Used to be, there'd be so many guests they'd spill into the bedchambers up here." They reached the corridor lined with doors, and Gracia jerked her chin toward them. "Now the bedchambers are closed and dusty."

"We'll have to cure that, won't we?" Cate answered.

Gracia wore consternation plain on her face. "Gives me the spooks, ma'am, to be up here."

"When we clean, we'll use an army of workers." Cate intended to comfort her.

If anything, Gracia looked more dismayed. Opening the first door, she started up another staircase, this one narrow and dim. "Watch your step, sir. There's no rail here."

And no light, either, except what came from below and above. They made their way up to the top floor and turned down the corridor. Doors were shut here, too, and Gracia led them to the door opening into a corner room. "Here you go, sir. Tis the best room up here under the eaves. It's been aired and dusted every day, waiting for the new housekeeper."

"Did the previous housekeeper stay here?" Taran asked.

Gracia shifted uncomfortably. "Nay, she wanted to be down the stairs in the guests' quarters, and no one could tell her different. But we thought you'd be ... safer up here."

Taran nodded. "That's a good thought. Thank you, Gracia."

The room was almost as big as Cate's bedchamber on Mull and faced east to catch the morning sun. The scarred wood floor was covered by a faded wool rug of indistinguishable origin and muddy colors. An odd assortment of furniture filled the room — a mahogany dressing table and mirror by Heppelwhite, a green-painted klismos chair, a scarred dark oak cupboard which would have been better suited for a medieval dining hall, and an end table in eighteenth century French style. The bed had a gilt headboard so hideously adorned with Egyptian sphinxes Cate would probably have nightmares, and was so narrow there was no question of Taran sharing it with her, even if they were in accord, which they were not.

Gracia eyed it doubtfully. "Do you want me to have the footmen bring in a bigger bed?"

There was an old, overstuffed chair and ottoman that would be too short for Taran. Cate smiled. "Not at all. This is ideal." Let him pay for coming up with this brilliant plan.

With uncanny accuracy, Taran caught her wrist and kept a tight hold. "Aye, if the bed is small, we can snuggle close and stay warm."

Gracia grinned. "Me folks like to snuggle like that, too."

Cate hoped the chair was lumpy as well as short.

Gracia rubbed her hands on her skirt. "If you don't need anything else, I'll go back to me scrubbin'."

"Have Gillies bring extra blankets," Taran said, "in case the snuggling is not enough."

Gracia giggled. "There're extra linens in the cupboard — and sir, you're a wicked one, you are."

"Thank you, Gracia," he said gravely.

She giggled again, and left.

Cate snatched her hand free. "Do you have to embarrass me at every turn?"

He pulled the bandage off his face and removed his hand — as well as a long, thin, sharp dagger — from the sling. He placed everything on the dressing table. "A small payment considering you intend to make me sleep" — his gaze swept the room — "there." With disgust, he indicated the dingy chair.

"Exactly." She smiled as he pressed his hand on the cushion. "Is it dreadful?"

"More dreadful than even you could have hoped."

She braced herself for an argument, but without another word he returned to the dressing table. He pulled a short knife from one boot, a cutlass from the other, and a pistol from his belt.

"You came prepared," she said.

"Sir Davies is an accomplished swordsman and a dangerous

man. I intend to defeat him, but like a badger, when cornered, he will come out fighting." Going to one of the windows, he threw open the casement, and gazed out as if the view captivated him — and as if she did not.

She wanted to knock him out of that window. Instead she made her way to the bed. The ropes squeaked as she leaned on it, but the mattress was goose feathers and the green and gold eiderdown thick and soft. She, at least, would be comfortable.

She glanced again at Taran. He had thrust his hands in his pockets as he gazed his fill, and his profile filled her with inappropriate dismay. The marks of his barroom brawl were still with him; his lips were puffy, his chin cut, and one eye was almost swollen shut — but he was still handsome.

The trouble was, she couldn't imagine him settling down on Cenorina or anywhere at all. They were alike in some ways, and one of those ways was a wildness that couldn't be contained by four walls.

But he was not her kindred spirit ... he was *not*.

Going to the other window, she opened it. Fresh, cool air flowed over her hot face, and she took a deep breath. Directly below her was the stone-paved courtyard. Beyond that she saw the road they'd traveled from the village, and above it all soared the mountains in a vista that made her forget her disgruntlement and confusion. The sun kissed each blushing peak goodnight, and she was moved to whisper, "Isn't it beautiful?"

"It is. As beautiful as I remember." With abrupt briskness, he turned from the window and clapped his hands together. "If I have to sleep on that chair, I'd best make it."

To Cate's surprise, he did just that, taking linens from the cupboard and tucking them in around the chair cushions. Then he removed his boots, his coat, unbuttoned his trousers ...

Covering her eyes, she cried, "Wait! What are you doing?"

"Going to sleep. I'm tired."

To her disgust, he tossed a blanket over himself and did exactly that.

She stood there, waiting, expecting some trick. But he was really asleep, instantly, as if he'd learned to snatch sleep when he could.

Her trunk and his bag arrived, hauled by the puffing Gillies and one of the footmen. They glanced at Taran; his face looked battered enough to satisfy their curiosity.

She had them place the trunk beside the cupboard, saw them to the door with a courteous thanks, then set to work unpacking her gowns and undergarments.

Still Taran slept, so she left him to it, returned downstairs, and began the long process of organizing the duties and labors of her servants.

CHAPTER THIRTY-ONE

That night, when Cate entered the room, Taran woke and listened as she undressed and washed, then put on her nightgown and slid into her comfortable bed. As if she had too much on her mind, she tossed and turned, then finally stilled and slept.

He rose and hobbled across the chamber, trying to work out the kinks formed by that instrument of torture where she'd forced him to sleep.

He was getting soft. When he first joined the pirates, he'd slept in worse places. But when he first joined the pirates, he had only dreamed of Cate. Now she was within reach … and he was banished to the chair.

The moon illuminated the countryside; pale light leaked through the open window. Taran stood over his wife and stared at her features, relaxed in slumber. He wanted so badly to slip between the sheets with her and remind her of the vows she'd taken with him.

But he had other duties tonight.

At midnight, dressed in a dark brown shirt, a pair of black trousers, and his comfortable black boots, Taran walked the gallery. He descended the stairs and saw no one; no one at all. In a house that, day and night, used to bustle with life, there was no sound except for … the single clink of glass against glass.

At the foot of the stairs, he froze.

"Who's there?" a man's bleary voice questioned.

Taran recognized the voice — Harkness, drunk again. Drunk still. Taran stared into the shadowy recesses of the library.

A hulking form emerged from the darkness, swaying, his head thrust forward. He waved a glass, and the cut facets glinted in the moonlight. "Who is there?" His voice rose. "Come forth, you villain, and make yourself known."

In a hushed tone, Taran commanded, "Be quiet, Harkness, and go to your bed."

Harkness gasped. The glass slipped from his hand, shattering on the marble, the sound loud and sharp in the stillness. "Your Majesty? Have you returned?"

Taran's heart sank. He might not look like his father, but apparently he sounded like him. "I am not His Majesty."

"I understand. You don't want anyone to know." Harkness threw himself at Taran's feet. "Your Majesty, I knew you would return."

The strong smell of whisky permeated the foyer, and if this scene didn't end, and quickly, Taran feared he would be discovered on his first night. "Get up, man, you'll cut yourself on the glass."

"Your Majesty." Harkness's trembling hand groped for Taran's, and he pressed his lips on the back. "I've tried to keep faith."

Taran gave up. With the bloody-mindedness of a drunk, Harkness would believe what he wished regardless of Taran's denials. And Harkness's devotion touched him, reminding him of those days long gone when Harkness had been devoted to Taran's father, the king. So Taran said, "You've done a good job, Harkness, but now you should go to bed."

"Bed. How could I go to bed when you're back?" Harkness's shaking voice was slurred. "I must summon the maids and the footmen.   I   must   prepare   the   house!"

"You can't do that. Remember? I don't want anyone to know I have returned."

"But   I   must   do   something   to   help   you!"

Hmm. Taran realized he could get information from Harkness. At least — perhaps he could. "You're right. I could use your assistance." Slipping his arm around the butler, Taran hauled him to his feet. "Harkness, could you give me a quiet, very quiet, tour of the house? Show me what has changed in my absence?"

"Everything has changed in your absence. Everything!" Harkness flung out a hand and waved it in a wide arc, and his voice grew louder. "None of it for the better!"

"Shhh!"

"Shhh!" Harkness repeated. "We don't want *him* to know you have returned. We don't want that devil, Davies, to know."

"We don't want *anyone* to know. Help me. Show me where Davies keeps his correspondence. Tell me who visited in the past year. Direct me to the firearms."

"Your Majesty, I would be honored. And you have asked the right man, for I am not the fool Maddox would like to believe." In an excess of drunken dignity, Harkness straightened his coat. "Let us go."

Go they did. They slipped through the moonlight in the foyer and walked — staggered — toward the huntsman's room. Outside the great double doors, Harkness called a halt. He fumbled with the keys that hung from his belt. He tried to put one in the lock. He dropped it once. Twice.

Taran waited, arms crossed.

At last, Harkness managed to insert the key and turn the lock. He flung wide the doors.

They crashed against the walls.

Taran froze and listened to the silence in the house.

No movement above or below.

"Everyone is truly gone," Taran said.

"No one wants to stay in this house — except me. I've been waiting for you ... for so long ... that I despaired..." Harkness choked up.

Taran put his hand on Harkness's shoulder. "You are a good and loyal servant. No one could ask for anyone as knowledgeable as you. But Harkness — you cannot have another drink."

"What?"

"I can't take the chance you'll tell anyone I'm back. That means I need you operating at the top of your capacities as a butler, as a spy, as the man who can confuse and delude the enemy. I need you, Harkness. Do you understand? I need you."

"I am yours, my king." Harkness's voice was fervent.

"I know I can depend on you." Taran wandered into the huntsman's room. The weapons were locked in glass cabinets, but glass never kept out a determined warrior, and... "Harkness, do you have the keys for these locks?"

Harkness sniffed. "Of course, Your Majesty."

Taran laughed softly. "You are a treasure."

They toured the house, upstairs and down, examining each room. On the second floor, Taran insisted they step out the back door onto the wide balcony to look far out over the magnificent, overgrown yard. There the rocky crag rose like a bleak stark finger pointing toward the eternal stars. "Harkness, the king has returned. When the battle is joined, is the beacon ready to light?"

Harkness swayed as he stared at the symbol of Cenorinian

hope. "It will be, Your Majesty. In secret, it will be done."

"How soon?"

"Within the week. I can manage it within the week."

"Sooner. We need that beacon."

"Yes, sire." Harkness led Taran up steep, narrow stairs to the third story. "You want to know where Sir Davies keeps his correspondence." He chuckled darkly. "When people are watching, he uses the king's study, and while he does he strikes cruelly at the reminders of royalty." His voice wavered, then he hurried on. "It is his belief that sitting his common buttocks on the king's chair makes him important. But I'm the butler. I know where he keeps his *secret* papers." Harkness opened a shabby door into pitch darkness. Striking a lucifer, he cupped the small flame in his hand, and hurriedly lit the candle beside the door. Lifting the brass candle stand, he waved it around the room. A small desk sat in the middle of a worn rug. Cabinets and drawers lined the walls. "They're here. In this room with no windows. Sir Davies hates the light."

"Then he will soon enjoy the confines of his coffin." Taran checked the desk. It was locked. The cabinets were locked. The drawers were locked. Taran asked, "Do you have the keys for all *this?*"

"No, Your Majesty. Only Davies holds these keys."

Ironic. On Taran's first night home, Harkness had in all probability led him to the place where Davies had placed the information Taran sought, and it was secure behind one of a hundred locks. Taran had seen how quickly Cate could work, but this … this would take time. And time they did not have.

Taran turned toward the door, and stopped.

Harkness stood like a statue, candle upraised, staring at him accusingly. "You *aren't* the king."

Now Taran had to proceed carefully. "Who do you think I am?"

Harkness's hand trembled. The candle wavered. "The crown prince. But he is dead."

"Why do you think that?"

"I was here when he was captured. I watched as they dragged him away to be delivered to the pirates." The candle trembled harder. "I knew … and I did nothing."

"Why not?"

"Because I am a coward." There was a world of self-loathing in those words.

Taran now knew what to do, what to say. "If you had tried to prevent the deed, you would have been most horribly killed. What good would that now do the prince?"

"Perhaps none." Harkness gave a dry sob. "But I would not now be trapped in this torment of guilt. I would not now be speaking to a ghost."

"I am not a ghost. Look at me. Touch my hand." Taran moved close to Harkness and grabbed his fingers. "I have returned to take my kingdom from the usurper. And I appoint you the general of my household. "

Harkness collapsed into Taran's arms.

With one hand, Taran caught the candle. With the other, he supported Harkness.

"This isn't a dream … is it?" Harkness asked.

"It is real. But you must sleep so you are prepared to take command." Taran maneuvered him out of the room. "I depend on you, Harkness. You will not fail me."

"No, I will not. But I don't want to go to sleep if you're going to be gone when I wake."

"I won't be gone. I'll be here … hiding in plain sight."

"That's all right, then." Harkness sounded as sleepy as a babe. "As long as you have in truth come back."

CHAPTER THIRTY-TWO

Cate dreamed...

In the early morning, in Granny Aileen's miniature hut, Cate woke and gave a long, languid stretch, feeling a pleasurable fatigue in each muscle, a soreness between her thighs. A sense of accomplishment brought a smile tugging at her lips. At last, she had seduced and conquered Taran Tamson. He was hers. She would keep him forever on the Isle of Mull, her husband, her lover.

She could hear him moving around the hut, stirring up the fire, setting the water to boil. His footsteps moved toward the bed. She shut her eyes and pursed her lips, ready for his kiss.

Instead, he leaned over the bed, placed a hand on either side of her head, and said, "Cate, look at me."

Her eyes sprang open, and she saw ... she saw Taran, dressed in his black traveling clothes, a lock of hair drooping over his forehead. She looked again, sure that she somehow must have lost her mind. But she hadn't. He even wore his greatcoat. Her voice had a squeak in it when she demanded, "Why are you dressed like that? What are you doing?

"I'm going back to my home."

"Back to ..." She tried to feel relief, but something in his expression warned her devastation approached. "You mean to Mull."

"No, I mean to my home."

"Your home? You don't want to go there. You never even talk about it!"

That made perfect sense to her, but his lips tightened as if she displeased him. "I'm leaving."

"But you can't. We're married!"

"I know." Leaning down, he pressed a kiss on her lips, a kiss that deepened of its own accord. But he drew back. "I have to go back and claim my heritage."

She flung her hands around his neck to hold him. "But you've got a home with the MacLeans now."

"Did you think I would live off of your brother for the rest of my life?"

Of course, she'd thought exactly that. "Why not? He's a great laird. He would be glad of your support."

Taran shook his head.

She thought he looked older, somehow. The rage that constantly simmered beneath his surface had been transformed into resolve. And she realized — before their impetuous marriage, they hadn't talked about where they would live or how. She had assumed things that weren't true, and now she had a choice to make.

Taking her hands, he loosened them from his neck. "I'll come back for you."

She sat up and kicked the covers off. "No, you won't. I'll go with you."

She expected her pronouncement to be greeted with joy, not a flat, "You can't."

"Why not? A wife's place is at her husband's side."

"It's too dangerous."

"I'm not afraid."

He straightened. "You can't come!"

He made her so mad! No one told her what to do. "How are you going to stop me?"

"Your brother is on his way. I left him a note telling him where he could find you. Inform him that we're married and he won't want to kill you. Tell him I'll be back for you — if I can."

"What do you mean, if you can?" Taran was abandoning her. Her husband was abandoning her after only one night!

Taran straightened his shoulders. "I face great peril."

She wanted to laugh at him for his posturing.

But he was serious as a tomb. "I'll be back. I can't allow myself to fail."

Her plans were all crashing around her ears. Nothing was going as it should. She came to her feet wearing nothing but a blush of fury. "I'm going to follow you."

He looked. She saw his gaze linger on her breasts and her legs, and everything in between. Then he looked at her face, and in the kind of tone she occasionally heard from her brother, he said, "You're not."

Taran couldn't talk to her that way. He was not her boss. Putting her hands on her hips, she asked, "How are you going to stop me?"

He stared at her for a long moment.

She taunted, "I'm as good at tracking as you are. No matter where you are, I'll be right behind you."

He took a long breath. "I should have thought of that."

She enjoyed one moment of triumph.

Then he removed the coil of rope off the wall, the one Granny Aileen used to tether the cow, and Cate realized she'd pushed him too far. "You can't do that to me."

He reached for her.

She tried to duck under his arm.

He caught her, tucked his foot under her knee, and tipped her back onto the bed.

She tried to box his ears. She got him, too, on the right side, with a resounding thump that made him stagger slightly.

But he caught that wrist, sat on her. Sat on her! As if she were a wild colt to be tethered.

And he tied her to the headboard.

She gave a shriek of rage. She kicked at his back.

His expression was intense. He frowned in concentration as if she were a problem to be solved.

She raked her fingernails across one side of his face. He caught that hand and tied it beside the other one.

Then he stood and looked down at her, chest heaving, blood welling from four jagged gashes in his cheek.

"I'm your wife," she shouted.

He sounded exasperated and looked harried. "Then act like one and stay where you're told."

"I am Caitlin MacLean. I'm not a dog to stay meekly where I'm ordered."

"You are Caitlin ... Tamson. You'll stay here, and I'll be back for you."

In a fury of rage and pain, she tugged at the ropes. "I'm not your wife. I will never be your wife. Not if you leave me like this."

"You promised you'd love me forever." He didn't leave her time to scream a denial. Instead he swept down on her, holding her captive with his knee across her legs. Holding her head in his hands, he kissed her swiftly, ruthlessly. Drawing back, he ran his hands down her, pausing to caress her breasts, caressing her inner thighs.

She trembled with a humiliating combination of hope and passion. "I hate you."

"You might hate me, but you'll never forget me. And you are my wife." He glanced toward the window where morning's light leaked through the shutters "I have to leave, but your brother's on his way. You'll be all right."

Cate woke with a start and clutched the covers to her throat. Taran. *Taran was gone.*

But she wasn't at Granny Aileen's. She was at Giraud.

It wasn't early morning, but the middle of the night. The moon was high, shining through the open window.

She could see an unmoving lump of pillows and blankets on the chair in the corner. She should have been comforted to know he had kept his vow and stayed out of her bed, but somehow she wasn't satisfied.

Something didn't feel right.

She looked around the strange room, noting the shadows, the furniture twisted into gothic shapes by the flat white moonlight. She saw no glowing eyes, nothing out of place. The curtains fluttered; perhaps that was what had woken her.

Cautiously, she sat up. She pushed the blankets away, swung her feet to the floor and stood, oh so carefully, her eyes straining as she looked at the chair. At Taran.

She couldn't hear him breathing. He lay motionless. She didn't know if he was feigning deep sleep to lure her into his grasp, or ... but how could he? He didn't know she would wake. Tiptoeing toward the chair, she watched the furniture, avoiding the fringe of the rug, giving the ugly cabinet a wide berth, only too aware of the dangers of wandering about a virtually unknown room in the moonlight.

She almost made it, she reached out her hand to pull back his covers — when the board beneath her foot squeaked. She froze, sure he would rise in a rage.

Nothing. He didn't move, he didn't ... "You faker!" She flung back the covers.

He was gone.

Again.

CHAPTER THIRTY-THREE

With many a reassurance, Taran put Harkness in his bed in
the butler's bedchamber. He returned to the entry hall, and stood in
the pale moonlight, listening to the approaching storm. Tonight he
would have liked to visit the stables, to assess if any of the king's
fine horses had survived. He would have liked to visit Arianna, to
see what was left of loyalty among his people. He would have liked
to visit the tower where his mother had been imprisoned, and where
Miss Jeannette Bennett even now masqueraded as the dowager
queen.

But the hour was late, thunder rumbled in the skies, and the
storm prowled closer, rampaging across the mountain peaks and
toward Giraud. He had accomplished more tonight than he could
have ever hoped ... and his bride was upstairs in her chaste bed.

Anticipation rose in him.

She hated him.

She loved him.

She wanted him.

And he wanted her, desperately, like a constant hungry
grumbling in his blood.

But he had left her sleeping. Tomorrow he could sleep, but
she had work to do, important work, work that would save his
kingdom. He could not wake her with seductions that would last all
the night through.

Yet how much longer could he hold onto his restraint?

He moved steadily up the stairs, not bothering to muffle his
steps. Why should he? Harkness had assured him that no one stayed
at Giraud. Only the ghosts.

The second flight was darker, narrower, the shadows deeper.
A landing cut the stairway in half, and as he climbed and turned,
ever-brighter flashes of lightning bit at the darkness in bursts of
stark white.

The flight to the fourth floor was narrower yet, lit only by
fading moonlight from windows far above. He put a foot on the
bottom step of the third flight, and halted, his ear caught by the
sound, above him, of his bedroom door opening, then gently

shutting. A soft tread moved purposefully across the landing.

He recognized those footsteps. He'd been caught. By Cate.

His heart leapt. She would be angry with him for leaving her alone, for making her worry. Very angry, her Scottish temper snapping and sparking like the storm outside. Anticipation of a tangle with Cate kept him in place, waiting ... waiting ...

She came down the first half-flight, then reached the landing and turned the corner toward him. In the gloom, she was a pale ghost in a long white nightgown, her auburn hair tucked into a short braid. As she descended, she kept her head down, watching her feet, and she was almost on top of him before some instinct brought her head up. She saw him. She gave a short, sharp scream and checked briefly.

He opened his mouth to say her name, to assure her it was him.

But lightning flashed, and thunder cracked. She saw him, recognized him. Her temper flared. She launched herself at him and grabbed his shoulders. "No wonder you didn't demand to sleep in my bed. You didn't intend to stay!"

"And that annoys you?"

She shoved at him, moving him down with the sheer force of her fury. "Where were you? What were you doing?"

"Reconnaissance."

Her voice rose in disbelief. "In the middle of the night?"

"Did you expect me to do reconnaissance in the daylight?"

"I didn't expect you to do reconnaissance at all. That's my job!"

And he hated that. "Being here is a chance like no other, and I seized it."

"Where did you go?"

"I looked around the palace. I sought knowledge that would help you in your search, but also ... I wanted to know if the situation was as dreadful as you'd said."

"Did you think I would lie?"

He reminded himself that she didn't know what Giraud had meant to him; that Giraud had been his home. "I had to see for myself."

Lightning flickered. The skies rumbled.

She said, "Tomorrow night I'll go with you."

"You will not. I'm here. I'll take care of everything."

She answered him in kind. "You will not. I came here for revenge. A person like Davies — he killed my brother."

"You don't have the strength or the ruthlessness to kill him back."

"I know that, but I can help bring him to justice. This" — she stomped her slippered foot on the step — "this is my job, my prospect for vengeance, my chance to leave scandal behind and find a new occupation out in the world. You will not get in my way. I am not going home in disgrace, and *I want my revenge.*" She turned and stormed up the stairs.

He had waited half his life to return to Giraud. He had expected that putting his plan into action would be easier than the anticipation. But his homecoming was more difficult than he had thought. To see his home devastated. To know his servants were gone or sunk in despair. To live every minute with the fear his wife would involve herself so deeply in the coming events she would be caught between the cruel millstones of duty and vengeance — and be killed.

He couldn't stand in her way.

He couldn't *not.*

He bounded after her and before she reached the top, he grabbed her sash and pulled her to a stop.

She twirled to face him. "Let go of me."

She stood above him on the stairs, fierce and proud as hell. He couldn't make out her features, but he knew she was glaring at him, eyes hot with fury, her lush mouth set in a stubborn line.

"Damn it, woman, why can't you simply do as you're told?" Taking hold of the lapels of her robe, he jerked her into him.

She stared down at him, her warm body resting against his, and he knew the lightning flickered on his features. What she saw there, he didn't know. Didn't care. He only cared that she wrapped her hands in his newly shorn hair, tilted her head, and pressed her lips to his.

It was like kissing flame. Smooth, excruciatingly hot, with tiny licks of her tongue that intruded into his mouth. Her scent rose from her, carried on the waves of heat, and all he wanted was to taste her, bury himself in her.

He would possess her. She belonged to the one part of his

life that was truly his. He slid his arms around her waist, relishing the slow slide of material across her skin.

Yes ...

Then, in a sudden reversal of affection, she grabbed his shoulders and pushed him away from her as hard as she could.

He staggered down two steps, almost lost his balance and tumbled the rest of the way down.

"Bastard," she hissed. "Don't think you can rob me of my role in this game." Turning with an elegant sweep of her robe, she climbed the stairs.

She didn't understand. He had to have her. Now. Life was brief. Justice was cruel. And death ... death was forever, and very close. Savage, senseless with desire and frustration, he bounded to her side. "Not tonight, my darling. You're not leaving me tonight."

CHAPTER THIRTY-FOUR

Cate wasn't afraid.

She was angry. Angry that Taran dared to try and tell her what to do. Furious that he imagined he could kiss and cajole her out of doing what she must to avenge Kiernan.

Doubling up her fist, she hit Taran as hard as she could on his wounded shoulder.

It had to have hurt.

He didn't even flinch.

She wound up to hit him again.

He caught her fist, kissed the knuckles, and backed her against the wall. This time when he kissed her, it was without her cooperation.

He didn't care. He thrust his fingers in her hair, tilted her head to meet his lips, and leaned his body against hers.

With his weight, he thought to still her rebellion.

That wouldn't work. Did he really think she would simply … surrender to him? Because he manhandled her?

She broke his hold with a swift upward and outward thrust of her arms.

His fingers tore at her braid, bringing tears to her eyes.

All right, that had been stupid. Especially when, as if it had never happened, he clamped his hands back to her head. And kissed her again. Thrust his tongue into her mouth and massaged her with erotic strokes that took her, for one moment, to the brink of desire.

He couldn't do this to her. She wouldn't let him. So she bit him. Bit his lower lip, hard.

This time he did flinch. Pulled back … laughed softly.

He had to have gone insane. Coming here, to his island home, seeing the devastation, had driven him to the brink. What other explanation could there be for his impervious disdain for pain? For his driving need to … to mate. He wanted to mate.

She was not an animal, and he would not use her as one. She shouted, "I don't want you!"

Throwing back his head, he laughed aloud. "You have never stopped wanting me. We want … each other. We need each other.

We are one."

He used simple direct language more potent than poetry ... for it was the truth. Damn him. Damn him!

Leaning against her, he cupped his hands beneath her bottom. He lifted her, tilted her. His erection pressing hotly against her stomach, a long, hard memory.

She had only ever been with one man, and that was nine years ago. Never mind that that man had been Taran. Never mind that he had been her husband, that she'd given herself to him joyously and passionately. In the long and bitter time since, she had been her own woman, yielding nothing of herself ever, to anyone. Now he stunned her with the heat and the fury he generated, and the intimacy ... he was too close. She had to get away.

He wanted her. Oh, yes, he wanted her, and his wanting curled in the air like smoke and flame. She could scarcely breathe for knowing his desire.

Worse, as he shifted her, rubbed himself against her, her body reacted like dry kindling to a flint. Sparks shivered along her nerve endings, and she wanted ... she wanted ... With his mindless thrusting passion, he was turning her into a she-beast, and she wondered ... what would it hurt if she seized at passion? Just passion?

Not love. Not closeness. Only two bodies writhing together for their mutual pleasure.

But no. No! Cate would not descend to such depths.

Inching her hands between them, she shoved at him. "Taran. Get away, you oaf."

For a long moment, he didn't move. His chest heaved, and she could hear the rasp of his breath.

Alarm stirred in her.

Then he let her slide to her feet. He backed up, head down, hands dangling loosely at his sides.

She wanted to walk away, with dignity and pride. But she saw the glint of his eyes watching her, and she didn't dare. She told herself she used good sense; she kept her back against the wall. She slid sideways up the steps. One step. Two.

She could barely see the dark silhouette of his head turning, tracking her. He commanded, "Cate. Don't go."

At his guttural tone, the hair rose on the back of her neck.

Lightning flashed.

In that instant, she saw him clearly, saw his need, his intent, his determination.

Thunder boomed a warning.

With the instinct of a hunted doe, she knew she was in danger. She should continue to sidle away. She shouldn't incite him by fleeing. But —

He reached out and slammed one hand on the wall beside her. "Cate!"

She broke and ran.

He leaped after her. He caught her as she reached the corridor. He swept her up, one arm beneath her back, one beneath her knees. He held her tightly, a pirate's prize. She expected him to take her through the door into their bedchamber.

She prepared to fight. But she had underestimated his hunger and his lust.

He couldn't wait. He laid her out on the floor as if it were some pagan sacrificial altar. He pushed her knees apart, knelt on the top step, and leaned over her, trapping her between his outthrust arms.

Earlier, when she stood above him on the stairs, the lightning illuminated his upturned face in bursts of power he seemed to absorb. She'd seen the man then, and the facial structure she knew only too well. Now lightning flickered behind him, and all she could see was a creature of hulking shoulders, black eye sockets, and intentions that angered and thrilled...

No! She was not thrilled. Her heart beat so hard it thumped against her ribs, but that was ... fear. Yes. Fear. Fear was better than believing she could not resist Taran and his passion.

She didn't touch him, either, or move suddenly, or make the mistake of trying to flee again. Instead, she stared directly into his eyes — or rather, where she knew his eyes to be — and in a clear, slow voice, she said, "Taran, I am not amused by this display of bloody-minded masculinity."

"Then there's hope for you yet." Now he sounded smooth, warm ... too warm. "Cate." As he lowered himself onto his elbows, his lower body formed to hers. His thighs were between hers, his erection pressed against her, and it made no difference that she wore a nightgown and robe — a robe that hung open, damn it — and he wore his rough-and-tumble clothing. For her, at this moment, this was as intimate as flesh on flesh.

He rubbed himself against her like some great, purring, wicked cat, and she gasped like a virgin, embarrassed by the contact, horrified by her own body's uncontrolled reaction. Her nipples tightened. Between her legs, she grew damp and she wanted, needed to lift herself and move with him until she satisfied the desire that burgeoned within herself.

When had this happened? When had she lost the lonely contentment she had achieved with so much difficulty?

She closed her eyes, and in her imagination, she could see the two of them, naked and entwined, their limbs sliding across bare skin, dancing to the endless song that only they could hear. She could almost taste his skin, feel the scrape of his tongue as he tasted her ...

Her eyes sprang open.

She had to get away from him. Somehow, he'd trapped her with him in this mindless passion made half of rage and half of frustration. She was Caitlin MacLean, and she would not be trapped.

Putting her hands against his shoulders, she pushed.

He pushed back, leaning into her, pressing more of his belly and his chest against hers, and the heat of this man, this pirate, warmed her blood and her bones. His hands covered her breasts, just like that, an abrupt cupping that should have seemed crude, but thrilled with its boldness.

She began to breathe in gasps — harsh, deep breaths that wracked her and lifted her breasts closer and harder into his hands.

He took this as an invitation, sweeping her nipples with his thumb, pressing her flesh rhythmically with his palms.

Lightning. Thunder.

Desire. Satisfaction.

A turbulence in the air, and in her blood.

Her feet rested on the steps beside his knees. Her toes flexed as she fought to *not* rub her leg against his thigh in restless invitation. She turned her head to the side, imagining herself away from this ... this seduction, this bold and dramatic seduction.

"Cate." He almost purred in her ear.

Goosebumps sprang up on her skin.

Gently, he pressed his mouth to her throat, then sank his teeth into the cord of her shoulder.

He wasn't kissing her. He was … he was eating her alive.

And no matter how much she wanted to, she couldn't lie to herself any more. She liked it. She wanted it.

Dear God, she wanted him.

CHAPTER THIRTY-FIVE

Panic struck. In a savage, convulsive movement, Cate tore herself away and rolled onto her stomach.

Taran pounced, grabbing handfuls of cloth. The robe slipped off her shoulders, trapping her arms. The nightgown strained at the shoulder seams. She slithered out of the robe and made a frantic leap across the landing.

He flung the robe away and grabbed the hem of her nightgown. He twisted it sideways; she slipped and landed on her hip. The rug was not nearly enough padding. She'd have a bruise tomorrow, but she didn't notice. She only knew this was her last chance to save herself.

She flung herself onto her back.

He lost his grip on her nightgown.

She lifted her feet and caught him squarely in the chest as he charged her. She heard his grunt, saw him slam against the wall.

Before she could scramble to her feet, he shoved himself off the wall and on top of her again.

She gasped from the impact. "How did you do that?"

"Desperation." His hands grasped the material at her throat. He tore it down the front.

Desperation. *He* said desperation drove him.

She said he was a primitive, and she would treat him like one. She clawed at his face. She kicked at him.

He ducked away, slid down her body, grabbed her thighs in his arms and put his face … between her legs…

She screamed when his mouth tasted her.

"What are you … what … " She couldn't finish the question. It was obvious what he was doing. He was kissing her … there. He was sucking and nibbling, tasting her body, reveling in the way her hips moved and laughing, softly, when she moaned. "God. Taran. Please. Don't. You can't…" She should have been fighting him. She *was* fighting him, trying to get away again, still, but all the while her body responded, tightened, prepared for pleasure.

It wasn't right, the way his tongue stroked her, over and over, until she wanted to give up and do whatever he desired. And his hands moved, slid, stroked her inner thighs, then found the entrance of her body. His finger circled and circled, teasing her when all she wanted was Taran, inside her.

Rising up, she pounded her fists on his shoulders. "Stop! I can't bear this!"

In retaliation, he slid his finger inside her.

Orgasm swept from everywhere he touched to everywhere in her body, carried in her veins, by her nerves. She groaned. She threw herself backward, arms outstretched, taut with overwhelming pleasure. The sensation went on and on, blanking thought, making her a creature driven by passion, lifted on one wave of pleasure after the other.

She was helpless.

She was empowered.

She was woman incarnate.

And he ... he kept on, drinking in her orgasm as if it were the elixir of life.

When the first violence of climax calmed, Taran rose above her and called her name. "Caitlin." He made it sound as if she were his only lover. As if he'd longed for her across years and miles. "Cate, give in to me."

She opened her eyes.

She was crying. When had she started crying? Oh. She knew. When that last, mighty spasm had swept her, the sensation had been too much, too good, too strong, and she cried. Now her breath quivered as she tried to see ... him. Tried to remember why she shouldn't give in, when he offered — nay, demanded! — such amazing response.

He was still firmly between her bent knees. He could have taken her without struggle, in an instant. Instead, his hand stroked the skin on her inner thigh, soft circles that beguiled and entreated. "Cate, give in to me."

She had to remember. Who he was. Who she was. What yielding would bring. Her voice was scratchy. "No."

Then he proved why he was such a great warrior.

He never gave up. Putting his hand to the opening of his shirt, he tore the material just as he had torn her gown. He tore it clear to the hem. She flinched from the sound, thin and sharp in the dim recesses of the stairway. Then, taking her fist from her side, he uncurled the fingers, one by one, and placed them on his chest.

How did he know that that was what she longed to do? To touch his bare skin, to slip her fingers down his muscled abdomen to rest on the bulge in his trousers?

Her hand pressed on his chest. Beneath her fingertips, she could feel the throb of his heart. Her own heartbeat matched his, rapid, desperate to go on, to finish what they'd begun. Sweat dewed his skin, and her palm slipped to one side and came to rest over his nipple.

He threw his head back.

She saw his features in the moonlight. Strained, pleasured, wanting. She'd seen him look like this before ... one day in a peaceful Scottish valley in the daylight.

The memory hurt.

She jerked her hand away. "Nay!"

As if her touch led him, he followed it down, laid full length on her. He caught her hands before she could punish him — ah, he'd weakened her with his wiles! — and he kissed her.

He might ask for permission, but it was nothing but form, a minor detail before he ravished her body as he now ravished her mouth. Her nipples rubbed against his bare chest. His heat, his closeness, his scent surrounded her. His tongue thrust past her lips, demanding response, and she yielded.

Yielded. Ha. She responded, wanted, cradling him between her legs, moving her hips against him, wishing his trousers were gone and he inside her.

Desperate. He was desperate.

Now, so was she. She would climax now, simply from his taste in her mouth, from their movements, from the constant, rocking desperation of their bodies together.

He stood so quickly, the chill struck her, made her nipples pucker, made her clasp her arms around her waist and bring her knees together.

He stood one step down and unbuttoned his trousers. He never turned his glittering gaze from her. He didn't move quickly, nor slowly. He moved deliberately. Softly, he said, "How could you think we would not come together again? The only way I cured my longing for you was to forget about you altogether. If I hadn't, I would have died from the longing, and we would have spent eternity alone. I don't want to be alone anymore. You don't want to be alone anymore. Cate, I want you."

In between the bleak darkness and the blinding lightning, Cate couldn't quite make out his expression ... but she heard that voice, saying things she secretly believed. And she saw his body, sculpted by hardship, marked with scars ... lean, muscled ... his trousers slid down his thighs, and oh, how boldly his cock thrust toward her. She wanted to take it in her mouth, take it into her body, possess that piece of him that would make them one.

He pulled her up to face him. Knelt on the step, wrapped his arms around her body. Wrapped her legs around his hips. Let her feel the prod of his penis against the entrance of her body.

She was soft, swollen, so damp with desire she had tasted herself on his lips. And he made it worse, with his probing, his almost entry, his taunting touches.

She strained, wanting to thrust herself on him, impale herself and cure this need that hounded her now. Tonight.

Always.

Savage, deep and strong, he told her, "Cate. It's time."

"Aye." She caught his hips and pulled him into her. "Aye."

God. *God.* He slid into her in a smooth movement that filled her, that stretched her, that brought her instantly to the brink. She wanted him to stay there. All the way inside her. To give her a chance to savor this sensation. To avoid this fate that rushed at her so quickly she couldn't catch her breath.

That wasn't what he wanted. He crushed her in his arms, moving only his hips, drawing out from her, not all the way, but enough that her swollen tissues clung in desperation. Then he pushed back in, all the way to the entrance of her womb, groaning as if he'd found the pinnacle of pleasure in her body.

She shuddered to have him inside her. It was like dying. Like being born.

He held her so tightly, he controlled her movements, the very act of joining. She cried out and struggled, managed to free her arms and wrap them around his shoulders, and all the time he moved in and out, an instrument of exquisite torture.

She wanted him to stop. She wanted him to hurry. She wanted anything but this half-movement, this almost-pleasure. The rhythm was slow, the touch of his penis against her womb intermittent. She wriggled beneath him, trying to force the pace, and he kept … tormenting her.

"Please," she heard herself say, and realized she'd been saying it like a chant. "Please. Taran. Please."

He kissed her. Invaded her mouth, used his tongue to match the rhythm and the depth of his invasion below.

Speechless, now, her hips surged against him. She dropped her feet to the step beside his knees, pushed up harder and more desperately. She dug her nails into his shoulders.

And finally, finally, his discipline cracked. With a gasp, he released her mouth. He reared up on his knees, rising over her like some grand, pagan god of passion. Sliding his hands beneath her hips, he lifted her with him, matching them together ever closer.

She sprawled on the landing beneath him, demanding the same worship he inspired. Grinding her heels into the steps, she arched her back, and forced him to reckon with her as if she were a force of nature.

The heavens crackled as he thrust, shaking her with the force of his onslaught. They swayed, back and forth, wrestling for supremacy, groaning with a pleasure that bordered on anguish.

Cate clawed at the carpet beneath her.

Taran's fingers clenched her buttocks, as again and again they came together, lightning strikes to the fertile earth. She burned. She ached. She needed … more. He had to give her … more.

They struggled in silence, the roars of the thunder and the crackle of the lightning their only love sounds.

Yet when the deluge of climax arrived, it swept her away. The spasms hit her hard, shaking her whole body, squeezing him inside her.

"Aye," she heard him whisper hoarsely. "Woman, that's what I want. That's just what I want."

She didn't understand what he meant. She didn't care. The demands of her body held her in thrall. She whimpered. She screamed. She moaned. Her whole body twisted, trying to wring every last drop of pleasure from him.

And he gave in abundance. Pleasure — and his seed.

When they came to rest, breathing together, relaxing into the bliss of fulfillment, Cate kept her mind carefully blank. She didn't want to think what this would mean to them, to her.

But inevitably he moved, rising above her, to look into her face. She thought he would be triumphant. Instead, he whispered, "What happened to your hair?"

She braced herself for conflict. "I cut it."

"Why?"

"When the man who taught me to pick locks ... Billy was my only friend, and when he was killed, it was *my* fault. I wanted to do penance. I've always been vain of my hair, so I ... chopped it off."

He cradled the ends in his palm. "It's beautiful. As beautiful as always."

For once — just once — he had said the right thing.

She remembered her vow to keep him out of her bed.

Passion on the stairs was one way of keeping her vow.

Yet ... she turned her head, and kissed his fingers.

He extended his hand to her. "Take me again."

She stared at the hand, then into his shadowed face. Foolishly, so foolishly, she whispered, "I love you. I have always loved you." Slowly she wrapped her fingers in his, rose, and led the way up the stairs.

CHAPTER THIRTY-SIX

A knock on the open bedroom door distracted Blowfish Burnham from his study of the chart of Cenorinian waters. He glanced up, saw Lilbit looking hangdog and anxious, and handsome, blond and young. And perhaps … ambitious. Blowfish started to roll up the chart, then changed his mind and weighed down three corners with the inkpot, the compass, and the Cap'n's log. He gestured at Lilbit. "Come in, lad."

Lilbit stepped in. Twisting his hat in his hand, he said, "Blowfish, I think misfortune has visited the Cap'n. And us."

Blowfish removed his wire-rimmed reading glasses and placed them precisely on the island of Saint-Simone. "Shut the door."

Lilbit did as he was told.

"Now tell me."

"Mr. Cleary's been gone three days now."

"Aye, who knows what the untrustworthy swine has been doing. Betraying us to the English Navy, mayhap."

"No, sir."

"Selling us to the highest bidder, then."

"Not that, either, sir. I found him." Lilbit nodded his head toward the window. "Down in the alley. His throat's slit, sir."

"Throat slit? Really? Poor devil. I wonder what misfortune befell him." Blowfish wandered toward the window, turned and found Lilbit looming behind him. "How did ye discover the body? That alley's no place for a stroll. I can smell the stench without even opening the window. And I wouldn't ever lean out."

"Right. No reason to open the window and lean out," Lilbit admitted. "Unless you're throwing out the nightsoil. Which I was."

Blowfish walked back to the table and studied the chart. "Mr. Cleary's day maid is a pretty little thing."

Lilbit clomped over, his big boots striking the floor hard with each step, and craned his neck to study it, too.

"Ye saved her from the smelly job," Blowfish said.

"I did. When I did, I spied me a man-shaped lump. Covered with filth. Big." Lilbit gestured widely. But he kept his gaze on the chart, studying it keenly. " I remembered Mr. Cleary had disappeared and I wondered ... so I went down there."

"You went down and mucked around in the shit? Ye're a good man, Lilbit. A caring man." Blowfish was all admiration. "Who cut his throat?"

Lilbit flicked a glance up, then moved away from the desk. "I don't know, sir. I didn't see it. I just found him."

"Did he force the day maid, and fall asleep, and she sawed his throat through?"

"No one has to force her, sir!"

"Or was it a strong, clean cut, like a sailor would make with his dagger?"

"A strong, clean cut." Lilbit clasped his hands behind his back.

"Hm." Blowfish rubbed his finger across his lips. "That's not good. Not good at all."

"I thought that, too." Lilbit sounded eager. "That means foul play, right? And foul play means trouble, doesn't it? Someone is on to our plan to capture Cenorina and return the Cap'n to their throne?"

"It's a possibility," Blowfish said. "A real possibility. I'm just not as sharp as the Cap'n. I can't figure all the ways trouble might come at us."

"I can't either, sir. Perhaps we should set sail immediately, and leave trouble behind." Lilbit frowned as if he was thinking hard to come up with his line. "Ship at sail, leaves no trail."

"Yes. Thank you. I've heard that maxim before." Blowfish scratched at his chest. "Lilbit, I value your loyalty."

Lilbit bobbed up and down, grinning.

"I'll see to stocking the ship for the voyage. You send word to the crew. Tell them we sail tomorrow at first tide. Be there or be damned. We'll linger offshore from Cenorina for the signal from the Cap'n."

"A good plan, sir. Blowfish. We'll be safe out there."

"Aye, that we will. Be off with ye now." Blowfish watched as the gangly American ambled out the door. He listened as the boy wandered casually down the corridor. By the sound of his boots, Blowfish knew Lilbit sped up as he reached the stairs; he eagerly ran down them, out the door and into the street.

When Blowfish was satisfied the lad was truly gone, Blowfish shut the door and turned the lock. "Ye can come out now."

Gerry Williams, louse-covered, low-life pirate, crawled out from the far side of the bed and patted at the curls of dust that clung to his filthy jacket. "So. What's yer thinkin'?"

Blowfish rolled up the chart. "I think if all goes as planned, ye greedy blackguard, ere long ye're going to be the proud owner of two pirate ships."

Gerry grinned an evil, black-toothed smile. "Aye, that's what I wanted to hear. Mark my words — before the fortnight is out, the Scottish Witch will be mine."

CHAPTER THIRTY-SEVEN

Cate woke in her bed, and stretched, long and luxuriously, her body humming with satisfaction for the first time in far too long...

Her eyes flew open. "Oh, God."

She was in her bed in the housekeeper's room. She had given in to her baser urges. She had slept with Taran. Repeatedly. And he had pleasured her until she was wild and irresponsible again. Irresponsible ... she looked at the bright daylight and sat straight up. "Oh, God. I'm late!"

"You're the housekeeper," Taran drawled. "You can be late if you like."

She looked toward the window.

Taran stood there.

She was reclining.

He was dressed in fresh clothing, his hair brushed, his face washed.

She was nude and disheveled.

He was a shadowed silhouette against the morning light.

She was revealed by the sun.

They had made love for hours on end, and she had told him ... she had confessed her love.

He had not made similar assurances.

Why would he? He had what he wanted without resorting to a lie.

She dragged the sheet around her and prepared to stand.

At once he crossed to her. Putting his hands on her shoulders, he pressed her back onto the pillows. As if they were continuing a conversation begun only a few moments ago, he looked into her eyes and said, "Did you think that I would let you search for the papers and the money while I cowered upstairs in our bedroom?"

"You told the maid that you would stay *here*!"

"It doesn't matter what I told the maid. I'm a pirate. I sink ships. I steal gold. I fight. I kill. And now, I wear a disguise. Do you think I'll quibble about telling a lie?"

No. She supposed not. "Leaving the room is dangerous. You grew up here. What if someone recognizes you?"

"Then he is a dead man."

Taran's cool ruthlessness took her breath away.

He asked, "Do you know what happened during those five years I was a prisoner on that ship?"

"You were not a prisoner." It was a protest formed of instinct and fear. He was *not* a prisoner.

"Not a prisoner? I would beg to differ. I was given to the ship's captain with a fistful of coins. Instructions were given that when the ship had left shore far behind, I would be dropped off the side and left to drown."

She writhed under his hands, wanting to escape his revelations.

"Actually, pirates force their prisoners to walk the plank. Do you know what that means?"

Wordless in horror, she shook her head.

"They blindfold you, put you on a narrow plank overhanging the water, and prod you to walk until you fall off. If you don't fall off, they wiggle the plank until you do."

"That is barbaric."

"When I sailed away on that pirate ship, I watched Cenorina disappear over the horizon and believed I had been sentenced to death. But I couldn't give up. I thought of you, and how you always went after what you wanted. I thought of your brother and how he told me every battle was won and lost in my head. I turned to the captain and said, 'You're a smart old devil. You got paid to take on a new sailor.'"

"Clever."

Taran smiled, a smile forged from remembered pain and ongoing anguish. "He knocked me clear across the deck. I hit my head on the fores'l mast so hard red stars exploded behind my eyes. Then he walked over, kicked me in the ribs, and said, 'You're not a sailor. You're not even a cabin boy, and I don't need another mouth to feed.' The other sailors gathered 'round and jeered, and I thought … I'd feared drowning. Now I thought I'd be beat to death, dead before I even hit the water. But I staggered to my feet. God bless him, Kiernan taught us hand to hand combat, and I used my skills that day. I stole a knife away from one of the sailors, and said,

'You're a pirate, so you can mark a bargain when you see it. I can fight better than any three of these men. Throw them overboard and give me their food.'"

"And he did?"

"He picked out three and I fought them."

"All of them?" Pictures formed and shifted in her mind. A bloody, wounded Taran fighting three hardened sailors, one after the other. But no. That was too easy. "At the same time?"

"I survived."

"Did you kill them?"

"Only one. The captain flung the others to the sharks." His chest rose and fell in hard breaths. "Do you know how men struggle when they see those fins swimming in the sea and know that, even before they can drown, they are going to be eaten alive?"

"Please."

"And scream. My God, they scream. When they go over the edge. When the sharks take their first bite. They scream a long time after you'd think they should be dead. The water turns red with blood."

Appalled, she asked, "You watched?"

"Captain Valentine held me over the edge and forced me to observe so I'd know what my fate would be when I displeased him. I fed the fishes with my vomit."

She covered her mouth to contain her own sickness.

He sat down on the bed, his hip nudging hers. "For five years after, I thought I would have been better off if I'd lost that fight."

"Don't say that."

"Of the twenty-seven sailors who manned the ship when I started, only eleven of them are alive. The rest were killed in battle or died of starvation or went crazy for lack of water or were whipped to death or were murdered for a whim. Captain Valentine was the meanest son of a bitch that ever ran a ship — and that's saying a great deal."

"Were *you* beaten?"

"Beaten? Yes." Standing, he stripped off his shirt and bared his back to her.

His skin was a mask of crisscrossed lines.

Last night, in the dark, she had run her fingers over those

marks, but she hadn't thought… she had refused to think what they could mean.

"Shot?" He turned, pulled down his waistband and showed her an old, white scar on his hip. "In battle." He pointed to the still-healing wound on his arm. "And by you, my darling wife. Stabbed?" He pointed at his ribs. "Once or twice. But those stab wounds were worth it. They won me a hammock, by God."

She swallowed. For a hammock? He was in a knife fight? "My poor, dear Taran."

He stared at her in astonishment, and laughed. "By the time I got the hammock, I'd been aboard two years. Do you know what it's like to sleep for two years on a damp wooden floor with no blanket? No, that hammock was worth every drop of blood." He changed from laughter to somber intensity. "I think you were asking if I was raped, though."

She didn't dare move. She didn't dare speak. The horror of his world held her frozen.

"That first night. I had knife wounds. Captain Valentine told the sailors they'd better not let me die, because I'd cost him three good fighters. Blowfish was there, God bless him. He doused me with salt water."

She winced, imagining the pain.

"He let me have a blanket. I had broken ribs. I found filthy rags and wrapped them around myself. I kept two knives, the one I'd fought with, and one I'd stolen off one of the sailors during the bout. I put one up my sleeve and one in my boot. Huddled into a corner and woke with every sound. Killed a man that night. No one tried again." He squinted as if looking back in time. "Four men. I killed four men before the sun rose. No one tried again."

"You didn't *kill* all of them." And she wished she didn't feel so warmly compassionate toward him.

"One way or another, I caused their deaths." He pulled on his shirt, tucked it into his trousers. "It was them or me. That's the way the ship ran."

Why hadn't she noticed the marks on his body?

She had, but only to note his masculine beauty. She'd deliberately shied away from examining him, from actually seeing him, because then she would have to deal with the issues of the past, and she didn't want to do that. She wanted only to move on as quickly as possible. Now he forced her to face the reality that, after he left her alone in Scotland, she *hadn't* suffered the worst fate. He had suffered torture. He had killed and almost been killed. Worst of all, he had been torn from his home, from his family.

She didn't want to know any of this, but it was far too late now.

His shirt tied at the throat, and before he could close it completely, she reached up and touched the scar at the base of his throat. "This ... this looks like you ran into the end of a burning stick." She looked closer. "It has the shape of a lion's head."

He stood preternaturally still, as if her touch wounded him. "Does it?"

She looked more closely. She could clearly see the lion's piercing eyes, the pouty cheeks, the catlike snout. "It's almost regal."

"Yes. The lion is the symbol of kingship," he said in a flat tone.

She didn't know what to think, how to respond to his refusal to acknowledge her compassion. "You got this in battle?"

"A sword fight. I lost."

"You fought in many battles?"

"Battles. Yes. We went to the Caribbean first, raided a few ports, boarded a few ships, ran away from the American Navy, the British Navy, and some angry natives. 'Stay alive to fight another day,' Captain Valentine said." Taran nodded. "That was the most useful advice he gave us. But I almost didn't make it around the Horn. A giant wave damned near washed me off the deck."

If that had happened, she would never have known the truth.

"Every day, every fight, every battle, I thanked Kiernan for all that he taught me. I'm alive today because of your brother."

"Well ... good. He would be proud. Of you."

"He would be glad that I lived. He would not be proud of my career as a pirate."

No. He would not. "How did you go from cabin boy to captain?"

"About two years in, some of the men attempted mutiny. I was still too cowed to help. Captain Valentine killed them all. It taught me a valuable lesson about meticulous plotting. My mutiny didn't fail." He waved a hand around. "You want me to stay in this room. No. I cannot. This room reminds me of the coffin."

"The coffin?"

"It was really more of a closet below decks, below the waterline in the center of the ship. No light, of course. Stout beams running across the ceiling, with finger holds gouged out. You found out what they were for fast enough." For the first time, she saw in his gaze a total stranger, a man who had lived in hell. Who still lived in hell.

She didn't want to know. She did *not* want to know. Yet at last he had opened himself to her, and so she had to ask, "What were they for?"

"When you failed to do your duty, or Captain Valentine disliked you, or if he wanted to instill fear into the crew for no reason, he had you thrown in the coffin. You always went down when they were using the bilge pumps, pumping the water out that leaked through the seams and the wood into the bottom level of the ship. Captain would stop the bilge pumps, and the water would creep up. There was no place to sit except on the floor, so your arse got wet. You could stand, and your feet got wet. When your arse was so damp the skin was puckered and your toenails were rotting off, you could dig your fingers into the holds on the beams and hold yourself above the water … until your arms gave out. Then you were back in the bilge, stinking, dirty, salt water sloshing around your ankles and filling your crack. Rats swimming past taking a bite. No food. And the worst mockery of all — no fresh water. Water everywhere, and nothing to drink. Some of the men went mad and drank the water. It takes a long time to die that way."

"How many times were you locked in the coffin?"

"Twice. The first time I drank the water. The second time … when I got out, the captain did. His salt water was cleaner than bilge, though. I fed him to the sharks."

CHAPTER THIRTY-EIGHT

Taran watched the emotions change on Cate's face, like the sunrise on the ocean, like clouds fleeing before the storm. Late last night, when lightning and desire had burned away pride and all that mattered existed in the slide of skin against skin, in hurried breath and heated blood, in possession and submission and the slow, sure knowledge that in this moment, they lived forever ... he had wrung a confession of love from her. Words whispered in the dark... *I love you. I have always loved you.*

But she had believed him to still be the boy she had known, and until this moment, she had not absorbed the reality of him. Now she knew what drove him — revenge — and she truly understood what he was capable of — theft, mutiny and cold-blooded murder.

He watched as she came to grips with the truth: last night's passion and this morning's confessions had bound her to a ruthless stranger. She was uncertain of him; of course she was. But he would not allow even the tiniest bit of fear to change her mind.

Leaning close, he slid his hand around the back of her neck and tilted her face to his. "I will never harm you. I will never betray you. My men trust me implicitly. I promise, you may trust me exactly so."

She lifted those glorious eyes to his and with a bite in her voice, she asked, "Are you saying you will give me the same level of loyalty and protection you give your men?"

There was a trap in the question. He could see it, but he couldn't avoid it. "Yes. But I will give you more."

"Intercourse."

"Passion."

"Aren't I just the most privileged member of your crew?" She sat up fast enough to make him jump back. She threw back the covers and rose, long-limbed, gloriously naked and brazen, and strode to the washbasin. He watched as she leaned over — at the sight of that rounded bottom, he wanted to groan — and washed, then visited the cupboard and gathered her clothes.

Fear him? No, she did not fear him. He was foolish to entertain such a development. But he did not know what she was thinking. Would he ever understand the maze of her mind? She had told him so much about her life after he left; he knew that fury, guilt and vengeance drove her. Yet every time he thought he understood her, she removed another mask and showed him a different face.

She was always and forever a mystery.

Cate dressed severely, in black, like every housekeeper he had ever met, and pinned her hair tightly, erasing the memories of the night's dissipations. Or so she might imagine.

"Caitlin," he said.

She jumped. "What?"

"Come here to the window."

She eyed him, then with a swish of skirts, she joined him.

He put his hands on her rigid shoulders. "Davies the usurper will soon arrive, and we are in position to discover his plans and overthrow him. He has his mercenaries. I have my sailors. There will be fighting. Men will be hurt. If plans go awry, or I am unable or otherwise occupied, there are two tasks I ask that you accomplish."

"In addition to finding Davies's papers and stealing them?" she asked tartly.

"In addition to that."

"Of course. What do you need me to do?"

Ah, that was his Caitlin. Give her a job, and she was steady as a rock. "See the beacon pinnacle? There will be kindling and oil there. When it's time, the beacon must be lit to bring my men in from the sea, and Harkness is too old."

"And too drunk."

"Not anymore."

She looked at Taran in surprise.

"Last night, I accomplished more than a wild loving."

In the aftermath of passion, she hadn't thought to ask him what he was doing in the middle of the night. "I will do everything in my power to make sure the beacon is lit. After all, the pirates are my salvation and my way home."

Taran tightened his fingers.

She smiled, pleased to have irritated him. "What other task do you want from me?"

"The queen must be freed from prison. She must not be held in that miserable fortress any longer, and you are the only one I know with the ingenuity and the lock breaking skills to free her."

Cate turned to him. "I will get the lady out."

He leaned his forehead to hers. "I am not happy about having you here performing tasks better suited to a warrior, but at the same time — I find comfort in the knowledge you are noble and trustworthy and the person I want by my side in these perilous times."

For a moment, her eyes softened. Then she straightened. In a voice brisk and dismissive, she said, "I shan't be back until this evening when my day's duties are over. I do not know what you intend to do this day — sleep, I suppose — but if you do come down, please take care to be seen only in costume."

He followed her to the door, waited until she had walked into the corridor before he said, "I do indeed intend to come down, and when I do, I will show you the room where Davies has hidden his papers." He shut the door. And he locked it.

Not that the lock would keep her out for long, but seeing the expression on her face kept him smiling as he settled down on the bed to catch up on his sleep.

CHAPTER THIRTY-NINE

In late afternoon, Taran at last made his appearance in the kitchen on Gracia's arm. "Mrs. Tamson, I found your husband groping around the entry, lookin' fer you." The girl sounded faintly accusatory, as if she thought Cate had deliberately neglected him. In fact Cate had taken time out of a busy first day to twice go upstairs to see if he was dressed and ready to come down. The first time she'd had to pick the lock. Both times he had been asleep on the bed, snoring loudly.

She had been tempted to put the pillow over his face and press. Only one thing had stopped her; he would wake, then she would be flat on her back, the pillow behind her head, and she had far too much to do today for *that*.

Cate rose and left her well-deserved tea unfinished. "Thank you, Gracia, for caring for my poor, wounded, blind warrior." She put enough tenderness and gratitude into her voice that Gracia was appeased.

Beneath the bandage, Taran managed to look soulful.

Fraud. She knew he'd heard the sarcasm beneath her words. And if he thought she was going to spend tonight fluffing the covers with him, he had another think coming. She had spent the day blinking the sleep from her eyes and, for reasons she did not want to remember, trying not to groan when she bent or knelt.

She took his hand and put it into the crook of her elbow. "Come. We'll go someplace where we can converse." She smiled at Gracia, at Signor Marino, and at his staff, then headed Taran up the stairs to the main level. Quietly, intensely, she said, "Where are the papers, you incredibly rude and disgustingly rested swine?"

"Third level, to the left. Third door on the right."

She led him according to his directions. "Today I have made a thorough inspection of all of the lower rooms and some of the second floor. But not so far as the third level. How did you discover this place?"

He said, "Last night, Harkness gave me a tour of the house, and when I asked where Davies kept his papers, he led me … to the place we are going. In the moonlight, Giraud seemed much the same as when last I visited. In the daylight, it must look quite different."

"The house is dirty and neglected, but with the proper care, it would be a magnificent home."

He must have heard the reserve in her voice, for he said, "But…?"

"It would seem Sir Davies directed his bile and his enmity toward the royal family by desecrating the king's study."

"Desecrating … how?"

"Portraits and drapes are slashed. Vile bodily functions were done in the fireplace. Cigars were extinguished on the rugs." The butchery had horrified her.

"Davies is a vulgar man of foul habits. He led the prince astray into terrible dissipations. I cannot be surprised that he reveals his inferiority by seeking to destroy all that is good in Cenorina."

"If ever I had harbored a doubt about your accusations, the king's study would have dispelled them."

"Did you harbor doubts?"

"No, for Throckmorton upheld you." That would teach him to ask such leading questions. "Here we are." She opened the third door on the right. She led him inside, and found herself in a small, windowless room with a desk, a chair, and a wall full of locked drawers.

He shut and locked the door behind them. He removed his mask and waved a hand toward the drawers. "Davies might be a swine, but he is an accomplished swine. Is this not a brilliant way to hide an important paper, in a drawer among a hundred?"

"Not as brilliant as bringing an accomplished lockpick to find and open the drawer."

"Did you compliment me?"

"No. Throckmorton hired me." *Take that, Taran Tamson.* She walked along the walls, looking closely at the locks. About once out of every ten drawers, she would stop and touch the brass, close her eyes, rub softly, shake her head, and move on. Finally she rubbed her thumb across the lock on a high drawer, slanted him a smile, got her tools out of her capacious reticule and rolled them out on the desk. She had to pull a chair over and stand on it, and when she was eye-level with the lock, she worked it briefly, so briefly his jaw dropped when she opened the drawer.

"It's never a good idea to thrust your hand sight-unseen into a drawer," she said. "People have been known to set traps as a final line of defense against an intruder." She stood on her tiptoes and peered into the drawer.

She gasped.

He dragged over a chair and stood on it. He looked into the drawer — and he laughed, briefly, nastily.

Money. Cash. Paper wealth drawn on the Bank of England. A whole drawer full of it. And a mouse trap set and ready for anyone unwary enough to reach without looking.

"That would have broken your fingers," he said.

She whispered, "Welcome to the Davies Bank."

Taran slid a hand down the side to gauge the depth of the bills, then toward the back. "This is not nearly enough. A drawer full is simply not enough."

She turned stunned eyes on him. "God's mercy, how much has he stolen?"

"Stolen, extorted … He sold valuable art. He confiscated properties. Cenorina was a wealthy country. He embezzled a nation's treasure."

She looked around at the wall of drawers.

He nodded. "Yes. Probably there is more here."

"As well as the papers you seek. Let me get back to work." Again she tested the locks on the drawers, opened another, this one containing a bag of coins of all denominations — and another trap. She opened an almost empty drawer, containing only one torn half of a bank note worth one hundred pound sterling.

"Not worth bothering to collect," he said.

Her mind whirled a confusion of thought, instincts, fears and amazement, but as she climbed on a chair to open the fourth drawer, she was proud to note her fingers were steady. The lock opened easily — it had been opened many times, more than the others. She looked inside; a short stack of papers rested flat in the drawer. "I may have found what we seek." Gingerly she touched the stash. When no trap snapped at her fingers, she grasped the papers, stepped down off the chair and placed the sheaf on the desk. "I suggest you proceed while keeping careful track of the order, to leave no trace of our activities here."

He left the papers where she had placed them, bent and read

the first greeting. "This is a letter from a Colonel of Portugal ... accepting Davies's invitation to come to Cenorina two months hence ... for the auction."

"What auction?"

"I am not sure." But she could tell by the tone of his voice that he had his suspicions. He lifted the first sheet and read the next. "Another letter from a comte of Normandy, telling Davies that the money was deposited in the account in Switzerland."

"The money for what?" She looked at the sheet in Taran's hand. "And shouldn't these be in Portuguese and French?"

"Compare the handwriting." Taran showed both letters to her. "To safeguard the contents, Davies copied them and destroyed the originals."

"An auction for what? Money for what?"

Taran read from another sheet of paper. "From a baron of Prussia, 'I have written a check for required payment of five thousand pounds to be included in the auction and added another thousand pounds for your good will and favor should there be any chance of a tie. The islands of Cenorina would be a precious acquisition for me and my aristocratic family who wish nothing more than use Cenorina's position to strike at England's domination and, as we discussed, infiltrate their government...'"

Her voice rose. "Davies is auctioning off Cenorina?"

"Sh." Taran put this hand over her mouth.

She pushed it away and spoke more quietly. "That's absurd. No one auctions off a *country!*"

"Davies was bold and did what no one thought possible — he captured the queen, dispatched the prince and took control of the whole country. He has taken from it all wealth, and now he sells the land and the location to the highest bidder, to those men and women who seek power or land or, in the case of this baron, want Cenorina for its position close to England. England's enemies have long wished to be able to easily strike at her. Why do you think this has Throckmorton's attention?"

"So Throckmorton *knew?*" She fought to keep her tone level, but — no one sold a whole country. No one bought a whole country. This was madness!

Taran continued to leaf through the papers. He was calm, almost preternaturally so, as if now that his worst suspicions were confirmed, he could proceed with his plan. "Throckmorton did not suppose this situation at all. He paid no heed until I suggested this could be Davies's plan."

"Now you know, and you have time to stop him."

"Yes."

"You'll tell Throckmorton at once."

"No."

"But —"

Taran looked up, and his eyes were cold, bleak, steady. "If I do that, Throckmorton will intercept Davies and I will not have my chance for revenge. The man destroyed my family, my pride, my life. He kept me from my wife." Taran caressed her cheek with the back of his fingers. "I will not give Davies to Throckmorton first."

"I understand." She did. He was going to fight a battle. She … no longer had a function here. "Do as you like. My job is done, and now I will leave for another mission."

CHAPTER FORTY

Taran could not believe the gall of the woman. Cate was *his wife.* She belonged at his side, in his bed, at his right hand, and now — she talked about leaving?

Absolutely not.

"We didn't expect to discover Sir Davies's plan quite so quickly." She looked up, her eyes shocked. "But now that we have, I must go."

"You can't go. You're my excuse to live in Giraud."

"You're resourceful. You could hide in town, wait for your ship to arrive."

Damn her and her logic. "You have no way to go."

"I could go on the ferry."

He flailed for a moment, then seized on a random idea. "You've forgotten the crown jewels."

"What?"

"The crown jewels. They are here somewhere." Actually, not a bad random idea. "You are the housekeeper. You can find them."

Her green eyes narrowed on him. "That wasn't part of the agreement."

"No." He moved toward her, stalking her with temptation. "But think of it. The queen's tiara is gold crusted with diamonds, and at the top above the forehead is an emerald to rival the color of your eyes. It is the stormstone, named for the color of the sky when a winter-borne wind brings roiling clouds of green and gray." *Cate would be so beautiful with that crown on her head.* "The king's crown matches the queen's in splendor, but rather than an emerald, it holds a sapphire almost purple in color. It is the seastone, named after the color of the ocean when the storm is past and the sun shines on the still restless water. Cenorina's position in the Atlantic has brought us wealth and treasures, crown jewels without match, greater than any royal jewels in the world."

"Now no one knows where they are?"

"They are gone. Gone." It broke his heart.

She was intensely practical. "Sir Davies sold them."

"Davies used to gaze at the crown jewels with such greed, and it is said that after the king's funeral, he was seen modeling the king's crown before the mirror. He would not sell something that gave him such gratification." The memory burned in Taran's gut. He had been there. He had seen it. He had struck Davies a blow across the face that sent the crown flying, and hotly told him he was not worthy to shine the dead king's shoes.

For the first time, he had seen bitter resentment and rancor in Davies's eyes. But arrogant young prince that he was, he hadn't cared. Never had it crossed his mind Davies would dare ... what he had dared.

With a pragmatism that matched hers, he added, "Anyway, none of the stones have appeared on the world market."

"Stones can be cut."

"The color cannot be replicated."

"So you want me to find the crown jewels while I wait to leave Cenorina?"

"What else do you have to do?"

She gave a crack of laughter. "I know this palace is not really my responsibility, but it obviously once was a much beloved home. It calls to me to restore its spirit, and if I must remain, I would rather act as housekeeper than thief."

So she loved Giraud. He almost hugged her. But she had her arms folded across her chest, as if she knew she had too easily given up her intention to leave. And if he wanted to keep her from setting sail on a raft back to England, it would not do to smile at her pride. "That is a noble decision," he said.

"Yes." She stood on the chair and one by one, re-locked the drawers. She descended, placed her hands on her waist, and looked disapprovingly at him. "This morning you spoke of revolution. You asked that I somehow light the beacon. I agreed. You asked that I rescue the queen. I agreed. Now you want me to find the crown jewels. Is there no end to the chores you require of me?"

"I require you to warm my bed every night."

"It is my bed. Every night. A man who demands so much of a woman would be wise to remember and respect her boundaries."

"I hold you in respect above all women."

"What a compliment." She walked to the door. "Don your disguise. I must go. The servants dally at their tasks if I do not harry them."

"They will learn."

"Indeed." Clearly she had no doubt she could form them to her will. "While I do promise to watch for the crown jewels' hiding place, I fear Sir Davies will have taken them to some secret location and buried them deep."

"Digging is too much like labor for him. Perhaps he forced one of my people to dig the hole, and buried the fellow with the jewels."

"Horrible!" She turned the doorknob, then stopped. "One of *your* people?"

He cursed his own royal sense of possession. "I am Cenorinian."

Cate looked at him oddly, deeply. "You are risking everything for this venture, aren't you?"

"I am."

"But should I find the crown jewels and Sir Davies's fortune, your gain will be immeasurable."

"Greed is perhaps what drives me. And perhaps you, too? If you should find the jewels, you'll wish to pick out a piece or two."

She snapped, "If I find the jewels, I'll take my share without asking."

God, he loved her spirit. "You have a bit of a pirate in you." He stalked her. "As my wife, the jewels you recover are yours."

"Because if I find the jewels, I must want to steal them? I think not, sir! They are the queen's."

"The queen will be generous."

Cate's eyes stripped him to the bone. "You, sir, are a mixture of wicked pirate and noble prince. I can't decide which is real."

They were skating dangerously close to the truth.

Was that a bad thing? She might be — would be — furious to discover he was the prince, but it would explain much. Furthermore, she seemed unlikely to pull a pistol and shoot him again. Not here. Not now. "Why can't they both be real?"

She straightened her collar, her cuffs, her apron. "I have met the pirate. He slept in my bed last night, and was every bit as wicked as a woman might hope. But never have I truly met the prince." With a swish of her skirt, she was gone.

CHAPTER FORTY-ONE

Taran stared at the closed door. With Cate's departure, a remnant of good sense returned to him.

What was he thinking?

He had convinced Cate to stay here, in this place where treachery lurked in every shadow, where old resentments shimmered like oil in a heated frying pan and a battle waited to be fought.

She had been ready to leave, and he had coerced, coaxed, *bribed* her until she agreed to stay. Here. In Cenorina. In deep and grave danger. What kind of man was he, who kept his wife by his side rather than sending her to …

Well. He could tell himself he had convinced her to stay because she wanted to go on another mission for Throckmorton. She would be in danger there, too. But it would take time for Throckmorton to find her another assignment, and by that time, Taran would have won his battle and fetched her back to Cenorina, or he would be dead and she would be a wealthy widow.

He couldn't lie to himself. He wanted her with him because every morning he wanted to wake in her bed, look into her eyes and know she loved him, no matter how unworthy he was of such devotion. Every night, he wanted to lie down with her and make love to her while lightning flashed in exultation of her pleasure, and of his.

She gave him strength.

He had meant what he said that morning — he trusted her competence … and he needed her at his side.

Yet he should have let her go.

What was he thinking?

What was she thinking?

Cate strode down the corridor toward the gallery, taking long strides, trying to work off her frustration without flinging herself on the floor, screaming and kicking.

But she had spent the night in ecstasy, with no sleep.

She had worked all day to establish her authority over a

sometimes lazy and always wary staff.

She had discovered the very papers she had been sent here to find.

She should be triumphant. She should be preparing to go back to England and on to another mission.

Instead, she had somehow allowed Taran to persuade her to stay and search for the crown jewels.

She didn't care about the crown jewels.

She didn't care about Cenorina's poverty.

She didn't care whether these surly, standoffish servants were freed from their yoke of oppression.

So why had she agreed?

Because she did care — about Cenorina, its people, its queen, its struggle to overthrow Sir Davies, and most of all, about Taran.

About Taran! Her lousy, rotten, conveniently disappearing, tortured, broken, sometimes charming and always good-in-bed husband.

Why did she care? When had all her righteous anger turned to this maudlin puddle of love?

She wanted to think it was merely the pure physical passion.

But she knew better. This morning, his story of how he had survived those years on the pirate ship had changed forever her opinion of his character. He wasn't merely Taran, boyish betrayer of Caitlin and the wedding vows they had taken. He was a man, a leader: dishonorable, without pity or compassion. He didn't even love her.

She couldn't lie to herself. It was her fault she remained in this situation. Her fault. Her fault. *Her fault.*

She descended the wide stairs in a froth of rage, but proud of her maturity. Why, she was hardly stomping at all.

What a fool she was to linger in this place. To imagine a life with Taran. To want to help him in his quest.

She looked around the entry: worn, dusty, musty, in need of more care than the current staff could or would give it.

Foolish? She wasn't foolish. She was an *idiot.*

She should leave now. Right now! Out that front door. That front door … that was wide open.

She walked toward it, intending to vent a little of her fury with a good kick. She was halfway across the entry when she heard a mouse-like squeak in the library, then a young woman's frightened voice pleading softly for ... something.

Cate did not like the sound of that. She did not like it at all. She moved purposefully in that direction, looked into the library — and there was Gracia, struggling in the arms of a big, burly, unshaven beast of a soldier while another soldier wandered through the room, whisky glass in hand, examining the knick-knacks.

Gracia's brother, Gillies, was stretched unconscious on the floor.

Mercenaries. No doubt about it. Cate faced a situation, one that required immediate action.

She welcomed the challenge.

As Blowfish had taught her, she surveyed the room for weapons. A five-foot tall, sculpted iron candle stand stood beside one of the leather chairs.

Yes. That would do nicely.

She indulged her temper by slamming both library doors all the way open.

The soldiers looked up in surprise, then insolent as only big, brutal men could be, they looked her over.

Cate saw the tears in Gracia's eyes, and in a crisp and authoritarian tone, she said, "Unhand that young woman."

The one holding the whisky rudely laughed.

The one holding Gracia sneered. "Wait your turn, my pretty."

"I am not *your pretty.*" Cate advanced into the room, intent on establishing her authority. She planted her feet beside the candle stand and said, "I am the housekeeper at Giraud, I'm responsible for the staff, and I do not allow thieves and rapists to roam where they will."

The one with the whisky examined a jeweled dagger on a stand, then slipped it in his pocket.

In an even sharper tone, she snapped, "Put that back!"

He jumped.

The one who groped Gracia pushed the girl aside.

Gracia stumbled and tugged her bodice together.

That *bastard.* Cate flushed with an even sharper jab of rage.

Gracia fled toward her brother. She knelt beside him and

leaned her head on his chest, gave a sob, and grabbed him under his arms. Grunting with the effort, she began dragging him toward the wall, away from the confrontation.

The bully of a mercenary headed toward Cate, head down, scowl in place.

She pulled the candle free from the point that held it in place. Taking the candle stand in both hands, she pointed it like a lance at the advancing soldier. She narrowed her eyes, gave vent to her rage with a deep-throated roar, and charged.

Blowfish had instructed her that surprise was the best attack.

The soldier *was* surprised. At the sight of the incensed Valkyrie, he backpedaled, his arms flailing.

She shouted again, and chased him in a straight line toward the broad window. She hit him. The point stuck in his leather jerkin. His shoulders hit the glass. He fell backward. Dozens of diamond shaped panes of glass exploded out behind him.

He shrieked.

He flailed.

He fell ten feet to the ground.

He landed with a satisfying thump that forcibly drove the air from his body. He gasped. And moaned.

She mused, "I feel better already. " She faced the thief of a solder. She pointed her makeshift spear at him.

He looked into her furious eyes. He pulled the pilfered jeweled dagger out of his pocket, flung it aside, sprinted out of the room and the open front door.

She paced after him, absolutely livid that one man thought he could take advantage of her serving girl, and that the other thought he could steal from *her,* from the place where she was *in charge.* When she got to the outer door, she lifted her foot and kicked it shut. She stood, breathing hard, wanting to do more, cause more mayhem, fight more battles... Then she heard the soft, sobbing intake of a frightened girl's breath. Cate turned and saw Gracia crouched over her brother's prone body.

Abruptly, Cate banished temper with the brisk efficiency she had learned in a hard and lonely school. Placing the candle stand in its place, she went to Gracia's side. She knelt beside the girl and her brother, pressed her fingers to Gillies's neck, and felt the strong heartbeat. She nodded. "He's alive."

"Thank God." Gracia buried her face in her hands and cried.

He stirred, opened his eyes, looked around in alarm, tried to raise himself onto his elbow.

Cate pressed her hand to his shoulder. "Stay down." Lifting her voice, she called, "I need help!"

At once, a dozen servants surrounded her.

"Take him to a bed," she said.

Two footmen helped him to his feet, and with his arms around their shoulders, walked him toward the stairs.

Cate embraced Gracia. "How are you? Did that beast hurt you?"

The girl was trembling, but she shook her head *no*. "He tried... he wanted to... but you stopped him." Gracia pressed her face into Cate's shoulder.

"I promise you, while I am in charge, such an outrage will never occur again." She hugged Gracia tighter and rose to her feet, lifting the girl with her. She swept her gaze over the assembled staff. "Who were these men? What were they doing here?"

The men and women glanced at each other, then Harkness stepped forward. "Volker and Stein. The mercenaries who man the fortress protecting the harbor come once a week to collect their meals. Cook provides them, but each time, they grow more bold. We knew something like this would happen. That's why we work in groups. But we didn't realize ... we didn't know ... they weren't supposed to come until tomorrow."

"Were you going to do nothing?" Cate demanded in outrage.

Zelle straightened her shoulders. "I was making a plan to distract them, but you ... you came and—"

Harkness said, "We were going to save the two young people, but not impetuously!"

Cate's ire calmed. "I see."

The huge iron knocker hit the front door with a boom that shook the frame.

Everyone jumped.

Cate put Gracia away from her. "They have returned. And this time, they will be angry."

CHAPTER FORTY-TWO

Cate strode toward the door. Belated caution was overtaking her rage. But she'd started this. She had to finish it.

Behind her, Signor Marino said, "Wait!" He stood at the end of the corridor leading to the kitchen, holding a large wooden box. The scullery maid and the rotisserie boy stood behind him, holding smaller boxes. "I have their meals." He walked toward her. "And I have your back."

She looked around.

The staff — her staff — was gathering close to her, unified by her actions.

She nodded at them, acknowledging their support, and indicated to the footmen that they should open both doors.

They did.

With blood streaming from the cuts on his face and hands, his left arm twisted at an awkward angle, and his eyes red-rimmed and ferocious, Volker was a fearsome sight. He waved his well-honed dagger around at the assembled servants, then extended his right arm and pointed at her. "Bitch. I'm going to kill you." His voice sounded deeper than before, and with his hairy, hulking shoulders and his small black eyes, he resembled a rabid bear.

Stein held his sword and his pistol at the ready, and he grinned nastily, brave enough with his friend at his side.

"No, you will not." She looked him in the eyes and spoke with the full, firm strength of her authority. "We have the food for you to take back to the fortress." She stepped back to allow Signor Marino to walk out and place the box on the porch.

"You're not going to pretend this" — Volker gestured at his arm — "didn't happen. You're not going to get away with this."

"Indeed not," Cate said crisply. "This outrage on your part most definitely did happen, and because of your actions, you are banned from the house. In the future, you will come to the kitchen door and wait outside while Cook assembles your meals."

Volker stepped forward, knife waggling up and down as he indicated her figure. "I don't take orders from a woman."

Five men, Giraud's gardeners, walked around the side of the

house, holding rakes and pitchforks, pointed at the two mercenaries.

Stein eased back a step. He cleared his throat. "Volker."

Volker looked at the gardeners. "What do you think you're doing?" He slid his knife into his belt, pulled his pistol and pointed it in a half-circle. "Do you want to eat lead?"

From directly behind Cate, Taran said, "You have a single shot." Taking Cate's arm, he moved her to stand beside him ... and a little behind. "Choose your targets carefully, for that will be the last shot you fire — ever." The menace in his voice raised the hair on the back of Cate's neck.

Taran. Taran was here.

Cate found herself frightened for them both, and at the same time ... so relieved. Even blindfolded, she had no doubt he was a match for Volker.

"Now a blind man is threatening me?" Volker laughed harshly.

"A blind *soldier*." Cate tried to get around Taran. He stopped her with his hand on her arm. "Do mercenaries not know how to figure the odds against them? It seems that in your business, that would be a useful trait."

Volker was hurt and in an ugly mood. He would have attacked.

But Stein caught his coattails. "Captain will not be happy that we're fighting."

Volker shook him off, looked around at the hostile faces. "We'll come back with our whole troop."

"And leave the fortress at the mouth of the harbor unguarded? That seems unwise," Taran said.

Volker glared. He pointed his meaty finger at Cate. "Sooner or later, I'll make you sorry." Turning, he stomped toward the wagon parked on the road. "Get the food loaded, you lazy bastards!"

Signor Marino himself put them in the back of the wagon.

The two soldiers got in and drove away.

The servants stood in small, tense groups.

Harkness broke the silence. *"Will* the whole troop come back to get their revenge?"

"It depends on what tales the soldiers tell." Taran's voice was dry. "I doubt that they will admit the housekeeper, gardeners, footmen and maids defeated them."

The servants relaxed and chuckled.

"And a blind man," Cate added, with an irony only Taran understood. She linked her arm through his and faced the house staff. "Thank you for your support in this matter. Gracia, go with Zelle to the kitchen for a cup of hot tea, and some bread and jam. The rest of you — you know your duties. Go now and fulfill them."

With an alacrity she had not yet witnessed in them, they went to work.

Putting her fingers to her forehead, Cate gave a shaky sigh of relief. "That came out well."

Taran gave a huff of laughter. "It's not over. Be careful, my love, never to step out of the house alone."

"I am careful. But I could not allow that brute to … to rape that child."

"Of course you could not. You could never allow such an injustice to occur." Taran brushed the tendrils of hair off her neck. "I sense your foolhardy actions have won the servants' loyalty."

Foolhardy. Well. She could hardly argue that. "I believe so, yes."

"When I heard the ruckus, I almost pulled off my blindfold and charged to your rescue."

"That would have appeared to have been quite the miraculous cure, indeed, and one fatal to our mission. A good thing I didn't need you." But she *did* need him. She needed him now that the crisis was over, now that the rage that had bolstered her courage had seeped away. She needed him to hold her and whisper that she was brave and clever and he loved her.

But she couldn't say any of that; no one wanted to believe a woman who was six feet tall with a temper to match should suffer moments when she feared and trembled. And he didn't love her. He simply did not.

Yet her casual tone did not seem to fool him. His hand tightened on the back of her neck; he brought her into his embrace and held her while she took deep breaths, until fear subsided and she was herself once more.

In a dry tone, he said, "I didn't see what happened, but I heard the servants. You shoved one mercenary through the window?"

"With a candle stand."

"And chased the other out the door?"

"Yes."

His arms tightened. "My God, Cate…"

She heard the worry in his voice. "You have to trust to Blowfish's training."

"I do. But the faster I can finish Davies…" He shook her a little, and put her away from him. "Listen. After you left that room upstairs—"

"The bank?"

"Yes. After you left the Davies bank … I started thinking." Grim lines bracketed his mouth. "You should go."

"Go?" What did he mean?

"Back to England."

She should. She should go. That was exactly what she should do. She had told herself that staying on Cenorina was imprudent. But if she went, he would be alone to light the beacon, to free the queen, to fight the battle.

In her estimation, he had already been on his own for far too long. She could not bear to leave him. How many more scars would he gather ere the end of their mission?

So she laughed derisively. "You aren't getting out of your promise that easily."

"My promise?"

"You promised me the crown jewels."

The set of his mouth eased, and he sounded relieved. "So I did."

"Then I will stay until I find them."

CHAPTER FORTY-THREE

Taran leaned against the wall in the shadowy corridor outside their bedchamber, waiting for Cate to come out of the bath. When she did, dressed in her nightgown and rubbing her hair with a towel, he said, "I'm going out tonight."

She jumped, removed the towel, and snapped, "Do you find pleasure in startling me?"

His voice warmed. "It is not startling you in which I find pleasure."

A single candle lit the space, yet he saw the flash of her eyes and the enigmatic smile. Damn her, she had always been an accomplished flirt.

"What are you doing tonight? Chasing after another woman?" She didn't sound unduly worried.

"After last night in your arms, I can scarce stand, much less seek another's company."

"Humph." But she sounded pleased. She moved closer. "Why are you telling me this?"

"We are equal partners in this fight for freedom. Are we not?" He took her fingers and kissed them. "I go into Arianna to seek allies in the upcoming battle. I will be back at dawn."

"Very well. Take care not to wake me when you return." But she squeezed his hand.

He lingered. "A good wife would stay awake to welcome me."

With acerbic amusement, she said, "A canny wife, when faced with a husband who sneaks in after dark, greets him with a frying pan applied to the forehead."

God, how he loved sparring with her. When he was somber and serious with the weight of his duties, he had only to see her, to speak with her, and he felt his burden lift. "Perhaps you should sleep then."

"I intend to." Then, to his surprise, she kissed his cheek. "Be careful."

"I will."

"Be smart."

"I am. No one would recognize me as your poor blind husband. Few would recognize me from my previous years in Cenorina. And I watch and I listen. I have come too far to jeopardize this operation now."

"Humph," she said again. She gave him a shove and watched as he ran down the stairs.

Giraud's great outer door squeaked as he opened it, and he was out in the moonlight, striding toward the stables. He entered cautiously. His father's horses had been the king's pride and joy, but Davies had been an appalling rider, weak in the saddle, cruel to the horses, and Taran feared what he would find here.

Yet the stable smelled of clean hay and leather, and he could hear the faint nicker of a horsely greeting. He moved down the line of stalls, all of them empty, until he came to the stall that had held his father's favorite. He could see the outline of a horse … was it Narragansett? He moved to open the shutter, to let the moonlight in.

Without warning, strong fingers grasped his wrist. A knife's point touched his ribs. In a voice low and menacing, a man said, "Identify yourself."

At once Taran knew who it was. Only Wahkan, the man who had brought Narragansett from America, could have taken him by surprise. "I'll let in the light. Then you will know me."

The hand on his wrist loosened. He heard the smooth sound of the knife being sheathed. "No need for that, my prince. Faces can lie, but your voice tells the tale."

Taran flung open the shutter. He faced Wahkan.

In the moonlight, the two men surveyed each other, each looking for changes. Of course, there were many.

Taran well knew what he looked like. And Wahkan … well, Wahkan had aged. He had always been short and wiry, with a reddish-brown face weathered by sun and dark brown eyes that had once squinted across an American desert. He had always been proud, a native of the Americas, a man who loved and tamed horses. Now, clearly, he was old, distrustful, ready to fight or flee, whatever it took to survive a difficult life.

Taran's relief in knowing the man he trusted remained here mixed with his irritation at seeing the empty stalls. "When my father was alive, you stocked this stable with horses of impeccable breeding."

"Davies was going to sell them. So I released them."

The answer sent a surge of hope through Taran. "The horses are wild? They are ... free?"

A ghost of a smile crossed Wahkan's lips. "Wild and free. Yes, my liege, a fine herd of horses roams this island. If you have returned to stay, I will capture them and tame them again."

With deadly seriousness, Taran said, "I am here to take back my kingdom."

"That is the answer I have waited to hear." Wahkan gestured to the horse behind them. "Your father's gelding remains my companion."

Taran faced the stall. It *was* Narragansett, thin and old, but with a proud tilt to his head and uncanny intelligence in his eyes. "Why did he stay?"

"He's a smart one. Smarter than any horse I've ever worked. He wouldn't leave. I would chase him away." Wahkan flapped his hands in dismissal. "He would return. Then Davies realized that the one horse that remained in the stable was the king's horse. The chance to plant his skinny ignoble ass on the royal steed was a temptation Davies could not resist. He demanded to ride him."

Taran didn't know whether to laugh or groan. "Davies could barely ride the stable's oldest nag. Did he even make it into the saddle?"

In the moonlight, Wahkan's eyes glinted with merriment. "Yes! The horse let Sir Davies ride. Let him! Narragansett sought revenge on the man he blamed for the loss of his companions and his master."

"What did Narragansett *do?*" Taran hung on the reply.

"He was the perfect gentleman ... in the corral. When Davies believed he had mastered the horse, he demanded I open the gate so he could ride like a lord over his new lands." Wahkan's laughter got louder, less restrained. "Narragansett walked out of the corral. He trotted onto the road. He cantered toward the mountains. I swear the horse knew I was watching, because at the last bend of the road, he turned and looked at me. In irritation, Davies lashed him."

Wrath took the place of Taran's amusement. "He dared!"

"No, my prince. Listen. Do you remember how Narragansett could run, smooth and swift as the wind across the prairie whence he was born?"

"I do."

"This chief of all horses stretched out his neck, and he ran."

"Did Davies land flat on his back?"

"Indeed not. Afraid for his life, Davies hung on."

"For how long?"

The old man spread his hands and shrugged. "Three days later, he came limping back. In a fury, he tried to whip me. That did not turn out so well for him."

Taran could not believe Davies's audacity. Wahkan was slight, but he wielded a knife with a skill that had taught more than one stable boy respect.

"Then he told me to get out, that he would not give me a referral, and he damned me to hell."

"Yet you stayed."

"I did. Here in hell. The stables were abandoned. I ate with the kitchen staff. I slept in the hayloft. Davies was gone — is gone — much of the time, and when he is here, he ignores his servants. He has never realized I remained, or if he did, he didn't dare confront me."

"That is what I believe," Taran said.

Wahkan leaned on the gate of Narragansett's stable. "A year later to the day, Narragansett returned with your mother's mare as a companion."

"You cared for them." Taran reached a hand into Narragansett's stall.

The horse nipped at him.

Taran snatched his hand back.

"He doesn't allow familiarities," Wahkan informed him. "He hasn't allowed anyone on his back since your father died."

"Of course not." Taran examined his own fingers, then glanced around. "I need a horse I can ride. I need one now."

Like a ghost, Wahkan disappeared into the depths of the stable and came back leading a beautiful, sleek, long-legged mare, saddled and ready to ride. "Take Hanna. She is older now, but she will carry you far and fast."

Taran stroked her nose, spoke softly in her ear, then put his foot into the stirrup and swung his leg over her back. He settled into the saddle with the ease of a born rider. "Tonight, I thought to visit the noble families who cling to their lands."

"The Trujillos. The Martins. The Vincents. Most of the families will welcome you. But first" — Wahkan put his hand on Hanna's neck — "first, go to Arianna. Go to the cathedral. The rebels, they meet there. You must win them over before you can take your kingdom back — and keep it."

CHAPTER FORTY-FOUR

The moon lit Arianna's ragged thatch roofs and illuminated broken windows. The schoolhouse was empty of desks, the window shutters torn off. If anything, Cate had spared him in her description of Arianna. Misery ruled the city. In the twelve years he'd been absent, exiled in Scotland and then sailing the world on a pirate ship, his people had gone from prosperity and pride to poverty and humiliation. They were beaten down, set apart from the world, without hope. Taran had failed them, but he would not fail them now.

As he neared the cathedral, he heard a low murmur, like the wind in the pines. But no, it was voices. Wahkan had directed him well. Taran made his way to the back of the once-proud building. He tied Hanna to a post, then went to the side door. It yielded to his touch. As he made his way inside, his boots crunched in dirt and desolation.

From the inner sanctuary, a woman's low voice predominated. But several men argued with her. Who were these people? What were they doing?

He lifted the latch and opened the door a crack.

The woman was speaking. "If we rush Giraud, we win nothing. Sir Davies is not there. The servants are not our enemies."

"But we can take the house," one of the men said. "We can confiscate the firearms."

Two of the other men shouted their agreement.

"Shh," the woman said. "Do you want the mercenaries to catch us and set fire to the cathedral?"

No one replied.

"If we take the firearms too soon," she said, "the mercenaries will fight us. They will win, and Davies will still be in control. We must wait until he returns, and take *him.*"

The man wasn't ready to give up. "We need to move now!"

"Your impatience will get us all killed." Her voice was low and intense. "We have waited this long. We can wait another day or week or month, whatever it takes so we can rule our own lands."

The people of Arianna were planning to overthrow Davies.

Good. Taran wouldn't have to rouse them. But if they moved too quickly, they could interfere with his operation and get themselves killed. He needed to recruit them, to convince them that his cause and theirs were one and the same. Surely that would not be difficult.

He pushed on the door, opening it slowly. He looked; two torches lit the old church. Footmen and serving girls, mothers and children, farmers and fishermen, sat on overturned pews or stood with arms crossed or with pitchforks and knives in their hands. Zelle stood on the altar, straight and proud, directing the men with the force of her personality.

Zelle. Of course.

It appeared he was not the only one who hid leadership beneath a humble mien.

He stepped boldly into the room.

The good people of Arianna turned on him with a ferocity that left him in no doubt of their determination.

He held his hands up to show that they were empty. "I heard you," he said. "Let me help you."

The blades pointed at him inched closer.

Zelle examined him with a frown. "You are a spy."

"A spy would have turned you over to the mercenaries," Taran said.

She watched him as if trying to place him. "Why would we let a stranger help us?"

For the first time in many years, he declared himself by his full name. "Because I am Antonio Raul Edward Kane. I am your crown prince."

Profound silence met his announcement. In the faces turned to him, he read disbelief and outright fury.

"Antonio? Prince Antonio?" Zelle radiated hostility as she walked down the steps toward him. "Why should we care?"

He had imagined this scene many times; his people would recognize him, welcome him, take him on their shoulders and shout forth their joy.

Another dream crushed by the burden of reality. "I can lead you. I can help you."

"We have leaders," one of the men said. "Leaders who won't betray us."

One of the women with a pitchfork poked it toward his

belly. "Where have you been while we were suffering? Off living on the continent, drinking wine and chasing women. We laugh at your leadership. We spit on your help."

Taran flinched away from the sharp points.

"We're not going to have a king," Zelle said. "We are going to take over the country and run it ourselves."

"No, you're not." The many pointy objects moved suddenly closer. Taran lifted his hands higher. "I promise you, I was not off drinking wine and chasing women. I was the captain of a pirate ship, learning the ways of the world so I would be an able king. I earned a fortune so I could come back to Cenorina and right the injustices done to you. I wish — I intend — to make things right."

"A pirate ship." Zelle snorted. "Prove it."

Everyone laughed derisively.

As he had done with Cate, he stripped off his shirt and turned his back to them.

The jeering stopped. The silence was profound.

"I bear the scars." He faced them again. "Do you think I don't know what I owe to the people of Cenorina? I am responsible for my mother's imprisonment, my own exile, and your suffering. Listen to me. Please, just listen to me. I have a plan…"

As he rode back to Giraud, he laughed softly. He had, he realized, bribed his people with the promise of his fortune *and* Sir Davies's fortune, explained international politics as controlled by Britain, the most dominant country in the world, and coaxed them with promises of his own good behavior.

At one point, the men had wanted to hold him prisoner. Only Zelle had refused, holding him in her hostile gaze. "Let him go," she'd said. "He's no threat to us."

But he was. And she knew it, for unspoken was the knowledge that he led fighting men, pirates, and perhaps, just perhaps, he could take control of Cenorina with or without their cooperation.

Yet he respected their autonomy — to successfully return this country to prosperity, he did indeed need their cooperation — so he asked them to consult with each other, and in three nights, he promised to return to hear the consensus.

He hoped the consensus wasn't death to the crown prince.

Dawn lightened the eastern sky as he started down the long road to Giraud. He returned Hanna to Wahkan's care, then hurried into the house and up the stairs, aware that the staff would be arriving soon. Zelle would be on the lookout for the prince, wondering where he hid, and he needed give the sharp-eyed, resentful female no cause for suspicion.

In the bedchamber he shared with Cate, he discarded his clothing, stacked it in a neat pile at the base of the closet, and climbed into bed. He snuggled close to Cate's back and kissed the nape of her neck.

She murmured a sleepy rejection.

He kissed her ear.

She jabbed him with her elbow.

He chuckled and kissed her neck again.

She sighed loudly, then turned over and slid her arms around his waist. Her body was sleep-warmed and supple. Her slurred voice declared, "You are a villain to wake me now."

"Go back to sleep and I will hold you."

"Too late. I am already awake." She kissed his mouth.

God. "One kiss from you, my unknowing princess, and I am no longer a brigand without country or family. You make me a man on the brink of the most glorious adventure of my life — an hour spent in your arms."

She wrapped her arms around his neck and smiled into his face. "If you can make it last an hour, I will happily declare you a god."

CHAPTER FORTY-FIVE

A red sky heralded the new day aboard the Scottish Witch, and Blowfish stood on the fo'c'sle, a length of rope in his hand, and randomly lashed the four young sailors that cowered on their knees before him. "Mutiny? Mutiny? What in hell's hot blazes did ye think ye could accomplish with such a caper? Did ye really imagine ye could steal the Scottish Witch from the Cap'n hisself? And he would let ye do it?"

One of the lads said, "Cap'n's not here and we thought..."

"Ye thought ye could pull the wool over *me* eyes? Ye boys are dumber than dung beetles! Did ye not think an old dog like me could smell a mutiny ten leagues away? And did ye not think the Cap'n knew what ye were up to even before he left on his mission?" Blowfish saw their incredulous exchange of glances. "Yes, he did. Ye were doomed before ye started. Do ye know what we do to mutineers on the Scottish Witch? Do ye?"

One of the lads finally spoke in wavering tones. "Hang us?"

Blowfish lashed him. "Hangin's too good fer the likes of ye! Why bother to tie a noose when we can sit on a coil of rope, lift us a bottle of rum, and watch ye walk the plank?"

Still on his knees, one of the lads slumped into a faint, his head smartly striking the deck.

Blowfish kicked his drooping body. "Brave mutineers ye are! But one of ye could yet save yer lousy life. Tell us the instigator behind this asinine plan."

The one in a faint revived.

The other boys didn't hesitate. They babbled, they begged, they shouted a single name. "Lilbit!" "Lilbit!" "Lilbit!" "Lilbit!"

Blowfish nodded. As if he didn't know. He seated himself on the steps, leaned his arm on his knee, and examined their eager, hopeful, stupid faces. "Where is yer leader now?"

The lads glanced at each other and shook their heads.

Maccus stepped forward. "Blowfish, one of the longboats is missing."

"Missing? Missing? *Missing?*" Blowfish's voice grew louder with every repetition. "Do ye mean that young villain stole a longboat, abandoned his pitiful crew to pain and death to save *his own life?* Is that what ye're sayin'?"

Maccus looked solemn. "Aye, Blowfish, so it appears."

"Not death!" One of the boy-mutineers looked around wildly. "I told you who the leader was. You can't kill me now!"

The seasoned crew burst into raucous laughter.

All except Dead Bob. He didn't laugh. Instead, he put his foot on the lad's neck, leaned over and asked, "Are ye telling the man against whom ye staged a mutiny what he can or cannot do?"

The boy looked into Dead Bob's bony, cadaverous face and began to blubber.

One by one, all the boys began to blubber.

The seasoned crew exchanged annoyed glances and exasperated sighs.

Quicksilver said, "Blowfish, I have an idea."

Blowfish lashed desultorily at the boys. "We should swab the deck with their wet, whiny faces?"

"These lads are young," Quicksilver said. "They've learned their lesson."

That made the boys cease their crying. "Yes!" "Yes!" "Yes!" "We have!"

"Are ye then suggesting clemency for mutineers?" Blowfish slashed at the air so hard his makeshift whip whistled. "All they'll do is grow into more villainy!"

"We wouldn't!" they chorused.

"Clemency is not quite the term I would use for what I have in mind." Quicksilver smirked. "I say banish them from the Scottish Witch, with its comfortable hammocks and its ration of rum and its kindly captain."

"That might merit some consideration." Blowfish stroked his chin as if the suggestion surprised him. Which it did not. "We could sell 'em and make some money off their scrawny, ungrateful hides."

"Sell us?" the boys wailed.

"Where do ye think?" Blowfish asked. "Sell them to a pagan whorehouse?"

"Sell them to a Spanish pig farmer!" Quicksilver suggested.

"Sell them to an English hide tanner!" Dove shouted.

Each occupation they suggested echoed the workhouse jobs the boys had held before they joined the pirate ship — terrible occupations — and they cringed and begged, crawling on their knees toward the seasoned sailors until Blowfish was sick to death of them.

"Enough!" he roared. "We'll sell 'em to a sea captain. A pirate captain."

"A harsh captain so they will suffer fear and pain," Quicksilver said.

"Aye," Blowfish said. "Of course we'll warn the captain so he knows to take measures to keep 'em in line. Whipping every other night. Half rations every other day."

Maccus considered the boys. "At night, he can chain them in the brig. Horrible fate if the ship is attacked and sinks, but it's no more than they deserve."

"It's settled, then." Blowfish kept an eye on the eastern sky. Morning light was growing. "We'll sell 'em to that scum o' the earth, Gerry Williams."

The one boy fainted again.

Blowfish did not care. "A pirate's life they will lead, and every night, they will weep for the memory of the good times they enjoyed aboard the Scottish Witch. Get 'em out of me sight. Take 'em below and shackle 'em beneath the water line."

Two sailors grabbed the boys and dragged them away, begging and crying.

Quicksilver, Maccus and Blowfish watched them go.

"Dumb whoresons," Maccus commented, and headed below to settle the inevitable fights.

"Aye." Blowfish walked to the port side railing. He pulled out his spyglass and looked to the southern horizon.

There it was, Gerry Williams's ship, waiting, as they were, off Cenorina's shore. Waiting for the beacon to light.

"Those lads are getting better than they deserve," Quicksilver said.

"After Cap'n's years at sea, he's soft on the new crew." Blowfish indicated his disapproval with another flip of the rope. "Makes me happy to know Gerry Williams will watch 'em close and make their lives miserable."

The two weathered sailors stared at that speck of a ship on the horizon.

Quicksilver sighed. "I wish the action would start."

"Aye. The waitin' is always the hardest part." Blowfish rubbed the spray of salt off the handrail. "What do ye plan on doing when the battle is won? Are ye taking the cash and sailin' with the ship, or are ye stayin' on Cenorina?"

"I'm taking the cash. You?"

"I've seen too many battles. I'm stayin' on Cenorina. I want a bit o' land and a ripe Cenorinian woman to fix me meals and tickle me cockstand."

Quicksilver nodded. "Sounds good."

"What bothers me now is — did Lilbit sabotage us before he left? And where did Lilbit row that longboat?"

The two men walked to starboard. They didn't need the spyglass to see Trueno Ridge where the beacon would be lit. "Cenorina."

"Lilbit's been playin' us fer fools," Blowfish said.

"He's a murderer and a mutineer, ripe for hanging."

"All I got to say is — Cap'n had better watch his own back, and the Caitlin's."

"Amen."

CHAPTER FORTY-SIX

The night Taran returned to the cathedral in Arianna both enlightened him and made him aware once more of the treacherous game he played.

The men of the town agreed to listen to his plan and, after heated discussion, voted to follow him.

Zelle refused to trust him, demanded to know where he hid, and when he refused to tell her, stormed out, leaving embarrassed and angry men in her wake. And Taran knew that was dangerous. Zelle was canny and determined; she had schemed to free Cenorina and she did not appreciate being swept aside for a prince who had abandoned them — so it seemed — so many years before. If she reminded enough people of his failures, and undermined his authority as a warrior, she could cause trouble … especially among the women.

Yet for the most part, the women observed him and listened, and Taran knew he must live up to their expectations lest they lead an insurrection against their husbands, brothers, fathers and friends. Cate had taught him that — women had power, and they knew how to use it.

Taran discussed what weapons they could gather and use, observed their fighting skills, appointed captains and discussed strategies. He asked for someone willing to run his errands; Leon, a healthy young blacksmith, eagerly volunteered.

An element of certainty began to temper Taran's impatience. He was — they were — going to win this fight.

On previous nights, Taran had ranged far and wide over the island, finding allies — and enemies. Of the Cenorinian nobility who were left on the island, some welcomed him with relief, some with joy. One family, intent on starting its own fiefdom, first scorned him, then tried to lock him away. He had fought his way free from them and ridden through a hail of bullets toward Giraud. He was not hit, but he did sustain cuts and bruises and faced yet another moment where he realized this task he had undertaken would not be nearly as swashbuckling, adventurous or fun as leading a pirate ship.

Cate had used cold compresses and bandages to put him back together, and said, "At least I am now sure you're not leaving me for the arms of another woman. Or if you are — I'd suggest finding a different lover."

He laughed and tumbled her on the bed, and held her and kissed her, and thought that, even as he faced down rebel aristocrats and ungrateful citizens, he had never been so happy.

"Sir Davies, we're coming into Port Arianna."

Captain John Dunbar's voice brought Maddox out of the hammock and onto his feet, sword drawn, before he was fully awake.

Captain Dunbar thrust out his hands as if to ward off the point of the sword with a gesture. "Sir! You asked that I wake you before we docked!"

"Oh. Yes." Maddox shakily sheathed the sword. "Thank you. You startled me. I'll come on deck immediately."

Captain Dunbar looked at him oddly, murmured, "Quite so, sir," and with his characteristic limp, he disappeared out the narrow door.

Maddox stood in the ferry's dark cubbyhole that made up the captain's quarters, trying to calm his rapid heartbeat, to loosen the noose of panic that tightened around his neck.

He hadn't slept well since that awful moment when Mrs. Cabera had declared Throckmorton hunted him. All these years, Maddox had fooled the great Throckmorton, made a mockery of Throckmorton's secret spy network. Now ... now Maddox had come back to Cenorina quickly, but in stealth. During the journey, he wore hats and turbans, cloaks and ill-fitting coats. He spoke in accents and used false names. He had shaken any tail Throckmorton might have put on him. He was sure of it. Yet still he looked over his shoulder, afraid to see someone skulking in the shadows.

Reaching under the hammock, he pulled out two bags. Each contained clothes, shoes, a few souvenirs to prove he had been vacationing in foreign lands, and secret compartments with all the signatures he had collected and all the bribes he had accepted. He carried the bags on deck and took a breath of fresh sea air.

He was not confined in prison. He was not facing an English court. He was still Sir Maddox Davies, coming home to the islands he ruled.

The town was a silhouette against the pre-dawn sky, but he could see the bowl that cupped the town of Arianna, lights in the fortress where his mercenaries held reign, and here and there a lantern moving through the streets. He wondered what people were doing out at this hour; prostitutes looking for business, he supposed, although who had the money to pay them, he did not know. The Cenorinians had nothing, because *he* had taken care to clear out their pocketbooks and reduce them to destitution.

Why not? When at first he had gained power, he had been prepared to be magnanimous, a king they could adore. But they had worshipped their dead king and blamed him for their pissant little prince's dissipations, and after a year of wiping their spittle off his shoes, he had resolved to strip them of dignity, of wealth, of pride, of the most basic human requirements.

Now they were ragged and starving. Now they didn't have enough energy or spirit to spit on his shoes. It served the proud beggars right, and he hoped they all died miserable deaths under the reign of … of whoever won the bidding to control the islands.

During his flight back to Cenorina, he had taken the time to do one thing — send letters to the top five bidders calling for their final offers. As soon as he had the results, and a guarantee the money had been deposited in his account, he would be gone from here, and he would never again fear poverty or cold or … Throckmorton.

Maddox Davies, bastard grandson of an English lord, would live in luxury, surrounded by furs and warmth and women, until the end of his days.

Dawn was breaking. For the second night in a row, Taran was in consultation with the men and women in Arianna, explaining in detail how the beacons would light, his sailors would land (he thought it best not to call them pirates too often) and their arrival would draw out and overwhelm the mercenaries. He drew pictures in the dirt, then when he heard the bell that signified the arrival of the ferry, he erased the images with a sweep of his hand, tipped his hat, and again promised them a better life. Riding to the overlook opposite the fortress, he observed the ferry pull in and tie up.

The gangplank lowered.

Leon met the captain and spoke to him.

The captain looked around, as if seeking something or someone, then handed over a letter.

Taran knew what that meant; correspondence from Throckmorton.

Then he forgot Throckmorton, forgot everything except the sight of a single well-dressed gentleman who strode onto the dock carrying a bag in each hand.

Taran recognized him; his old tutor, Maddox Davies.

Taran had been expecting him, watching for him, yet still ice spilled through his veins.

From this distance, Davies's appearance was unchanged. He was tall, thin, long-armed, graceful, the kind of man able to wield a sword with enough finesse to defeat a defiant young prince — and he had. Taran would never forget the battle in his father's study. When he returned from his exile in Scotland, he had thought to teach Davies a lesson for daring to depose the Cenorinian royal family. Instead, the lesson had been taught to him by a master swordsman. When his own sword had been sliced in half, then removed from his grip with a single, skillful flip of the wrist, he had refused to beg Davies's pardon. He had refused to admit defeat.

His punishment had been brutal. Four mercenaries had held him down while Davies heated the king's seal over the candle flame and used it to brand the skin over Taran's heart.

Taran touched the place where the scar puckered his skin. The humiliation still burned.

This time, when they fought the results would be different.

Taran went to meet Leon and accept the letter from his hand. Then, turning Hanna toward Giraud, he galloped ahead of the oncoming confrontation.

Cate woke to the press of a hand to her shoulder. She flipped over and faced a grim-faced Taran.

"Davies is on his way here. You had best prepare. He'll want to meet you." Taran took his hand away. "And you will want to introduce him to me, your crippled, blinded husband."

She sat up and pushed the hair out of her eyes. "Do you think it necessary that you meet him immediately? Or at all?"

For the first time since they had made love on the stairway,

Taran seemed not to notice the thrust of her breasts against the thin material of her nightgown and the glow of her hair in the morning light.

"Davies returns because Throckmorton made him realize the dangerous game he is playing." Taran showed her a letter. "Throckmorton has written to say Davies will receive correspondence from the men who wish to buy Cenorina. Throckmorton wishes to know who the final players are, for he believes they will leave their homes to make their way here, and he intends to dissuade them from their purpose."

"Dissuade them?"

"Capture them. Imprison them." Taran smiled coldly. "It is to our advantage to wait for those letters to arrive before we make our move, since those letters will contain information about —"

"Payments to Sir Davies," she said.

"Exactly."

"More money with which to restore Cenorina."

Now he smiled in truth.

For the first time, she understood his intention. "You're *not* doing this to make a fortune. You intend to assume the role of governor of Cenorina!"

"Not quite that. Not the governor. When we have more time, I will explain … exactly …" He fumbled as he tried to find the words.

"What?"

Far below in the courtyard, she heard the clatter of hooves.

Taran went to the window. "Hail, the conquering hero … and his mercenary guard."

She joined him, and studied the gentleman who rode up in the back of the carriage that had brought Taran and Cate to Giraud. "He is handsome, for an older man. His clothing is elegant and his boots are polished."

"He is a tyrant," Taran said.

"Yes, he moves in a manner that clearly bespeaks his ownership and his contempt for those who serve him." She craned her head to see which mercenary drove the carriage. She didn't recognize him; he was not Volker or Stein. Good. That, at least, would make this day easier. "Sir Davies wears a long sword at his side. Can he use that weapon?"

"Very effectively." Taran spoke without inflection. "He is also skilled with pistols. He never takes any chances — to ensure his safety, he keeps a mercenary in the house with him at all times."

Taran always seemed to have information far beyond her expectations. "How do you know that?"

"I asked the servants."

A simple answer. Too simple? Or was she being overly suspicious?

"If we can wait for five days after the delivery of the letters, England will send a ship to enforce my power. Without them, I cannot guarantee we will win." Taran paced away to the cupboard and pulled out the stack of clothing he wore as a disguise. "So — until we can defeat Sir Davies, we must convince him we are what we say we are — a subservient woman who earns the living for her unfortunate husband."

"As you wish." She gathered her undergarments, her largest petticoat and her most severe black dress. "We will face Sir Maddox Davies as a couple."

"We will defeat him as a couple."

Startled, she faced Taran and saw his purposeful stance, and for the first time she realized rehearsal was over.

The curtain had gone up.

The final act had begun.

CHAPTER FORTY-SEVEN

Cate and Taran moved down the wide sweep of stairs. He walked with his cane hung on his elbow, his short sword at his side and his hand on her arm, and she knew them to be perfectly garbed for their parts. To anyone who studied them, she was the austere, yet brave housekeeper who cared assiduously for her husband, a man broken in battle and left without vision and with a withered arm.

While she had dressed, Taran used clay to perform some magic on his face. She hadn't viewed the finished product, she only knew he had tied his blindfold with great care, covering more of his upper face than usual. He had hidden his knife deep beneath several layers of clothing and he had slid his pistol into a leather fold in his boot.

Now, as they reached the entry, she saw that the servants were nowhere to be seen. Except for Zelle, who stood half-hidden in the drapes, observing Taran as if she found him as distasteful as a beetle baked into the bread.

What had occurred to make the woman watch him with such abhorrence? And why was her dislike mixed with such avid satisfaction?

Cate gaze met Zelle's; Zelle silently slid into the shadows of the library.

Cate recognized a troublemaker when she saw one; she would have to keep an eye on Zelle. As if she didn't have an ample amount of work and worry already!

"What's happening?" Taran murmured.

In a low voice, she said, "The young mercenary is armed with a thick oak club, and he…"

"And he's stationed before the closed door of the king's study, guarding Davies's privacy." Taran's voice was equally low and quite calm.

She stopped and faced Taran. "You can see through the blindfold!"

"No."

"Then *how* did you know where Sir Maddox Davies would

be?"

"I asked the servants."

"More and more I doubt you."

"Your mistrust breaks my heart."

Obviously, Taran was lying, at least about his heartbreak, but if he could remain calm in this crisis, so could she. With Taran on her arm, she walked to the tall, brawny young man. Ruthlessly and deliberately, she fixed him with her sternest gaze. "You are?"

He had been trained to respond to authority, and he snapped to attention. "Sergeant Fortunato Gouveia."

"Well, Fortunato" — she ignored his title quite purposefully — "*I* am Mrs. Tamson, the housekeeper hired by Sir Maddox Davies, and I wish to meet him."

Fortunato's brown eyes got wide. He swallowed. "I recognize you from Volker's description."

No wonder he looked frightened.

Fortunato continued, "But I cannot let you in. Sir Davies does not wish to be disturbed."

"I have waited several weeks to report to Sir Davies. I will do so now." She lifted her fist, prepared to rap on the door.

Fortunato reached to stop her.

She stared him down.

He stepped back. "Knock if you dare, but be warned — Sir Davies is respected and feared among all who meet him."

Ah. A warning. One she would not heed.

To Taran, she said, "Come, husband." Once again, she fixed Fortunato with her gaze. "Announce me," she said.

He straightened his shoulders, lifted his beardless chin, opened the door and marched inside. "Sir Maddox Davies, the new housekeeper requests to see you."

"Does she? Then show her in."

The cool, flat tones sent a shiver down Cate's spine.

Taran's hand tightened on her elbow, and he murmured, "You're doing well. Keep it up."

Almost at once, her nerves subsided. Taran had complimented her, and she couldn't help it — she felt flattered. No wonder he was the pirate cap'n, when a single assurance from him could give her confidence.

She led him in, and told him, "Sit in this chair and rest until

I've spoken with Sir Davies."

To her surprise, Taran played to her. Sounding as meek as any shrew-bit husband, he said, "Thank you. The pain is bad this day, and I am exhausted." He groped for a chair and seated himself, head bent, ankles and knees together like a schoolboy in a dunce cap.

Once again Cate marveled at his ability to don a disguise. He not only wore the clothing, he assumed the attitude.

She patted his shoulder, turned and strode toward the desk.

Behind her, she heard Fortunato softly shut the door.

As always, the size and opulence of the study dazzled her. Once upon a time, the painted walls had been marbled in shades of amber; the drapes had been swirls of blue. Her feet sank into the depths of a plush oriental rug, and an antique vase and two Chinese figurines still decorated the alcoves, proving that once this room had a showcase of exceptional beauty.

Yet more impressive were the spaces where works of art had once stood and stood no more, where royal portraits hung in shreds and tiles had been knocked from the fireplace mosaic. The chamber smelled of excrement, of cloying tobacco and burnt wood, and a smoking cigar overhung the surface of the imposing desk, its glowing tip backing toward the polished surface. All around the desk's rosewood edges, burned spots glared like blackened eyes. A marble ashtray sat atop the jumble of letters, ignored and used as a paperweight by the handsome and elegant Sir Maddox Davies.

Cate came to a halt before his desk.

Davies ignored her as steadfastly as he ignored the progress of his burning cigar.

His hands were pale, his fingers long. He lolled in his fine leather chair and scribbled on a sheet before him. He wore a black velvet smoking jacket with a white, shiny, starched shirt and a black cravat held in place with a jeweled stick pin. His countenance was not displeasing; a little bony, perhaps, and his ears stuck out, but most women would call him comely. Looking at him here, surrounded by the broken shards of royal ceremony, he seemed a lesser man, ineffectual, easily overcome. She knew that was nothing more than a guise he donned, for both Taran and Throckmorton had warned her he was vicious.

But he might also underestimate her because of her gender.

In fact, she knew he would. Too bad for him that she was more than she seemed.

Folding her hands before her, she examined the painting behind him; a stylized portrait of Sir Maddox Davies, posed like a monarch among his hounds and his horses, with a glistening and beautiful Giraud as a backdrop. At one time, he must have intended to become Cenorina's monarch; she wondered what had changed his mind. Probably he had imagined only the pleasures of reigning and none of the work.

Davies dipped his pen repeatedly into the ink well. He frowned fiercely, and once even glared out the window before continuing to write in large, looped handwriting.

The cigar's fire inched closer to the wood.

The sideboard behind him did not match the desk; yet it was a fine modern piece with drawers on one side and a long cabinet door on the other. Before Sir Davies had arrived, she had searched inside; he kept slippers, handkerchiefs and a blanket in the cabinet as well as some revolting personal items in the drawers.

Before he arrived, the surface of the sideboard had been dusty, but pristine. Now papers littered the top; her fingertips itched to examine them, to see what correspondence he had carried back with him. She wondered if he would be careless with his information, or if he left those papers out deliberately, hoping to lure in a spy. If he was so artful, he would use the information therein to disseminate duplicity and half-truths.

She was a straightforward woman; all these possible layers of deception made her head spin. Perhaps Taran was right; perhaps the game of espionage was an ill-fit for her. Yet she had no other way to avenge the death of her brother, and no other future that she could see. And so she would learn…

CHAPTER FORTY-EIGHT

At last Sir Davies finished his letter, shook sand over the paper, folded it and sealed it with wax. Only then did he stick his hand out to Cate. Yet he did not look at her, and he offered the hand not in friendship, but in demand. "What have you brought me?"

With her best imitation of naïveté, she took his ink-stained hand and shook it firmly. When he looked up to glare, she smiled. "I am the new housekeeper, Mrs. Tamson."

He jerked his hand away. He looked her up and down. Apparently nothing he observed in her lean figure gave him pleasure, for he looked away without interest.

As Taran had told her, men who were intimidated by her height would pretend disinterest when it was their own masculinity at fault.

He said, "A letter, Tamson. You must have brought a letter, and I wish to have it — now."

She didn't allow her smile to diminish as she reached into her reticule for her letter of recommendation, and passed it to him. "This is from Lady Bucknell, the director of The Distinguished Academy of Governesses."

He weighed the letter in his hand. "What does it say?"

"Do you wish me to read it to you?" He was not illiterate, she knew.

"I assumed you had already read the letter." The cigar began its slow burn of the rosewood, and the stink of tobacco, bee's wax and finish curled into the air. "Don't women always know clever ways to open mail that is not theirs?"

At first Cate didn't understand.

Then she did.

He had insinuated — no, he had *said* that because of her gender, she was untrustworthy and inclined to open mail that was not addressed to her.

The ill-mannered *bastard.*

She wanted to blast him with the full wrath of her formidable rage, yet here, in this land, she was not the sister of a Scottish laird. Instead, she was a stern, hard-working woman who supported a blind husband. A single, indrawn breath gave her control over her temper. With deliberate artlessness, she said, "I don't read other people's correspondence, but if you have trouble deciphering the writing, I'm sure I can assist you."

His chin snapped up. "You're insolent."

She managed to look amazed. "No, Davies."

"You will call me Sir Davies!"

"When you call me Mrs. Tamson!" Before he could draw breath, she continued, "You're foreign, and everyone knows foreigners are ignorant."

Color rose in blotches on his forehead. "I am not ignorant, nor am I foreign. I am English, born and raised in England."

"That's different." He was a traitor to his own country. *Every day, every hour, she cursed these people who hated everything and everyone in the British Isles, who envied the Empire, who sought to harm her and hers.* The black rage that had brought her so far from home writhed in her belly, but she presented a knowledgeable façade. "So perhaps you do read."

"Exceptionally well. However, you, *Mrs. Tamson*, are not English."

"No, *Sir Davies*. I am Scottish."

He leaned back in his leather chair, picked up his cigar, took a puff and smiled for the first time. "Scottish … I am the son of a British lord."

"I am the *legitimate* daughter of a Scottish laird."

Sir Davies's smile disappeared. "You brought a husband, Mrs. Tamson."

"That's right, Sir Davies."

"Housekeepers don't have husbands, Mrs. Tamson, especially not husbands who are blind and require care."

"This housekeeper does, Sir Davies."

"I do not take in charity cases."

She placed her fists on the desk, leaned forward, looked him in the eyes, and took a terrible gamble. "If Mr. Tamson is a problem, please say so, and we will swiftly pack and catch the ferry to England before it leaves. As you know, housekeepers trained at The Distinguished Academy of Governesses are in great demand, and I can secure another position in England, and for a better salary."

He leaned forward and glared back at her. "If you are displeased with the salary, Mrs. Tamson, why did you take this position so far from home?"

She straightened. "My husband's wounds will benefit from sunshine and warm air, and those are not readily available in the British Isles. They are here."

As Sir Davies began to replace the cigar on the desk's bare wood, she could contain herself no longer. Snatching up the ashtray, she thrust it at him.

He glared at her. He ground the cigar out on a piece of untouched wood. "Bring your husband here."

She was proud of herself. She did *not* call Sir Davies a swine. Instead, she placed the ashtray by the cigar, returned to Taran's side, and said, "Come, dearest, Sir Maddox Davies wishes to meet you."

Taran groped for his stick, knocked it over, waited while she retrieved it and hung the crook on his elbow. He stood, put his hand on her arm, and together they walked to the desk.

To Cate's surprise, Sir Davies was pleasant and faintly smiling."Mr. Tamson, how good to make your acquaintance." He rose to meet them. "You appear to be a youthful man. How did you come to such ill-fortune?"

Taran stopped and bowed. "Sir, I was a soldier in Her Majesty's army."

Sir Davies extended his hand.

Taran continued, "I was stationed in India where one of the rajahs gained access to our munitions and —"

With a startling and vicious intent, Sir Davies seized the sword from Taran's side.

"What are you doing?" Taran's hands reached out. "That's mine!"

Sir Davies pointed the point at Taran's throat. "What does a blind man need with a sword?" Tearing the blindfold off Taran's face, he flung it aside.

Cate cried out in fear and shock.

Taran staggered forward.

She caught his arm, and for one shocking moment, she saw his eyes, sealed shut as if by a searing explosion, his nose, crooked and covered with scars, his hair, burned back from his forehead. She didn't know how he had done it, but he had created a disturbing, misshapen countenance.

A convincing countenance, for Sir Davies stepped back in revulsion. "I had to see what was under that wrap. A man of my position and wealth cannot be too careful."

My God. The man was a monster.

And Taran was an incredible actor. He clutched his forehead. He sank to his knees, whimpering.

She didn't have to stage a performance. She was truly appalled by Sir Davies's actions. "Sir, that was reprehensible!" Kneeling beside Taran, she caught up the blindfold and tied it back over his eyes.

None too soon, for Sir Davies's heartless unmasking had shoved some of the clay off Taran's temple, and if she didn't cover him soon, his disguise would fail.

As she helped Taran pull himself together, she told Sir Davies, "You could have hurt him badly. Hurt him more. Shame on you!" Sir Davies was as vile as Taran claimed. More important, Sir Davies stole Taran's sword and used it as extension of his arm. She extended her hand. "Return the sword to him at once!"

Sir Davies examined the hilt. The blade whistled as he slashed the air. "It is a good sword. What is he doing with it?"

Taran's voice quavered. "After the explosion, it was given to me by my colonel in honor of my sacrifice."

"He cannot have this sword," Sir Davies said. "He might hurt himself with it."

Cate put her hand under Taran's arm and helped him to his feet. "Sir Davies, you are talking about my husband as if he is invisible. Not only is he here, but you are attempting to steal from him. From him!" She indicated Taran, who was doing a credible job of trembling and drooping. "Now, give me that sword!"

Sir Davies clearly wavered.

"Very well." She crossed her arms over her chest. "We are leaving."

"I suppose it doesn't matter. He is helpless. I will give in to your demand." With a smooth motion, Sir Davies slid the sword into the scabbard at Taran's side.

She cast a glance at his chair. His belt hung on the back of his chair; his sword hung in the belt, the hilt was both beautiful and worn by much practice, and she could clearly see the man was an expert.

"Such a fuss," Sir Davies said. "I didn't hurt him, and even if I did, he's used to pain and unpleasant to view."

Taran whimpered again.

Sir Davies continued, "Get him out of my sight, then fetch me something to eat. I'm hungry from my journey."

Fixing Sir Davies with a stern eye, she said, "Sir Davies, I am the housekeeper, not the cook or the chambermaid. If you wish for a meal, I will pass the message onto Signor Marino, our cook, and he will tend to the matter. But let us make one thing clear — it is my intention to return Giraud to the proper appearance for a royal palace. I hope you appreciate my intention to restore this room, and all the rooms, to their former elegance."

Sir Davies considered her, and for the first time, she spied the sharp intelligence that had brought him from prince's tutor to the position of Cenorina's governor. "I admire your frankness, Mrs. Tamson. Please do keep busy. Observing you will be my greatest pleasure."

That sounded like a threat, to her employment, or to herself.

She looked longingly at the sideboard behind the desk. It would appear her investigations there would have to wait.

CHAPTER FORTY-NINE

Ten days passed in stately progression.

The first week, Cate hired more staff, ordered more of Giraud's main floor and major rooms cleaned, and surreptitiously searched for the crown jewels.

The first week, Taran stayed close to Cate, night and day.

The first week, Sir Davies spent hours closed in the king's study or closeted in his room on the third floor fondling his money — so Taran claimed — and filled his evenings with drinking and brooding. While he proved his indifference to all the servants by treating them as if they were invisible, Cate frequently felt the skin on the back of her neck crawl, and when she looked around, she would discover him avidly observing her.

He had said he would watch her; he meant it. But for what purpose? Was he one of the lechers who preyed on his female employees? Or did he suspect her of working for Throckmorton?

Both options put her teeth on edge, for she never, ever got the chance to investigate the king's study with an eye to finding the crown jewels.

On day eight, Cate grew tired. She was tired of working to the point of exhaustion — and she was more and more easily exhausted. She was tired of Sir Davies and his less-than-stealthy scrutiny. Most of all, she was tired of Taran trailing after her like a lost puppy all day, and lecturing her on how to safely handle Sir Davies all night. Listening to him harp on Sir Davies's evil nature was *not* how she wanted to spend her few remaining private hours with Taran.

If she had to describe her mood, she would call it irritated.

But justly irritated, damn it.

She snapped at the staff, asked Sir Davies who he had watched when she was not present, and in full view of every maid who adored him — and that was all of them — she told Taran to go away, to leave her alone, to set sail to distant shores.

The staff looked at her reproachfully.

Her outburst seemed to satisfy Sir Davies in some perverse way. He became less avid in his observations and more relaxed in his approach. In fact, he seemed interested in a different way, a way that made her want to knock that knowing smirk off his face. Did he dare imagine that because she was married to a man who suffered from blindness and infirmity, that she would willingly cuckold that husband? Even if Taran was truly so disabled, his attitude insulted *her*.

Taran ... ah, Taran. He seemed as alert as ever, yet he did allow her time to herself.

In the daylight, he remained close, spending hours in the kitchen being coddled by the scullery maids or sitting out in the sun as Cate supervised the cleaning of the carpets and the airing of the linens.

After midnight, when she was secure in their room, he rode out and was gone for hours. His behavior had the effect of making Cate even more irritated. Didn't he understand she needed him to hold her through the dark hours when imagination flared, when she remembered how her brother had been murdered and she feared for Taran's life in the upcoming battle? A battle that would, if all went on schedule, be delivered by pirates to Cenorina within the week?

No. Of course he didn't. Men were fools, all.

CHAPTER FIFTY

On the morning of day ten, Taran waited at the harbor overlook. Hanna moved impatiently beneath him. Not far away, he knew his pirates waited for his signal to come sailing in and launch the fight that would free Cenorina. He hoped Blowfish could handle any problems that the young sailors might present; inactivity wore on them, and the crew would be restless.

Restless ... hell, he was restless, on edge, anticipating the battle ahead. His newly commissioned Cenorinian soldiers were as ready as they could be in such a short time. His sailors would do their duty. Yet Davies's mercenaries could not be discounted. They were well-trained, well-armed, and held the high ground. From here, he could see the black eyes that marked the barrels of the cannons. One heavy iron ball shot accurately could knock down the town, or sink a ship.

Yet more than anything, Taran feared Maddox Davies himself. In their previous conflict, he had proved himself a brilliant, ruthless tactician — and devious. So devious. As more and more people found out Taran had returned, his chances of surprise diminished.

In the days ahead, timing was everything.

Then he heard the sound he had been anticipating — the bell that announced the ferry. It was the sound of hope for all Cenorina.

His heartbeat sped up. Surely today he would at last take into his possession the letters that would give him control over all of Davies's fortune. There it could be used to bring Cenorina back from the brink. He watched as the ship made its slow progress through the channel and into dock. One of Taran's new recruits met Captain John Dunbar and spoke with him. A leather bag and a tall, narrow Italian alabaster vase were delivered into Leon's hands, then Leon strode away, up the road toward Giraud.

Taran rode to the grove near the crest of the hill.

Leon arrived and presented the goods.

Taran searched the bag, an excellent piece of Italian workmanship, and found nothing but two sealed letters.

He opened one. It was a demand from the Italian merchant

for payment for the vase. Taran snorted. "Good luck with collecting, my man."

The other letter was addressed in a child's painful handwriting and sealed with nothing but a few splattered blobs of wax. He opened that, too, and scanned the first lurching lines: *To Maddox Davies, greetings from one who would know you better. I know things you would like. You would like what I know. I can sell you these things you would like…*

Not from a child, then, or at least he hoped not. From a woman, an almost illiterate prostitute who knew of Davies's licentious proclivities and sought to sell him her services.

These letters were not the ones Taran sought. He wanted correspondence from foreign sources of wealth and power, and he did not believe Davies had lingered at Giraud for a bag, a bill, a proposition, and an alabaster work of art. The letters Taran sought had to be here somewhere. They had to.

"Maybe in the vase, sir," Leo said.

"Yes." Taran took the vase into the sun and peered into the interior. He could see a shape inside. But he couldn't shake it out, nor could he slide his broad hand into the narrow neck. Damn. Perhaps Cate could retrieve them.

So he handed the merchandise back to Leon with instructions to give it to the new housekeeper.

Then, in broad daylight, he rode back to Giraud. He was taking a chance, yet he had to return. Cate had said nothing about Davies's attention to her, and because of Taran's blindfold, he had not witnessed any misconduct. But he had heard the tone in Davies's voice when he said, "Observing you will help pass the time." Taran knew the challenge his tall, self-assured wife must present to Davies, and he knew, too, the fact she had a husband was no deterrent to the man.

Who better to know Davies's propensities than Taran? Taran supposed he should be grateful that Davies had seized power, kidnapped him and shipped him away on a pirate ship. He *should* be, but he wasn't. Who could be grateful for years of anguish and pain? Yet he knew that if Davies had kept him close, he would have become a dissolute brute, a man who reveled in brandy, in opium, in the dissipations of the flesh…

He resolved that on the day he revealed himself to Davies,

Taran would thank him for his malice. Sarcastically, of course. But he would thank him.

Taran pulled his hat low over his eyes, pulled his collar up around his chin, and boldly rode into the stable, sure a confident mien would play better than skulking. Wahkan greeted him and when Taran had dismounted, led Hanna to her stall. She greeted five new horses along the way. Young horses, with good bloodlines.

"I have culled them from the king's herd and am breaking them to my hand," Wahkan told him. "When you take your place as ruler of Cenorina, you will need more than two aging horses."

"One of which I cannot ride." Taran got a carrot and offered it to Narragansett.

Narragansett snapped his teeth close to Taran's fingers.

Taran dropped the carrot.

Narragansett picked it up off the floor and chewed it noisily.

Wahkan's dry laughter sounded like the rattling of autumn leaves. "He is the king's horse, and you have not yet proved yourself worthy to be the king."

Taran placed his hand on Wahkan's shoulder, felt its bony strength, and again he realized — Wahkan was strong, he was resolute, but he was old. "Can you do what needs to be done? Can you carry out our plan?"

"Whether I can or not, I will. Do not worry, my prince. I will achieve whatever is possible in my own time and in my own way."

"I have faith in you."

Going to the door, he looked across the long expanse of lawn toward the house. In a second floor bedroom, he saw a curtain twitch.

"Someone is watching." Wahkan might be old, but his sight was keen.

"Yes, stealthily." Taran took the path through the walled garden to a narrow side stairs that led to the second floor. He moved swiftly through the empty corridor to the bedchamber, hoping to catch the watcher, but the spy had fled. He examined the dust before the window. A woman's medium-sized shoeprint was clearly visible. Who was she? Was she an idle maid hoping to escape Cate's zealous drive to restore Giraud to its former glory? Or was she, like him, in disguise?

His mind went to Zelle, the maid who sought the position of

revolutionary leader. He could not underestimate her intelligence or her rage, or ignore the fact that she had known him as a youthful debauched prince. Would she recognize him now? Would she unmask him to destroy their plan?

He wanted to find Cate, to make sure she was safe and to warn her about the letters. He raced up the stairs and changed into his disguise. He gathered his weapons — his dagger and pistol he hid in his boot and his sling. His short sword he wore at his side ... allowing him to keep possession of the sword had been a serious mistake, one for which he hoped Davies would soon pay dearly.

He took a chance and tied his blindfold in a manner that allowed him to see through it, and ran back down the stairs. On the second floor, one of the young maids spotted him.

So he stumbled and fell.

She helped him rise, and advised him to slow down.

He thanked her and made a show of groping his way to the top of the stairs. He surveyed the entry.

The mercenary, Fortunato, stood before the king's study. He was a sturdy, strapping young man, rather dull and without guile. Now Fortunato looked bored as he practiced tossing his club in the air and catching it.

The door to the study was closed.

So Sir Davies was within.

Taran adjusted the blindfold so he was in total darkness, and descended, using his cane as a guide. "Young man!" he called. "Can you tell me where my wife can be found?"

It didn't occur to Fortunato to wonder how Taran knew his location. "I last saw her back there" — apparently he waved a hand. "Go toward the kitchen. You can follow your nose." He laughed.

Taran laughed, too — nothing like a cruel joke to lighten the atmosphere — and made a show of banging his cane on the tables and walls as he navigated the large entry and found the corridor going toward the kitchen.

He began to call Cate's name; one of the footmen led him to the housekeeper's room and ushered him inside.

"Shut the door," she said.

He did, and removed his blindfold.

She stood holding a stack of letters, looking at him with a mixture of triumph and terror. "This is it. They're here," she said unnecessarily.

"Where were they?"

"In the vase, in that leather packet."

He took them from her, sorted through them, and examined the wax seals on each folded sheet of paper.

"I believe that one is from Italy." She pointed at a seal that included a symbol of the Vatican. "See the shape of the cross? That one must from Austria. That one from France. Russia. That one ... I don't know."

"Nor I. Nor do I care. Can you really do as Davies suggested and open the letters?"

"Without him knowing? Some women could, perhaps. Not I." She put her hand on her temples and massaged as if her head ached. "Every day we stay here, we face a greater and greater possibility that Sir Davies will discover the truth and kill us. Kill ... us."

She looked worried and worn to the bone. She had been impatient with him and the servants. She had not been trained to this kind of work. Of *course* she was agitated. He put his arm around her. "I gave Throckmorton a deadline. Only five more days and we'll light the beacon and the revolution will begin."

"Five more days? Are you mad?"

He hadn't realized how anxious she was. "I could hide you in town —"

She slapped him away and plucked the letters out of his hands. "I'll take them to Davies."

"Is something wrong? Are you ill?"

"If I don't stay here, you cannot stay here." Her voice was sharp. "So I'll take them to Davies."

Taran wanted to argue. But the abrupt way she moved and the flash of her eyes made him very aware he would not win this battle. Instead he said, "Delivery of letters is the butler's task. Have Harkness take them."

"Certainly! As you wish! But if we are to discover where Davies places the letters so I can later retrieve them, I've got to go in with Harkness."

She was right. "I will go with you."

She sighed in palpable irritation. "Then get ready. I'll fetch Harkness. I can't wait for a new round of dramatics played out in the king's study."

With Taran on her arm, Cate followed Harkness into the study.

While she settled Taran in a chair against the wall, Harkness intoned, "Sir, your latest deliveries include a vase and a leather valise, and are in the dining room awaiting your inspection."

Sir Davies sat behind the scarred hulk of the king's desk and looked almost as fractious as Cate felt. "What are they doing *there?*"

"Sir?"

"Why didn't you bring them in *here?*"

"The king always inspected his purchases in the dining room," Harkness said.

"I   am   not   the   king!"

"No, sir." Harkness managed to infuse absolute disdain into his agreement.

Sir Davies flushed the deep red of humiliation.

"In the meantime, your mail has arrived." Harkness presented the letters to Sir Davies on a silver platter.

Davies's humiliation turned to rage, and he demanded, "Damn your eyes, where did you get those?"

Harkness's brow knit. "Sir?"

Sir Davies gripped the arms of his chair. "Were these sent in a courier package?"

"No, Sir Davies." Cate kept her hands folded demurely before her. "They were crudely stuffed into your alabaster vase. I found them, retrieved them, and presented them to Harkness. I hope you are pleased."

What could Davies say? That she had snooped into the hidden contents of his vase and discovered what he wished to keep hidden? He took the letters. "You have done well, Mrs. Tamson."

"Thank you, sir." She turned away. Because she knew what he would do.

And he did. Men were so predictable.

"Stay, Mrs. Tamson," Sir Davies said. "You, Harkness — you go."

Harkness narrowed his eyes; he suspected her of illicit behavior with Sir Davies.

She shrugged and waved him away.

On his exit, the door slammed a little too hard.

Taran jumped as if the sound terrified him, and he sat trembling.

In a reassuring voice, she said, "Don't worry, dear husband, no one will harm you here." Turning back to Sir Davies, she said, "I hope your overseas correspondence is satisfactory, sir."

Sir Davies heated the short, thin blade he kept at this right hand. One by one, he eased the razor-sharp steel into and through the wax seals. With trembling fingers, he opened the letters and stacked them. Then head bent, eyes fixed, he began to read.

While he concentrated on his correspondence, she stepped behind him to the sideboard, the one piece of furniture which he had installed in this room, the one piece he had not marred or scarred in any way. The one that had attracted her attention only after he had arrived … and now, at last, she had the chance to examine it.

In a display of housewifely tidiness, she stacked the papers he had scattered on the top. She opened a drawer and noted it should have been deeper, extend farther back into the cabinet. She dusted the surface, and as she did, she ran her fingers around the edges of the wood, seeking a latch, a lock, something. And found a clasp cleverly hidden from sight, and secured with a brass lock.

Hm. Whatever did Sir Davies keep in here in safety and in secrecy? She half-smiled. She thought perhaps she knew.

She glanced at him.

He was still reading, grinning widely, scratching figures on a separate sheet of paper.

She took a chance. She tapped the stack of papers sharply above the back end of the cabinet. It sounded hollow.

By God, she had found Sir Davies's hidden treasure!

His harsh voice made her jump.

"Woman, what are you doing? Get away from there!"

She turned to him, papers in hand, and blinked innocently. "Sir, while you are busy and wished to be private, I thought to organize your —"

"No! Get away from there." He moderated his tone. "I have only two more letters to read, and you're distracting me with your shuffling and your tapping."

"I do beg your pardon, sir. Distracting you was not my

intention." She had not succeeded in her intention. Close, but not quite.

He pointed to the place beside his desk. "Stand here where I can keep track of you."

She took her place, folded her hands, and watched him read the fourth letter.

Apparently, he found the contents displeasing, for he muttered under his breath, "Parvenu Portuguese villain."

"Portugal!" she said.

Sir Davies viewed her oddly. "Mrs. Tamson?"

"I confess," she said. "I examined the seals. I am without foreign experience, and viewing correspondence from so far away thrills me. I thought I recognized seals from Italy, France, Austria and Russia. I could not identity Portugal."

Taran took a surprised breath.

Sir Davies's jaw dropped.

Perhaps she should have dissembled, but she was too impatient with this man who cared only for himself and nothing for the world's future well being. He and his ilk had murdered her brother. "What does this villain write?"

"He writes that he will take Cenorina away from me without —" Sir Davies took a breath — "that he will sail into the harbor and conquer Cenorina, and I will be able to do nothing to stop him!"

"Yet I believe the mercenaries in the fortress would be a powerful deterent."

"No one has ever taken the fortress, and so I shall tell him!" He groped for his pen.

She placed it and his inkpot near to his hand.

"Thank you, Mrs. Tamson. You are most" — he ran his gaze up and down her — "most helpful."

She smiled. Coldly. "I live to help my employer in all matters while maintaining a respectful distance to his station." *Take that, Sir Davies!*

Sir Davies looked flustered.

She glanced at Taran. He was as disconcerted as Sir Davies. "Please, Sir Davies, write."

After one resentful glance — he seemed to imagine she was ordering him — he did. His large, looping letters filled the bottom of the Portuguese letter, expressing some great emotion that contorted his face and made him breath so loudly it sounded as if a steam engine had invaded the room. When he was done, he folded the letter.

She pushed a lit candle and the stick of sealing wax toward him.

He melted the wax into a blob, picked up the weighty gold seal at his elbow, and pressed it into the wax. He lifted the seal away from the hot wax.

She tilted her head to look at the image. It looked familiar. Like … a lion. In fact, it *was* a lion, with a lion's piercing eyes, pouty cheeks, and a cat-like snout. "That's … very regal." Where had she seen it before?

"Yes." Sir Davies turned the seal toward him, and smiled into the lion's face. "It is the dead king's seal. I have taken it for my own."

Cate plucked the seal from between his fingers and stared, mesmerized, into the golden face. Memory clicked into place. "It looks like the brand on my husband's chest."

CHAPTER FIFTY-ONE

Cate didn't know what she'd said or why the two men froze in place.

Then two things happened simultaneously.

Taran tore the bandage off his face. He slipped his left arm out of his sling; he pointed his pistol at Sir Davies.

Sir Davies stood, grabbed her arm, pulled her toward him, and stuck the tip of his dagger under her chin.

Once again, the two men froze.

"Perhaps one of you gentlemen could tell me why we are at odds?" She tried for cordial, yet she managed to sound sarcastic.

Sir Davies laughed shortly. "Did you think I would welcome the Prince of Cenorina, come to take back his throne?"

"Who?" *What was he talking about?*

Taran bowed. "Such a pleasure to see you again. I can't quite remember … who are you? The governor of Cenorina? An English nobleman? No! You are nothing more than a tutor, a usurper, and a filthy murderer."

Why had he ripped off his disguise? Why hadn't he denied Sir Davies's accusations? Cate cleared her throat. "I am confused. What are we talking about?"

Sir Davies arm tightened. "And this beautiful woman is your wife. You always did have good taste. Oh, wait. No, you didn't. When you were young, you would rut with anything that moved, even the pigs."

"I learned debauchery at your hands, tutor of mine, and I paid the price."

They were ignoring her. Ignoring her as if she was a pawn and they were the … the kings. Black and white. Bad and good. Well defended and defiant.

Sir Davies asked, "However did you manage to survive the pirates?"

"Better ask whether the pirate captain managed to survive me." Taran seated himself and waved his pistol negligently. "I am rather more lethal than I used to be."

"It doesn't matter." Sir Davies used the point of his blade to nudge at her chin. "As long as I've got this knife under your wife's chin, I hold all the trump. Isn't that right, little prince?"

Frustration grew in Cate. These men knew each other. They spoke to each other. They taunted each other. But they spoke in riddles. "Why do you keep calling him a prince?"

Sir Davies was focused on Taran, and answered absently, "Because he is Crown Prince Antonio Raul Edward Kane of Cenorina, long-vanquished heir to the throne."

"No, he's not!" *He wasn't. That wasn't his name at all.*

"Yet I rise from the dead." Taran gestured with his sword.

Why didn't he deny it?

"I had no idea I would be lucky enough to have the Princess of Cenorina as my housekeeper." Sir Davies stroked her jaw with one cool finger.

"I am not a princess." *They had both run mad.*

Sir Davies squeezed her throat once, hard. "She's quite the little flirt, your wife."

"I am not little." *Even without his grip on her throat, she felt as if she was on the verge of suffocation ... she was going to kill Sir Davies. Or Taran. Or both.*

Sir Davies never took his gaze away from Taran. "Your mother, the queen, will never approve the marriage."

"She does not," Taran acceded.

"But then, your mother, the queen, is under my control."

A faint smile touched Taran's mouth.

About this, Cate was absolutely certain. "His mother is in England. I saw her there. I met her there."

Sir Davies held her close, and she felt the tremor that shook him. "No. I assure you, Queen Sibeol is here in the fortress tower."

Cate could not breathe. She could not.

Sibeol.

With absolute certainty, Sir Davies spoke her name.

Sibeol.

Taran's mother was Sibeol.

Cenorina's queen was Sibeol.

Cate had thought the woman at the inn behaved with the imperiousness of a queen…

The room took a spin. Cate fought to get breath into her suddenly constricted lungs.

That brand on Taran's chest. She understood now. Sir Davies had done it. He had used the king's seal to brand the king's son.

All the pieces of the puzzle at last fell together: Taran's misery in Scotland, his determination to succeed in war and in diplomacy, his reluctance to marry her and then his insistence on marriage. His disappearance. Sir Davies selling him to the pirates...

"You are telling the truth," she said thinly. "Taran is ... not Taran. He is the Crown Prince of Cenorina."

Sir Davies stiffened. Pulled her closer. Pushed the point of his knife into the skin above her jugular vein. "You didn't know."

She looked at Taran. At her handsome, perfidious, seductive husband. "No. I didn't know."

"No, she didn't know." Taran wasn't looking at her, though. All his attention was focused on Sir Davies.

"You didn't *really* marry a housekeeper, did you?" Sir Davies asked. "You didn't *really* stain the proud name of Kane with a common working girl?"

Neither of them paid Cate a scrap of attention. And she was done. Done with their stupid rivalry, with their pretense that she didn't exist or didn't matter, with their irritating masculine superiority. She was *done*.

She said, "No, Sir Davies, Taran did not stain his proud name by joining it with a serving girl." Her voice shook — with anger.

But Sir Davies thought she was going to cry.

Taran was taken aback. "What are you—?"

She overrode him with a voice that soared with crackling emotion. "But I thought he might. When I thought he was a mere pirate captain, I thought he might wed me and give our child a name."

"Our child?" Taran's eyes were popping out of his head. "We're going to have a child?"

"As if you didn't know, you blackguard!" She pressed her hand to her belly. "And now, instead of being a prince, he'll be a bastard — like *you,* you lying hound of a ... pirate!"

Sir Davies started cackling, quietly at first, then with more vigor. "You led the girl on, Crown Prince Antonio Raul Edward Kane."

She sniffled and hid her dry face in her cupped hands.

Sir Davies patted her shoulder — ah, if only he comprehended how thoroughly she had duped him — but he spoke to Taran. Only to Taran. "You learned the lessons of dissipation I taught you, and now you have surpassed the master. You, sir, are a cad."

She lifted her utterly dry face from her hands, looked at Taran, and in her weakest, most feminine voice she said, "Yes. He is." Then she slammed her elbow into Sir Davies's stomach just below his sternum. He wheezed, and when he doubled over, she smashed his face with her knee.

Sir Davies fell backward, cracked his head on the desk, and slumped to the floor.

She stood over him, breathing hard.

He didn't move.

She gave him a kick in the side.

He flopped over.

My God. Blowfish would be so proud. She was magnificent in her own protection... *Too bad she had to defend herself. Too bad her husband spent the whole scene exchanging banter with the villain who held a knife at her throat.*

Too bad she had trained Taran to have absolute faith in the fact she could take care of herself...

Leaning down, she plucked the knife from Sir Davies's fingers. To his inert body, she said, "You, sir, are a buffoon, and yet you *dare* threaten me. You *dare* mock me. You *dare* laugh at..." She looked up at Taran.

By the flame in her eyes, he knew the depth of her fury. Awe, respect and caution washed through his veins, and he tried to lighten the atmosphere. "So you're not expecting a baby?"

"What do you care if I am?" She advanced on him. "It all makes sense now. *Queen* Sibeol. *Crown Prince* Antonio of Cenorina. The names, the titles make sense now, a horrible, humiliating sense. The deference with which my brother had treated you. Your leadership. Your languages. Your knowledge. Your determination to rescue Cenorina from the usurper."

Taran kept his pistol trained on Sir Davies — he would be a fool not to — but he watched Cate move toward him with one stiff, affronted step after another, growling like a cat who had been teased too often.

"You are Crown Prince Antonio Edward Raul Kane of Cenorina." It was an accusation.

"Crown Prince Antonio Raul Edward Kane," he corrected. "You switched two of the names."

She growled again.

Hastily, he confirmed, "I am."

"And you *married* me? I am not the commoner Sir Davies imagines, but I am not of royal blood." She reached Taran, stood before him, proud and tall and angry as hell. "When you regain your throne, do you intend to cast me aside?"

"You are my wife." As a precaution, he grabbed the wrist that held the knife. He spoke with sincerity and utter possessiveness. "You will be my wife until the day you die, or I die, and all the world can go up in flames before you ever get away from me. You are *mine*."

He should have paid more attention to the hand without the knife, for she lifted it in a fist and punched him in the nose.

He felt the bone crack. Blood spurted.

He dropped her wrist, staggered backward, grabbed his face. "Damn it, Cate, why did you do that?"

"Revenge." She stalked toward the door. "Your wife I may be, but you'll have to catch up with me to keep me."

This was not the time or the place Taran would have chosen for this confrontation. But all unwittingly, Cate had revealed him. Now she stood in mortal danger, and he could do nothing but to beg her for help. "Cate, you can't leave."

She flung herself around to face him. "Watch me!"

"Remember what you promised."

She paused, her hand on the doorknob, her back to the room. To him.

"Remember," he said. "The beacon. The prisoner."

Her spine straightened. Without looking, she said, "I will keep my promises."

He turned back to Davies, determined to finish the traitor.

Davies was conscious. He was on the move. He reached up on the desk, grasped the short, sharp knife he had used to open the letters. He held it balanced on the tips of his fingers. He threw the knife.

At Cate.

Cate, who was opening the door. Cate, who had her back to them both.

Taran shouted and flung himself forward, shooting as he leaped.

He missed Davies. The knife whistled past his shoulder.

Cate turned.

The blade buried itself in her arm up to the hilt. The shock made her stagger.

"Caitlin!" Taran reached for her.

She looked down at the knife. She looked up at Taran. She offered him the dagger Davies had held at her throat.

Taran dropped the useless pistol and took the hilt.

"Finish him." She walked out and slammed the door.

CHAPTER FIFTY-TWO

Taran drew his cutlass and faced Davies.

Davies dragged himself to his feet. His face was bloody. Like Taran's. His nose was broken. Like Taran's. He dabbed a lace handkerchief against his skin.

Not like Taran. Taran didn't give a damn about his broken nose, the blood, the pain. He anticipated the taste of sweet, slow revenge.

In a fury, Davies looked at the crimson that stained the fine linen. "That bitch!"

"Yes." Taran loudly turned the key in the lock.

Davies looked incredulously at him. "You love her."

"I do. And for hurting her, I'm going to make you suffer." Taran watched Davies sidle around the edge of the desk and unsheathe his sword from its scabbard.

"My dear little student, you won't kill anyone today." Davies pointed the long, narrow épée at Taran. "As always, your sword is half the length of mine."

Taran threw back his head and laughed. "Ah, but my sword is sturdier. Sharper. It has been christened with blood in many a battle. And I wield it so much better." He ran. He leaped onto the desktop, kicked the inkpot into Davies's face, and while Davies sputtered and gagged, Taran said, "Thanks to you, my dear tutor, I am no longer a gentleman. I am a pirate." He gripped Davies's own dagger in one hand and his cutlass in the other. He looked down at his erstwhile tutor. "I fight to win."

CHAPTER FIFTY-THREE

Cate found herself standing in the entry, in pain, committed to two missions — and facing young Fortunato.

He held his oak cudgel high over his head. But he looked at her uncertainly, as if he didn't quite dare strike the female who ordered his meals served and his uniform cleaned. "Mrs. Tamson, you're hurt!"

"Yes. And this" — she gestured at the knife protruding from her arm — "makes me less than my usual good-natured self."

"You're not usually that good ... natured..." He seemed to realize that was not the thing to say to an angry, agonized female.

She extended her hand. Her good hand. The one that wasn't attached to an arm with a knife. "Give me that."

He hesitated.

In the sharp tone that made young footmen jump, she said, "Give me that!"

He handed it over.

The oak cudgel weighed heavy in her hand, and she let it sink slowly until the end rested on the floor.

Inside the king's study, they heard shouted insults. Feet thumped. Glass broke.

Fortunato gawped at the door. "I should go in there."

Something smashed against the wall. Someone gave a cry of pain.

"Didn't you hear the key turn?" she asked. "It's locked."

"I am a mercenary. I was hired to protect Sir Davies. I should break down the door." Fortunato backed up, half-turned, and prepared to fling his shoulder at the wood.

She sighed, and with a resurgence of strength, lifted the club and knocked him cold.

He fell sideways against the wall and slid down in a slump.

"You did your best," she said to his unconscious form, and placed the club beside him.

She looked around. The corridor was empty. Where were the servants? ... Hiding from the sounds of violence, she supposed.

She placed her good hand on the wall and moved, step by

step, toward the kitchen. She had to get there, had to fulfill her promises to Taran. Had to get the beacon lit. Had to ... to free the queen.

No, not the queen. She'd met the queen. Queen Sibeol. If Taran was the crown prince, then there was not a doubt that Sibeol was, in fact, Cenorina's anointed queen. So if the queen wasn't in the prison, then who was? Who concerned Taran so much he asked for Cate's word that she would free an imposter?

Cate glanced down at the knife wound.

Oh, God. Blood oozed from around the blade and stained her sleeve, but she didn't dare remove the knife. Not yet. When she did that, blood would spurt and she would ... faint...

Focus!

The imposter in the tower. Who was she?

Who else could she be, but Taran's virgin bride, the woman Queen Sibeol had told Cate would replace her in Taran's affections?

But no. That was impossible. Whoever she was, the imposter had to pass for a woman in her fifties.

On the other hand, Taran had passed for a blind and enfeebled soldier. Disguise was his specialty, and perhaps also the specialty of this woman. This ... this virgin bitch.

Sight unseen, Cate hated her.

Without warning, a figure appeared at Cate's side. "Mrs. Tamson, you've been stabbed!"

Cate hadn't seen Zelle for days, yet here she was. "Where have you been hiding?"

"Upstairs. In the house. Where I could keep watch," Zelle said sullenly.

"The war has begun."

Zelle stepped back. "I don't give a damn about this war."

"You do. If you didn't, you wouldn't be so angry." Cate tried to maintain eye contact. But the world wavered, and she staggered.

Zelle caught her. She slid her arm around Cate's back. "I don't give a damn about the war. But you ... you have been kind. Lean on me."

"Thank you." The floor dipped and rose like the deck of a ship.

Cate would not faint. She would not. She would land badly and do herself irreparable damage. And she had to keep her promise to Taran. "I need to find someone who can take care of this … of removing this knife."

"That would be Signor Marino."

Cate thought of the cook, competent and kind. "Good. I'm glad he can … help me. After that … I need you to do something for me."

Zelle stuck out her chin. "Why would I?"

"If I do not live through the day, someone must know —"

"You won't die of that little stab wound." Zelle was brisk.

"No. I won't. Not from this. But I have another duty I have promised the prince I will perform —"

"The prince." Zelle couldn't have made her scorn more clear.

"He's my husband."

"I know."

"He's Crown Prince Antonio of Cenorina."

"I know."

"How did you know?" *How?* Cate hadn't known. But if she pointed that out, she would look even more stupid than she felt.

"Servants know everything."

Cate stopped, leaned against the wall, and cradled her injured arm against her body. She stared at Zelle, silently demanding an explanation.

Zelle sighed in exasperation. "He came to Arianna, presented himself to our meeting in the cathedral, tried to cajole us, convince us he had changed. He fooled the others. But not me. And I knew he had to be hiding somewhere close. So I thought and I watched … he is so proud of himself for ruining Cenorina once before, and even now he is making plans to ruin it again."

"He's going to kill the man who did ruin Cenorina."

"So he can take his place."

"He's not like that." Taran had not told Cate who he was. But Cate knew him so well. His intentions were good. He was determined. He would succeed. "He came to save his country, make reparations."

"You came along to enjoy his life of luxury."

"Me?" Cate chortled, then winced at the fresh shot of pain that brought her. "I've cleaned. I've organized. I've cared for the staff. Do you sincerely believe I'm here for luxury?"

"Not you," Zelle admitted.

"Not him, either. Because … why? Why would he do that? He was a pirate captain. He was free. He had no responsibilities, and he made a fortune! Then he came here, to Cenorina, ravaged by Sir Davies. Reviving this country will be difficult and costly, and his duty will take all that he is." Cate was explaining Taran's motivation and his intentions to herself as well as Zelle. It wasn't as if she really knew this, what with him not telling her the truth about who he was, the conniving phony. But she was speculating, and she knew she was right.

Zelle turned her face away and studied the front door as if she longed to escape that direction.

Fine. If Zelle didn't believe her, Cate couldn't help it. She didn't have time to say more. She pushed herself away from the wall and again started toward the kitchen. "I believe I have found the crown jewels."

Zelle caught up with her. "The crown jewels!"

"I'm not sure. I didn't get the chance to investigate. So if I die — "

"You will not!"

"— someone I trust must know of the crown jewels and how to retrieve them."

"Please don't tell me, lady." Zelle covered her ears.

"It must be someone who is competent and clever. Someone I trust."

Zelle took her hands away. "I am not that person. My loyalties are not to the prince. They are to my people."

"Your people are his people." Cate staggered again.

Zelle put her arm around her waist. "I wish I could believe you."

"You can. You should. For only he has the strength to save you from your enemies … and your friends. Without a royal family in charge, I promise you, England will swallow Cenorina."

Zelle's chin jutted out. "Let them try."

"England has a long tradition of winning. A ragtag mob of Cenorinians will not stop them." Again, Cate halted and leaned against the wall. "The crown jewels are Cenorina's national treasure."

"The crown jewels should be used to feed the hungry!"

"The prince has already recovered much of the money Sir

Davies stole, and I promise, Taran will bring Cenorina back to prosperity. Now ... about the crown jewels and their location."

Zelle looked away. "I already know where they are."

"You found them?"

"I have been observing you since you arrived. I didn't know about the prince, but I realized almost at once *you* were not what you seemed. You searched the house. I followed you, saw you pick locks, rifle through drawers and cabinets, tap wood and walls looking for hollow spaces. I started wondering what you sought. I thought ... I knew no one had seen the crown jewels since Davies had taken power, so I began to search, too."

Cate's excitement rose. "Did you actually *locate* the crown jewels?"

"I didn't get the chance. If Davies left the king's study, he stationed the mercenary at the door. But once I went in on the pretext of cleaning and found —"

"— found the hollow space in —"

"— the cabinet behind the desk!"

The two women grinned at each other.

Then Cate's exaltation faded. "So I cannot extract a promise that you will bring them forth and give them to the prince."

"No. I found them. If I can retrieve them, they are mine." Zelle looked bitter, resolute ... and ashamed.

Cate thought perhaps the shame could overcome the bitterness. "In that case, I shall have to try with all my strength to fulfill my last vow to Taran."

"What is that?"

"I must rescue the lady in the tower."

Zelle's face hardened. "The queen."

"No. The queen is no longer Davies's prisoner."

"She worked with him willingly. She was never his prisoner."

"Then why would she have to escape?"

Zelle had no reply to that.

"A brave and noble lady took her place." Cate pressed Zelle's hand. "Now if you'll help me, I will get this damnable knife removed."

CHAPTER FIFTY-FOUR

The rush of the oven's heat and the outcry of the assembled servants made Cate lift her drooping head. She had just made the longest walk in the world, but at last they had reached the kitchen.

Zelle eased Cate down on the bench by the table.

Signor Marino came to her side.

The servants crowding the kitchen gathered behind him.

Gently he lifted her arm and placed it on the table. "Mrs. Tamson, what happened?"

"They're fighting. Taran and Sir Davies ... are fighting. Sir Davies tried to ... kill me." For the first time, Cate faced the truth. "He tried to kill me. If Taran hadn't shouted, if I hadn't turned, the knife would have struck me in the back, entered my lungs, and ... he tried to *murder* me!"

"He's treacherous and a bully. We all know that." Zelle met her gaze. *"We've* lived with it for years."

"I know. But that is not my fault, and Taran seeks to make reparations!"

Zelle looked away from Cate's vehemence.

Cate needed to calm herself, to get over her shock of coming so close to death. After all, right now, Taran was fighting for his life, and she did not underestimate Sir Davies's prowess with a sword. "Signor Marino, this blade in my arm is not long, but we need to remove it and I understand you have skill with such wounds."

"All will be well." He waved at his scullery maid.

She sprang toward the cupboard and pulled out a roll of linen and some clean white rags.

"In my day, I've seen much worse than this." With a pair of long scissors, he cut the sleeve away from the knife. "Here in the kitchen, we're always cutting and stabbing ourselves." He spoke to the assembled staff. "Aren't we now?"

"That we are!"

"All the time!"

"Keeps us strong!"

Signor Marino nodded. "With a good sharp knife, you

hardly notice the pain."

Cate blinked away tears. "It must be very dull, then, or else I am a complete milquetoast."

The footman offered her a glass of rich, red wine.

"Sip," Signor Marino urged. "It's good for the blood."

She did.

He said, "If you would like me to pull the knife for you—"

"No!" She didn't want to do it herself, but she couldn't stand the thought of anyone taking the hilt, possibly twisting or ripping her muscles.

"I knew you would say that. It's always the brave ones who insist on doing it themselves." He folded the linen into a pad, laid strips of rag out on the table. "Pardon me for being so impertinent, but if you ever retire as housekeeper, you would make a fine cook."

Gracia wiped Cate's face with a cool, wet cloth.

"I think being a cook requires more than bravery." Cate tried to smile, but it wavered terribly. "But you have made me feel better, more steady."

"That's the way," he encouraged. "Pull that knife out now."

Cate stared at the hilt protruding from her sleeve. The wound burned as if the steel was hot, and the blood seeping from around the edges dribbled onto the table. She put her hand on the hilt, took a deep breath, and pulled: fast and straight out.

Was it supposed to be easier coming out than going in?

It was not.

Yet Signor Marino moved so quickly, pressing the pad hard onto the wound. He lifted it and looked. "It needs stitches."

Immediately his scullery maid appeared with a thin curved needle threaded with silk.

They had planned for this. They had known it would need stitches!

Signor Marino pressed the skin together. The girl poked the needle through and around, and tied off the thread with each stitch.

Cate gave up on the bravery façade. With each thrust of the needle, she squeaked and moaned and whimpered. But she didn't move. Not an inch.

"That's it!" Signor Marino dabbed the holes with brandy, then pressed a new, clean pad on the wound and wrapped strips of cloth around and around Cate's arm.

Somewhere during the process, her head got woozy, she took a few long breaths, and when she opened her eyes, the butler had joined them.

Harkness looked worn, thinner, older than he had before. Harkness…

Abruptly, Cate remembered Taran's battle, her vows, and the need to make haste. With Harkness here, she could fulfill the first promise. She said, "You must go light the beacon."

Harkness staggered back. "Now?"

"My husband is your crown prince," she told the gathering, and waited for an outcry of surprise.

Heads nodded.

Smiles lit faces.

"Ah," Signor Marino said. "So the rumors are true."

"Rumors? There are rumors? " Damn Taran. *Did everyone but Cate know?*

"Many of us have pinned our hopes on his return," Signor Marino told her. "Some have said he was here, now, bringing the fresh air of freedom to this land."

Zelle scowled and slipped out of the kitchen.

One of the maids rushed in. "They're still fighting. In the study. You should hear it!"

One of the service bells rang violently. Everyone looked.

"It's the bell from the king's study," Gracia said.

"Does Sir Davies imagine he can ring and *we* will come to rescue him?" Harkness was incredulous.

Eyes alight, one of young footmen ran out. "I want to listen!"

The kitchen began to hum with excitement.

"Taran is your crown prince," Cate repeated. "He has come to free Cenorina. He needs to call in his warriors, and Harkness" Pressing her good hand to tabletop, she stood, she stood — "he wants that beacon lit *now!*"

Harkness straightened his jacket. "Mrs. Tamson … Your Highness —"

No. Not that. Not your highness. "Just Mrs. Tamson, please."

"I would do as the prince requires, but every night, I have been working, hauling wood and oil up to the top of the pinnacle, and the last time…" Harkness pressed his shaking hand to his chest.

"I don't think I would again make it to the top alive."

Cate placed a hand to his sleeve. "Then you must not try." She looked around. "Who else can fulfill this duty to Cenorina?"

Using a pair of tongs, Signor Marino removed coals from the fire and put them in two empty iron pots. He handed it to young Gillies and one to Gracia. "You heard the princess. Go and ignite the beacon."

The young people's faces lit up, and they ran out the door.

After another sip of wine, Cate followed them.

"Where are you going?" Harkness asked. "The prince might get hurt. He might need you here!"

"He will win this battle." She had to believe that. "The queen escaped the tower, and the prince requires that the brave lady who took her place be rescued."

"Let me help you," Signor Marino said.

These were such good people. Taran would be happy living in Giraud. "I'm afraid rescuing the lady is something I must do myself. If the lock must be picked, I am the only one who can do it."

Signor Marino caught up with her as she crossed the lawn. "Please, Highness, I cannot pick a lock, but I can give you this." He held out his hand, palm up.

A small pistol rested in his palm.

"It is loaded," he said. "I keep it hidden in the kitchen, where I am always prepared to defend my crew. But you are a heroine, walking into the deepest danger, and we have agreed — you need it more than we do. Please. Take it."

She did. Reluctantly, because she couldn't face the idea of killing someone. And willingly, because she knew her use of this gun might be necessary to save a life: the lady in the tower, or her own. She tucked it into the reticule she wore at her side. "Thank you, Signor Marino. I will return it." She meant, she would survive.

He understood. "See that you do."

CHAPTER FIFTY-FIVE

The flush of energy carried Cate from the kitchen across the lawn, through the garden and into the stable. She stood in the doorway, blinking into the dim silence and wondering what to do now. She could ride, of course — she had galloped across many a wild Scottish mile — but she had never saddled her own horse. She needed help. "Halloo?" she called. "Is anyone here?"

No one answered.

As her eyes adjusted to the light, she strolled along the stalls, looking for a horse capable of carrying her into Arianna and up the hill to the fortress that guarded the harbor.

As Taran had discovered before her, only a few of the stalls were occupied and most by young horses who gamboled and flirted and made it clear that, even if Cate tried to ride them, they would be more than she could now handle. Only one horse captured her interest, a large, elderly gelding that watched her with standoffish dignity.

"Aren't you a handsome boy?" She leaned over the wall and offered her hand.

With a look of almost comical disdain, the beautiful old horse stretched out his neck and sniffed her fingers. Then he curled his lip at her.

"Don't be that way. I'm the Crown Princess of Cenorina." Might as well impress him with her credentials, no matter how recently she had learned them, how terribly she feared for her prince, and how likely it was that she would be ousted from her position before she had even taken the throne. "If you would consent to carry me into town, I will free an important prisoner and fulfill my duty to my husband and sovereign lord."

The horse tilted his head in equine derision.

She *loved* this guy. "Come to me, my darling boy, my king, my savior."

The horse leaned his head closer, put his nose under her hand and slid it up his head to his mane.

He was *her* horse. She knew it now. She scratched his forehead. "If you would let me, I could put the bridle in your mouth, but even if I knew how, I cannot place a saddle on you." She showed him her bandaged arm. "Will you carry me bareback?"

A voice from behind her said, "No need for that."

She jumped so hard she startled the horse.

"I can saddle him for you."

The man who stepped forward was an American — after meeting Lilbit, she recognized the accent — and appeared to be a native of that continent, with dark, straight hair, cool eyes, and copper skin. All the natives in America were portrayed as savages, but this man introduced himself eloquently and with an undertone of humor. "I'm Wahkan. I am in charge of the stables, what is left of them. I would do anything our future queen desires."

Her temper rose. "Damn it, *everybody* knows Taran's true identity."

"I heard you introduce yourself to Narragansett. That was is courtesy many riders neglect."

She looked from Wahkan to the horse. "How did you hear me? I didn't know anyone was near."

Wahkan laughed, and something about that dry, cool amusement made her think Wahkan had a way of hiding in plain sight. But he said, "Also, I knew the prince as a child. I taught him to ride."

Appeased, Cate said, "I suppose that makes sense."

"You can ride a man's saddle?"

She had ridden a man's saddle since she was three. "Yes. Please."

He disappeared into the shadows and came back with a fine saddle of tooled leather. "'Tis the king's saddle, for the king's horse."

Startled, she looked at the large gelding. Of course. That explained the tinges of gray hair on his muzzle, the length of graceful neck, and the dignity and beauty that lingered around the old boy's shoulders.

"This is Narragansett," Wahkan said. "His days of carrying a king of Cenorina are over. Now he resides in peace. Not that a noble steed like this wishes for peace." He finished saddling the horse, then cupped his hands and offered them as a mounting block. "I'll help you up," he said. "Have a care with that arm."

She glanced at her arm. Blood still seeped through the pad, but she told herself it felt better. "I will." She took a breath, put her good hand on the saddle horn, held tight and put her foot in Wahkan's cupped hands. She jumped, and he pushed, and she got her leg mostly over the horse's back.

The horse, God bless him, stood stock-still while she arranged her skirts and took the reins.

"You look good up there," Wahkan said. "Do you know, since the king died, Narragansett hasn't made up to a single soul until you. He likes you. That means he recognizes your nobility. Don't forget."

"I will remember." She leaned forward and gave the gelding a gentle kick.

As they walked out of the stable, Wahkan followed, and pointed. "Look!"

Giraud's beacon leaped with flame. She saw the tiny figures of Gracia and Gillies scampering down the stairs, and even from such a distance, she could feel their infectious excitement. "The revolution has started," she said.

Wahkan pointed at the study as someone — Taran or Davies — shrieked, and tore the velvet drapes off the window. For one moment, the outline of both men was visible, and sunshine danced across two deadly swords. "Fire did not begin the revolution. The prince did. And he will finish it!"

Wahkan saluted her. "Go forth, Crown Princess Cate, and do your duty!"

She nodded in return. Narragansett trotted through the yard. Then Narragansett moved into a smooth gallop. They traveled up the road toward Arianna, leaving that battle behind, carrying Cate to a new confrontation.

Cate held on with all her strength, and at the top of the hill, she brought the gelding to a halt and looked back.

In response to Giraud's beacon, fire touched the beacon at the top of the Trueno Ridge. Flames grew slowly, then suddenly, the beacon blazed, spreading its light far out to sea.

The pirates had been signaled.

Cate's first vow had been fulfilled.

Turning, she spurred her mount toward the fortress, and the tower, and the lady imprisoned within.

CHAPTER FIFTY-SIX

Someone pounded on the door.

Taran didn't seem to notice. He kept attacking Maddox, not with the elegant grace of a true swordsman, but like the bully he was. He used a chair as a shield. He launched himself off the wall. He swung on the bell pull.

Of course, Maddox prided himself on being the premier swordsman in all Europe, and he scored hits. He had slashed Taran's cheek, his ribs, and in one moment of triumph, pierced his thigh.

But as this battle proceeded, one truth became escapable — this crown prince, with a passion for combat, a laughing disposition, and a pirate's sharp sword, would triumph.

Wherever Maddox turned, Taran was there. Smiling. Mocking. Slashing.

Maddox dripped blood from a dozen shallow slices. He was in pain. He was growing weak. And afraid. Sir Maddox Davies was *afraid* of the arrogant boy he had once so easily bested.

Would no one come to his rescue?

The servants? … No, probably not. The cook? … No. That savage in the stable? … Most definitely not.

Yet the battering at the door continued. The mercenary! Yes. If he could get in…

Maddox didn't have time to wait. Taran's sword whipped through the air with a humming sound. The point stung like a thousand bees. And everywhere Maddox looked, there was Taran's face, smiling, smirking … the little brat was enjoying himself!

Finally, irrevocably, Maddox panicked. He *panicked.*

His sword work became less polished, his thrusts less precise.

Escape. He had to escape!

The window. The window was open.

Yes! He could flee through the window. He turned his back to Taran. And he ran.

Just as he reached the king's battered desk, Taran brought him down with a graceless tackle.

Maddox landed hard with his arm underneath him. His arm separated from his shoulder. He screamed. He lost his grip on his sword.

Taran flipped him over, planted his boot in his chest and pointed his sword at his throat. Taran — Antonio — whateverhisname was — was still laughing, but his eyes were cold and black and intent. And purposeful. And expectant.

Taran intended to execute Sir Maddox Davies.

The door rocked on its hinges. The mercenary — what was his name? — would surely break through soon.

Fortune somebody.

Fortunato! That was it.

Sir Maddox Davies paid an exorbitant fee for his mercenaries, and the soldier had damned well better get in here fast.

Because the maniac who held Maddox down with a boot to his chest didn't intend to kill him ... yet. Now he heated the king's seal in a candle's flame ... and smiled.

Davies knew what Taran intended.

Revenge. The boy wanted revenge.

Maddox babbled. "I'm sorry. The sword fight. The mess I've made of your father's study. The pirates."

"My mother?" Taran suggested.

"Yes! Your mother. In the tower. Dreadful place. I never meant to cause trouble."

"The betrayal?"

"Awful betrayal. Dreadful. Very bad form." Maddox watched Taran fearfully.

Taran laughed out loud.

That mercenary needed to try harder. Slam the door harder. Shoot off the lock. *Get me out of here.*

Oh, God. Oh, no. Taran looked almost sympathetic as he pulled the king's seal out of the flame.

Maddox grabbed for the feeble shreds of his courage. He needed to remember — he was not done yet. By God, his spirit had not been broken by this fight. He was strong and resolute. He could yet win his freedom and escape with at least some of his fortune intact. That was what mattered. No matter how scarred and slashed and beaten Maddox might be, if he had his money, no one would dare mock or hurt him. He was secure.

Outside, the mercenary shouted worthless commands and Spanish swear words. Over and over, the door rocked and swayed.

The point of the sword pricked Maddox's throat. Taran leaned down and looked into Maddox's eyes. He spoke with clear intensity. "I wouldn't move if I were you."

He extended the heated seal. The gold glowed; the air around the metal wavered with heat. Closer and closer it came, moving deliberately toward Maddox's eyes; he could see nothing else but that golden disc, so small, so hot, so deadly.

He gave up all pretense of courage; he shrieked pleas and begged in moans.

Taran no longer gave the impression of pleasure; instead he was intense, focused, determined.

He applied the seal to Maddox's forehead.

Flesh sizzled. All of existence narrowed to one single point of anguish.

Outside in the entry, the mercenary threw himself at the door over and over, and at last — at last! — he burst in.

Taran looked up. In that insouciant tone that made Maddox hate him even more, he said, "That took you long enough."

At once, Maddox realized several things.

Taran no longer held the seal to his forehead or the sword to his throat.

And Fortunato couldn't rescue Maddox. The stupid mercenary held only a club for a weapon.

But Maddox could turn the tables. He could even now impale Taran.

He used his good hand to grope for the hilt of his épée. He grasped it, lifted it ... it felt different. Lighter ... he gave an appalled shriek. His blade of Toledo steel, the blade he had had specially made for him — had been snapped in half.

He should be enraged.

He was petrified.

Taran met his eyes. The boy's smile had returned. "Revenge," he said, "tastes sweet." Then he used Maddox's chest as a launch to leap toward the mercenary.

Ribs cracked. Maddox gasped and choked. And rolled. And stood.

And while Taran fought the mercenary into a corner,

Maddox ran out the broken door. He raced past Signor Marino, past a gauntlet of grinning servants.

They jeered.

Something struck his back. Something hard. Something that broke.

The smell of rotten egg filled the air.

Something splattered against his cheek. He wiped it off. It was red; a moldy tomato. A handful of decayed berries sprayed his shirt.

The servants. They were throwing things ... at him! At their master!

It almost seemed as if that realization brought a hail of flying projectiles.

He raced toward the entrance.

One of the footmen smoothly opened the door.

Maddox sprinted outside, down the steps — and a formation of gardeners.

Those peasants didn't waste time with rotting compost. They used stones. They used fresh manure from the cows and the kennels. By the time Maddox stumbled to the end of the long driveway, he ached and wept, and smelled as bad as he had the time his schoolmates had locked him in the privy.

Then the road stretched out before him. He turned away from Arianna. He had to reach his secret cove. There he had cash, bank information, gold, and an escape plan. He would signal the fishing boat. They would come and take him to Gibraltar. There he would be safe.

Safe from Taran.

Maddox's heart pounded in his chest. Again and again, in terror, he glanced back at the house.

Taran intended to kill him. Chase him down. Slaughter him like a peasant.

Would that big, dumb mercenary keep Taran occupied long enough for Maddox to flee this cursed land of Cenorina?

His feet pounded on the gravel. He stepped into a rut, fell, tore the knees out of his trousers, scraped the skin on his palms, and his shoulder ... oh, God. His dislocated shoulder! Bleeding, stinking and in agony, he got up and ran again.

At last he had to slow. Gasping, he turned, walked backward

and looked. And realized … he had escaped! Escaped. The road was empty.

His arm hung useless at his side.

His bloody wounds and the filth that covered him attracted flies.

The king's seal blistered his forehead.

But he was safe. Safe. All he had to do was cross the mountain and reach his private cove.

No one would find him now.

Wahkan slipped along the edge of the road. He held a rifle in one hand. He kept out of sight of Davies's limping, staggering figure, but he never lost him from view.

Because … Maddox Davies had destroyed the land Wahkan had come to love.

Maddox Davies had wrecked the stables Wahkan had worked so hard to build.

Maddox Davies had harmed the royal family Wahkan served.

Maddox Davies's life was about to take a ghastly turn.

CHAPTER FIFTY-SEVEN

Cate galloped along the outskirts of Arianna, high over the harbor. In the streets below her, the townspeople were stirring, gathering, pointing at the beacon on Trueno Ridge. She saw people disappear, then reappear with weapons. She watched as they grew from a few to a mob. Carried on the breeze, she heard their shouts of defiance. When they turned toward Sir Maddox Davies's warehouses, she whispered, "Take everything."

Over and over, she glanced toward the harbor, hoping to catch a glimpse of the Scottish Witch sailing across the ocean toward the harbor.

She saw no sign of the ship and the pirates who would save them. Were they negotiating the winding channel? Would they appear in time to give Taran the warriors he needed to take Cenorina?

When she and Narragansett reached the winding path that led up to the fortress, the horse truly showed his breeding. Along the places where the trail had sloughed off, he picking his way through the rubble with grace and as much speed as he dared.

At last they reached the top. She slid from the saddle; when her feet hit the ground, the jolt reverberated all the way up to her wounded arm.

She had never been a good patient. But she had never been such a weakling before, either. Perhaps she had simply lost too much blood. Or perhaps she enjoyed the *idea* of being a heroine better than the responsibilities attached to the role. She wrapped her fingers around Narragansett's bridle, placed her other hand on his neck, and confessed, "I am a chicken heart."

He rolled his eyes.

"I know. It's a little late for that."

He dragged her by the bridle toward the fortress.

"You don't want to go there," she told him, and slipped the bit out of his mouth. "Thank you for carrying me so far. Now you should go home."

He tossed his head contemptuously, turned and made his way down the slope again. Before he disappeared around the bend, he turned his head and looked at her, and inclined his head.

"Have a care!" she said, but she had no doubt he could care for himself.

Straightening her bodice, she walked around to the tall, wide and grim door, lifted the heavy iron knocker and let it drop.

The sound echoed in the vast hollow of the fortress.

As she waited for someone to answer, she looked up. And up. And up. The fortress's stack of forbidding gray stone rose thirty feet in the air, ending in a crenellated wall where the black cannons aimed toward the town and, she knew, out to sea. Above that, the tower rose another twenty feet.

And she had to rescue the lady who lived at the top.

Desperately, Cate glanced out to sea, and her heart leaped with joy.

There. There! A ship was sailing toward the mouth of the harbor. The pirates had arrived! But that left her little time to flush out the mercenaries.

Hastily she pressed her hand to the blood-soaked bandage and smeared her face with red.

The peephole in the door opened, and a man's broad, dark, mashed face looked at her in surprise. "What do you want?" he bellowed.

"The beacon is lit. The pirates are attacking!"

He stared at her as if she was impaired. "So?"

Greed. She needed to appeal to their greed. "The people broke into Sir Davies's storehouse! They're carrying off gold and jewels. He'll never be able to recover all the wealth, and he'll never know what happened to it."

His eyes kindled with interest.

"You must help!" she said.

He shut the window. Just shut it, leaving her standing there.

She stared at the impregnable door. What was she going to do if they didn't take the bait? She would never get the future princess out of prison, the girl would be held for ransom, and Cate would have broken her promise to Taran.

Cate's wound throbbed in time with her panicked heartbeat.

Then the great door creaked open.

Two dozen mercenaries, armed to the teeth, strolled out. They were big, burly men with ham-sized fists and hulking shoulders. They grinned when they saw her and one man, the captain, stopped and chucked her under the chin. "Stay close, little one, and when I return, I'll share my wealth."

He stood half a foot taller than she did.

Nobody, not even her Taran, not even her brother before his death, stood half a foot taller than she did.

She hoped the townspeople, and the pirates, lived through their encounters with him.

He yelled back into the fortress, "Lich! Sheffer! Go up to the parapet. Man the cannon. Sink the pirate ship!"

From inside the fortress, she heard two enthusiastic voices yell, "Yes, sir! That we will!"

From the dim interior, another man roared, "To hell with you, Captain! I'm not staying here while you go to steal a fortune!"

The man with the mashed face shouted back, "We can't take you, Volker. There might be unarmed women down there who will beat you up!"

Cate's heart sank. They were leaving Volker. They were taunting Volker about his encounter with her. And she had to get past him to rescue the lady.

She had no choice. So she smiled and rippled her fingers at the captain. "Later."

She *really* hoped there would be no later. She intended that today Taran should win every battle, kill every enemy, take every prisoner. Even if he intended that she rescue the woman who would take Cate's place at his side and in his bed, she wanted him to live, to flourish, to be king of this land. She wanted this because through all the pain, the effort, the drama, she thought of him first. She acted for his good.

Damn him, she was a fool in love.

And damn him, he had better have defeated Sir Davies, for the only alternative was … his death …

One pained breath followed another. Then she slipped inside the gloomy fortress.

"Volker, we're leaving you a tasty morsel," Mashed Face shouted. "Try not to let her hurt you!"

The mercenaries rumbled with laughter as they headed down the path toward the tumultuous town. The last one out slammed the door; it sounded like the roll of doom. Cate blinked, trying to get her bearings.

The chamber was huge, tall and filled with shadows. Candles flickered on a table scattered with playing cards. Soot streaked the rock walls. And like a stain on the darkness, Volker stood, his mean blue eyes fixed on her. "You!"

But he posed no problem, because she had her hand inside in her reticule on the grip of Signor Marino's loaded pistol.

Except, as Blowfish surmised and Taran knew, she couldn't kill anything. Not in cold blood. Not if she wished to retain her sanity.

If she killed this man, she would be guilty for the rest of her life.

If she didn't save the princess, she would regret it forever.

So she tried a tactic with which she had little experience: tact. "Sir Volker, I came to beg your pardon for pushing you out the window. That was wrong of me."

He paid no heed to her words. "Do you know how the men have goaded me? Mocked me?" He lumbered toward her. "Do you realize the humiliation you put me through?"

Stupid, worthless tact. Stupid, worthless pistol. She stole a quick glance around, saw a stout walking stick that leaned against the wall. Never taking her gaze from his hostile advance, she edged toward the staff, grasped one end and brought it in front of her.

"What are you going to do with that?" he snarled. "There are no windows to push me out of here. You've lost your element of surprise." His voice got louder, echoing through the stone chamber. "And I'm going to get my revenge!" He charged.

She sidestepped.

He smacked the corner of the table and gave an audible, "Oof!" He whirled and grabbed her arm — her wounded arm — and yanked her toward him.

She felt the stitches tear the skin.

Agony vanquished her misgivings and brought her to instant, blinding rage.

She thumped the narrow end of the staff onto his instep.

He roared with surprise and distress, and gave a hop backward.

Fiercely, she swung the staff and slammed it between his legs.

He went down, swearing, clutching his ballocks. He writhed on the floor.

Flipping the stick, she used the heavy end to bash him on the side of the head.

His skull made the sound of a ripe melon splitting, and he collapsed, unconscious.

She stood, breathing hard and weeping with pain. She was bleeding again, not the slow oozing but blood gushing from a deep, now-open stab wound.

She had to get to the imposter in the tower before she lost consciousness.

But she could see the rise and fall of Volker's chest. She hadn't killed him. So first, she had to somehow secure him.

A coil of rope hung on the wall. She dropped the staff, fetched the rope and using good Scottish knots and her uninjured hand, she tightly trussed him with his hands and legs twisted up behind him.

She hoped he woke in agonizing discomfort. It would serve him right.

Next she wrestled the wooden bar across the outer doors; she could not have the mercenaries return and interrupt her mission.

Two men remained above on the parapet, preparing to shoot the cannon at her pirates, but surely loading the cannon would keep them busy long enough for her to free the prisoner.

She looked around for keys. She found them tossed on the table, two heavy, well-worn keys on an iron ring.

Finally. Something had gone right.

She had the pistol in her reticule. She took the walking stick as both weapon and support.

The first flight of stone stairs rose straight up to the second level, and ended in a long corridor. Many men's footsteps marked the dusty floor. She followed the trail to a heavy, armored door. She opened it, stepped through and saw the round base of the tower … and the long, bare, narrow stairway winding up and out of sight.

She sagged against the cool stone wall. She had been doggedly ignoring the fact that she had to climb those rickety steps, steps with no handrail, all the way to the top.

But she could do this. A slight breeze slipped down like a cool waterfall. Long, narrow arrow slits lit her way.

She risked a glance at her bandage.

Blood soaked it through. Just looking at it made her squeamish. Squeamish! Her, wild Caitlin of the proud MacLean clan!

She put her foot on first one step. Then the other. Then the other.

True, she had never before been stabbed. But she had fought with the boys, fallen from trees, broken her arm, landed in a wasp's nest, swum in a frigid Scottish stream ... when had she turned into such a sissy?

She climbed around and around. She used the staff to test the steps.

She could probably blame Taran for her cowardice. In fact, she intended to.

She huddled close to the cold, dirty gray stones, and kept one hand against them for balance. As she ascended, the drop-off grew greater and greater; she didn't dare look down for fear she would get dizzy.

Yes. She had become a mincing, delicate flower. Taran had a lot to answer for.

About two thirds of the way up, the fingers holding the heavy iron ring went suddenly numb; she almost dropped the keys. "No, no," she muttered. "No, no, no."

She needed those keys. Using one would be so much easier than picking the lock. And faster. Time was of the essence. She *needed* those keys.

She hung them on her arm like a bracelet.

She didn't look down. She had already come so far. She could do this.

She paused two steps from the top landing. She needed to catch her breath, exalt at her success — and consider the oak door, armored with steel plating. At the bottom, a slit had been cut to pass through food and water.

The poor woman was truly a prisoner, cut off from daily human contact. Cate felt sorry for her. Or she would, if the hussy wasn't in line to take Cate's place. She hardly sounded sarcastic at all when she said, "Hang on, Princess, your liberator is here."

The oak was thick. The slit was small. The lady probably couldn't hear her.

But Cate's own words kept her focused.

She climbed the last steps, fumbled with the keys, grasped one, inserted it into the lock.

It didn't turn.

Wrong key.

She grasped the other key. She poked it at the wavering keyhole once, twice. She inserted it. She turned it.

She turned it! She stared, dumbfounded. She had done it. She had rescued Taran's princess!

Gently, she pushed the door open.

The chamber was round, with windows that opened at intervals all the way around to let in light and air. The furnishings were luxurious for a prison, and neat, which showed an orderly disposition. But nothing moved. She could see no one, no young woman shrieked at her appearance or demanded an explanation for taking so long with the rescue. Of course, the replacement princess was probably shy. Or she thought one of the soldiers had appeared. Cate could take comfort in knowing she wasn't the only milquetoast involved in this mission.

Was the girl cowering under the bed? Hiding in the cupboard?

Cate moved cautiously into the room. "Miss? Lady? Princess?"

She heard a noise behind her.

Instinctively, Cate ducked. Something whistled pasted her ear, barely missing her head. She swiveled to face the woman holding a half-inch steel bar.

This female — petite, young, beautiful, with blazing blue eyes and curly blond hair — thrust the point of the rod under Cate's chin. "Who are you? Speak now, before I kill you where you stand!"

CHAPTER FIFTY-EIGHT

"I'm the woman who was sent rescue you." A little shocked and a lot tired, Cate staggered backward. "If you're going to be bullheaded about it, do you mind if I sit down?"

The fake queen frowned. "Rescue me? Why? Who sent you?"

"His Highness Prince Taran —"

"Who is Prince Taran?"

"Prince Antonio. He's using an alias." Which called to mind a question Cate had been steadfastly ignoring; was their marriage valid? She supposed that in the current circumstances, it didn't matter … but it did to the young bride she had been. It mattered to the woman she was today.

"An alias," the female said. "Yes. I suppose he *would* use an alias."

Cate did not so much decide to sit down as the act of sitting became imperative. A straight wooden chair beckoned; she took it. "He made me promise to get you out of here safely."

Dark lashes surrounded those blazing blue — and disbelieving — eyes. "Why you? Why should I trust you?"

Cate had to quell her irritation before she could reply, and she didn't quell it very well. "I didn't trick the mercenaries into leaving the fortress, lock the door behind them, knock out Volker, and drag my bleeding body up those interminable stairs because I was worried about *you.*"

The fake queen got an arrested expression on her face. "You knocked out Volker?"

"I tied him up like a Highland sheep for the shearing."

"How?"

"In my time, I've tied a few Highland sheep."

"No, I meant how did you knock him…? Never mind." The lady smiled and offered her hand. "I'm Miss Jeannette Bennett."

"I'm Caitlin MacLean." Cate could have taken the preferred hand, but such an action required a depth of courtesy and charity beyond Cate's shallow being. So instead indicated the bloody pad on her arm, using as an excuse to withhold that gesture of friendship.

Miss Jeannette Bennett was immediately sympathetic and helpful. "That looks bad. Let me look at it."

"We don't have time." Cate really needed to get up.

She really didn't know if her legs could hold her.

"If you bleed to death, you'll be no good to anyone." Jeannette unwound the soaked rags, lifted the bandage, and tsked. "Two stitches are torn." With brisk efficiency, she cleaned the wound with soap and water.

While she worked, Cate distracted herself by scrutinizing Jeannette Bennett. Lovely girl. Really lovely. "How did *you* come to replace the queen?"

"I'm Cenorinian. My family lives in exile in England, and my grandparents want sunshine and warmth before they die. They wish to come home." Jeannette pulled a length of soft cloth from her trunk, fashioned a square and placed it over the wound. "So I volunteered for the duty. When Sir Davies ordered Queen Sibeol to make an appearance in her open carriage, we — the prince and I — arranged an accident. The switch was made. The mercenaries did not suspect, and Sir Davies was none the wiser."

"But you look nothing like Queen Sibeol. How have you fooled the mercenaries all this time?"

"Prince Antonio — or Taran, as you call him — taught me the details of disguise. Cosmetics, a scarf, my hair is white-blond, and most important — why would the mercenaries look at me? They believe me to be an old woman. They are a dastardly lot who, if they had to live by their wits, would be bankrupt." Jeannette smirked at her own turn of phrase, then turned serious. "If Sir Davies had returned, *then* I would have been in trouble."

"You are clever and brave ... for a princess." Oops. Bitterness may have seeped into Cate's tone.

"I'm not a princess." Jeannette grabbed a beautifully embroidered canvas and pressed it over the pad.

Cate tried to pull away. "Don't use something so fine!"

"Working on the wearisome thing is all I've had to do these last months." Jeannette extracted a velvet ribbon from her sewing basket. "If I never see another embroidery frame, it will be too soon." She wrapped the ribbon around Cate's arm and prepared to tighten it. "This is going to hurt."

It did. Tears dribbled down Cate's face as Jeannette tied the knot.

When Jeannette was done, she said, "Sip some water. It will revive you, and we can escape this accursed fortress."

Cate sipped, at first cautiously, then eagerly. "Before we leave — two of the mercenaries stayed in the fortress. They are loading the cannon and —"

A massive boom shook the tower.

"I've got to stop them." Cate stood up. "They're shooting at my pirates!"

Jeannette ran to the window and looked out. "Two ships are in the bay, one flying the flag of Cenorina — those must be your pirates — and other flying a foreign flag. Portuguese, I think. They are engaged in battle!"

Another boom shook the tower.

"And the mercenaries are firing at both!"

Cate half-expected Jeannette to say two women could not affect the outcome of this battle and insist on escape.

Instead she came to Cate's side and offered her arm. "We must aid your pirates!"

As they descended the winding stair, the cannon roared again.

Cate jumped.

Jeannette patted her shoulder. "Don't worry, we'll save the day."

"You are very brave." Cate felt as old and sour as a wrinkled grape.

"*I* am brave? You were stabbed in some terrible struggle, came straightaway and captured an impregnable fortress, then overcame the meanest mercenary in the troop. You put me to shame! Anyway" — Jeannette stopped to allow Cate a moment of rest — "I pretend to be brave to fool everyone else, and if I fool myself too, all the better."

Cate doused the unwanted stirrings of empathy with a vat of exasperation. She did not want — could not stand to — like this woman.

When they reached the bottom, Cate stood panting while Jeannette checked the bandage.

"The blood loss has eased," Jeannette said. "We must make

our way to the ramparts, but first — if you'll stay here, I'll go find weapons."

"Here. It's loaded." Cate handed over the pistol, and saluted her with the staff. "I used this to smash Volker's ballocks … he fainted."

"Caitlin MacLean, I adore you. This way." Jeannette helped Cate down the corridor and then up another flight of stairs, not so high this time, and with sunlight streaming from the open door at the top.

As they got to the top, they slowed and peeked outside.

There, high on the fortress's ramparts with the wind blowing, Lich and Sheffer were laughing, although Cate was unsure which one was which. A dark-skinned fellow with white hair poured gunpowder into the muzzle, placed a patch at the end of the ram and drove it home, then with a grunt lifted a heavy iron ball and rolled it inside.

Another man with the bright red hair stood back, holding the fiery torch, and he shouted, "Ram it again, Lich, to make sure it's seated!"

Sheffer. He was Sheffer.

"When I ram 'em, they know they've been rammed!" The two men guffawed, and Lich applied the ram again.

Cate stepped back. "We cannot stop two determined mercenaries with a pistol and a stick."

Jeannette lifted her pistol, and her eyes snapped. "We can if we aim well."

Cate put her hand on Jeannette's wrist. "We need a ruse. We can scream and pretend the invaders have taken the fortress, and when the mercenaries run downstairs, we can lock them out."

"I like that. You are clever! No wonder the prince sent you. Your scheme needs only a little modification." Jeannette took down her hair and mussed it. She unbuttoned her high collar and the bodice of her dress until the lace of her chemise was showing. With her hands, she plumped her breasts. "Now. When I have their attention, you run behind the door and wait. When they dash into the citadel, slam the door shut and we'll barricade it against their return." Without waiting for Cate's agreement, Jeannette sprinted out into the sunshine, tossed her hair, threw her shoulders back, breathed deeply, and screamed, "They're taken the fortress! They've taken the fortress!"

The two men froze, staring in bug-eyed amazement.

"Who the hell is she?" Sheffer asked.

Lich shook his head and cupped his two hands in front of his chest in blatant admiration.

Cate stared, too, impressed with Jeannette's masterful impression of a maiden in distress. Then she remembered her role, and scuttled around and behind the door. At once she realized the glitch in their plan; back here, there was no iron rod, no heavy timber. No way to bar the door.

Jeannette glanced back. She met Cate's gaze.

Cate indicated her own empty palms.

Jeannette showed a remarkable ability to think on her feet; she raced to the edge of the wall high over the ocean. She looked down, down to the bottom of the fortress, down to the base of the cliff where the ocean waves battered the rocks. She pointed. She shrieked, "Oh, no!"

For no reason except that her acting ability was so persuasive, Lich ran to her side and also leaned over to look.

She put her hand in the middle of his back, grabbed his ankle and while he flailed wildly, she tipped him over the wall and into the ocean.

Cate could scarcely contain her shout of admiration.

Jeannette faced the other man, lifted her pistol and pointed it in his face. "Jump!"

Sheffer stood there. He edged closer to the precipice. He leaned over and looked. He looked back at her. "I could die!"

"Jump hard. Jump far."

"You're crazy!"

She cocked the pistol. "Yes."

Something about her — the way she stood, the way she stared, her blossoming smile — convinced him.

He dropped the torch and jumped.

Jeannette leaned out, craned her neck, and looked. "They're both in the water, swimming for the rocks."

Cate strolled over and looked. She applauded softly. "Masterful!" And inventive and quick-thinking.

It wasn't fair. Why, why did Taran's betrothed have to be beautiful *and* clever?

"I wish one of them had resisted. After these last months in prison, I have quite *longed* to shoot a mercenary." Jeannette placed the pistol on the wall, looked at the cannon and rubbed her hands. "Instead, I will sink a foreign sailing ship. How are you at judging distance and angle?"

Cate looked out to sea.

The small, swift Portuguese ship was well-armed with cannon and packed with sailors shooting rifles at Cate's pirates. On the bridge, a rotund, well-decorated officer shouted orders.

Cate itched to take him out. *Buy Cenorina, indeed.* "I've never shot a cannon before, but I can pick a squirrel off a branch with a slingshot."

"Good enough." Jeannette picked up the still-burning torch and handed it to Cate. "Instruct me. When I have the right angle, light the fuse."

"Up a little. A little more. No, too much." Cate eyed the muzzle, the ships, tried to calculate how far the blast of gunpowder would send the shot.

Jeannette strained as she maneuvered the screw mechanism that moved the heavy barrel up and down.

The gun carriage creaked and groaned as Jeannette used her iron rod to change the direction of fire.

And all the time, out on the bay, the combat raged.

From the town below, Cate heard shots and the ever-increasing yells of men and women.

"We've got to hurry!" Jeannette said.

"If I get this wrong I could shoot the wrong — there!" Cate held her hand in a stop gesture. "Right there!"

Jeannette stepped back.

Cate lit the fuse. They covered their ears, and watched in hope and terror as the fuse burned down.

For an interminable moment, nothing happened. Then … the cannon roared. Smoke billowed. The iron ball blasted from the barrel.

Cate stumbled as she ran to the edge of the low wall that surrounded the battlements. The breeze blew the smoke away, and she watched the cannonball rise through the air in a graceful arc, over the sea, toward the Portuguese ship.

"It's too high." Jeannette slapped the stone beneath her

hands. "We aimed too high!"

They had overshot the Portuguese; the cannonball was headed for the pirate ship.

Cate had sunk her own dear pirates!

With a crack, the iron ball hit the fores'l mast of the Portuguese vessel and sheared it off. Splinters flew as the broken mast fell straight down, penetrating the deck, then slowly, like a falling tree, fell gracefully over the rail dragging its sails and rigging with it. The ship halted, quivering in the water like a rabbit confronting the hounds.

Taran's men immediately seized the advantage; they brought the Scottish Witch smartly about and returned to rake the foundering Portuguese ship with a broadside. Doing a swift turnabout, they raked it again.

That was enough. The Portuguese ship began to tilt and take on water.

The Portuguese sailors were jumping and swimming for shore.

Across the waves, Cate heard her pirates cheer. "Good lads!" she shouted, although of course they could not hear her or even see her as more than a speck so far up in the fortress.

The Scottish Witch turned toward Arianna's pier.

Jeannette caught Cate in her arms and hugged her. "We did it. *You* did it."

So Jeannette was nice, too, taking credit when they thought they had failed and giving credit to Cate when they realized they had succeeded beyond their wildest dreams.

Cate should be glad for Taran. His mother had found him a brave, beautiful, smart and kind mate. How great for him. With a healthy helping of sarcasm, Cate said, "When we see the pirates, we shall tell them that was exactly what we planned."

Jeannette laughed. "We shall!"

The noise of the battle in town below intensified.

Cate and Jeannette hurried around the corner of the ramparts to look.

Arianna's streets writhed with soldiers, mercenaries, citizens of the town. Cate's pirates landed on the dock. While a contingent secured the ship, the rest leaped off and met a charge led by the massive mercenary leader himself.

From the fortress, Cate screamed instructions.

Jeannette screamed warnings.

Carrying knives and swords, the soaked Portuguese sailors ran up from the beach and joined the fray on the side of the mercenaries.

Servants and gardeners from Giraud, armed with pitchforks, rakes, clubs and knives, fought the surprised, affronted and now desperate mercenaries.

But Cate couldn't see Taran.

She couldn't see Sir Maddox Davies, either.

But mostly, she couldn't see Taran. Where is he? He had survived … hadn't he? He had prevailed against Sir Davies, had he not?

Her heart started a slow, steady, anguished thumping. Her ears buzzed and her vision blurred.

Dear God, he can marry Jeannette, I won't mind, as long as he is alive.

She must have been speaking aloud, for Jeannette asked, "Why would he marry me?"

Dear God, I'll go back to Scotland and live a quiet, chaste life if that is what you require, as long as Taran is alive. Dear God —

"No fears," Jeannette said urgently. "There he is!" She pointed at a vicious battle in the middle of the square.

Taran burst out of the crowd, leaped up onto a wagon, and took out a mercenary with a swing of his sword. He looked up at the fortress, spotted them, and even from such a distance, they could see his beaming smile. He lifted his sword in salute.

And behind him, Lilbit burst from the crowd. He aimed a pistol at Taran's back.

Cate screamed and pointed.

Taran swung to face Lilbit.

A gout of flame and smoke blasted from the pistol barrel.

Taran fell to the side, into the crowd, and disappeared from sight.

Lilbit fell back and was gone.

The battle raged on.

In an agony of grief and shock, Cate stared. He was dead. Taran was dead. The man she loved had forever vanished from this earth. His laughter, his determination, the pain of his past and his plans for the future … gone. He was gone.

And she was alone. Forever.

Hard and fast, she fell to the ground, unconscious.

CHAPTER FIFTY-NINE

Cate opened her eyes and realized ... heaven was a large, strange bedroom with a comfortable bed covered in clean, fragrant sheets and piled with feather pillows. And glowing with sunshine. Lots of sunshine illuminating a sky blue ceiling painted with clouds and fat, naked cherubs.

She wouldn't have thought heaven would have to paint the sky or the clouds or their cherubs. Shouldn't the cherubs be there in person, playing zithers and hiking up the scraps of cloth that covered their nether regions?

Off to the side, someone said softly, "She's awake, sire."

Footsteps sounded. Cate turned her head.

Taran stood beside the bed. But not the Taran she'd come to know. This Taran wore a gentleman's attire. He looked good, although she hadn't realized men wore suits and cravats with diamond stickpins in heaven.

He leaned over and smoothed her hair, and she thought his hand trembled. "My darling, you scared me half to death."

Obviously, she was dead. Ergo, he was dead, too. He had not survived Lilbit's shot. Of course not. How could he?

Her eyes filled with tears.

He deserved to live, to bring his beloved Cenorina back to health, to enjoy the fruits of his labors.

"Are you in pain?" As if he had done it many times before, he eased his arm beneath her shoulder and held a glass of water to her lips. "Drink."

She drank, tentatively at first, then eagerly. "That's good."

He pressed his lips to her forehead and sighed. "Her fever is gone," he told someone. "She is better."

Cate glanced around, trying to see to whom he spoke, but that person stood just out of her range of vision.

Or else ... Taran was talking to a spirit. That was it! Her brother was dead, too. Taran was talking to Kiernan. She asked, "Can I see Kiernan?"

Taran lowered her back onto the pillows and frowned into her face. "Kiernan?"

"He has to be around her *somewhere.*"

"Why are you...? How did you...?" Taran swallowed. "No, he's not here right now."

"Then where am I?" Maybe ... she'd gone to hell.

But that wouldn't be fair. Not to her, and not to Taran.

Taran took her hand and stroked her fingers, over and over, as if he needed to touch her. "You are at Giraud in the master's bedroom, exactly where you should be."

It took her long minutes to assimilate that information. "At Giraud? How is that possible?" She tried to put the facts together. "Are we *alive?*"

"Very much alive. Look." He pointed to his bruised, gashed face. "When you broke my nose, you gave me two black eyes."

"Served you right," she mumbled, and touched his face with her fingertips. He needed a shave. Were men unshaven in heaven? Or hell? Yet his skin was neither cold, like a corpse, nor hot like a man tormented by fire, but warm ... perhaps he was telling the truth. Perhaps they were at Giraud. "How nice. "

Once again, he slid his arm around her shoulders and lifted her. Looking nowhere but at her, he held out his hand; it came back holding a cup. "Drink some broth, Cate, then you can sleep."

She drank, then asked, "Are my pirates well?"

"All survived except — we have lost Lilbit."

"He's dead?" She remembered that scene in Arianna's square, Lilbit's gunshot, Taran's fall, her scream of anguish." Good."

"No. But he's hurt, and he has disappeared." He smoothed the frown lines on her forehead. "Don't worry. All is well."

"I want to know all that happened."

"You have been unconscious three long days. You lost a lot of blood. When you next wake, you will hear the whole tale. But you must sleep now."

"Will you be here?"

He took her hand. "I will not leave you."

That sounded like a promise.

CHAPTER SIXTY

The second time Cate woke, the room was lit only by a branch of candles set on the desk. Taran sat there, his coat and cravat discarded, his shirtsleeves rolled up to his elbow, writing on a sheet of paper. He looked intent. And tired.

So she hadn't dreamed it.

She moved her wounded arm, and in that moment knew she was definitely alive, because the discomfort made her whimper.

At the sound, he came to his feet and to her side. As he had done before, he slid his arm under her shoulder. He held a cup of water to her lips, and encouraged her to sip. "My darling, are you in pain?"

"Yes." The truth. "And I wish you wouldn't call me that." A lie. She liked it.

"But you are my darling." He smiled with such devastating charm, she wanted to punch him in the nose again.

Before she could try, he went to the door and spoke to someone, then returned. "During your illness, Signor Marino and his staff have been preparing foods just for you — I swear his broths have kept you alive — and now he is sending some soup. Then I can give you something to ease the discomfort."

"A narcotic would put me to sleep. I don't want to sleep. I want to know whether you killed Sir Davies and what happened in the battle and why Lilbit tried to murder you and how you escaped."

Taran seated himself on the mattress by her side. As he had done before, he picked up her hand and stroked her fingers. He acted as if he needed to touch her, lived to touch her.

She was fine with that.

"Maddox Davies. We fought. I prevailed." Taran smiled, as if the memory of the fight gave him pleasure.

"You killed him."

"No."

She tried to sit up.

Mistake.

She laid back on the pillows. "No?"

"I hurt him. I slashed him. I branded him. I made him

hideous in every woman's eyes."

With pointed logic, she said, "If he was dead, he wouldn't care."

"True." Taran arranged her pillows behind her and helped her sit up. "But if I had killed him, I wouldn't now have in my possession all of his wealth, as well as a revenge of grand proportions."

"*All* of his wealth?"

He laughed at her skepticism. "You and I found *some*, but there was more. During my years with the pirates, Wahkan watched all that happened in Cenorina. He has been an immeasurable help, and he wanted one thing in return — he wanted his own revenge on Davies. He informed me that Davies had prepared a bolthole in case of rebellion or bad fortune. Wahkan also told me Davies could not be allowed that escape. So together we plotted..."

Cate thought back on her memories before all had blurred into unconsciousness. "I remember Wahkan. He's the man in charge of your stables."

"Yes, and in America, he was a warrior and a tracker. I allowed Davies to flee, scarred and bleeding. Rifle in hand, Wahkan followed him to the other side of the island to an isolated cove where long ago conquerors — and pirates — would drop anchor, and come ashore for fresh water and whatever food they could forage."

Cate became caught up in the tale. "That's where Davies had hidden his ill-gotten gains."

"In locked metal boxes." Taran still smiled, but his eyes had grown dark with remembered intent. "When Davies arrived in the cove, he dug up his treasure, built a signal fire, and waited for his transport to arrive."

"Who was his transport?"

"Wahkan had searched out that information, too. Long ago, Davies had made a deal with local fishermen. They agreed that when they saw his fire, they would come to take him to the mainland. Wahkan offered them more to ignore his signal." Again, Taran lifted her fingers to his lips. He pressed a kiss on them. He invited her to smile. "Instead of the fishermen Davies had hired, another small vessel rowed into the cove..."

"A small vessel sent by you?"

Taran smirked. There was no other word for it. He smirked. "It was more of a runabout from a ship."

"Whose ship?"

"Gerry Williams's pirate ship."

"Gerry Williams?" She hung on Taran's every word. "When did Gerry Williams become your ally?"

"He is buying the Scottish Witch, and with my ship and his as the beginning of his fleet, he has started an import business. He'll bring exotic goods from the Far East to the English middle class. He's a good sailor, a good fighter, and a shrewd merchant. He'll make a fortune. For part of the profits, I'm giving him a good price on the ship." Taran touched her cheek. "Your eyes are big with surprise."

"I missed so much!"

"I've been waiting to tell you."

A knock sounded on the door.

He went over, opened it, accepted a tray and shut the door. As he walked back to the bed, he said, "Everyone wants to see you and congratulate you on your heroic actions. But I will have to share you soon enough. I'm not sharing you now." He smiled at her, and his eyes looked … fond.

He was fond of her. How jolly.

He placed the tray on the bedside table, placed the napkin around her neck, poured the soup from the pitcher into the bowl, and fed her the first bites of chicken soup flavored with morsels of fresh vegetables and with tiny snips of egg noodles.

She had never had anything taste so good. She wanted to eat all of it right now.

But after three bites, Taran slowed her down with a question. "Don't you want to know all that happened to Davies?"

"So tell me."

He dropped a chunk of bread into the soup, stirred it around, and fed it to her. "Before Davies could realize the boat that approached was not the one he had hired, Wahkan started shooting at Davies. He missed every time … deliberately. Davies was dodging and dancing, a silliness that Wahkan said gave him a good laugh. The sailors in the runaway were shouting for Davies to come or be abandoned. So Davies stuffed money into his shirt and pants, splashed out to the boat, and … "

"You gave Sir Maddox Davies over to Gerry Williams." They had a steady rhythm going now. He fed her a bite. He talked. She talked. He fed her again.

She was enjoying herself. Enjoying the food, enjoying Taran's service to her, and most of all, she was enjoying the story. "What will Gerry Williams do with Sir Davies?"

"I *heard* from a good authority —"

"Who?"

"Blowfish." They exchanged smiles. "I heard that Gerry Williams and his men hauled Davies aboard. Davies began to empty his shirt, wave his money about, and give orders. Gerry Williams upended him, shook the paper and coins out of him, reset his shoulder —"

"What happened to his shoulder?"

Taran widened his eyes in deceptive innocence. "At some point during our battle, he dislocated it."

"Such a shame."

"Yes, poor, poor Maddox Davies."

She remembered Sir Davies's elegant grace, and could not imagine him laboring on a ship. "What is he doing on a pirate ship?"

"Sir Maddox Davies is now living the carefree life of a barefoot cabin boy, sailing the seven seas, drinking foul water, eating bread full of weevils, sleeping in a damp hammock and when he malingers, feeling the lash of a cat-o-nine-tails." Taran stroked the lion-shaped scar over his heart. "I hope he enjoys that lowly occupation as much as I did."

Cate contemplated how carefully Taran had planned his retribution, and how long he had waited to visit it upon the traitor. She thought any enemies of Cenorina should take heed. "Is Gerry Williams as cruel a captain as yours was?"

"No, but I don't think Davies will survive much beyond his first attempt at mutiny." Taran offered red wine.

She sipped, then pushed it away. "No more of that."

"So the affair with Davies didn't turn out as I had planned." Taran lightly stroked her arm. "And I will never forgive myself for allowing him to harm you — but beating him was damned satisfying."

"Good. I will take pleasure in knowing you did that."

"What else can I tell you?" He thought. "The battle went well. After a good fight against very angry townsfolk and Cenorina aristocrats, Davies's mercenaries retreated to the fortress, found themselves locked out—"

Now Cate smirked.

"—And found themselves the perfect target for the marksman above."

"That was Miss Bennett?" *Of course, Jeannette would be a marksman.* "She is beautiful. And petite." *Short. The woman was short.*

"More to the point, she shoots well and ruthlessly."

Oh, good. He admired her.

"The mercenaries surrendered. The Portuguese fought with the ferocity of men who planned not to pay for the islands, but to steal them. Those who survived are now in a prison ship headed to England." Taran put the bowl on the tray. "And you have finished your soup. Signor Marino will be so proud."

She watched him carry the tray to the door and hand it out. Even with a broken nose, he was handsome. And noble. And he had a well-formed backside…

When he returned, she said, "So you now hold possession of the islands."

"We do."

"I am happy for you."

"For us. My people were angry, and they would have taken the islands back anyway. But my men helped win the battle, and I will keep Cenorina free of foreign domination." Picking up her hands, he kissed the open palm of first one, then the other. "And my wife won their hearts with her quick thinking, courage and kindness. So now I have a second chance to rule Cenorina, and to prove myself."

Her gaze fell beneath his. He seemed so warm, so appreciative, so supportive. What did he mean by it? She should question him. But she was tired, fading fast. "I know you will … what about Lilbit? Why was he trying to kill you?"

"Ah, Lilbit. Mutiny was his first objective. While I was gone, he and a few of his comrades tried to take my ship."

Remembering the men's loyalty to their Cap'n, she asked, "How could he think he would succeed?"

"He did succeed, in a way. He put the ship into disarray and sabotaged the guns, which Blowfish did not at first realize. That's why they came into the harbor late and almost lost the battle to the Portuguese. But why he thought to kill me, I did not understand until I went through Davies's correspondence for the last few weeks. Then I was thoroughly abashed." Taran looked more than abashed. He looked embarrassed.

"What happened?"

"Lilbit had written a letter to Davies, offering to sell him information. Information about you. And me. It came with the other letters, the ones bidding on Cenorina. I saw this letter. I held it in my hands." He showed her his hands as if she could see the evidence written on his palms. "But the blackguard could barely write, and after reading the first lines, I arrogantly tossed it aside. I cared only for the other letters from foreign powers."

"I can see how you might have missed that clue."

"You are being kind."

"No." She squirmed. "I saw the letter too, and did not consider that it could be important. What did Lilbit say about us?"

"He warned Davies that the prince had survived the pirates and had returned to Cenorina, and without identifying me, he offered to kill me — for a price."

Cate could scarcely believe it. "But he seemed like such a nice boy!"

"I thought so, too, for a very long time. But I had begun to have my suspicions about him, and told Blowfish to bait a trap and see if he could catch a traitor. Thus Blowfish was able to thwart the mutiny."

She nodded. "You're very astute."

"If I was astute, I wouldn't have missed the letter, which also offered information about the identity of the princess." Taran circled her finger where the wedding ring should rest. "The princess, who is also the wife I married so many years ago."

That took her breath away. "How did Lilbit know that we were married or when?"

"When we sailed for Cenorina I left a letter for my mother, confessing that you were now and had long been my wife."

Had Taran lost his mind? "Why would you do that?"

"In case of my death, I wanted her to treat you with all the honors you deserve."

"So your mother knows?"

"She is delighted."

"How wonderful!" How horrifying! Queen Sibeol *knew*. Cate shut her eyes. She could only hope the queen didn't have her assassinated to make way for … Jeannette.

"You, my darling, are drifting off. I will leave you to sleep." He started to turn away.

Her eyes popped open. She caught his hand.

Oh, she was weak. So weak. But she'd been to hell and back, and she didn't care. "Please," she whispered. "Would you lay down with me? And … hold me?"

"I would love to hold you more than anything in the world." He pulled off his boots, lifted the covers and slid into bed. He gathered her into his arms.

As she breathed in his scent and basked in his warmth, she felt as if she had come home. "Taran?"

"Yes?"

"You didn't tell me how you escaped from Lilbit's assassination attempt."

"With the well-timed slash of a sword, someone saved me."

"Who saved you? I must thank him."

Taran chuckled, deep and amused. "That is a surprise for you, one you will enjoy in the morning."

CHAPTER SIXTY-ONE

Cate woke alone, hungry and cross. Bright sunlight streamed in the windows. Two women stood nearby, brows furrowed, heads together and speaking in low tones.

Queen Sibeol. And Jeannette Bennett, aka the princess.

Cate heard her name spoken. So they were talking about her. Discussing how best to oust her, she supposed.

Her testiness increased in leaps and bounds. Right now, she was still Taran's wife and Cenorina's crown princess, and maybe she didn't feel like being ousted. She sat up in stages, testing her arm and her temper, and announced, "I want my breakfast."

Both women jumped guiltily.

"What were you talking about?" Cate asked. As if she didn't know.

Jeannette said, "Her Majesty just wagered me that —" Queen Sibeol elbowed her in the ribs, and hard, too, if the way Jeannette doubled over meant anything.

Queen Sibeol smiled as if she was pleased to see Cate awake and glaring. "You're better."

"Of course I'm better." Cate moved her arm experimentally. "It was just a little knife wound."

"You passed out and scared me to death," Jeannette said. "I was afraid you were dead. You were burning with fever, and that infection was serious!"

Queen Sibeol put her hand on Jeannette's arm and shook her head, then walked to the tasseled velvet bell pull and gave it a healthy yank. When Gracia entered the room, the queen said, "The princess will take her breakfast now."

Gracia beamed, bobbed a curtsy and disappeared.

"Don't try to pretend you want me here," Cate said. Or rather, she muttered.

Because Jeannette and Queen Sibeol hurried to her side and arranged the pillows behind her, and fussed like they cared.

Gracia arrived carrying a tray loaded with melon, bacon, oatmeal, a pot of tea, and a rose in a vase, and placed it across Cate's lap. "With Signor Marino's compliments, and he hopes you enjoy this meal."

The smell of the bacon alone made Cate forgot her testiness, and the way everyone acted, as if she really was a princess ... well, that was nice.

Ravenous, she fell on the food. When she had consumed everything except the rose, she looked up.

Everyone was watching her and smiling.

"What?" Cate asked.

"We have been worried about you." Queen Sibeol said. "Taran especially. Since the battle, this is the first time he has consented to leave your side, and only with a guard at the door and Miss Bennett and I in attendance."

"Oh. That's nice of him." And Cate felt the heat rise in her cheeks.

Jeannette and Gracia exchanged smiles. Queen Sibeol chuckled indulgently.

Cate blushed harder. Last night, for the first time since her injury, she had slept well and deeply, and she knew it was because Taran had held her and she felt safe in his arms. An awful thing, to be dependent on the man. An even more awful thing to be married and blushing about sharing a bed. It wasn't as if they had done anything except sleep. More was the shame. Hastily she said, "I do feel much better. I can get up and go to work."

Jeannette eyed her oddly. "Doing what?"

"I suppose I am no longer needed in my position as housekeeper."

Gracia took the tray away. "No, Ma'am. Prince Taran has sent for someone to fill the position."

"He took care of *that* quickly enough." Cate's irritation was back in full force. "Nevertheless, I would like to freshen up and go outside into the sunshine."

Queen Sibeol declared, "Yes. The sunshine would do you good."

It quickly became apparent the queen's word was law. With the appearance of four chamber maids and no effort of her own, Cate was washed, her hair brushed and arranged around her shoulders, and her tired nightgown changed for a clean gown with a loose, lacy, flattering dressing robe. She was placed in a rolling chair and alternately pushed and carried down to the main level and out onto the sunny terrace. She was transferred to a chaise lounge and covered with a plaid wool blanket in the tartan pattern of the Clan MacLean. How kind of someone to seek out a covering such as this for her. Yet a query niggled at her mind — how had someone brought this from Scotland so quickly?

Then Gillies came out, carrying a basket of fruit from his father's orchard, and offered his family's thanks to Cate for her leadership and bravery. In the ensuing conversation, Cate forgot her question about the tartan.

When Gillies had gone back to his duties, Cate looked around. Already the house and the gardens looked better, neater, brighter. The staff was happier; one by one they followed Gillies example and brought flowers from their mothers' gardens, lace their grandmothers had tatted, a basket full of fresh brown eggs. Each servant expressed gratitude for her all she had done for Cenorina.

Gracia took the gifts from Cate's hands and arranged them on a table nearby in an attractive display that gave Cate pleasure every time she looked at it.

Queen Sibeol served her a cup of tea, then with Jeannette retreated to chairs set a little to the side and behind. Queen Sibeol pulled out her knitting. Jeannette did *not* pull out her embroidery, and after a few minutes excused herself to go walk in the gardens.

Cate sipped her tea, then she heard a call, "In the mood fer a chinwag, lil one?" She looked up to see Blowfish poke his head around the corner of the house.

With a grin, she extended her hand.

He scampered over. "I thought ye taught ye better than to get in a fight where ye got no chance of winnin'!" He frowned, but he squeezed her fingers gently.

"It was a battle I had to face. As it was, I was scared to death. Yet thanks to your training, I knocked out the bully and trussed him up." She gestured to a chair beside her.

He seated himself, and looking innocent as only Blowfish could, he asked, "Did you geld him, too?"

"No, didn't have time to search for his tiny little—" From the chair off to the side, Cate heard the queen gasp. "That is to say — no."

"Ye done good, lass." Blowfish beamed with delight.

"You shouldn't ask such improper questions of a lady." Cate

looked him over. Blowfish was dressed like an old-fashioned gentleman, in a striped green coat, a paisley green waistcoat, a blue cravat and brown knee breeches. She said, "You don't look like any pirate I ever imagined. Why are you here? I thought you would be sailing away on the Scottish Witch!"

"I like Cenorina. The Cap'n promised a bit o' land for us pirates what want to retire, so I'll be stickin' around."

"Oh, I'm so glad!" Cate started to put the tea down.

Gracia rushed forward and took it from her.

Blowfish chortled. "Aren't ye just Her Majesty High an' Mighty?"

"I like it. I could get used to this kind of attention."

"Yer ego could get used to it, too."

"As long as you are around, I don't think I'll have to worry about keeping my ego in check." Cate leaned back with a sigh of pleasure. "So you will settle down."

"Aye. I met this woman. She's skittish. Bossy as hell. Not in love with the Cap'n, but she likes ye." Blowfish stuck his thumbs in his lapels. "I've decided to marry her."

Something about Blowfish's tone of voice made Cate ask, "Does she know she's going to marry you?"

"She'll figger it out. Either before the ceremony or after. " His blue eyes twinkled. "She's got somethin' fer ye."

"What?" Visions of more bright flowers, more white lace, more blushing fruits filled Cate's head.

"I dunno. She's awful proud of herself, though." He looked up, caught someone's eye, stood hastily and bowed. "I'll go fetch her, and she can tell ye."

Cate glanced behind her.

Queen Sibeol had her gaze on her knitting, but Cate knew she had signaled to Blowfish that his time was up.

Cate smoothed the wool blanket across her lap. "Your Majesty, where did you get this plaid? It is pleasant to see — it is the tartan of my family, of the Clan MacLean."

The queen said, "A guest brought this gift for you. He has been waiting most anxiously for you to wake and rise."

Cate came to attention. "A guest? From Scotland? With our clan plaid? When did he arrive?"

"A most fortuitous circumstance brought him here on the

day of the battle. Indeed, when the coward and traitor Lilbit tried to kill my son" — Queen Sibeol's eyes grew steely and cold — "this most welcome visitor saved my son's life by slashing the traitor with his sword."

Cate tried to understand whom in her family would arrive here, now, carrying the MacLean tartan, and would be strong and swift and save Taran's life. She could think of only one man ... but that was nothing but the wistful thinking of a woman who had lost a beloved brother. "I will be most pleased to see any visitor from my homeland."

Queen Sibeol gestured into the house, and a gentleman with a badly scarred face stepped out. A lady walked beside him, her hand resting on his arm.

Taran walked behind them, his eyes alight with anticipation.

The group walked toward Cate, and her heart began to thump — hard. With trembling hands, she pushed the throw aside.

She knew she had never seen the lady before, and the gentleman was a stranger to her ... except he was not. He was as tall as Kiernan, he moved like Kiernan, and his eyes ... his eyes were her brother's eyes. Yet his features were wrong, changed, transformed by some great catastrophe.

Then he smiled, and she knew.

Cate leaped up and flung herself toward him. "Kiernan!"

CHAPTER SIXTY-TWO

Kiernan met Cate halfway and caught her in his arms. "Damn, lass, do you never do what's proper? You've been hurt. You shouldn't be flying around like a witchy-woman!"

His voice was the same. His scolding was familiar. He looked into her face, and kissed both her cheeks, and she thought her heart would burst with joy.

Then he said, "There she goes."

He was right, of course. Her head spun. Her knees collapsed. Another, even more familiar pair of arms took her, lifted her, and carried her back to the chaise lounge. Taran placed her tenderly, then seated himself beside her. She leaned her head against his chest. "You did this, didn't you? You sent for Kiernan?"

Taran kept his arm wrapped tightly around her. "I didn't know he was alive. I simply thought it was worth sending a message to your mother telling her where you had landed, and that we were reunited. I gave her my promise to keep you safe."

"I came immediately." Kiernan knelt beside the lounge. He looked sternly at Taran. "You could have done a better job keeping her safe, man, but I know my sister's reckless bravery, so I'll not scold too much."

The lady who had held Kiernan's arm watched the reunion with a smile, but she scrutinized Cate, too, as if she had a right.

That told Cate all she needed to know. "Kiernan, introduce me to … your wife?"

He stood, fetched the lady, and escorted her to Cate and Taran. In a proud tone, he announced, "This is indeed my wife. Caitlin, this is my Enid."

Cate and Enid shook hands. They would get to know each other in the years ahead, through correspondence and occasional visits. For now, they loved Kiernan and found their connection through him.

Jeannette came back from the garden. A love-besotted young gardener carrying an arm full of flowers trailed after her. Harkness ordered more chairs and supervised the serving of lunch while Cate heard Kiernan's tale of danger and disaster, and how

Enid had nursed him back to health and then again saved his life in an adventure that made Cate gasp and her heart race. Cate would never have thought her brother would marry an Englishwoman, but hearing of Enid's courage and dedication made Cate adore her as much as Kiernan did.

Then Kiernan turned a stern eye on Cate and Taran, who sat side-by-side, hip-to-hip on the narrow chaise, and Kiernan's Scottish brogue strengthened. "Taran tells me you two are also married, and have been all this long time."

Cate glanced uneasily at Jeannette and at Queen Sibeol. "Yes, but—"

Taran talked over the top of her. "I've hired as many people from town as can be spared to clean and repair the cathedral so we can repeat the ceremony while you visit Cenorina."

Kiernan nodded. "'Tis right and proper that I represent the MacLean clan and give the bride away. Our mother will be most pleased."

Cate glanced at Jeannette again. "But Jeannette — "

"I think Jeannette can be convinced to stay long enough to enjoy the celebration. You will stay, won't you?" Taran asked.

Jeannette shuffled her feet. "I had hoped to go on to my next assignment."

"Of course she will stay," Queen Sibeol said. "She is one of the heroines of Cenorina and should be celebrated as such."

Jeannette looked at Cate as if seeking sympathy from a kindred spirit. When Cate spread her hands helplessly — the plans had been made, and they were sweeping her along without caring about her input — Jeannette glared at Queen Sibeol's back, crossed her eyes and stuck out her tongue.

Cate changed her laughter into a compulsive cough. She was starting to think her suspicions of Jeannette had been foolish and a trick of pain and fear and thwarted love.

"It is always good to plan a coronation early enough to allow foreign dignitaries to grace the ceremony and prove the lineage is safe, but in this case an earlier coronation is definitely in order to reassure our people that all is well and … for other reasons. I do wish we had found the crown jewels." Queen Sibeol studied Cate's auburn hair. "Cate would be lovely in the queen's crown with the stormstone above her forehead, and she has handsome hands and long fingers, and the wedding ring would sit well upon … well. It is sad to lose those traditions, but we will soon make new ones."

Cate began, "I'm afraid—"

Taran half-turned on the lounge to face her. "You are not to reproach yourself for not finding them."

"I'm not."

"No, indeed," Queen Sibeol said. "Since I have returned, I have also searched the house. I thought I had discovered Davies's hiding place in the king's study, but alas, the case was empty."

Cate didn't want to explain, but she had to. "That's because Zelle —"

Taran took her hands, massaged them, and looked deep into her eyes. "Zelle has disappeared."

That irritation was back. "I *know*. Zelle believes strongly that—"

Zelle stepped around the corner of the house holding a silver tray covered in a cloth. "I believe the crown jewels are for all Cenorina. "

"Ohhh." Cate lit up with pleasure. "I was right about you. I knew I was."

Zelle came forward.

Blowfish bobbed along behind her and pointed, grinning like a lad under the spell of his first infatuation.

With his help, she knelt at the foot of Cate's chaise lounge. Looking Cate in the eyes, she said, "I couldn't do it. You were right — the prince is generous and just, and these are for all Cenorina." She told Taran, "Your wife, the princess, *did* discover the jewels. She knew where they were. She told me about them."

"Zelle took them for safekeeping until the battle had been won." Cate was so proud, of Zelle, of herself, of these people who surrounded her and looked with anticipation to the future of their country.

Taran slid his arm around Cate, hugged her, put his face into the curve of her neck, and laughed deeply. "You darling!"

Zelle gestured to Blowfish, who pulled the cloth off the tray.

A gasp rose from every throat.

Taran looked up, and laughed again.

A pile of rings, necklaces, earrings and bracelets sparkled in the sunshine. Atop them sat the king's crown, with the massive seastone glowing as purple as the deepest sea, and the queen's crown, with the stormstone sporting a bright strike of lightning deep in its heart.

No one on the veranda could look away. Every eye was riveted to the glorious display.

From the bottom of the stairs, a rough voice spoke, "Beautiful jewels. Thanks for finding them for me. Now I'll take 'em." Lilbit walked up the stairs, a knife in his belt and a pistol in each hand.

CHAPTER SIXTY-THREE

On the sunny terrace, everyone's gaze moved from the crown jewels to the intruder. The sight of Lilbit froze them in place. No one spoke except for a lone, frightened female voice — Cate thought it was Gracia — who said, "He's a living corpse!"

Lilbit's adventures in the wilds of the island had changed the handsome, strapping sailor into a cadaverous monster. He had lost weight, so that his grimy clothes hung on him. Patches of sweat stained his armpits and stuck the white linen of his shirt to his belly. At the same time, his face was puffy and red, so swollen his skin was peeling off his cheeks and his eyes were mere slits.

Taran groped at his waist for his pistol or his knife, but he was dressed like a gentleman. He wore no weapons.

Kiernan was the same.

Jeannette half rose in her seat, then sank back down.

Blowfish eased back. He pulled a knife from his sleeve and cradled it in his palm.

Lilbit knew Blowfish too well; he waved the pistol at Cate. "Drop it, Blowfish."

Blowfish looked between Cate and Lilbit.

He whispered a curse word and dropped the knife.

The clatter of the steel onto the stones broke the profound silence, and made Cate jump. If Blowfish, who had taught her to defend herself, couldn't disarm Lilbit, what could anyone do?

She wet her lips. She looked for anything that would serve as a weapon.

She saw nothing.

None of the servants were prepared. No one had foreseen an attack. Why would they? Here, at Giraud, in the middle of the island, knowing the first moment of peace they had enjoyed in nine long years?

The only sound now was the wheeze of Lilbit's breath, and beside and behind Cate, the slow and steady click of Queen Sibeol's knitting needles.

If Lilbit rushed them, Cate could take him out with those needles.

He wasn't going to rush them; not as long as he held loaded pistols in his hands.

"Bring those jewels here ... Zelle." Lilbit had been hiding in the bushes, listening to their conversation. He had listened as they exchanged affections, he understood their pleasure in their triumph, he knew how close the connections were that bound them ... he knew their names. With one pistol pointed at Zelle and one at Taran, he said, "Zelle, bring them now."

Zelle glanced at Taran.

Taran nodded to her, a slow, deep nod.

As Zelle got to her feet, she staggered. The jewels clattered on the tray.

"I'll kill you if you drop it," Lilbit promised.

Cate believed him.

So did Zelle. The tray trembled in her hands; the jewels shimmered and flashed.

Perhaps it was a trick of the light, but to Cate, it looked as if Lilbit's eyes had lost their color; the irises were an eerie white.

His failed mutiny, his failed attempt to murder Taran, his lonely trek into the depths of a strange island, had driven him mad.

Zelle dragged her feet as she walked across the porch.

In a clear, steady voice, Taran said, "Lilbit, you can't get off the island with those jewels."

"Not all of them. But I only need one to be a wealthy man. And I'll take all I can carry." Lilbit wheezed when he breathed, his skin glistened with perspiration, and his gaze slid from side to side, encompassing every man and woman on the terrace.

He hated them all; for surviving, for thriving, for their moments of happiness.

His gaze touched Cate.

She shrank back. He hated her most of all.

And why? She had done nothing to him ... except survive, thrive, be happy.

Beside and behind, the click of Queen Sibeol's needles slowed.

"Stuff the rings into my bag," Lilbit told Zelle.

Zelle slid toward him like a skater afraid to advance.

"Ye insolent young whoreson." Blowfish vibrated with fury. "I should have killed ye while I had the chance."

"Old man," Lilbit said with lethal intensity, "you're a dog panting to stuff your nose up your master's arse."

Blowfish started to rush forward.

"Stop!" Queen Sibeol snapped.

Blowfish came to a halt.

Taran eased around to fully face Lilbit, to present him with a larger target. "You realize we will hunt you down."

"Really? Will you? You destroyed my ambitions, and for trying to kill you, you sentenced me to die." Lilbit lifted his shirt and showed them the red streaks across his skin and the oozing, festering wound on his side.

Jeannette winced and turned her face away.

Zelle made a gagging sound.

"You smell like decay," Taran said.

Cate smelled it, too — the faint trace of putrefaction wafted on the breeze.

Lilbit snarled, showing gray teeth and red gums. "So, prince, will you kill me like a mad dog who has destroyed everything you love?"

Slowly, so as not to alarm him, Taran waved an arm around. "Look at us. There are too many. You can't kill us all."

"Hold your tongue," Cate said out of the corner of her mouth.

Taran continued, "You can't destroy everything I love."

"I can. All I have to do is this." Lilbit held one pistol pointed steadfastly at Taran's chest. His hand tightened on the trigger. At the last moment, he turned his aim toward Cate —

Taran flung himself at Cate.

Cate flung herself at Taran.

A pistol roared.

Cate screamed in rage. "No!" She would not lose Taran now.

But when she looked up, Taran was alive, holding her with trembling hands, asking, "Are you all right? Were you hit?"

"No. No. You?"

"No. But —"

Lilbit was sprawled on the steps, a smoking bullet wound in his chest.

Kiernan helped Enid up off the floor; he had shoved her down and out of the range of fire. She cupped her wrist as if she was in pain. Jeannette hurried to assist as Kiernan helped Enid into the house.

The crown jewels were scattered across the terrace, ignored while Blowfish embraced Zelle.

The palace staff was standing, stunned and bewildered, until with a gesture Harkness directed them to face Queen Sibeol.

She stood calm and straight, a pistol held in her firm grasp. She said clearly, "After Davies took me prisoner, I swore I would never again be unprepared. So I always carry a loaded pistol in my knitting bag. And I can shoot, you know. I *am* the queen."

Cate could almost see the change come over the servants. Before, even though they knew better, they had remembered only the queen who lived in the tower and oppressed them.

Now Queen Sibeol was a heroine in her own right.

The servants bowed and curtsied, ignored everything but their awe of their queen.

"My God." Taran gathered Cate close against his chest. His voice was choked. "My God, I never thought to worry about an assassination attempt."

She burrowed close, trying to rid herself of the teeth-chattering fear that would forever haunt her dreams — that Taran had been killed. "We were so happy, we forgot about Lilbit."

"Maybe I should let you go," he said. "Maybe you would be safer."

She muttered into his chest, "I could go on adventures with Jeannette." Jeannette, who Cate now knew had never been a threat to her. Jeannette, who he had never loved.

"You taunt me. You terrorize me. You love me ... you give me courage to do the right thing. It is you who makes me work to be a better man. And when ... when I thought you were dying, I wanted to die, too. When Lilbit was going to shoot..." Taran took her hand and placed it over his pounding heart. "I can't live without you. Tell me you'll stay. Tell me you'll marry me again. I will make you happy. I will crown you with the jewels of my family. I will worship you."

She wanted to laugh at him, but he looked so intense, so desperate, and his heart pounded so frantically beneath her palm, she had to try and bring him to sense. "Taran, you must be not serious. If we stay married—"

"There is no other choice."

"You won't worship me. We'll fight. You'll try to boss me around. I'll do what I think is best. When I wear the crown, it will slip sideways or I'll put it down somewhere and lose it. You know I don't care about those things." She choked up. "I only care about ... you."

"You love me."

"You know I do." Tears rose in her eyes. "And I wish I could make you love me."

"My God, woman!" He tugged at his hair until it stood up in all directions. "When you were unconscious, I carried you here all the way from Arianna in my arms. I bathed you when your fever rose, made you drink water and broth, changed your nightgown and held you in your delirium."

"Queen Sibeol said you had stayed with me, but I didn't know..." She was balanced between laughter and weeping. "Did you really do all those things?"

"Yes! Yes, I did! Don't you recognize love by its deeds?"

"I do." She slid her hand around his neck and looked into his eyes. "I like the words, too."

He resisted. He really did. But how could he resist the woman who had loved and married him in his callow youth, who had haunted his fantasies and in his mind accompanied him on all his pirate adventures, who had helped him reclaim his kingdom and gave her soul to his passion? "Crown Princess Caitlin MacLean Kane, you have captured my heart and all my love, and as your punishment you are sentenced to a lifetime in my arms." He pulled her into his embrace. "Starting now."

"So you love me."

"You are a terrible nag."

"I am your wife."

"As I said..." He kissed her, and he was home. "I love you."

At last, when they came up for air, he looked around and realized — the terrace was empty, with no one in sight. In a few short minutes, the crown jewels had been gathered and whisked away. Even Lilbit's body had disappeared. Everyone at Giraud had mobilized to allow the Crown Prince and Crown Princess their moment of privacy.

Taran lolled back in the lounge and pulled Cate's head onto

his chest.

Cate relaxed and said, "If I marry you again —"

Taran corrected, "When you marry me again."

"— I will be queen." She frowned with genuine worry. "I am not raised to be royalty!"

"I was, and look at the good it did me. Being a pirate was a more fit training. You know I'm right."

"Yes… So you will be ever known as my pirate king."

"And you are the picklock princess." He ran his fingers through her shining auburn hair. "You know, we should treasure this time."

"Why is that?" Cate yawned.

"We are alone. With the busy schedule we now face, this moment will probably never come again."

"Actually, lately it has occurred to me that…"

"Yes?"

"It's just that, I suspect … we are not quite alone." Sitting up, Cate took his hand and placed it low on her belly. And smiled into his stunned eyes.

In the king's study, Jeannette slid the window shut and with a groan, placed five gold coins in Queen Sibeol's extended palm and stormed out of the room.

The woman who had just been crowned with the title, *Grandmother*, smiled and slid the coins into her reticule. Reaching into her knitting bag, she pulled out the lacy white baby cap she had begun a week ago and finished only yesterday. She smoothed it with her palm. Sitting down in her dear husband's chair, she took up her needles, and prepared to make a matching sweater and pair of tiny stockings.

In a voice pitched to reach to her husband, and no further, she said, "Antonio, it is as we hoped. Our son is happy with his darling wife, and he is ready to be king. Our newest crown prince is on the way. And for another thousand years, our family will rule Cenorina in peace."

THE END

*Christina Dodd here! Thank you for enjoying **A PIRATE'S WIFE FOR ME**! Please accept my invitation to explore my worlds and join my **free mailing list** at http://christinadodd.com for news, book sales and exclusive excerpts!*
And read on to find more thrilling Christina Dodd romances!

<u>*The Governess Brides series*</u> *in order*

<u>THAT SCANDALOUS EVENING</u> (prequel)

<u>RULES OF SURRENDER</u>

<u>RULES OF ENGAGMENT</u>

<u>RULES OF ATTRACTION</u>

<u>IN MY WILDEST DREAMS</u>

<u>LOST IN YOUR ARMS</u>

<u>A PIRATE'S WIFE FOR ME (You just read this one!)</u>

<u>MY FAVORITE BRIDE</u>

<u>MY FAIR TEMPTRESS</u>

<u>IN BED WITH THE DUKE</u>

<u>TAKEN BY THE PRINCE</u>

<u>Want more Christina Dodd historicals?</u>

<u>*The Well Pleasured series*</u> *in order*

<u>A WELL PLEASURED LADY</u> (A controversial story with challenging sex scenes! Read at your own risk!)

<u>A WELL FAVORED GENTLEMAN</u>

The Lost Princesses in order

SOME ENCHANTED EVENING

BAREFOOT PRINCESS

THE PRINCE KIDNAPS A BRIDE

Historical Novellas in eBook to enjoy on your phone, computer or eReader!

THE SMUGGLER'S CAPTIVE BRIDE
A wicked English earl, a woman determined to avenge her brother's death, and a little bit of bondage... But it's okay. He gets to tie her up, too.
Read an excerpt of this Regency romance e-novella:

Kent, England, 1813

Miss Laura Haver listened as the two men spoke in the taproom below. It was probably nothing, probably the first of the villagers arriving for an ale, but the events of the night had made her wary, and she slipped over to the door and laid her head against the boards while straining to hear.

The knock made her jump backward, stumbling on the thin carpet that covered part of the floor.

"M'lady?"

Only the inn-keeper, called her by that title. Because ... well, because she had told him she was married to his lord, Keefe Leighton, the earl of Hamilton. That was not quite true ... or even slightly true. But he didn't know that.

"What?" she called, and her voice quavered.

"'Tis Ernest, m'lady, with a surprise for ye."

"What kind of surprise?" She feared suspicion colored her tone, but Ernest sounded as cheerful as ever.

"Something to warm yer bones." Metal rattled against metal. "Shall I unlock the door and pass it through to ye?"

She stared in horror at the metal lock. She'd thought herself inviolate in the inn's bedchamber, and now Ernest announced he had another key. Should she fling her weight against the door and block it? She looked down at herself and at another time, she would have laughed. "Bird-bones," Ronald had called her, and "Shorty."

And why was she worried, really? As far as she could tell, Ernest had been trustworthy, keeping the secret she'd entrusted to him with perfect consideration. Only her recent trip to the cliffs, where she had seen smugglers — and they had seen her — had frightened her and made her suspicious of everyone in this small village.

"I'll open the door," she called. She wanted to retain control of access to her room, and not have Ernest thinking he could enter any time. She produced the key and turned it in the lock, then opened the door a crack. Nothing more. Just a crack. She was smart enough to peek before she swung the door wide.

Ernest stood beaming, a dusty bottle in one hand and a candle in the other.

The earl of Hamilton *loomed* beside him.

Shock held her frozen for the briefest of moments.

Had her thoughts summoned him here?

She rammed the door closed.

Before the latch clicked, he gave a shove.

She stumbled back, caught her heel on her hem, and fell backward.

Before she hit the floor, he swept her into his arms. Lifting her, he smiled ferociously, looked into her eyes, and in a voice meant to carry, he boomed, "Darling!"

And he pressed his lips against hers.

Order **THE SMUGGLER'S CAPTIVE BRIDE**
and read it on your phone, your computer or your eReader!

Another historical e-novella you might enjoy:

WILD TEXAS ROSE

Jumping Jehoshaphat, Rose was nude! Not a stitch on! Bare-beamed and buck-naked! In the open, in full daylight, without a shred of self-consciousness or guilt.

Thorn gulped. What a woman. What . . . a . . . woman.

Was that a rifle she was holding?

Oh God, it was.

She had her Winchester, and her hands were mighty steady.

And she'd called him a bastard — the first curse word he'd ever heard her use. Deep in his gut, he had the ugly suspicion she would, without remorse, shoot him through the heart.

He'd better think fast.

But she was naked!

*Order **WILD TEXAS ROSE** and read it on your phone, computer or eReader!*

*For you collectors, enjoy **LADY IN BLACK**,*
a full-length romantic suspense about a straitlaced lady-butler, a powerful billionaire, and kidnapping, conflict, and steamy sex in the shower...

Margaret Guarneri has found sanctuary managing the home of a rich, elderly man...until the day he receives a threat of kidnapping. Enter Reid Donovan, dynamic, wealthy in his own right, and suspicious of the gorgeous young widow who so diligently cares for his grandfather.

Distrust, extortion, and the shadows of the past drive Reid and Margaret apart. Wild, uninhibited passion brings them together. They must learn to trust each other before they can vanquish a killer...and in the process, they discover a passion more powerful than anything either of them could imagine. But has love come too late for the handsome billionaire and his lady in black?

*Get **LADY IN BLACK** in eBook and in paperback.*

Who is Christina Dodd?

Readers become writers, and Christina has always been a reader. Ultimately she discovered she liked to read romance best because the relationship between a man and a woman is always humorous. A woman wants world peace, a clean house, and a deep and meaningful relationship based on mutual understanding and love. A man wants a Craftsman router, undisputed control of the TV remote, and a red Corvette which will make his bald spot disappear.

So when Christina's first daughter was born, she told her husband she was going to write a book. It was a good time to start a new career, because how much trouble could one little infant be?

Quite a lot, it seemed. It took ten years, two children and three completed manuscripts before she was published. Now her more than fifty New York Times and USA Today bestselling novels — paranormals, historicals, romantic suspense and suspense — have been translated into twenty-five languages, recorded on Books on Tape for the Blind, won Romance Writers of America's prestigious Golden Heart and RITA Awards and been called the year's best by Library Journal. Dodd herself has been a featured author at the Texas Book Festival *and* a clue in the Los Angeles Times crossword puzzle (11/18/05, # 13 Down: Romance Novelist named Christina.) Publishers Weekly praises her style that "showcases Dodd's easy, addictive charm and steamy storytelling."

Christina is married to a man with all his hair and no Corvette, but many Craftsman tools.

More ways to connect with Christina Dodd
tsū - ChristinaDodd
Goodreads - Christina Dodd
Google+ - ChristinaDoddBooks
Facebook - ChristinaDoddFans
Twitter - @ChristinaDodd
Pinterest - Christina Dodd

Explore Christina's worlds, get writing tips, and join her FREE mailing list for book news, book sales, and exclusive excerpts!

Printed in Great Britain
by Amazon

43040061R00188